The Identity Wars

Utopia is Dystopia

JP Tate

Copyright © 2015 James Tate.

The right of James Tate to be identified as author of this work has been asserted in accordance with the Copyright, Designs and Patents Act 1988. All rights reserved. No part of this publication may be reproduced or transmitted without the express permission of the author. All characters in this novel are fictitious. Any resemblance to real persons, living or dead, is purely coincidental.

ISBN-13: 978-1519306890 / ISBN-10:151930689X

Other publications by JP Tate

http://jptate.jimdo.com

Contents

Chapter 01: Ritzy in the year 2035

Chapter 02: Lines on a Map

Chapter 03: The Red Squirrels

Chapter 04: Alfred in the year 1975

Chapter 05: Michael in the year 2005

Chapter 06: Utopia is Dystopia

Chapter 07: "E Pluribus Unum"

Chapter 08: Spare a Copper

Chapter 09: The Last Generation

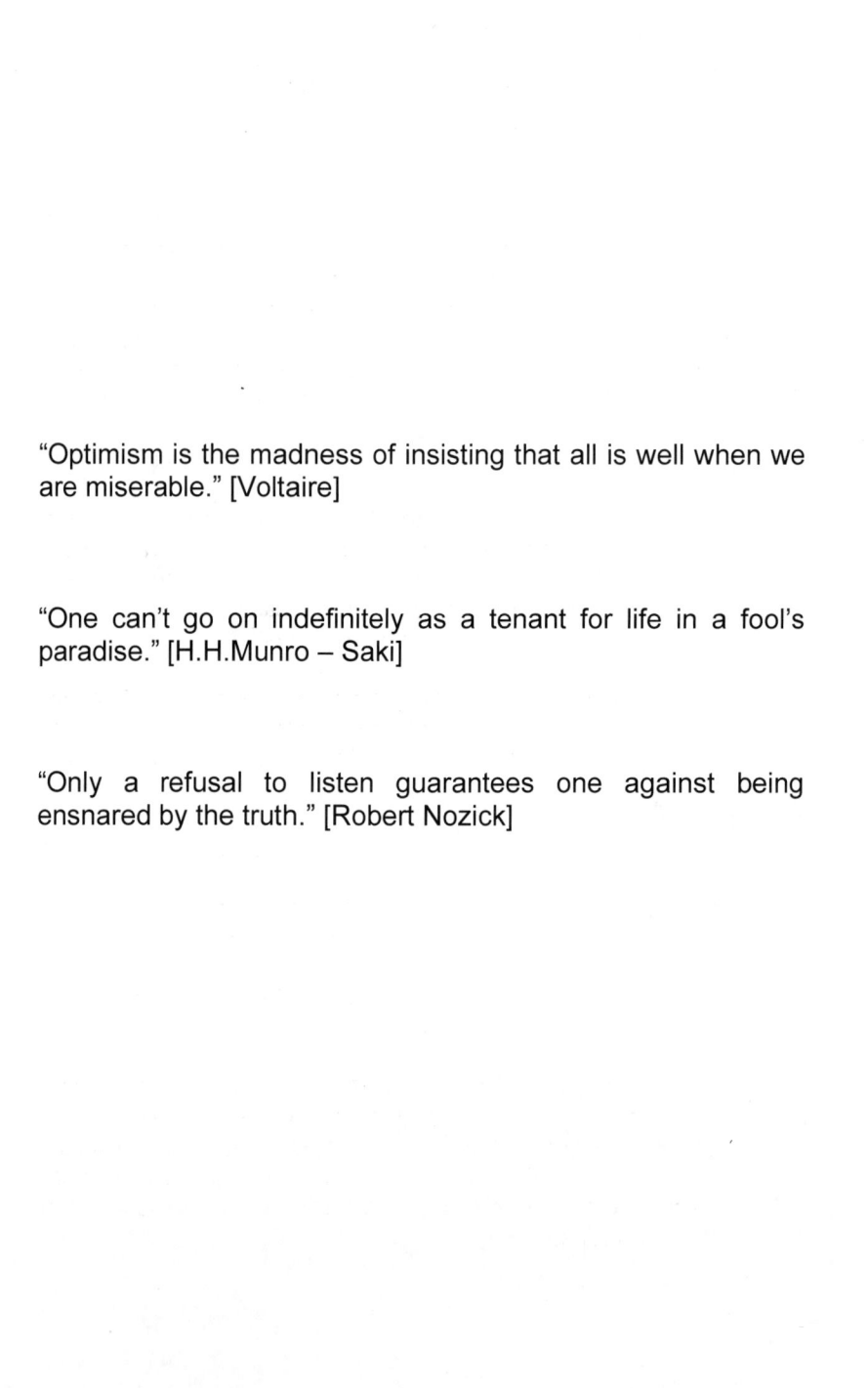

"Optimism is the madness of insisting that all is well when we are miserable." [Voltaire]

"One can't go on indefinitely as a tenant for life in a fool's paradise." [H.H.Munro – Saki]

"Only a refusal to listen guarantees one against being ensnared by the truth." [Robert Nozick]

Chapter 1

Ritzy in the Year 2035

The furniture of the room was deliberately confrontational, with the interviewee's isolated chair set apart and directly facing the panel of three bureaucrats who sat in judgement from behind their communal desk. The furnishings themselves were quite ordinary, no different to what might be found in a million other government offices, it was their positioning in the room that created the antagonistic effect. With an array of state officials in front of him the solitary interviewee, presented for their inspection, was given the strong impression that he was about to be dissected and have his innards exposed.

Confrontational it certainly was, but the three bureaucrats would have denied this fact had it been pointed out to them. They were firmly of the opinion that their interrogatory procedure was: "inclusively cooperative to maximize emotional sensitivity and to minimize the inducement of psychological trauma".

They believed this unquestioningly because it was clearly laid down in their department's mission statement that their professional methodology had been designed to be inclusively cooperative, and so the three women on the panel couldn't imagine that it wasn't. Mission statements could not be challenged. They were holy writ. It was certified in an official document so it must be true. To suggest that their procedure was anything other than what it ought to be would undermine the proper functioning of the department. That was unacceptable. Consequently, if an interviewee found the procedure confrontational, then this demonstrated an unhelpful attitude, possibly even a hostile attitude, on the part of the interviewee. Such an attitude would be viewed with disfavour.

Moreover, "confrontational" was a word of which the bureaucrats staunchly disapproved. It was far too masculine. It had no place here. Inclusivity did not include the masculine. Besides which, all three bureaucrats were female and therefore by definition they were supportive and non-confrontational. To think otherwise would be a misogynist hate-crime.

Ritzy sat in the chair of isolation being interviewed by the panel with an expression of bland insolence on his face. If Ritzy had been female or transgender he would have been entitled to be interviewed via a webcam to further desensitize the situation. But he was categorized as hetero cis-male, so he was not entitled. In practice, interviewees were never entitled because they were always male. The webcam was never used. But it had been purchased at taxpayer's expense because, strictly speaking, it was possible for females and transgender persons to be interviewed which meant that a webcam must be available even if it was never actually switched on. To have neglected to make special provision for vulnerable groups would have been another hate-crime, regardless of the absence of any victims because of the uniform maleness of those being interrogated.

These proceedings were a Civic Investigation. Ritzy was under suspicion of bad citizenship. It was a serious charge. The authorities could dismantle your life and deprive you of whatever liberty you had, if they could get a conviction. There were numerous grounds for Ritzy being under suspicion: he had never married or fathered children and he'd had so little to do with women that there had been no allegations of domestic abuse or sexual assault made against him. This too-good-to-be-true personal history wasn't fooling the panel of his judges. Besides, the primary reason that he was presumed guilty of bad citizenship was that his record of income taxation was unsatisfactory. He wasn't paying any.

Today was Ritzy's fortieth birthday. Neither young nor old, he was very much a man of his times. His body was sinewy and firmly muscled despite his forty years, looking wolfishly lean in his baggies. Food was hard to come by these days and the former obesity epidemic was over. Ritzy still had the same waist measurement that he'd had ten years earlier. The saggy drapery of his blue-grey camo shirt and long military shorts hung loose from his wiry frame beneath the sleeveless utility jacket with its proliferation of pockets that he habitually wore. All of Ritzy's limited wardrobe was similarly functional. But this wasn't merely a matter of practicality. Clothes were an important form of self-expression and Ritzy's attire told a tale of his pride in his masculine physicality.

He had removed his bowler hat for the interview at the request of the panel who eyed the offending article disdainfully. Ritzy was one of the Red Squirrels and they all wore bowlers as an assertion of allegiance to their dying ethnicity. The panel may have guessed as much, hence their disdain. Ritzy's bowler was grey to match his sleeveless jacket. He liked to be colour-coordinated.

His scalp and jaw were stubble where he had taken his electric razor and shaved the hair of his head and face to the lowest setting on the razor. It wasn't so much a hairstyle as the lack of a hairstyle. There was no sign of grey in the naturally dark stubble. He didn't carry colour-coordination that far. This fashion in home-barbering was called a "Con". Some thought it witty to claim that "Con" was short for "convict" since the style was somewhat reminiscent of a Victorian convict in a Dickens novel. But this wasn't so much wit as malice. "Con" was actually an abbreviation of "convenience" which was the true motivation for the style.

Under the dim ecologically-sound lighting in the unornamented severity of the room with its molded plastic walls and plexiglass windows, all of which had been built into the room's design in the name of ergonomics, Ritzy looked as physically alienated as he was psychologically estranged. From his own point of view he couldn't have been more out of place, in a tribunal created by people who were utterly different to himself in pursuit of an agenda entirely contrary to his own. But from the perspective of those who sat in judgement over him, this was exactly where he belonged; under the eye of their microscope like a substandard specimen in a scientific experiment whose findings were unsatisfactory.

"You persist in giving no adequate account of your means of livelihood," said the woman in the centre of the trio of judges. She appeared to be the presiding magistrate since she was doing all of the talking. "Nor can we find any verification of your submission of self-assessment taxation documentation. Not merely for this year but for any annual submission since 2026. You are not in compliance with law."

There was almost no inflection in the way that she spoke. If her brusque voice had any cadence at all, then that cadence was flat. Her every utterance was delivered as if she wished to disassociate herself from the subject of her statements. She held aloof from their object too. Both Ritzy and his actions were distasteful to her.

"I live with friends," responded Ritzy. "They support me."

"So you have said in your previous formal evidence," intoned the judge before listing those friends as they appeared in Ritzy's case file: "You claim to be financially provided for by Misters Barker, Kidd, Reynolds, and Hastings. But our cross-checking reveals that none of these persons has identified any source of income either."

The woman with the monotone voice was about Ritzy's age but she spoke down to him like a schoolteacher consigning an unruly child to detention. This condescension was matched by her physical appearance. Along with her sister judges she presented that bone dry persona which typified the inhabitant of hygienic white-collar working environments. Hidden out of sight her perspiration might stain her underwear but her exterior image would never reveal a single bead of sweat. This sartorial smartness was supposed to signify her intellectual superiority. It certainly contrasted dramatically with the wrinkles and creases of Ritzy's loose-fitting baggies.

The interview was being digitally recorded, of course. Anything a man might say could be used as evidence against him when it had been appropriately interpreted by the officials in charge of his case. Their talent for misconstrual was an important part of their job description. They did not lower themselves to any technical trickery in editing the recording to omit phrases or anything crude of that sort. They simply chose to understand the words used by the interviewee to mean what it suited the panel to believe that those words meant. Even the most innocuous of comments could be made to appear culpable if it was viewed in the correct ideological light. Context was everything; manipulate that and anything could mean what you wanted it to mean. The officials of the Civic Investigation were rightly feared for their lawyer-like capacity for misrepresentation.

In recognition of their skill in this regard, Ritzy made no attempt to speak truth to power. There would be no point in the attempt. Power, as represented by the establishment bureaucrats on the panel, had no interest in hearing the truth. They were concerned only with implementing ideology. Truth counted for nothing; conformity to feminist multiculti correctness counted for everything. Speaking truth to power was like trying to engage a dog in moral debate, its canine brain could understand obedience to its master's commands but it could never grasp the conceptual complexities of rational justification and refutation. Ideological correctness was the alpha dog. It didn't have to justify itself, it merely had to maintain its status as the alpha dog.

Ritzy looked into the judgemental faces of the three magistrates on the panel and saw only the self-aggrandizing complacency of the indoctrinated. They were automata programmed with the software of feminism and multiculturalism. They had no minds of their own, they simply complied with the procedures of their intellectual programmes in accordance with the binary coding of the Correct and the Incorrect. Of what use would it be to speak truth to power? To explain what was true and why it was true to the drones of the establishment would require that they break their programming and start thinking for themselves. This they would never do. Even had they been capable, they would have adamantly refused to abandon their conformity to political orthodoxy.

So Ritzy's answers to the Civic Investigation's questions tended to consist of procrastinations, equivocations, and evasions. Most interviewees didn't even offer them that much and instead refused to speak to the panel at all beyond confirming their names and certain other uncontroversial information. Or what should have been uncontroversial. The abdication of common sense in the systems of the political state ensured that controversy could be found in pretty much anything. In Ritzy's own case the Monotone Woman had found an anomaly which she considered a cause for dissatisfaction:

"You gave your name to us as Mr Kyle Eldridge but the national data reserve clearly lists your name as Mr Kyle Thorpe-Eldridge. Can you explain this discrepancy to us Mr Thorpe-Eldridge?"

"I don't use the hyphenated name of my childhood," explained Ritzy placidly. "For some years I've only used my paternal surname."

The Monotone Woman didn't like this. Gratuitous name changing made the records untidy and she sniffed the smell of misogyny in Ritzy's use of the word "paternal". Apparently, Thorpe had been his mother's surname and Eldridge his father's. Why, then, had the mother's family name been dropped? Why not the father's? The Monotone Woman stiffened in her chair.

The story of Ritzy's dehyphenation was not one that he intended to reveal to his interrogators. Nor the story of his prenatal hyphenation. His mother had related the tale of his name to him more than once when he was a child, never without a certain sense of grievance.

She'd told him that initially, after her marriage to his father, she had quite liked her husband's family name, Eldridge, because she associated it with a prominent figure in the black civil rights movement in America, Eldridge Cleaver of the Black Panthers, about whom she had heard in school. His principle that "If you are not a part of the solution, you are a part of the problem" perfectly encapsulated her own political perspective. Her maiden name had been Thorpe but, as the name Eldridge had pleasant associations, she had taken the married name of Mrs Thorpe-Eldridge.

Unfortunately, when she looked further into Cleaver's life she found out that prior to his political career with the panthers Cleaver had been a serial rapist. His commitment to the violence of armed struggle for black liberation from white oppression she had viewed favourably but his earlier view that the rape of white women was an insurrectionary act she held to be unforgivable. Her enquiry further disclosed, what she had not known before, that after his time with the Black Panthers the fickle Mr Cleaver had subsequently become a born-again Christian and a supporter of the Republican party before adopting Mormonism. Having discovered these unsavoury facts, Ritzy's mother had thereafter felt soiled by the name of Eldridge and she had been quick to revert to her maiden name of Thorpe when she got divorced. But her son had kept his hyphenated name of Thorpe-Eldridge because his mother had conceded that it was probably too late to do anything about it now as far as he was concerned.

Some years later Ritzy had dropped the name Thorpe. He'd done this at the same time as he had stopped calling himself Kyle. His parents had named him Kyle, partly because they liked the name and partly because of the character in the movie Terminator. His mother had despaired of her husband's penchant for action movies but she made one of her rare exceptions for Terminator because, after all, the main hero was a soon-to-be pregnant woman and the secondary role was played by the male hero who was simply there to protect the woman and her unborn child. A role he fulfilled perfectly by conveniently getting killed before the child was born. So there was much to recommend the subtext of the film. It would have suited her better if the unborn child had been a girl because she profoundly believed that the future was female, but since she was now the mother of a son herself, she didn't mind so much.

It wasn't until Ritzy had reached puberty that he transformed himself from his mother's vision of who he ought to be into the man that he had actually become. He did not find the gender role of male self-sacrifice in the sacred cause of womankind to be quite to his taste. It bothered him that his mother seemed to care more for other people's daughters than she did for her own son. So a change of name had been included in this transformation. He had called himself Ritzy in recognition of one particular but prolonged episode from his childhood. When he was a kid the authorities had subdued him with Ritalin. This form of state-sponsored social control had targeted boys like Kyle. Fidgeting was disobedience. Worse than that, in boys fidgeting was an illness requiring treatment. It had been conventional practice back then for the medical profession to drug boys into conformity at the behest of the education system. One arm of the feminist state supported another in this imposition of obedience. Shackled by the biochemical manacles and fetters of Ritalin young Kyle had been a good boy. But when he had grown up enough to understand what had been done to him in his infancy, he had taken the name 'Ritzy' as a kind of constant reminder of his declaration of independence from the system. He had cast off his slave name.

He was not alone. His transformation had been a microcosm of a macro-level social phenomenon. Society changed on the day that men gave up. Not that it actually happened on a single day, of course, but the societal change had occurred pretty quickly once the idea had caught on. It wasn't done in any organised fashion. There were no leaders of a political movement, there was no ideology instructing them to take this decisive step. Men just came around to the idea of not trying any more. They gave up on bending over backwards to satisfy those who would never be satisfied. They abandoned their millennia of effort to do what was expected of them. They abdicated their role of serving the interests of women and the larger society. They reached this decision individually and personally rather than collectively. Men just gave up. They left everyone to their fate. It wasn't worth bearing the burden any more. Society had rejected men as deficient and inferior and obsolete, so they embraced their obsolescence and gave up working for no reward.

Countless generations of men had held things together, working their guts out to keep the world turning, carrying the responsibility of generating the wealth that everyone in society depended upon for survival. On whose aching backs had civilization been carried forward? They had built it brick by brick. But then the time came when they were told that all this effort and striving had been nothing but their male selfishness. After all the centuries in which men had made civilizational progress and technological advance to increase the comfort and convenience of people's lives, they were told that all these achievements had been nothing but their patriarchal oppression of women. All the generations of men who had lived and died protecting and providing for their families were declared to be women's worst enemies. Men were told that all this male self-sacrifice had been nothing but a selfish hate-crime against women.

This was explained to them at interminable length throughout several decades of insults and abuse from the feminist establishment in a society which viewed the systemic disrespecting of men as a moral undertaking. It was all a part of the establishment's puerile Politics of Name-Calling. Disagree with them about anything and you were a racist sexist Islamophobic misogynist far-right extremist woman-hating Nazi rape-apologist. And if you still dared to disagree with them after all that, then they'd call you all the same names again. And ten thousand times again. Name-calling was their idea of an evidence-based and rationally justified argument. It had worked splendidly for them and they had acquired immense political and cultural power by using this strategy. Everybody else was far too intimidated to disagree. Nobody bullies as effectively as the establishment because they've got the big guns. Yet, as the decades rolled by, the effectiveness of this bullying had waned.

Men had withdrawn. Since their children were no longer their own, they ceased to want to have children. Since their marital home was no longer their own, they ceased to marry. Since their contribution to society was no longer valued, they ceased to aspire to contribute to society. Their working habits changed. In the old days they had sought the highest paying jobs they could find, even though that meant doing the dirty jobs and the dangerous jobs and the high-stress jobs, because they needed those jobs to financially support women and children. But now that they had withdrawn, they no longer supported women and children. This meant that they could make do with easier forms of employment, less dirty, less dangerous, less stressful forms of employment. Now that they had only themselves to financially maintain they could afford to make far less of a contribution to society.

When the political class and the cultural elite realised what was happening they had tried their perennial male-shaming tactics, propagandizing the idea that men should "man-up" and accept the responsibilities of their traditional gender role. The establishment ubiquitously and endlessly reinforced the gender-construct which said that men were supposed to take it upon themselves to work and earn money in order to pay for women and children in accordance with the archaic stereotype imposed upon men since time immemorial. Men who rejected this gender-identity were ridiculed as "man-boys", they were belittled as "losers", they were vilified as "failures", they were mocked as "unmanly". But the keen edge of this weapon had been blunted from overuse. It no longer cut deep. Who was going to accept the traditional male gender role of hard work and self-sacrifice as a husband and father if they were only going to be insulted for it? No amount of propaganda made any difference. Men had been verbally abused by feminist name-calling all their lives, and they knew that they would certainly be disparaged with smears and slanders whether or not they tried to satisfy the demands of society. So they stopped trying. After more than half a century of female entitlement, the traditional male-shaming tactics no longer worked. And, to a significant extent, neither did the men.

With the realisation that their formerly reliable shaming tactics were now out-of-date, the political state had responded by implementing more draconian measures. The government had repeatedly tried to introduce bachelor taxation or, as they called it, the "parental premium". They had initiated so many tax remits for families that citizens with children now paid scarcely a fraction of the contribution which single persons were expected to pay. Conspicuously, single women were exempt from bachelor taxation due to the women's rights legislation which held that the state could not exercise any authority over a women's body. She must not be penalised for her choice to not have children because, if she were, that would amount to the state forcing a woman into pregnancy and childbirth. The state must not be allowed to own a woman's ovaries. A woman's right to choose was sacrosanct. So a "female equity premium" was incorporated into the tax system to compensate single women, thereby ensuring that the "parental premium" did not unfairly curtail a woman's entitlement to exercise her rights.

But single men were not exempt. Their bodies had always been the property of the state, both in peace and in war. There was no men's rights legislation forbidding the state from exercising authority over a man's body. Generations of fragile male bodies had been marched off to the mass slaughter of battle whenever government had waved a patriotic flag. The state might have to call upon men to walk into machine gun bullets again if there were another war, so there could be no suggestion of men having the right to deny the political state ownership of their bodies whenever the state considered it necessary. The state considered it necessary now. If men were selfishly refusing to accept their age-old duty of providing financially for women and children through marriage, then bachelor taxation would guarantee that they paid anyway. Any man who didn't wish to pay for other people's children had better get himself married.

But this coercive policy of punitive taxation had radically failed because single men increasingly lived and worked off-the-grid in a cash economy and the government could not levy taxes on incomes which were not officially declared. This, needless to say, constituted tax evasion and the bureaucracy had lumbered into action to come down hard on those single men who were guilty of bad citizenship. Not that the state dared to attempt imprisonment as a punishment for this criminal lifestyle because there simply wasn't the space in the penal system for hundreds of thousands of new convicts. Instead, the penalty was enforced community service; a system of indentured labour. Yet this had also failed due to the inability of the system to cope with the sheer scale of the tax evasion. There had been a thriving shadow economy for many years because the extensive population of illegal immigrants within society had created a culture of cash-in-hand working practices. Following the instructive example of the illegal immigrants, single men had retreated into this culture.

The practical upshot of all this chaos had been a crushing loss of overall tax revenue to the exchequer. The whole system of taxation had collapsed under the weight of the ideological dogma it was being made to serve. Yet still the bureaucracy persevered with their futile attempts to force single men to take up the slack, for they lacked any alternatives within the confines of their establishment doctrines. Hence the bad citizenship investigations which chased relentlessly after men like Ritzy as the state went in pursuit of bachelor incomes, indefatigably searching for the pot of gold at the end of the rainbow.

Ritzy was, in this respect, a fairly typical case. He lived as one of five single men who shared an apartment. For ethnic reasons they called themselves the Red Squirrels. The other four were the men that the Monotone Woman had named: Barker, Kidd, Reynolds, and Hastings. The rent for the apartment was paid in cash like everything else they purchased. All five had shadow economy jobs with mediocre wages which were nonetheless sufficient for their needs with a little left over for a few luxuries. As they were all hetero, none of them felt able to avoid the bachelor tax by marrying each other, but this did have the advantage that their shared sense of persecution and oppression kept them fiercely loyal to one another. The state offered financial inducements to informants willing to betray men who could be caught for tax evasion and set to work as indentured labour in the service of the community. But if any of the Red Squirrels had informed upon their housemates, they would have been putting their own head into the same noose when the others retaliated in kind. The five had other reasons for their mutual loyalty, not least their ethnic kinship, but it never hurt to have some reciprocal self-interest on their side too.

Today was not the first occasion that Ritzy had been summoned by the Civic Investigation to give an account of why he was not paying taxes at the rate expected of single men. Yet, to the best of his recollection, he had never sat before the same bureaucrats twice. Every time it was a different set of faces. However, in every way that mattered, the panel of three officials conducting the interview this morning were indistinguishable from all the others he had sat in front of in the past.

Ritzy's participation, if it could be called that, in the investigation was unrewarding for the panel of judges conducting the questioning. He prevaricated in a manner which they found frustrating and provocative, although he was never openly defiant or aggressive. His replies were often simply silly but they were always stated with complete sobriety. He appeared compliant yet none of his answers seemed to provide them with any definite information from which they could proceed. This was a standard tactic for those under suspicion because if he were to admit anything he would immediately be fast-tracked through automatic prosecution procedures. But if he refused to admit anything or gave incoherent answers, then they couldn't touch him because they didn't have the resources to send an investigator to find out where he worked and catch him in the act.

All five men in his household were under investigation and all five gave more or less identical answers whenever they were brought in for interview. Each claimed that they were being financially supported by their housemates and if the Civic Investigation couldn't get anyone to admit to earning an income, then the situation remained status quo. Only those men who admitted things were ever prosecuted. Honesty was the worst policy. Total denial and rambling unintelligibility was safety.

Continual denial did not resolve the investigation, it merely extended it indefinitely. But that was good enough because most men had ongoing legal difficulties, one way or another, and Ritzy's case was just one file on an overpopulated hard-drive. These days men lived and died with their legal cases pending. It was a mundane ritual of the way the world turned.

"Mr Thorpe-Eldridge," continued the Monotone Woman, "as the five persons resident at your address, yourself included, have all failed to register any legitimate source of income, this Civic Investigation must remain open until such time as a satisfactory account of your financial position has been submitted."

"I understand," affirmed Ritzy. He did, too, but not in the way that his interrogator would have wished. Ritzy had a firm grasp on the situation.

There was a moment of whispered conferral amongst the members of the panel. They were deciding to put the case forward for due process of further investigation, as they did at the end of every interview. The nods and whispers were collaborative and were the only genuinely supportive action taken by the judges since the interrogation began, in that they were being supportive of each other.

Ritzy noticed the strong smell of perfume that emanated from behind the magisterial desk. Each of the three women was wearing her own perfume of choice and each on its own might have been a pleasing scent, but in such close proximity the three different aromas mixed together cloyingly in the still air of the enclosed room. They combined into one malodorous artificiality which did not enhance nature with a pleasantly aromatic fragrance, it was merely a manufactured disguise intended to camouflage the human truth beneath. Collectively the perfumery became an overpowering stench.

"Frankly, we're very disappointed in you," said the Monotone Woman. The condescension in her voice was the only trace of emotion that passed her lips. "We had expected greater cooperation."

"I'm sorry to hear that," replied Ritzy with a bogus sincerity that the Monotone Woman found intensely irritating although she didn't allow this irritation to register on her implacable countenance. "Perhaps it would be better if you had no expectations of me," went on Ritzy helpfully, "because if you had no expectations, then you couldn't be disappointed."

"Your sarcasm is inappropriate Mr Thorpe-Eldridge," opined the Monotone Woman. "This is a very grave matter. You could find yourself in very serious trouble."

Ritzy, despite the masculine stubble on his chin, adopted a facial expression which was so diffident that it almost amounted to being demure. Then his features settled into a dignified sobriety that was so overdone that it contrived an imposture of the woman's own pomposity.

"Innocence is no defence against the law," he observed solemnly.

*   *   *

At that moment, and in many places, the law was under attack by the guilty. One of the more enterprising crimes was being carried out by a multiethnic street gang known as the Rudý, named for the red bandanas they wore to identify their gang affiliation. A metallic blue electric car, stolen earlier that morning, pulled up at the kerb in Prince Albert Street and the seven members of the Rudý climbed out with the self-assured nonchalance of people who view the law as somebody else's problem. Only one of them carried a concealed firearm because guns weren't easy to come by and ammunition was scarce, but all of them were armed with the weapons of the street which they wore as the tools of their trade, secreted in the long pockets of their overtly paramilitary clothing.

Ghetto gangs, known as ghangs, came in a variety of sizes and were formed for a variety of reasons. Most common were the territorial ghangs whose *raison d'etre* was to occupy and control a certain area of the city. They generally had a large membership but poor organisation because they had an inclusive policy of accepting anyone that lived locally who was willing to fight when called upon to do so. The Rudý were very different. They were a specifically criminal ghang whose collective purpose was to earn a living in hard times. They kept their numbers small and recruited selectively, not inclusively. The prime movers within the ghang were two Slovak brothers called Marek and Matej whose Slovak cousin Nina was their lieutenant, but they had non-prejudicial employment practices and the remaining four Rudý were non-Slovaks. The discrimination they exercised when accepting or rejecting a new member was the usefulness of the applicant's abilities. A capacity for physical violence was essential but other skills, especially IT skills, were particularly valued. Each person, male or female, was judged solely upon what they could bring to the table. To be one of the Rudý you had to have something worthwhile to contribute. If you were of practical value, then it didn't matter what else you were. But equally, if you had nothing to contribute then you were rejected and it still didn't matter what else you were. There was no ethnic nepotism. As professionals they were a meritocracy.

Their target today was a disused ATM cashpoint machine at a branch of a formerly well-known bank. It was located in the outside wall of the abandoned bank and so it was accessible without having to breach the steel defences that secured the building itself. The once-mighty banks had always been a curious mixture of the spendthrift and the parsimonious, and the latter trait was evident in the way they ensured that their now useless vacant properties were impregnable to squatters. It wasn't worth the effort of trying, and the buildings remained empty. But with an ATM in the outer wall the Rudý could attempt to hack into the bank from the street. There was no need to get inside.

All such cash dispensing machines had long since been disconnected, ever since the economic collapse had decimated the corporate banking system, but not all of the machines had been physically removed. Some had merely been plated over with a riveted sheet of steel. Perhaps the corporations envisaged a time when they would be restored to their former majesty and wanted to keep their infrastructure in place. If so, this was a mistake. It was possible, for those with the technical knowledge, to hack into the machine and access the dead accounts. Active bank accounts were unhackable from a disused ATM because of recent changes to the system but there were old accounts which still had small amounts of money in them even though, for one reason or another, they had ceased to be active. Many of these abandoned accounts were those of deceased customers whose executors hadn't tidied up all the bits and pieces of their residual estate properly during probate. There were a lot of these, partly as a result of the current suicide rate, and they remained accessible from the ATM. If a hacker could transfer a lot of these small sums of money into one account of their own, then the total could add up to a significant amount. The machine no longer dispensed any cash, of course, but that wasn't the intent of the hack.

Three of the Rudý huddled around the metal plate covering the cashpoint machine. The two brothers, Marek and Matej, were carrying hammers and chisels. Carbon copies of one another in their brawny athleticism, they began smashing lumps out of the brick wall around the plate to remove it. Just behind them was a Latvian girl called Taz, whose nickname was an abbreviation of Anastasia. She had the essential knowledge to make the hack into the machine.

The men were pounding vigorously with their hammers, knocking fragments of brick and plaster in all directions. The physical break-in to remove the metal plate would take longer than the actual hack itself. The two Slovaks made no attempt to muffle the noise that they were making or to conceal their actions. They were working fast but their haste was not for fear of police intervention because that would be very unlikely in this neighbourhood. Nor would they suffer any interference from pedestrians passing by in the street. None of the citizens would put themselves at risk over something which was no business of theirs. The danger, and therefore the reason for haste, was the possibility of being discovered by a rival street gang who would take advantage of the opportunity to cause a little mayhem and perhaps to rob the Rudý of their hack.

For this reason Marek and Matej had deployed their troops to spot the approach of enemies and to block any possible interference if the Rudý were so unlucky as to be discovered. Nina, a woman with a similar build to her cousins, stood guard with Painter, a Scotsman with a terrible complexion who was named for the colourful style of his extensive tattoos, on one side of the ATM. Poontang stood guard with Mars on the other side. Mars was a mixed race British-Jamaican who had taken the name of the god of war and he certainly looked suitable for the role. He was six foot five inches tall and weighed around 230lbs, none of which was anything other than muscle and bone. The stab-proof ballistic body armour strapped to his torso was sleeveless to display his Herculean arms. Standing beside him, Poontang was a stark contrast.

She was only of middle height and her gymnastic physique was strong but slender. Of Irish heritage, her short spiky blonde hair was encircled by the red bandana of the Rudý folded flat against her forehead and tied at the back. Apart from the crimson of her scarf she was dressed entirely in black; her military shirt, tactical body armour, combat trousers and army boots were all matte black. The other six Rudý were attired almost identically but only Poontang's nubile figure managed to make this militaristic uniform appear chic. She had the kind of gamine femininity that could make a woollen cardigan look fashionable. Not so with her fellow gangsters. It enhanced the masculinity of the four men and lent them a dangerously forbidding appearance. It de-feminised the other two women, making them androgynous. Yet on Poontang's lithe body the soldierly apparel, although intimidating, also displayed a definite hint of erotic mystique.

This sexual suggestiveness wasn't self-consciously deliberate but neither was it entirely unpremeditated. She was fully aware of the provocative temptation inherent in her naturally seductive girlishness. Why else would she have taken the name Poontang? Her original name had been Sarah but when she dressed to express herself she didn't feel like a Sarah, she felt like a captivatingly badass young woman called Poontang. A man had to have permission to touch her but she didn't mind them looking. And if their tongues were hanging out, that just reminded her of where the real power lay. She was nineteen years old and as fit as a greyhound. Sensibly she had been a student of freestyle combat martial arts since she was a young girl. Her fighting style wasn't traditional, she'd studied at the school of 'whatever works'. She specialised in dirty tactics. But her training had been hard and she was in superb shape so any clothing, no matter how drab or utilitarian, tended to become eroticized when it was wrapped around her supple contours.

The metal plate broke off the wall of the bank and hit the pavement with an almighty clang. The four black-clad gangsters standing guard swivelled round in response to the sudden noise but then resumed their vigilance. The street had noticeably emptied as a result of the hammering. Pedestrians could see the raid taking place ahead of them and were opting for alternative routes down side streets. It was mid-morning but the road would soon be deserted apart from the occasional car.

Taz had her portable interface wired into the inner workings of the machine. It wouldn't be too long now. Her fingers flew over the icons on the touch-screen. Accounts were automatically scrolled and non-active ones selected at a speed no human eye could follow. The programme engaged the transfers. It was easy when you had the software.

Then a chunky SUV with reinforced bumpers came roaring around the corner. It was petrol fuelled and made a hell of a racket, in low gear for maximum acceleration. Nina and Painter shouted the alarm as it came straight for them. The nearside wheels, front and rear, mounted the pavement and the chrome grate on the bonnet hurtled forward with deadly intent. Behind the SUV were a dozen teenagers in sky blue berets. Their clothes were ordinary street fashions but they all wore the light blue berets made famous by the military peacekeepers of the United Nations. They were a neighbourhood gang called the UN. They were a shabby mean-spirited bunch but they could call upon considerable numbers of bodies. They must have had to scrabble to put together a raiding party in the short time that the Rudý had been breaking into the ATM, yet they had at least twelve on foot plus however many were crammed into the SUV.

They came from the Rat Run, a shanty town half a mile away. All major cities had these cobbled together villages, constructed from cardboard and corrugated plastic and a scattering of charity tents, with their populations of the dispossessed and the superfluous. What was left of the welfare system consisted most importantly of food vouchers which could be redeemed at municipal depots. The distribution of public welfare could not stretch to address issues of homelessness. Those folk for whom private accommodation was as unrealistic an ambition as paid employment had found their way to derelict areas and created the shanty towns as somewhere to live that they could call their own. Their oil-drum bonfires and barbecue braziers kept the cold at bay in the winter. The number of residents had been copiously supplemented by the last few waves of legal and illegal migrants who had discovered nowhere to make a home in the no longer wealthy West. When the municipal authorities in many cities began spending some of their limited store of public money to provide portable toilets for the shanties it was a tacit acknowledgement that the authorities had accepted the situation as a long-term reality of modern urban life. The cardboard villages housed a great many young people.

No one was sure whether the ghetto gang had taken the name United Nations as a deliberate act of satire or whether they just happened to steal a bunch of blue berets from a warehouse, made use of them as their gang affiliation sign, and as a result had acquired the name by accident. Either way, this mattered far less than the storming ferocity of their attack. They rained down like hailstones.

The approaching vehicle tore along the street at the Rudý clearly intending to drive them down like bowling pins. Taz rapidly disconnected her interface as Marek drew an extendable baton from his armoured utility vest. Matej pulled a 10mm Glock handgun from his belt and began firing at the windscreen. Mars and Poontang ran to join their comrades, apparently unconcerned about the oncoming car. They both had sizable knives in their fists. The one that Mars carried was more like a meat cleaver or a machete. The car's windscreen shattered and Matej poured bullets into the interior. The SUV swerved wildly, bouncing down the kerb and veering drunkenly. The sixteen year old girl at the wheel was dead and soaked in blood from three or four gunshot wounds.

The remaining UN came on, screeching and yelling as they ran. A couple of them threw petrol bombs but their aim was poor and the fireball explosions didn't hit anybody. Their average age was around seventeen and they knew no fear. They owned these streets, or they believed they did. A wild-eyed lad with a baseball bat arrived first, shrieking a war-cry and swinging for a home run, but Marek evaded the crude swipe and bust the lad's face open with a backhanded strike of his baton. The weapon was blunt but the whipping impact ripped the skin apart, creating a ragged gouge through the nose and cheek. The lad put a hand to the wound and retreated, swinging the baseball bat blindly to cover his escape.

Nina was wielding a hunter's axe, light enough to use one-handed but when applied with sufficient force its keen edge could slice inches deep into flesh. A young woman in a green fleece sports shirt ran directly at Nina and launched herself in a jumping kick. It was energetic but clumsy. Nina's hatchet swung overhead as she dodged backwards and the axe blade chopped down to cut into the acrobat's shin, breaking right through the bone. The woman screamed as she dropped to the ground and lay clutching at her leg, staring at the grisly wound in horror.

A bulky UN thug, somewhat older than his comrades-in-arms, who charged in at Painter had his eyes fixed firmly on the stun gun in Painter's right hand. The electric weapon was emitting a loud crackling noise and the fighter in the blue beret knew that he had to avoid letting it make contact with his body. He clattered to a sudden halt and faced-off against his opponent, holding a stiletto dagger high in a reverse grip, ready to strike down at Painter's right arm to disable the man. Vigilant for any movement of the stun gun, he closed in to narrow the gap between them. But when he came within striking range Painter snapped out an unexpected front kick which caught the thug in the balls and doubled him up. As the assailant collapsed to his knees at Painter's feet the tattooed man calmly pressed the stun gun between the thug's shoulder blades to make a firm contact and sent a high-voltage pulse of electricity into him. The defeated fighter shook as the current ripped through him and he fell face forward.

Mars raised his muscular arms, waving the machete in his fist, and roared like a bear. But no one came near him. He was a scary fucker. Nobody wanted to try him. Mars ran into the group of oncoming youngsters but they broke apart to scatter, leaving the big guy with no opponent to fight.

But a solidly built eighteen year old fancied his chances with Poontang. He darted toward her with a butcher's knife held out in front of him. Poontang held her own knife defensively. The young man came in fast and lunged but Poontang sidestepped. His momentum meant that he couldn't stop and as he plunged passed her she slashed laterally in a tight circle, bringing her knifepoint into his body. Poontang was aiming for his chest but the blade caught his throat, slicing through tendons and raking a trench in the side of his neck. The careering body spun crazily and crashed to the pavement.

The initial rush of the UN had spent its force and, with surprise no longer on their side, they ran to positions of relative safety to regroup behind the closely packed Rudý. But it was a shock to the UN to see four of their number writhing in agony in the gutter and their car fifty yards down the street crashed into the concrete post of a streetlight. A pause of uncertainty swept over them.

The Rudý's own vehicle was parked on the other side of the road. Marek, the tactician in the gang, made use of the momentary hiatus in the fighting to make their exit, and yelled to the others to get in the car. The black figures in the red headscarves ran across the street and bundled into their vehicle, the women sitting on the laps of the men in the back seat. The UN saw that their prey was escaping and rushed the car. Matej fired the engine and they squealed away in the stink of burning rubber. He drove into a couple of UN gangsters who were knocked aside by the weight of the vehicle. The Rudý sped off with Matej changing up through the gears with an impressive nought-to-sixty acceleration. No one was going to catch Matej when he had a set of wheels under him.

It hadn't gone entirely to plan but all's well that end's well. They were away clean with nobody hurt except a few of the UN and nothing damaged except the unregarded estates of a few thousand deceased customers of corporate banking. Both enemies could afford the loss. And who cared if they couldn't afford it? The big banks of the past had robbed everyone blind when they'd had the upper hand. Now that the world had changed they couldn't expect any mercy, never having shown any. The Rudý liked to target the relics of the former society. It was a kind of justice to feed off the people who had fucked up the world.

The political beliefs of the Rudý did not allow them to steal from the local community banks that were cooperatively run within communities, operating on a purely local level, which had taken the place of the big corporate banks in the lives of those ordinary people who still made use of a banking system. But the old dinosaurs were considered a legitimate target by pretty much everybody and there was a special satisfaction to be derived from raiding them. The Rudý were thieves with principles.

Chapter Two

Lines on a Map

Outside the imposing edifice of the Civic Administration Offices the street was scarred with graffiti and a little smoke-blackened from petrol bombs but you could tell that this was an area serviced by the police because the kerbs were choked with cars and none of them were burned out. The authorities still exercised control here. Ritzy walked briskly away from his latest encounter with the officers of the Civic Investigation and set off toward the northern quarter. He had no vehicle and would have to walk home on a route that would take him passed several disputed neighbourhoods.

He kept mostly to the shopping streets. These were neutral ground. Each ethnic community had its residential area with recognised boundaries but the high street shops were a no-man's land where all the different communities met. Culture-specific shops could be found within each community but retail businesses that drew their custom from diversity were necessarily located in-between the community borders. They occupied ground in the gaps. These were the streets where the riots most often took place because people weren't such fools as to trash their own residential areas, they rioted in the places that belonged to nobody in particular and where there were plenty of shops to loot. But the advantage of these streets was that anyone could walk along them without getting hassled for being somewhere that they didn't belong. These were the arteries of the city where the pedestrian traffic could move relatively freely.

More and more, life was becoming about geography. Cultural and ethnic divisions were laid out on the ground like a demographic map. You had to be aware of which streets were safe to use, how to get from one street to another, which junctions used to be okay but which weren't any longer. Everyone carried a diagram around in their head to plot a reasonably safe course from where they were to where they were going. The lines on this mental map were variable and impermanent. The shifting power-balance between communities meant that the map had to be continually updated. Security was transitory. If you wanted to make it home without being blooded or robbed, you had better be sure you knew who was dominating which roads and housing estates at the moment. It was all about keeping up with the geography of jeopardy and sanctuary.

Ritzy hummed to himself. It was an old tune whose lyrics he couldn't quite remember, but the melody was one of those that went round in a satisfying circle without any beginning or end. Ritzy was an inveterate hummer, although he never described himself as such because to some people a "hummer" was a type of blowjob and any confusion in the matter would have been unfortunate. But it didn't stop him humming. He crossed an intersection. Ahead of him was a large mural inexpertly painted on the side of a house. It depicted the Khanda, the symbol of Sikhism, with its three swords. The next few streets ahead were a Punjabi Sikh area. He hesitated. Sikh communities were usually okay for a white foreigner like himself to pass through, but he decided to play it safe and skirt the area by taking Cromwell Avenue which connected with Tennyson Lane.

Territories were often identified by murals. It was a method borrowed from Northern Ireland where sectarian divisions on the ground had been signalled by huge wall paintings supporting the Catholic/Republican cause or the Protestant/Loyalist cause. In England nowadays the sectarian divisions were very much more complex because there were far more than just two sides. It was the multi-sectarianism of pluralism. Since the economic collapse even the multicultis had been forced to admit that multiculturalism had descended into multi-sectarianism, although they refused to accept that the descent had been predictable and inevitable. Nor did they accept any blame for what they'd done. They were still blaming everyone except themselves and insisting that the situation could be saved with sufficient good will. The establishment never changed their tune because their vanity wouldn't permit them to confess that they'd been wrong. They were still parroting the same old multiculturalist propaganda that they'd been endlessly regurgitating all their lives. But the murals proved otherwise.

A common feature in these paintings were gun-wielding paramilitaries. If the paramilitaries wore beards, it made a big difference whether they were wearing headscarves or turbans, the former being Muslim and the latter being Sikh. If the paramilitaries wore dreadlocks, then they were African-Caribbean. If the paramilitaries were white, then they were East European, although whether they were Russian, Polish, Rumanian, Bulgarian or something else was another matter. If a mural displayed images of blood-soaked people, then this confirmed that the area would be particularly hostile. Images of men with guns was an explicit warning, but images of people being killed was a declaration of war.

The most ubiquitous mural was the prohibition symbol, a red circle with a diagonal line through it. All communities used this sign in their murals. If you saw a prohibition symbol, then you had better be sure that whatever was depicted inside that circle didn't include you. If it did, then you were prohibited. A lot of murals were brightly coloured Arabic script which Ritzy couldn't read. Most graffiti was unintelligible to English speakers but that was okay so long as you could identify the language. It wasn't important to know what it said but it was vital to know which community had written it. What mattered was to connect the murals with their corresponding cultures, since that was the whole point of them. They were about sectarian identity. You'd be a fool to walk where you weren't welcome.

There were some areas that you obviously didn't venture into at all. Not under any circumstances. The central government called them Exclusion Zones. The mail was not delivered there because postal workers could not enter the area without being set upon by the local ghetto gang. Ghangsters were extremely territorial and proud of their borders. Nor could firefighters or ambulances cross the ethnic threshold without being stoned with bricks and bottles, so naturally they didn't cross it at all. When the police reluctantly acknowledged that they could no longer be expected to maintain the rule of law within these neighbourhoods, the segregation of these districts was complete and they were officially classified as Exclusion Zones. The majority of these zones were Islamic but the practice of ethnic self-segregation was spreading. There were very strict laws within these neighbourhoods by which everyone had to abide, but the laws were enforced by whichever ghang or ethnic culture exercised power in the area. Writing their own laws entailed imposing their own punishments which were as harsh as they were immediate. Ghang enforcers literally took no prisoners, having no facilities for confinement, so beatings were the standard penalty. Mistakenly wandering into an Exclusion Zone could turn very nasty very quickly. But what made them especially dangerous was the way that their boundaries shifted. You had to be cognisant of who was in charge of which streets at any given time.

Ritzy consulted his touchpad. It was a multipurpose device, like all electronics. His finger jabbed the icon for his local map. The GPS tracker had been modified and encrypted, of course, as no one who worked in the shadow economy could have done business safely if their location were easily identifiable by those who thought it proper to take your earnings to finance their own agenda. The local map on the touchpad was an aid to memory. Free streets were shown in green; foreign but accessible streets were shown in amber; forbidden streets were shown in red. Ritzy kept it updated as best he could.

He put his touchpad into one of the many pockets of his sleeveless utility jacket, tipped his bowler hat over his eyes, and stuck his fists into his blue-grey military shorts. He was unarmed because he wouldn't have been able to get anything passed the metal-detection scanners at the entrance of the Civic Administration Offices. Going inside any public building involved a certain amount of undressing and x-rays, so the only blades you had any chance of smuggling through were ceramic blades and Ritzy didn't own one. But he walked along with his fists bunched inside his pockets in a way to suggest that he might be clutching a concealed weapon. The lean muscularity of his body was apparent in his baggies and Ritzy wasn't too worried. He travelled today with a fair degree of confidence. Recent months had been reasonably quiet compared to the kind of civil unrest to which people had grown accustomed. The long series of race riots which had burned through the country during the worst couple of years of the global financial meltdown had left a permanent mark upon urban life and had produced a thousand further outbreaks of rioting as the aftershocks of this earthquake. Those two years were known colloquially as "The Rupture". Societies in the western world had been limping heavily ever since. The wound wasn't about to heal any time soon.

This time around the economic collapse hadn't been like the 20th century crash of the great depression. In the 1930s, despite the political divisions caused by social class, each nation had at least been unified by its ethnic integrity; a common national identity shared by its citizens. It had allowed for the idea that "we're all in this together", even if that idea had been somewhat naïve. But the 21st century crash had occurred in pluralist societies which were radically disunited by diversity. They had no ethnic integrity at all. Without a national community there was no national identity and without a national identity there was no *nation* in any meaningful sense. There was only a multiplicity of cultures. So when money got tight, when resources got scarce, when people got hungry, each ethnic community was concerned to take care only of their own people. Society became an internecine conflict of each community against every other community, and the devil could take the hindmost. The sectarianism of multiple cultures had become entrenched behind ethnic barricades.

Ritzy strode along, his demeanour only slightly furtive, his mental radar not setting off any alarms in his head. The world in which Ritzy had grown to manhood was an uncertain place, and it wasn't always easy to know how best to stay safe. But Ritzy understood his world and he did not fear it.

He nodded a passing hello to Renata who was standing at her usual pitch under the railway bridge. Renata was of indeterminate ethnicity but she bore the impressively strong facial features of a Slavic heredity along with the yellow-brown fingers of a dealer in tobacco. Renata sold black market cigarettes for the Romanian mafia who had controlled the trade in this district ever since they'd driven out the Russians. That had been a bloody turf war. But Renata was one of nature's survivors and, having previously worked for the Russians, she now had the same job with the Romanians. She did okay for herself. She paid her own way in life. Ritzy admired folk who stood on their own two feet, even if they had to dance around from time to time when circumstances changed. Renata was around thirty years of age and didn't wear cosmetics, which was a sure sign that she didn't live off a man. She'd taken a beating from the ghangs once or twice, like any street trader, but she was still earning a wage from illicit cigarettes rather than climbing on to some man's back and expecting him to carry her. Despite the occasional beating and the ethnic vagaries of her employment Renata sold her ciggies and paid her bills. Ritzy respected her for that.

Tobacco smokers had been forced into buying from the illegal trade by the incredible expense of this luxury item when prices had been set by central government. Legal cigarettes had been done to death by inflated prices, three quarters of which had been taxation. Those smokers who hadn't given up the habit entirely couldn't afford anything but the duty-free weed supplied by international smugglers. The sale of tobacco had never been officially criminalized but the trade now belonged entirely to the underground merchants. The black market straddled the shadow economy of self-employed workers who were off-the-grid and the criminal economy that was operated by the ghetto gangs and the ethnic mafias. These two economies divided the black market between them depending on what type of product or service was being purchased. Tobacco, which required warehousing and wide-scale distribution, was very much in the hands of the ethnic mafias.

The loss of tobacco tax had been bad news for the legitimate economy but the huge drop in revenue had been remedied by the simple expedient of legalizing several other drugs which had previously been illegal, especially marijuana. The growing of marijuana remained illegal because that undermined the government's ability to levy taxes on the product but the sale and smoking of grass was unfettered. It had become a major money-spinner, almost equalling taxation on petrol now that far fewer people could afford private cars. The new policy was beneficial all-round. Criminal drug barons were cut out of the equation and so buying marijuana became much safer. Millions of ordinary people were decriminalized. The exchequer made an absolute fortune. In fact, the only disadvantage was that the grass smokers and other recreational drug users now had to pay much higher prices for their drugs because these were now taxed as heavily as tobacco had formerly been. The price of marijuana quadrupled as a result of legalization. Governments were even greedier than drug barons and, unlike the barons, central government had a monopoly on the taxation of imports. The barons had found themselves having to settle for the smaller but still substantial profits to be made from tobacco.

By and large, however, the legitimate economy with its government restrictions and legal permissions struggled to compete with the shadow economy with its tax-free entrepreneurship which enabled it to under-price and out-perform its law-abiding rivals. In the current circumstances illegitimate commercial trading was flourishing. When legitimate businesses are on their death bed coughing up blood, it's the underground suppliers and dealers who own all the antibiotics. The criminal economy was going from strength to strength also, with its cyber-crime and extortion. The protection rackets, which threatened commercial companies with a cyber attack that would destroy their business if they didn't pay off regularly, were incredibly lucrative. Identity-theft was also a growth industry.

This ongoing commercial struggle between the lawful economy and the unlawful economies was the overriding concern of politicians these days, even more than internecine ethic rivalries and public violence. They knew that they couldn't do anything about the latter two social problems but they still nurtured the fond hope that they might be able to regain control over the money supply. Central government's main strategy to achieve this was their attempt to end all use of cash. This policy was represented to the public as a necessary measure because paper money had lost its value almost entirely in The Rupture, but everyone understood that the government was actually just trying to circumvent black market trading by restricting all commercial transactions to electronic finance. If all money was nothing more than numbers on a computer screen, then whoever controlled the computers controlled the economy. In this way the government and the banks could recover their monopoly of control.

The strategy hadn't worked. Since the sequestration of financial resources from private bank accounts during The Rupture, when all private holdings of money over a set limit had been appropriated by the government to pay for essential public services, most people were even less willing to trust their personal wealth to electronic banking than they were to trust cash. They had learned that central government could grant themselves the authority to change the numbers on a computer screen without your permission and suddenly you only had half the money in your account than you'd had the day before. So, although the authorities burned vast quantities of paper money in the civic furnaces, enough cash remained in circulation to keep the shadow economy in operation.

Renata returned Ritzy's nod of hello as he went by, but she didn't speak or move from her pitch, nor did he pause in his walking. Business was being conducted. Renata was in brief conversation with a teenage girl dressed in street-whore-chic who was buying a packet of twenty pre-rolled. In her tiny skirt and skimpy top she appeared slightly undernourished yet too fleshy in the thighs. The aesthetic effect fell short of the image she was attempting. Somehow she managed to look both skinny and flabby at the same time. Ritzy told himself that she was about as erotic as the steam coming off a dog turd. He told himself this although it wasn't strictly true. Ritzy noticed the pert peaches of the girl's arse but his eyes didn't linger. He couldn't afford flesh and he couldn't afford crotch-rot. Medication was hard to come by. The remains of the healthcare system wasn't able to provide for everyone and, in time-honoured fashion, men tended to be relegated to the back of the queue. They were expected to crawl away and die stoically so that the limited supply of available medical treatment could be given to women and children first. A stoical acceptance of death had always been the recommended procedure for the expendable sex.

Before the financial system had caved in upon itself the number of male suicides had been three, four, or even five times higher than the number of female suicides. Men had killed themselves in droves to escape a world that had no role for them except that of a beast of burden and a political guilt-object. Society had failed men, yet it was men who had punished themselves for society's failure. Society had failed to recognise their value as men, but a guilt-object could not blame anyone but himself for this. So they killed themselves. It was hard for men to find self-esteem in a society that was not conscious of their intrinsic worth but saw them only in terms of their utility value to women. For men to learn to live for themselves, they first had to learn that they, as men, were worth living for.

But since The Rupture it wasn't only men who were killing themselves. Life was hard, and the suicide rate had spiked for women. Suicides among the over-sixties of both sexes had skyrocketed. No one could actually put a figure on it because there weren't the highly paid researchers and academics to collate the statistics any more. Their non-essential occupations had been downsized to nothing when public spending had been cut to essential services only. But everyone could witness for themselves how many old people were making the choice that they'd rather end their lives than continue to live in the present circumstances. They didn't have the resilience to endure. Those of the baby-boomer generation who were still alive in The Rupture had been the first to go. This was ironically apposite as they were the generation who had started the political policies of demographic revolution which had made the consequences of the economic collapse so much worse. They received very little sympathy from their juniors when they killed themselves rather than face the consequences of what they had done. Besides, they were very old and people didn't have much respect or consideration for the elderly. Humanitarianism, like cigarettes, was a luxury item and people couldn't afford it any more.

Ritzy wasn't heading straight home, first he had to see a client about an estimate. He was a freelance mechanic and his skills were much in demand now that spare parts were difficult to find due to the reduction in imports. Fewer people had cars than formerly but those who did own vehicles generally had no idea of how they worked and had no one to teach them. Legal garages were prohibitively expensive because they had to comply with all the cripplingly time-consuming regulations and licensing which doubled their prices and, having jumped through all these bureaucratic hoops, licensed garages were reluctant to work "off the books" because the penalties would probably bankrupt them. By contrast, Ritzy had no paperwork, charged a cash fee, and did the job to the customer's specifications without informing their insurance company. These advantages ensured that customers were not too hard to find. It was individual freelancers like Ritzy who kept most cars on the road, although they had to get creative in their substitution and adaptation of spare parts. It was a make-do-and-mend approach. But people were growing accustomed to that in these straightened times. Ritzy was content in his work. He could make a living wage and he was his own boss.

He didn't have his bag of tools with him this morning because he didn't fancy lugging them all over town. Besides, he would've had to leave the bag in the property office when he went through the metal detectors at the Civic Administration Offices and it was more than possible that someone might have peeked inside. In which case they'd have seen his tools and could have put two and two together to answer the question that so preoccupied the panel of the Civic Investigation: how did he earn his living? Better to just visit the client to view the wreckage this morning and quote the woman a price to fix it. She was a new customer, recommended by one of his regulars. Like the rest of the shadow economy, Ritzy's one-man business was bespoke.

He took Dixon Street to avoid the primary school in Wilmot Road. Men of Ritzy's age didn't go anywhere near what the authorities termed "child-oriented locales". Too damn dangerous. Any man could get accused of anything at any time. When Ritzy had told the Civic Investigation that innocence was no defence against the law, he hadn't limited the principle to tax evasion. Why risk Wilmot Road when he could take an alternative route. Dixon Street was mostly boarded up housing and it was populated by a poor but thriving community of squatters whose unity was strong enough to keep the local ghanghs at bay. Despite their diversity they had a powerful community bond because of their shared illegal occupation of the premises in which they lived. They viewed themselves solely in terms of economic class, not race, ethnicity, or gender. Dixon Street was wide open to anyone except official representatives of the state and rich people. Squatter communes like Dixon Street were the best of diversification because their class-politics made multiculti diversity a complete irrelevance. The harsh realities of hard times had caused them to abandon the victimology of The Correct. The doctrines and dogmas of the PWKB had no influence here. Ritzy strolled along, able to more or less relax for the length of the road.

With it being his fortieth birthday today Ritzy was in a reflective mood. As usual, a meditative frame of mind sent his thoughts in the direction of contemplating the radical changes he'd witnessed in his lifetime. That happened to people in early middle-age and Ritzy was no different. Besides, when social disruption occurred on such a vast scale you couldn't really ignore it. Reality intruded willy-nilly. The revolutionary transformations Ritzy had seen since his father's time were as dramatic as those which his dad had witnessed from the world of Ritzy's grandfather.

His father, Michael, had been born in 1965, right on the cusp of the New World Order of feminism and multiculturalism. He'd watched "political correctness" become the intransigent cultural establishment known subsequently as "The Correct" or the PWKB, the "People Who Know Best". Michael had been a young man when the judgemental intelligentsia of the PWKB had seized power and he'd been a loyal follower of their credo. He'd endorsed all their mission statements. It had cost him his self-esteem, his son, and ultimately his life when he joined the male suicide statistics. But he had tried to keep his faith right up until the end. He had spent his wasted life trying to conform to the restrictive thought control and behavioural norms of those who knew what a man like him ought to think and ought to be. He had approved of the things that he had been told to approve of, and he had disapproved of the things that he had been told to disapprove of; he had said the things which he had been told to say and he had avoided saying the things which he had been told he was forbidden to say; he had welcomed the things that he had been told to welcome and he had shunned the things that he had been told to shun. Michael had been a good little boy and followed his teachers' instructions. He had believed what he had been told to believe. In this regard Michael had been merely one among hundreds of millions.

The New World Order had acted as if they had a natural right to rule, as if they were the only people who were fit to rule, fit to make political decisions, fit to have an opinion. Debate between The Correct and ordinary people had always been impossible because the establishment had treated all opinions contrary to their own as illegitimate. The PWKB believed themselves to be opposed to prejudice, and with childish over-simplicity they had assumed that anyone who disagreed with them must therefore want to perpetuate prejudice. As their own politics were all about fighting *against* prejudice, they felt entitled to take it for granted that anyone who disagreed with them must be fighting *in favour* of prejudice. If you didn't support their policies, then you must be motivated by prejudice. What other reason could there be? So the PWKB decided that whenever anyone disagreed with ideological correctness these contrary opinions could be dismissed because, of course, prejudice invalidates an opinion. This left feminist multiculturalism as the only legitimate point of view. All opposing opinion was bigotry.

They had never once doubted that they occupied the moral high ground, which meant that those folk who disagreed with them must be immoral. To express a contrary opinion was wickedness. Political opponents were necessarily ignorant oafs who were spouting hate-speech. Consequently, any genuine discussion had always been unworkable because the feminist multiculti establishment were a political class who refused ever to come down from their high horse and treat their opponents' point of view as a valid opinion. Anything ideologically incorrect was by definition invalid.

They were like The Guardians in Platonic philosophy; an elite class of correctly educated persons whose rule over society was justified by their superior knowledge. How ironic that the Guardian should have been the name of their favourite newspaper. How foolish that this situation should have been confused with any idea of democracy. Plato would have told them that his Guardian class of philosopher-kings were dead-set against democracy. It was rule by the People Who Know Best.

Ritzy's contempt for his betters made him feel bitterly resentful toward the arrogance of his parent's generation. They had been so wrong for so long and yet so blithely unaware of it. Mind you, many of his own generation weren't much better. It had taken a global economic catastrophe to wake some of them up from the self-aggrandising slumbers of The Correct.

He left Dixon Street behind him and traipsed along Devonshire Avenue, down passed the monument erected in stone to the fallen in two world wars. The 20th had been the century of nationalist wars but the 21st was the century of civil wars. Ritzy wondered which was worse.

If you judged it solely on body-count, then the nationalist wars had been far worse. But that was because they'd been fought with tanks and planes and artillery and suchlike. Heavy armaments. Not to mention gas chambers. Whereas the fighting during The Rupture had only killed a few tens of thousands across the whole European continent. Small potatoes in comparison. The weaponry had mostly been nail bombs and other IEDs and small arms. Lots of skirmishes but no set-piece battles. And since it was a civilian conflict it was hampered by the fact that the majority of people had no idea of how to fight. They'd always expected men in uniform to do that for them. Militarily it might have been considered a damp squib.

Yet what made the civil wars throughout Europe so terrible was that your enemies weren't the people from a neighbouring country, they were the people from a neighbouring street or a different area of your own home town. People couldn't take the sustained level of terror and insecurity. It may have been the first conflict in history in which the most common war wound was post-traumatic stress. The feminised populations of Europe hadn't been tough enough to bear the relentless psychological pressure. That stress hadn't decreased much even after the worst of the fighting was over.

No one had forgotten. It wasn't just the multiethnic confrontations, it was the loss of welfare provision when the nations went bankrupt. The underclass, deprived of their means of livelihood, had set about burning to the ground the society which had betrayed them. They had no other weapons but their fists, kitchen knives, hammers from the toolbox, but they had risen in their rage. They had no weapons of mass destruction. The closest thing they had to it was fire, so that became their weapon of choice. They had burned and burned. Nowadays they lived in the shanty towns and united as ghangs. They hadn't forgotten either.

It had been hunger and homelessness which had re-established some kind of peace. For most people feeding themselves and their families took priority over cultural and territorial disputes. But nothing had been settled. Diversification didn't permit any overarching political structure to be put into place that could settle it. The future remained up for grabs.

In the meantime people had to find a way to get on with life. Ritzy smiled at the thought because he was looking straight at an example of that, right now. Up ahead was a kiosk in the street, an octagonal booth just large enough for one occupant to work in comfortably, with the word "Translations" written on it in several different languages. In the past the kiosk had been a state-owned information centre serving tourists and visitors to the city. These days it was privately owned and had another function.

Barbara the translator was sitting behind the reinforced plexiglass window of her booth. Ritzy didn't know her personally but everyone around here knew of her. Barbara was a landmark in this part of town. She had a nice little business translating both the written and the spoken word for a very diverse clientele. She was fluent in five languages and spoke a couple more passably well. In today's society there were plenty of people whose command of English wasn't reliable enough to extend to matters that involved the exchange of money. Local traders and suppliers needed to know exactly what their mutual agreements and commitments entailed. So Barbara was consulted to ensure that the various partners in prospective business ventures were fully cognisant of the contracts into which they were entering. It was worth their while employing Barbara in order to avoid expensive contractual disagreements later. On rare occasions, this included contracts of marriage in which precision of vocabulary was especially important. At the moment a young man in Arabic clothing was discussing something with Barbara through the grill in her booth window. It must have been something of vital significance because he was gesticulating like a semaphore signaller.

Barbara was one practical solution to the mess that everyone was in. She didn't negotiate but she did facilitate negotiation. She provided a valuable service precisely because it was practical and immediate. Nobody had any time to waste on the verbiage and procrastination of the political class with their policy solutions. Their academic studies and political speeches about long-term inclusively proactive sustainable solutions weren't convincing anyone but themselves. Harsh economic circumstances were quick to cut through the bullshit. People had to live.

Not that The Correct gave up trying. They had always seen themselves as the vanguard. As far as they were concerned, small scale solutions organised by ordinary people like Barbara were no doubt admirable but such things could never replace the larger vision. Only the vanguard could point the way forward. The role of everyone else was to follow their lead. They had always paid lip-service to democracy but they had never actually practiced democracy because that would have required permitting the common people to make the decisions, and the PWKB did not trust the common people to decide correctly. The people had to be led by the progressives. This was the only way that progress could be achieved. Who but they could take society in the direction that it ought to travel? Who but they understood these things? After all, they were the educated elite, the cultural elite, the ethical elite, the ideological elite. The PWKB, who viewed their politics as being *anti-elitist*, preferred the reassurance of complaisant self-congratulation over the unpleasant cruelty of self-knowledge.

They called themselves progressives because the word 'progress' has such a positive ring to it. Progress had to be a good thing, right? Upwards and onwards and all that. It had never occurred to them that progress is simply forward motion. Whether progress is good or bad depends upon what it is that you're progressing toward. If the growth of cancer in your body is progressing, this is not a good thing. If two cars are progressing swiftly down the road toward an imminent collision, this is not a good thing. If you're a bunch of lemmings progressing toward the edge of a cliff, this is not a good thing. If the economy is progressing steadily toward financial meltdown, this is not a good thing. If you're pursuing policies which alienate men from women, alienate men from children, fragment society into ethnic sectarianism, and facilitate the imperialist ambitions of Islamic fascism, then okay this is certainly progress but it's progress in the wrong direction. Not that the progressives could believe this of themselves because they couldn't get passed their ideological conceit. They couldn't believe themselves mistaken. How could they, the elites, possibly be wrong? They were the progressives and the word 'progress' sounds so optimistic and upbeat that it just had to be right.

Ideological conceit had always been central to their belief-system and not even the crushing events of the last twenty years had been able to change their minds. They had always been so convinced that in the end everyone would come around to seeing things from the correct point of view that they had never once questioned or doubted their faith. Like any other religious ideologues, they did not deal in knowledge they dealt in certainties. To doubt the truth espoused by The Correct was sin. To think differently was heresy. Eventually all the doubters and dissidents must come to realise that the People Who Know Best had been right all along. On that great and glorious day when the policies of The Correct finally came to fruition no one would be able to deny that the progressives had been fully justified in steamrolling over all opposition. The establishment elites had been so certain that their policies must have utopian outcomes that they had given no thought to the probability, or even the possibility, of dystopian consequences.

Meanwhile the social divisions had increased exponentially and society had fragmented. A bull in a china shop may be intending to buy a Crown Derby tea set, but that's not what's going to happen. Multiculturalist intentions bore strikingly little resemblance to the real consequences of their actions.

They had ruled in blind, deaf, closed-minded, authoritarian conceit as the decades rolled by until The Rupture had finally brought society crashing down around them. They had squandered everything bequeathed to them by earlier generations, they had collapsed the economy with unprecedented national debt, they had created internecine divisions with their socially divisive policy of multiple cultures, they had set women and men at each others' throats, yet many of the PWKB remained entrenched in denial about the actual consequences of their misrule. They had never cared much for evidence. Ritzy's interview with the panel of the Civic Investigation was a choice example of that. The imposition of a bachelor tax had been a miserable failure but the bureaucrats persisted in their attempts at enforcing it. They continued to behave as if they were still in charge, regardless of how ineffectual they had become. They'd been in power for so long that they couldn't imagine power being taken away from them even after they'd lost it. Their political naïveté bordered on imbecility and their ignorance was matched only by their inability to conceal it.

Ritzy had it in mind to stop for his lunch in the small park at the corner of Walpole Road, which was on his route, so he dropped into the Polish grocers on the edge of the park. The heavy metal shutters were down over the plate glass window, as they always were day and night, but the door stood wide open to indicate that they weren't closed. The shop was only Polish in terms of ownership, not in its consumer products. He took a can of Oak & Acorn ale from the refrigerated unit, and a double-size pack of ham and mustard sandwiches. The young woman behind the counter had a swarthy skin and dyed-blonde hair. It didn't suit her but that was her affair, not Ritzy's. She offered him the machine for an e-payment but he held up a cash note and she gave him a lop-sided smile. The transaction was illegal but that was the government's affair, not hers.

The weather wasn't great and the park benches were occupied but he loitered near the trees drinking and munching. Oak & Acorn was a Dorset brewery and one of Ritzy's favourites. He didn't know where the sandwiches came from and it didn't matter. There were no litter bins in the park because they'd been removed when someone in authority had decided that they were too likely to be used as bomb drops, but there was an unofficial litter bin in the form of an oil drum which some considerate citizen had placed near the park entrance, so Ritzy threw his empty can and package in there. He sighed. No one was going to use a litter bin in a park as a bomb drop because the loss of life wouldn't be sufficiently impressive. A railway station or an airport, yes, but not a park. But it was easier to remove litter bins than it was to put them back. The person in authority had doubtless made their decision from within the bubble of bureaucratic regulation without consulting the local people who actually used the park. It was typical. Ritzy went on his way.

Heading for Doncaster Road, he took a shortcut through the multi-storey car park. No one parked here any more, of course, as their car would have been trashed in the first five minutes. But it was still used by pedestrians who didn't want to traipse all the way around the no-access gated community of Mayberry Square in order to get to Doncaster Road. The deserted multi-storey was a route that could be a bit dicey sometimes but Ritzy thought it was safe enough if you kept your eyes and ears open.

As he walked across the ground level he heard excited shouts coming from the basement level. They weren't cries of alarm or distress, they were the whoops and hollers of a sporting contest. It piqued his interest. He wasn't a gambler, as he wasn't fond of giving his hard-earned money away to bookies who were already richer than he was, but he didn't mind being a spectator. He strolled toward the downward slope to the basement level, his eyes checking ahead in case of trouble.

He descended the slope only far enough to see what was going on. There was a large group of men and women standing in a circle around two contestants who were slugging it out in a brutal fist fight. They were a multiracial crowd but all had a short yellow scarf tied around their left arm above the bicep. Ritzy recognised it as a ghang affiliation sign. They were, if memory served, the Jean Jammers.

The two fighters in the centre of the ring were pounding on each other with serious intent. Ritzy knew what this set-up was. A couple of ghangsters had quarrelled over something and had decided to settle the matter in time-honoured fashion with their fists. It happened a lot. In the absence of any recognised legitimate authority it was necessary to have some formal method of resolving disputes. The rest of their enclosed community were present to bear witness to the result and to enjoy the sport.

The fight may have been primarily a settlement of the personal quarrel between the two women but that didn't stop the audience from gambling on the outcome. These staged combats between individuals were usually single-sex contests because in a fair fight most women couldn't hold their own against most men, which not only made women reluctant to challenge men but it also meant that such contests were useless for gambling purposes when so few punters were willing to bet their stake on the female fighter. In a single-sex contest, however, betting was brisk.

It was amongst the ghetto gangs that women and men mixed most freely and had the greatest measure of equality because the female ghangsters behaved exactly as the male ghangsters behaved. In the ghangs there were no gender roles to speak of; no disparity in the way that people were treated. There was a lot of fucking, of course, but no gender roles. Ghang life, especially in the shanty towns, was too poor to permit anyone to claim privileged treatment and the female ghangsters had ceased to expect any. They took their lumps like the men. Nobody shed any tears for either.

In their crude fashion the ghangs practiced a meritocracy. You got ahead by proving your own worth without any help from anyone else. The strong took the lead and the weak did what they were told. It was a hard school. The proof of that was evident in the condition of the two fighters. Their faces were badly cut and bleeding, their chests heaving with exertion, as their struggle continued.

Both women were black, although one was much lighter-skinned than the other. Ritzy identified them in his mind as 'red vest' and 'blue shirt' which is what they wearing, along with identical pairs of stretch-denim skinny jeans. There was a certain amount of girly hair pulling when they grabbed hold and wrestled, but for the most part they fought as men would fight, toe to toe and punching with a closed fist. There was a long-standing hostility between the two ghangsters which gave the fight real venom and they were providing their fellow Jean Jammers with an entertaining bout of grappling and bare-knuckle boxing. The crowd around them were having a high old time.

Red vest had an impressive pair of breasts and, naturally, blue shirt was targeting her opponent's bust with body punches. It was a rule followed by everybody: when fighting a man, hit him in the balls; when fighting a woman, hit her in the tits. Blue shirt was obviously familiar with this common sense combat technique because as Ritzy watched she caught the women with a strong right hook to the left breast which sent a shudder of pain through red vest and set her jugs quivering. But she countered quickly with a crunching straight right to the forehead. Blue shirt walked right into it as she tried to get in close to work the body and it rocked her back on her heels.

The crowd roared their approval with each solid thump that landed. They appeared to be unpartisan, cheering on both fighters equally. What they wanted was blood and glory, and plenty of it. Red vest sent a wild haymaker scything around at blue shirt's head but missed as her cagey adversary ducked underneath it in a crouch and attacked the tits again. The lancing agony of an uppercut to the jugs caused red vest to lower her guard, wanting to protect her torso more effectively by tucking in her elbows, and blue shirt immediately went high and caught the other woman with a sweet little left jab to the nose.

From what Ritzy could see at a distance, red vest was getting the worst of it but she wasn't ready to give best to the other woman. It was a matter of pride. The pain of the damage to her body was less frightening than the threat of damage to her reputation. She didn't have to win to preserve her reputation but she did have to put up a good fight. Surrender too soon and you were diminished, but lose courageously to a superior opponent and you kept your respect. Also, she hated the other bitch and the desire to punch her face through the back of her head was a powerful motivation to keep battling.

Unfortunately Ritzy saw nothing further because at that moment one of the crowd happened to look up from the spectacle and he noticed Ritzy loitering on the downward slope. The guy drew the attention of some of the other gangsters to this intrusion by an outsider. Ritzy knew better than to hang around. He was up the slope in a flash and running across the car park toward Doncaster Road before any of the ghang had decided to chase him. He knew that they weren't likely to bother, as the fight was a good one and they'd want to see it to the finish. He would have liked to himself.

Ghang culture wasn't something which had developed overnight after The Rupture. It had been a long time in gestation during the preceding decades. Ritzy could remember, when he was a child, his mother expressing astonishment at a television news report showing CCTV footage of a violent attack committed by an all-girl gang. His mother had been aghast because she'd always taken it for granted that street gangs were an exclusively male social phenomenon in which women played no part. Ritzy seldom wondered what his estranged mother thought of the world these days, as he had no doubt that she would blame it all on the usual suspects. Her own political opinions had ruled unchallenged over the decades which had created the society that Ritzy now had to live in, but he'd never known her to accept any responsibility for it. What happens in the present is so often determined by decisions that were taken in the past. But just try to get the decision-makers of the past to admit it.

Although the powers-that-be might repudiate all blame for what they had done over the last fifty years, they wouldn't be able to fool themselves for much longer. Brutal reality had caught up with The Correct, as it inevitably had to, including those at the highest levels of political office. It wasn't just the economy over which they were failing to exercise their customary power. Government structures were being compelled to adapt also. Everything was slipping out of the control of the Westminster politicians and the oligarchy of Brussels eurocrats. Their loss of authority had been a steady process of forced abdication.

The nation-state was a concept that was rapidly passing out of political relevance. In times past nations and ethnicities had gone together; Sweden had been the country of the Swedish, England had been the country of the English, France had been the country of the French, and everyone had understood where they belonged. They'd each had a place of their own in the world. But that had changed with the success of the policy to eradicate national identity in favour of pluralist global citizenship. With so many people living in the country whose ethnicity was derived from elsewhere in the world, and with no single ethnicity having precedence over any of the others, the idea of a nation was now far more shifting and inchoate.

Most people had identities which were either purely local or which were a mixture of the local and the international. A young Muslim living in Bradford-Islamabad would have a strong communal identification with his local neighbourhood and an equal identification with the global ummah, but the country of England or the nation of the UK meant little or nothing to him. Why would it?

The country had a multiplicity of cultures with a multiplicity of identities, all but one of which were *not his*.

Similarly, a Somali born and raised in Bristol might only identify with his Somali neighbourhood. The rest of the Bristol population were foreigners to him, let alone the rest of the UK. The empty shell of the political nation-state still existed but it's population no longer had a national community or a national character. Central government tried to cling obstinately to the idea of one nation but the citizenry had moved on. Eventually the structures of civil administration had been obliged to follow the same path.

Multiculturalism in England had led to the concept of Metropolitanism which advocated the dismantling of the central government of a nation-state and its replacement by a federation of largely autonomous regional states or metropolitan areas called "Metros". These Metros had the authority to levy their own taxes and control public spending within their own areas. This fundamental change was implemented on the basis that political decision-making had been over-centralised in the Westminster state machine and that devolved government would boost the economy. In the same way that the nationalists in Scotland had demanded independence not simply from England but more particularly from London and the Westminster government, the metropolitan regions had demanded and received a large measure of independence for the same reasons. And just as the age-old Scottish racism against the English had emotionally motivated the demand for an independent Scotland, the overly diverse foreignness of London fuelled the desire for Metro-independence.

It was an expression of the ethnic apartheid of multi-sectarianism. The dominant ethnic identity of the different regions of the country varied enormously. Some cities or areas within cities were majority Asian, others were majority African-Caribbean, others ethnically English, and in others the emergent Sharia Muslim communities were dominant. But London had no identity at all. It was foreign to everyone. The advocates of these autonomous metropolitan states had declared themselves unrepresented by the so-called national leadership of the Westminster government, and the new age of the Metro had replaced the dead era of the nation-state.

There were ten Metros in the former England. Many had a dominant ethnic culture which gave the region some cultural coherence although some were simply areas of mass diversity without any ethnic social cohesion. Ritzy lived in the *East Anglia Metro* which was usually abbreviated to "Anglia" because it was still principally English but with ever-increasing East European communities. The comparative prevalence of ethnic populations was shifting and uncertain. The expansion in the Polish, Russian, Romanian and Bulgarian presence had caused a significant proportion of the Asian residents in the *East Anglia Metro* to relocate to the Midlands where they could be in the majority. One of the prominent features of the Metros was how many people from every culture wanted to relocate to somewhere that they could be in the majority.

The population of the *Greater Northumbria Metro* was primarily ethnically English although most locals preferred to call this region "Geordieland" in keeping with its persistent regional ethnic identity. Some of the other English regional identities, especially Cockney, Scouse, Yorkshire and Brummie, had largely disappeared but Geordies remained tenaciously Geordie. The only other Metro that was predominantly English was the *Southwest Metro* but here the English ethnicity was flavoured with a strong Celtic identity because it included Cornwall where many people customarily referred to themselves as "Celtic-English" or simply as the "Cornish" to emphasise their allegiance to their own distinctive identity.

The *East Midlands Metro*, which was sometimes called "Greater Leicester" was predominantly Asian, as was the *West Midlands Metro* or "Greater Birmingham". Together these two regions were generally referred to as "Little Asia" and the ethnic conflicts in the Midlands therefore focused largely on the antagonism between Pakistani Muslims and Indian Hindus with the Pakistanis greatly outnumbering the Indians, though the Indians still had a much stronger middle-class. There was also a notable Sikh presence despite their smaller population. The religious divisions within Little Asia increased steadily as time passed, and those of Bengali or Punjabi ethnicity in particular were often caught in community conflicts between Islam, Hinduism, and Sikhism. Competition for representation in the Metro legislature had led to both the East and West Midlands Metros being notorious for electoral corruption.

The internationalism of identity added fuel to the fire. Whenever events abroad involved a conflict of ethnicities, it frequently produced an echo of violence in the former England. If Sikh Punjabi separatists in India blew up a bus in Delhi or the Indian government, identified with the Hindu majority, cracked down on the separatists, then it was almost inevitable that clashes between Sikhs and Hindus would also take place on the streets of Birmingham or Leicester. But there was nothing to be done about this because nobody could control events taking place abroad.

The *Southeast Metro* was a battleground between what was left of the ethnically English and the colonising power of mass immigration. Its multi-sectarianism was sliding steadily into "total diversification" where there was no prevailing ethnic identity across the confused and bewildering plurality of disparate ethnicities.

The distinction between multiculturalism and diversity was now very clear, although for a very long time the multicultis had believed that these two things were actually one and the same thing; that multiculturalism and diversity were synonymous. But in the Metros it was apparent that this was not so. Where distinct ethnic communities lived side by side in recognised territories within a city, society had multiple cultures. Each of these cultures had an internal continuity and an established identity of its own. This was the multiculturalism which led to multi-sectarianism.

In contrast, where the mixture of ethnicities amongst the population could not sustain distinct communities of any significant size, it created the melting pot of diversity. Local areas were in a continual state of modification and could change their character very rapidly, and repeatedly. There was no continuity of population in such areas. They were highly unstable and subject to constant changes in their ethnic permutations. It had turned out that multiculturalism and diversity were, in fact, two very different social contexts in which to live.

The descent into the social unintelligibility of total diversification had already gone beyond the tipping point in the remaining four Metros where the level of diversity had fallen into what the demographers called "civic incohesion" but which was popularly labelled as "social incoherence".

The *Greater Bristol Metro* was an instance of civic incohesion, as was the *Greater Manchester Metro* and the *Greater Merseyside Metro*. There was no predominant ethnicity in any of these regions. And, of course, the *Greater London Metro* was the archetype of social incoherence. It had an international reputation for it. London had ceased to be English by the end of the first decade of the century and by the fourth decade it had forgotten that it had ever been English. Londoners had lived in social incoherence for too long to be able to imagine anything else. Its lack of a dominant ethnic culture was still being hailed as the chief virtue of the city, even while its buildings burned. No city had surrendered itself to diversity more unstintingly than London and when the global economy had collapsed no city had suffered the consequences of total diversification more painfully than London. It had virtually been a war-zone during The Rupture and the other Metros had been too busy with their own internal struggles to lend a hand. London had been left to its fate for a couple of years.

However, although these four Metros had undergone total diversification there were nonetheless towns and cities within them that were almost uniformly of one ethnic culture. This caused distinct sectarian cleavages to occur within these Metros. Bradford-Islamabad in the *Greater Manchester Metro* and Blackburn-Islamabad in the *Greater Merseyside Metro* had amended their names to celebrate their status as Cities of Islam. But whilst they may have bent the knee in submission to Allah they certainly didn't submit to anyone else. The Islamic civic structures of both cities were well-established and they constituted an institutionalised counter-culture to the social incoherence which was to be found elsewhere in the Greater Manchester and Greater Merseyside Metros.

This devolution of political power to the ten metropolitan regions had been an unavoidable accommodation to the loss of national identity. It was the logical next step in the ideological policy of social engineering which had been pursued through decades of unrelenting mass immigration to embrace diversity. The Metros were simply a necessary continuance of the same demographic revolution; a consequence of the same social engineering by the same blind engineers. In little more than a generation they had set in train the chain of events that would end the continuity of an ethnically English culture which had lasted for around fourteen centuries. Yet they expressed no regret. Ethnic cultures begin and end. After all, Englishness wasn't the only European culture that was well on its way to becoming extinct, even if it was one of the oldest of those being killed off.

In Doncaster Road Ritzy passed a destitute man sitting on a suitcase, homeless in the street. The suitcase was what was left of the life he'd once had. Ritzy saw him but the man didn't register on Ritzy's consciousness beyond that. The destitute were like streetlights, they were all over the place but who paid any attention to them? The dispossessed who'd been reduced to living rough were mostly men. There was nothing new about that, the legion of homeless males had always vastly outnumbered the number of homeless females. The Rupture hadn't changed that. Nothing short of an act of god was likely to change that. If it came right down to basics, a woman under forty could put a roof over her head by offering herself to a man who had one. Destitute women tended to be middle-aged or older. She was more likely to be homeless if her tits had dropped. But men of any age were on their own. Men had always been on their own since the dawn of time. Ritzy understood this but there was nothing he could do about it, which is why he paid no attention to the man on the suitcase as he passed by.

For his part, the homeless man barely noticed Ritzy either, apart from his bowler hat. That was the only feature which stood out. Lots of men wore the type of sleeveless utility jacket that Ritzy had on, and the baggy shorts were commonplace among men in a society which cared far less about glamour than had been the case once upon a time. When most people got dressed in the morning they didn't make a choice between comfort and style, they opted for comfort every time. There was very little choosing involved. There were some young women who still aspired to glamour, or at least to a glamorous eroticism, but they tended to be seen as mercenary. It was assumed that they were looking to exploit the commercial advantages of glamour rather than enjoying it for its own sake; they weren't taking pleasure in the aesthetic artifice of gorgeous glamour, they were looking to hitch up their sale price as they hitched up their hemlines. This judgement may have been harsh but it was the general assumption. The fashion for men like Ritzy was entirely practical. "Modern Utilitarian" it might have been called, if anyone had bothered to give it a name. As far as the homeless man was concerned, as he sat on his suitcase watching the world go by, Ritzy was an unremarkable specimen of humanity except for his bowler hat. That was a stylish hat.

Political opposition to Metropolitanism had come, predictably, from the centralists in the Westminster government whose power was rapidly draining away and their livelihoods with it. But opposition also came from the ethnic minorities within Metros because they feared that the greater community cohesion of the dominant ethnic group within each Metro would eclipse any political consideration for themselves. Previously they had been able to count upon the support of central government whose favouritism toward ethnic minorities had been inveterate and uncompromising. But they were far less certain of how well or how badly they would be treated by the devolved regional governments. The dominant ethnic group within each Metro might be less favourably disposed toward multicultural policies now that they were the majority community in their region. The Poles, Romanians, Roma, and other East Europeans were especially vocal in this regard when resident in Little Asia. Just as there was a steady drift of Asians in the *East Anglia Metro* relocating to the Midlands, there was a corresponding drift of Europeans from the Midlands to East Anglia.

The ethnically English organised very little opposition to the end of the nation-state because they understood that if Englishness was to survive at all as a living culture, then it could only survive in the form of sectarian communities. The nation would never again be English because they didn't have a competitive birth-rate so they wouldn't have the numbers. Besides, there wasn't going to be a nation in future. Consequently there was far more concern among the English to create small but sustainable ethnic communities of their own where their children could grow up English and preserve their culture. Whereas for the increasing populations of the colonising cultures the future would be a competition for dominance, for the diminishing population of the colonised English the issue was one of avoiding cultural extinction. Unsurprisingly, therefore, they had very little concern about a nationality which had already been irreparably lost and focused their ambitions on ensuring the survival of their ethnicity in small pockets of Englishness.

The Celtic-English or Cornish in the *Southwest Metro* were developing a fearsome reputation for their hostility to anyone moving into their territory from "up country". But no one resented such attitudes any more because this provincial defensiveness was nothing more than the kind of territorial demarcations signified by murals in any major city. Anyone who wanted a place of their own for their community had to be ready to defend it. Nowhere was this more true than in the Metros of total diversification, where territorial demarcation was often reduced to single streets or tenement blocks, and a twenty minute walk might take a pedestrian passed a dozen different murals displaying ethnic boundary lines.

Hostility to ethnic outsiders was also conspicuously the case in the Midlands. The conflicts between immigrant colonies which had existed since the 1960s and the much later incursions from Eastern Europe meant that local attitudes in Little Asia were becoming egregiously anti-white. The multiculti reactionaries of the establishment got themselves very befuddled over these racial conflicts in Sikh, Muslim and Hindu areas when the local brown-skinned residents reacted hostilely against the inclusion of white-skinned Romanians, Poles, and Bulgarians in their territory.

In the old days the multicultis had always sided with the brown-skinned immigrants against the local white-skinned residents, and it had been easy for them to present the situation as one in which the white locals were nothing but a bunch of ignorant racists resisting the "browning" of their country. But now that the Asians were resisting incursions into those same residential areas by white Eastern Europeans, the multicultis had to choose between siding with the immigrants, in which case they'd be *siding with white people against brown people*, or alternatively siding with the Sikh, Muslim and Hindu communities, in which case they'd be siding with the dog-in-the-manger local residents *against the immigrants*. Neither of these options were acceptable to the set-in-stone beliefs of the multiculturalists. Their ideological faith had always told them that people with brown skins must invariably be defended and that immigrants must invariably be defended. These two beliefs were now in direct contradiction, and so the poor baffled creatures were left with no one to side with and no one to blame but themselves.

Elsewhere these lessons were being learned. Since gaining their national independence at the second time of asking, the Scottish Nationalists had abandoned their former nominal endorsement of multiculturalism and were now vociferously opposed to it. Outside of Glasgow, Edinburgh, Dundee and Aberdeen, all of them urban sprawls, Scotland had never really been a multicultural country but it was a very strongly nationalist country. These days, with England's catastrophic example close at hand, the Scottish Nationalists could see what had happened to the old enemy and they realised how very much they didn't want to have the same thing happen to them. So they'd dragged their politicians kicking and screaming into opposition to mass immigration. The politicians had never understood that 'multicultural nationalism' was a contradiction in terms, but their voters had gotten the message. They could be nationalists or they could be multicultis but not both. They chose the former.

Wales had been divided into two metropolitan regions, north and south. The *South Wales Metro* could no longer claim to be predominantly Welsh as diversification had increased sufficiently throughout its population to make any such claim tenuous at best.

What was left of Welsh Nationalism dominated the *North Wales Metro* and it took a similar position to the Scottish, rejecting multiculturalism and embracing monoculturalism. The Cornish Nationalists of the *Southwest Metro* liked to emphasise their joint ancestral heritage with the ethnically Welsh who were still the majority in North Wales and they agitated for a "Celtic Alliance" with them. The Cornish Nationalists were gaining in popular strength as a result.

Across the sea the Irish were waking up to the grim irony of their demographic condition. The phrase "Ireland for the Irish" had once been a rallying cry against the British presence in Ireland but since the Irish had been required to embrace diversity the cry of "Ireland for the Irish" was considered to have a pronounced whiff of anti-immigrant prejudice. It had been declared a racist slogan. The Irish were confronted with the realisation that after generations of trying to get the British out and reclaim the whole island for the Irish, their country had now been taken from them by the PWKB. Suffering the fatal combination of both ethnic Irish emigration and non-Irish immigration, it was unlikely that Ireland would ever be Irish again.

These demographic realities were the background context of Ritzy's life, as they were for everyone outside of the gated fortresses of the rich, but whenever he reflected upon them it was always with a fatalism that took it for granted that nothing could be done to resist the tide of history. His abiding thought was to wonder what his father, and especially his grandfather, would have made of the current situation had they been alive to see it. Would his grandfather have been able to believe it?

Ritzy checked the map on his touchpad again. The job he'd been offered was taking him into neighbourhoods that were on the periphery of his normal stamping grounds. He went quickly down Garvey Avenue.

Whether dear old Marcus, for whom the avenue was named, would have appreciated the compliment was debatable. Garvey Avenue was one of those streets favoured by pimps and prostitutes. It was a business which had undergone many changes in the 21st century. Long before The Rupture feminist legislation in England had targeted any and all men who were connected with prostitution. It wasn't just the pimps who profited from a woman selling sex that were committing a crime. Crucially, to pay for sex was a crime and even to offer a women money for sex was a crime, so the customers were also eminently arrestable. The girls' clientele became less inclined to approach sex workers in public. Consequently, most sex workers had retreated behind closed doors into brothels and private houses which they advertised online to pursue their trade "off-street" as the police described it.

Not only had the FemiNazis driven sex workers underground but the Islamic fascists were doing so too. Street hookers were a particular target for the Jihadis. The soldiers of Allah never felt more piously virtuous than when they were assaulting sex workers to drive them off the streets so that the eyes of Muslims would not be soiled by the sight of them. There had been a great many assaults upon women by Sharia Patrols, including a lot of women who weren't actually selling sex but who looked like they might be. To ply their trade in the street was therefore a hazardous occupation, especially in areas that bordered on Islamic territory, and the pimps had to do some work themselves to protect their girls. The Russian mafia ran the business in most of the major cities, and the murderous battles between the mafia boys and the Jihadis were very brutal.

Prostitution had predictably mushroomed since the economic collapse but changing times were undermining the oldest profession. Technology had arrived. One of the shops in Garvey Avenue had a window display of erotic accessories and sex aids. The thick metal grill over the shop window obscured the display somewhat but, unlike many of the shops which had their panel shutters down permanently, this one had its wares on exhibition. Prominent in the window were the robotic sex dolls called "synth-lovers" which were proving to be more popular that their passé human counterparts and which were steadily putting whores out of business. For many consumers, the girls in the street were becoming the cheap alternative for those who couldn't afford a synthetic.

Comparisons did not favour the merely human. The synth-lovers, both male and female, were astonishingly lifelike in their perfectly sculpted silicone. It wasn't easy to tell them apart from actual humans at a glance, and they had a full range of physical movements so they retained their anthropomorphic imposture even when in motion. Their animated eyes were programmed to follow the sound of a voice when it spoke to them. Their lips moved convincingly when they said the things that the consumer wished to hear. Their sighs and whimpers were as realistic as they were gratifying to the man or woman who liked to pretend that these sensual exhalations were genuine. The only thing which gave them away as mechanised counterfeits was that they were too flawless to be real. Anatomically they were better than nature.

Synthetics had other advantages too. They were programmable with a wide variety of erotic software to suit personal taste. All predilections were catered for without bias or judgemental censure. Cruelty to a machine carried no moral guilt. The simple fact of their artificiality made everything permissible. Obscenity was liberated. Consent was not an issue. Nor were the bruised feelings of the object of desire. For the consumer they offered sex without rebuke and pleasure without criticism. There was no rejection, no infidelity, and no reproaches. They weren't just better than girlfriends or boyfriends, they were better than whores.

Adjacent to the shop full of synthetics was a bakery which had a sign on its reinforced security door saying "Open 2pm to 3pm". The limited supply of ingredients available meant that the bakery could only bake enough bread each day to satisfy one hour of customer demand. They would be sold out after sixty minutes. Rather than spend their days turning away angrily dissatisfied shoppers, they did the obvious thing and only opened for one hour each day.

As Ritzy walked by he noticed these two shops right next door to each other and it struck him as an apt comment on contemporary commerce. There was plenty of product when it came to robotic and electronic sex aids but there was a seriously insufficient supply of basic foodstuffs. It spoke volumes about the current state of society.

Ritzy ignored the catcalls and solicitations from the cattle market of whores working the street. They had nothing he wanted and certainly nothing for which he would be willing to pay. In his eyes they all had the lacklustre tawdriness of the over-fucked. Their flamboyant fake-eroticism was cheap and wholly unconvincing. The lies of their phoney flirtation rang hollow. They had the cynical fatigue of someone whose job entailed long hours of standing around waiting. Even the young ones had a mercenary detachment etched into their faces. And their bodies weren't particularly arousing either. They presented no temptation to him.

He was similarly dismissive as he passed another destitute. These were not charitable times and the pathos of the tragic derelict did not touch Ritzy's heart. Homelessness was commonplace, after all. This vagrant was propped up against the wall sitting on the pavement in a pool of his own piss. At least, Ritzy assumed it was his own.

The address that Ritzy had been given for his potential customer was northeast of Temple Grove, which was getting perilously close to Islamic territory. It was right on the murals. Had it been one more road further on, it would have been beyond the boundary and Ritzy would not have accepted the commission. As it was, she apparently lived right on the border. He found the address and discovered that the customer lived over a shop selling new and second-hand carpets. There was a car parked outside; a twelve year old electric Nissan. Ritzy pressed the intercom buzzer on the private door next to the shop and waited. There was a mechanised spluttering and he heard a metallic voice say:

"Yes, who is it please?"

"Mrs Hanif?" enquired Ritzy. "I was told that you wanted a mechanic. I'm here to give you an estimate for the job."

There was a fairly long pause before she replied:

"Yes, that's right, but I cannot see you now. My husband is not at home."

Ritzy understood at once. Her accent was recognisably western but the house rules were evidently middle-eastern. She could not let him in, nor could she step outside to speak with him, because her husband would have disapproved severely of her speaking alone with a man to whom she was not related by birth or marriage. Ritzy muttered a curse under his breath. He had wasted his time in coming here. He was too close to the Muslim area. He was disappointed but he wasn't surprised.

Her accent was the giveaway. An increasing number of western women had reverted to Islam over the preceding decades. Some did so out of a genuine religious zeal but for the most part their motivation came from one of two sources. The first group found their way to Islam because they believed it to be the best option for a woman who wanted a financially supportive husband predisposed to allow her to occupy the purely domestic role of wife and mother. Alterations to mainstream gender relations in western cultures had left maternal women, drawn to a life based around motherhood, with far fewer options than had once been the case. Religion seemed to promise a solution to this.

The second group, bizarrely, had bought into the idea that the wearing of hijab was a free choice exercised by women who wished to avoid being sexually objectified by men. They rejected the overt eroticism prevalent in western cultures and the media-fuelled obsession with the sexualized feminine physicality which typified the women in those cultures. By covering themselves in the modesty of hijab these reverts to Islam believed that they could escape being judged on their physical appearance and find the type of respect which they felt they wanted from men.

In this way, feminism had primed these women to become Muslim. They chose a life in Islam because they thought it offered an escape from the objectification of the female which feminism had so industriously criticized and condemned. The colossal irony of this was not lost on those who observed the social trend. For many women the illogical outcome of feminism was to embrace the most patriarchal of religions; to surrender themselves to an ideology in which god's law could not be defied or disputed; an unchallengeable patriarchy. How ironic was that?

But it was of no relevance to Ritzy's life what the dumb bitches did to themselves. All it meant to him was that she wasn't in a position to employ him. This wasn't a neighbourhood he cared to loiter in, nobody felt comfortable on the borders, and he didn't intend to come back another day. If she couldn't speak to him now then it was just too bad. Ritzy would get no payday here.

Frustrated, although only mildly, he shrugged his shoulders and gave it up as a lost opportunity. He didn't even bother to say anything further into the intercom. He didn't owe her an explanation. Ritzy didn't owe her anything. He just turned and walked away.

Chapter Three

The Red Squirrels

"How was your interview, Spart?" enquired Chippy.

The slang term 'Spart' was a mark of respect. It was derived from the name Spartacus and signified resistance to oppression. Chippy called every man of his acquaintance Spart and even a few women.

"Same as," replied Ritzy.

He hung his hat on the crowded rack with the other four bowlers, but he didn't remove his sleeveless jacket as they tried not to use the heating any more than was necessary. Fuel bills cost the earth. This meant that their home was always a little colder than they would have liked. Ritzy entered the living room, which was almost the entirety of the apartment. Aside from this one big room there were five tiny converted bedrooms, a serviceable kitchen, and a basic but functional bathroom tucked away unobtrusively. The décor centred largely around the sofas and armchairs on which five men could sprawl and surf their channel screens online. It was a real home. The only house rules were those that all five of them had agreed upon consensually without any passive-aggressive bullying or crying. Consequently, there were very few rules apart from those dictated by common sense. Emotional blackmail and manipulative weeping were not tools that were employed in this community of five.

Barker and Gravy were viewing their channels on handheld screens, sitting side by side on the sofa ignoring each other. Barker was exploring an ancestry website, trying to track down a married aunt of his great uncle but it was proving difficult because he didn't know her married name. Barker was fascinated by family trees and knew a vast amount about his forebears going back to the eighteenth century. The other four housemates were never quite certain that he wasn't making it all up but, in fact, he was scrupulous in his veracity. He had assembled a remarkably extended and accurate record of the lines of descent which had led to his own existence. The intricate pattern of lineage was a precarious cobweb of lives, each surviving to the next generation, handing on the guttering torch. It was an awe-inspiring realisation to survey so many disparate lives connecting to span the centuries to the present day where Barker sat on this sofa, the very flesh of his ancestry preserved in his own body. He used his family name of "Barker" as his mononym. He was, however, the last of the Barkers. In common with his housemates he had no progeny. Perhaps this was why, lacking any other posterity, they would all have liked to relocate to one of the rural Metros in which there was a smaller population but an English majority. It was Barker who proposed this plan most often.

Gravy was watching a news channel with an update from South Africa. The incessant wave of asylum-seeking migration from Zimbabwe was bringing further turmoil to the streets. The army were in the townships because the police only had water canon and rubber bullets, not armoured personnel carriers and live rounds. But unfortunately for the South African government the army were unwilling to fire upon their own people and so the civilian war continued apace with the South Africans taking the machete to the Zimbabweans along with their classic method of summary execution: a burning tyre thrown over someone's head called a "necklace". The migrants were going to continue coming into South Africa all the same because it was the third year of famine in Zimbabwe, but it was out of the frying pan and into the fire. Literally into the fire. On Gravy's channel screen the bodies were ablaze from the petrol-filled car tyres.

Gravy contemplated the way that the effect of mass immigration was the same wherever it occurred and how it seemed to occur everywhere. The humanitarian impulse always succumbed to resentment eventually. It was the mercilessly unrelenting character of migration tsunamis that broke people's spirits and robbed them of their former charitable compassion. No one could tolerate it forever. It was like Chinese water torture; at first it didn't seem so bad but over time it drove you crazy. As the interminable became the intolerable, people turned violent. The South Africans had taken up arms in their resistance to Zimbabwean mass immigration. They weren't the only ones. Gravy watched the images of human immolation and shook his head sadly.

Ritzy lived with four friends, all men of English ethnicity, who called themselves the Red Squirrels. Five men in an apartment might once have been thought a trifle overcrowded but it wasn't considered such nowadays. The accommodation shortage which had grown so acute during the decades of mass immigration had been amplified enormously by The Rupture. Not only had most of the construction companies gone bankrupt but a lot of the existing residential property had been made unfit for habitation by the rioting when the underclass had done their best to burn society to the ground for having let them down so badly. The accommodation crisis gave people few options and, as the only practical solution, communal living had become commonplace. Joint tenancies between up to a dozen people were increasingly the only viable alternative to homelessness, and due to the poisoning of gender relations by toxic feminism these joint tenancies were frequently single-sex households. The laws being what they were, men felt safer living with other men. This left women with no one to share a home with but each other. It was a far from ideal situation but the lives of both sexes were ruled by economic necessity and political mismanagement, leaving people in the position of having to choose the lesser of two evils. Each of the five Red Squirrels would have preferred to live alone but none of them had a financial income that could afford such luxury. A bachelor apartment shared between the five of them was the best available option.

With five guys who all worked in the shadow economy sharing a living space, the apartment was a bit of a revolving door of housemates coming and going at different times of the day and night. By chance, they were all at home this morning when Ritzy arrived although Chippy was about to leave for his lunchtime round. Chippy got his name from his profession. He sold polystyrene trays of chips from his fast-food van. His business was a one-man operation. He bought sacks of potatoes from a contact who grew them in prodigious quantities in his back garden. Chippy was his only retail outlet and took his whole harvest. It was an arrangement that suited them both. The chip-van had a large deep fat fryer installed so that Chippy could slice the potatoes, fry them, and ladle them out into the little plastic trays, all without leaving the vehicle. It would have been easy money but for the security issues. Finding safe locations to park the van within reach of residential areas was a problem. Chippy was an absolute expert on routes around this part of the city. Also, he carried a pickaxe handle and a huge carving knife in the van.

Ritzy slumped down on an armchair next to Captain and picked up his channels screen from a cluttered table, the engrained habit making the action almost a reflex upon returning home. Captain looked up from his own screen long enough to acknowledge Ritzy's arrival. Captain was the only member of the household who was black English rather than white English and he was admired by the others for having found his was to an English ethnicity despite all the barriers which had been put in his way by the power-elites whose policy was always to encourage people of his skin colour to reject Englishness. To assert their own ethnicity it had been necessary for all of the Red Squirrels to resist the top-down social pressure from the cultural elites, but the struggle had been harder for Captain and he was respected for it accordingly.

Ritzy's dextrous fingertips began sliding over the skin-sensitive biometric touch-screen which continually authenticated the identity of the user and thereby ensured that only the legitimate owner could use the device. He plugged his speakers into his ears. The audio-visual display of the channels screen was the system of information dissemination which had superseded all others. A vast multitude of channels were uploaded by a society full of media-savvy individuals with a desire to reach out and connect with others like themselves. This had destroyed the mainstream media's stranglehold on the dissemination of news, just as it had broken the iron grip of the PWKB on the dissemination of ideas. Now the orthodox and authorised media who propagandized the establishment narrative had to compete against opposing voices. The provision of information had been democratised. Everyone had their say. Such television or radio stations as still existed were now accessed in the way that all information was accessed, via the online channels. They were everyone's window on the world; the means by which the planet communicated with itself.

Each person had two basic forms of human interaction; online and offline. Their relationships with other people, whether personal or generalized, were conducted in both ways. It was common for people to speak of their "onlife" and their "offlife". Most people found that they valued the former more than the latter. They didn't like to find themselves without access to their onlife. Channel screens came in a variety of shapes and sizes but the Red Squirrels, traditionalists in such matters, preferred the portable convenience of the old-fashioned tablet. You could take it anywhere, including the lavatory.

Ritzy's touchpad had been bleeping with incoming messages during his walk home but he hated to text in the street because when a person got involved in online conversation they stopped paying attention to their physical environment and that could be dangerous. It was smarter to wait. His tablet was synchronized with his touchpad, so now he downloaded his messages to his channels screen. They were mostly junk but there was one item that piqued his interest.

It was from the daughter of a friend of Ritzy's, or at least it purported to be. The friend was Brendan, whom Ritzy hadn't actually spoken to for several years, but he was still nominally a friend. Brendan hadn't been around much because he was repeatedly in and out of prison for non-payment of child support. He was inside again at the moment. The message from the daughter was asking Ritzy to meet with her to "get my dad out of jail". There was a sender-image included which showed a pretty young woman with short blonde hair. More than pretty, she was sexy. Even when photographed from the neck up. Ritzy remembered Brendan's daughter as a cute fourteen year old and this woman definitely did resemble her so it might be a genuine contact. But the message was signed "Poontang". It wasn't the name that her parents had given her. If this was the same girl she must have called herself that.

The last Ritzy had heard, from a friend of a friend, was that Brendan's daughter was a ghang member with an impressive track record of criminal violence so, doubtless, Poontang must be her ghang name. Could this message mean that she was planning some kind of jailbreak? That wasn't the kind of thing with which Ritzy could be of any assistance. He had no talent for gangster violence. But, by the same token, how could Ritzy help with any legal processes to liberate a man from prison either? His only involvement with the law was in trying to keep out of jail himself. But it wasn't the oddity of her asking for his assistance that worried Ritzy. It was the sender-image that struck him as a cause for concern. Pretty blondes weren't likely to send him a picture of themselves unless it was intended as an inducement. A lure. Did she think that her beauty would make him compliant and easily exploitable?

It was a brief but intriguing message which he decided needed some thought before he replied, if he replied. He would get back to it after he had checked his favourite channels. He was just settling down to a finger sashay through his icons when his onlife was interrupted by his offlife. It happened a lot.

"The DiD called by earlier," said Captain.

The acronym DiD stood for "Damsel in Distress" and was a term of acerbic abuse in the Red Squirrel household, as in so many others. Her actual name was Abbi, short for Abigail, but they never referred to her by either version of her name. She was always "the DiD" because she only ever appeared at their door to appeal for some assistance on behalf of herself and her eight year old daughter. She lived with her child in a tiny one-room studio flat on the second floor of their building. The DiD had some kind of remunerative occupation at the local pizza takeout but it didn't pay much. The child support payments that she received from her daughter's father were sporadic because he'd only occasionally been in paid employment since she'd kicked him out of her life. Consequently, she was invariably short of cash, utility credits, food, and babysitters. None of these items were available from the Red Squirrels, not that she would have trusted them with child-minding duties, but once in a while the DiD received charitable donations from other male residents in the building. She had a fair figure and her long brunette hair had a natural curl, but it was her big Manga eyes that served her best when looking for a handout. When she filled those saucer orbs with soulful distress she came across like a Hentai cutie and the erotic effect could be compelling on the male instinct for gendered self-sacrifice.

But her allure didn't get passed the psychological defences of the Red Squirrels. They respected women who carried their own weight, like Renata the tobacconist and Barbara the translator. Life gave nothing to men that they hadn't earned, and it cut both ways. The five of them chose to live with other men because men expected nothing from them. Women who could do likewise were okay. Plenty of women had accommodated themselves to the new social arrangement. Such women received the respect that they had earned and which was their due. But women who expected preferential treatment and unearned respect merely for being female had no place in the lives of the Red Squirrels. They permitted no female privilege or prerogatives. They had a communal and justified contempt for damsels in distress. The DiD in the apartment downstairs got nothing from them but she persisted in trying from time to time because to her mind it didn't seem possible that an apartment containing five hetero males could be entirely immune to feminine petition.

"Was she after money or services?" asked Ritzy.

"A temporary loan, was how she phrased it," Captain answered, his bullish face contorted in scepticism. "About as temporary as the snow in Antarctica, probably."

"And wearing the camel-toe leggings again?" asked Ritzy wryly.

"As usual. They show contours without showing stretch-marks," replied Captain.

"I hope you gave her nothing," said Ritzy.

"When do we ever?" responded Captain rhetorically.

Ritzy took the rhetorical question seriously and reminded his housemate: "She got a dinner out of us once."

"Only because she called by with the kid at the exact moment that we were all sitting down to a collective meal together," clarified Captain defensively. "We were using the big tureen and the kid took a bowl without being invited. If the kid was staying for a bowl, then there was no point in denying one to the DiD. She benefited from fortuitous timing, that's all."

"It's surprising she doesn't come knocking with the kid in tow every dinner time," chimed in Barker from across the room.

"Fat chance of that," said Gravy over his shoulder from the sofa. "That must have been the only collective meal we've all shared together since we set up shop in this gaff. I haven't seen that tureen used again, have you?"

He'd acquired the nickname "Gravy" from his habit of having gravy with everything. Fish, flesh, or fowl, he poured gravy all over it. This was one of several reasons why they all preferred to cook their own meals and not collaborate in culinary matters. Each to his own taste was the rule.

"Why would we want to eat meals together?" asked Chippy belligerently as he strode off to work. "This isn't a bloody commune. I live here because I can't afford to live anywhere else. You don't think I live here because I like you bastards, do you?"

The other four placed their right hands over their hearts and sarcastically sang in chorus: "And so say all of us."

It wasn't the first time that they'd chorused thus in response to a less than brotherly sentiment, and Chippy might have joined in the laughter on another occasion, but he was never in the best of moods when he was starting work for the day and he wasn't inclined to appreciate their sarcasm right now. He left the apartment. Chippy did a lunchtime round, a dinnertime round, and a long evening round every day. His regular customers would go elsewhere if he wasn't reliable, and he couldn't afford to lose trade to a rival.

Gravy had switched channels from the South African news and was now reading a blog on paternity injustice. Like all men of their generation the members of this household were highly politicized on issues of gender, although inclined more to abjuration than to stridency.

The blogger was arguing that for as long as women had control over the fertility of men, the latter should refuse outright to father children. The basic argument was very well known. Women could control their own fertility through the oral contraceptive and abortion rights, but men had neither oral contraception nor parental abdication rights. Men were in the invidious and inequitable position of becoming fathers when, and only when, *women* decided that they would. Men could neither exercise the negative choice of not becoming fathers by means of a male contraceptive pill nor choose to reject the legal obligations of parenthood if the woman decided to take the pregnancy to full term without the father's agreement. Contrarily, if the man wanted the child in the womb to be born but the woman decided to terminate the pregnancy, then he again had no rights in the matter. The man could be forced to accept termination even when he wanted the baby, and he could be forced to accept fatherhood even without his consent. He became a father if *she* decided that he would, and he did not became a father if *she* decided that he wouldn't. Women, in short, had total control over men's fertility.

For many years Men's Rights Activists had been demanding both a freely available male pill and parental abdication rights so that if a man didn't consent to becoming a father but the women went ahead and had her baby anyway, then he could choose to exercise the option of disclaiming all rights and responsibilities for the child. He would have no rights regarding the child but neither could he be made to pay child support or be made to fulfil any other parental duties because her choice of childbirth had been non-consensual as far as he was concerned. Women's rights accorded a woman the absolute right over her own body to choose to terminate a pregnancy or to have the baby. MRAs didn't want to repeal a woman's right to an abortion, her legal right to an abortion could continue, they simply wanted men to have the nearest thing to an equivalent right in the form of parental abdication. It would still mean that his child could be terminated without his consent, but at least he could no longer be forced into fatherhood.

But of all the sexist double-standards practiced by the reactionary feminist establishment, parental gender inequality was one of those which they valued most highly. The MRAs demand for greater equality in parental rights was a reform that the feminists had fought against with all their strength. However, science had intervened. The male contraceptive pill had now been invented, although it was not free because the economic collapse had caused a major diminution to the National Health Service and all forms of medication had to be paid for by the consumer. Nonetheless, it was a step forward.

Yet, despite this small advance, men were still being denied parental abdication rights. The authorities latest excuse was that the introduction of a male contraceptive pill meant that men could exercise their non-consent to fatherhood by this means, so that parental abdication rights were no longer necessary. The blogger was incensed at this duplicity by government parties, who had denied the need for abdication rights even before the male pill was invented, and his blog damning their fraudulence was so incendiary that it almost set Gravy's touch-screen on fire.

"There's a blogger here who's insisting upon the need for all men to refuse to father children under any circumstances on moral principle until the powers-that-be equalize parental rights," said Gravy to no one in particular.

"Since the beginning of civilization those in power have expected men to support women in the raising of children which may or may not be his own," observed Ritzy, "but feminism made the family an unrelenting battleground of misandry. We're better off out of it."

"So only the non-western cultures will have babies in future," said Gravy. "That should please the Muslim Supremacists. They've been telling us for ages that they're going to inherit the future. It's looking like a pretty safe bet."

Barker, having overheard the exchange, threw his arms wide and proclaimed: "My fellow Red Squirrels, we proudly present the downfall of western civilization!"

"And about time too," smirked Captain.

Barker raised a comical eyebrow and enquired: "You're pleased?"

"When the world's been going to the dogs for as long as it has," explained Captain, "you can't blame me for getting impatient to see the dogs devour it."

"He's right," agreed Gravy, "Society should slash its wrists and have done with it, that's what I say."

"There is something depressingly undignified about a long lingering death," said Ritzy dolefully.

"Slash 'em", insisted Gravy enthusiastically, "get the razor out and cut deep."

"So much for western civilization," said Captain lugubriously.

He was called "Captain" because his surname was Kidd. Captain earned his living as the plumber and electrician and repair man for a block of flats owned by an Arab absentee landlord who lived abroad. The tenants were extremely ethnically diverse and they all lived off-the-grid. Mostly they were illegals. The volatility of this situation had worsened lately because a slowly increasing prevalence of East Europeans and Roma was causing an escalating hostility from the Asian and Southeast Asian residents who have been living there for longer and who resented losing their building to these more recent arrivals. The Asians referred to them as Euros, a commonplace term of racist derision because the former Euro currency had become a joke before it was finally abandoned during The Rupture. Referring to the East Europeans as Euros was a way of saying that they were a useless joke. However, the reality was that many of the Euros were self-employed and financially better off than the Asians which just bred further resentment.

Captain did not live in the block of flats himself, of course, as he had more sense. The building was a shambles and a firetrap. But the Red Squirrels' apartment was nearby and he was called on his touchpad whenever repairs to the plumbing or electrics were needed. Captain had never met the owner but received his monthly wages cash-in-hand from the building manager who worked for a letting agency. The letting agency managed a lot of rented accommodation that was off-the-grid, in addition to legal rented accommodation, and Captain was hoping to get further work in some of their other properties because he was only paid piece-rate and there weren't always enough repairs needed in a single block of flats to keep his income at a tolerable level.

"I didn't notice the DiD and her kid at the door today, when did they come round?" asked Gravy, who had a slightly annoying habit of returning to earlier conversations which everyone else had already finished.

"She didn't have the kid with her. You were in the shower when she called," answered Barker indifferently.

"She looks her best in camel-toe leggings," mused Gravy.

"You sound ready to fall on your knees and worship at the Alter of Cunt," sneered Captain, a little testily.

"There's no need to turn nasty," objected Gravy. "I wouldn't act upon the impulse. I merely said that the camel-toe pageant is decorative, that's all."

"After what you went through with Monica I thought you would have learned your lesson," Captain reminded him. "You were a punchbag, verbal and otherwise."

"Monica was four years ago. Anyway, you had worse from Saskia," countered Gravy.

"Calm down," advised Ritzy. "We don't fight over women."

"The sage-like voice of sweet reason," mocked Barker. "You're not the only one with a functioning brain, you know."

"I'm glad to hear it," said Ritzy sarcastically. "I sometimes wonder."

"Doubtless women have their place and uses," lectured Barker drolly, "but that place isn't here."

All the Red Squirrels had synth-partners. Now that sex-dolls were so realistic and responsive, having a programmable lover was definitely the way to go. There were no quarrels, no nagging, and no feminist bitching. Who'd want a woman? As the advertising slogan said: "Synthetics give happiness". Or as the Red Squirrels said apropos relationships: "With a synthetic you get the best and you dump the rest". They'd all had sexual relationships with women in the past, although only rarely and usually by accident, but they'd reached an age where they'd moved on to a self-sufficient lifestyle. If you weren't capable of learning from personal experience, then you weren't capable of learning at all.

Each of them kept his synth-lover discreetly out of sight in the corner of his bedroom behind the door, except for Gravy who had his girl sitting up in his bed. He was the only one of the five who had given his synthetic a name, although since her called her "Angel" it wasn't much of a name. Their virtuporn visors were plugged in nearby because they all preferred to supplement their synth-lovers with a 360 degree virtual reality experience, heightening their sexual pleasure by immersing themselves in a variety of erotic contexts. There were a hundred different characters they could become, inhabiting a hundred different worlds in which the consumer could be whoever he wanted to be, limited only by the extent of his imagination. Immersion in a total-surround virtual pornography environment made every fantasy possible.

Synthetics were very popular with women, too, in addition to the usual vibrators and dildos. Women were fond of saying that their male synth-lover was a big improvement on an actual man. He always listened, he always said the right thing, he never got tired when fucking, and he didn't fart in bed. Some women referred to their sex-doll as a "synth-partner" and a few would engage in conversations about their day with their synth-partner when they weren't using it to induce their orgasms.

The widespread use of automated synthetics by both genders had seen the sex-aid industry experience an unprecedented period of financial growth. It was a trillion dollar industry and one of the few areas of commerce in which imports and exports were still being conducted profitably. Synthetics were of substantial benefit to the economy in promoting jobs in manufacturing, engineering, design technology, as well as retail sales. On the stock market they were considered a safe investment. Only communication IT was more important in the field of technology and that would soon be a redundant distinction as the two technologies were combined in virtual reality synthetics. Synth-lovers were rapidly becoming just one more type of hardware on which to run VR software programmes.

This change in sexual habits was a reflection of, and a consequence of, the systemic political modifications made to gender relations over the preceding two generations. The Asian family unit was still secure but African-Caribbean family structures had always been shaky and the European family unit had largely been dismantled by the social engineers of the PWKB. This was another reason why women of western ethnic heritages were reverting to Islam in such significant numbers, and why the other monotheisms were also becoming more popular with women. With the exception of people who were committed to a religious faith, whose god guaranteed fidelity and commitment, there were few men willing to seriously consider marriage or long-term cohabitation. Western women and men, if they came together in anything like intimacy these days, only really came together for sex and even that was on the decline with the enormous commercial success of synth-partners.

Society's level of misandry relating to hetero sex had become so extreme, culturally and legally, that men had been forced into correspondingly extreme levels of basic self-protection. Many considered sex with women to no longer be worth the risk. Feminism had managed to curtail male promiscuity in a way that not even AIDS had been able to achieve.

The presumption of guilt held against any male accused of a sex-crime by any female was well-established, although the judiciary was still pretending that requiring a man to prove consent was a different thing from requiring him to prove himself innocent. In reality it was exactly the same thing. The reason he had to prove consent was to prove that he was innocent of the crime of which he'd been accused, and if he couldn't prove this then he was considered guilty. They called it "affirmative consent". It was very obviously a presumption of guilt. But everyone was so accustomed to the feminist establishment lying through its teeth that no one expected anything else from them. What it came down to in the end was that it was impossible ever to prove consent because any woman who had consented could always claim that she had changed her mind later. So receiving her consent in advance wasn't enough. To avoid being found guilty a man had to prove consent throughout the entire sexual encounter.

The practice of ABR, "Always Be Recording", where a man kept an audio-visual record of any sex he had with a woman for the purpose of proving her consent if the matter came to court, wasn't a very satisfactory way for him to defend himself. Not only were there problems with poor quality recordings, but this whole method of defence was often thrown out by the judge on the grounds that the woman hadn't given her consent to being recorded. The man was then charged with the additional crime of "illegal monitoring" unless he could prove her consent to the recording as well as her consent to the sex.

The impossibility of adequately proving consent made it similarly impossible for a man to prove himself innocent. This meant that any man who risked having sex with a woman could be found guilty on her fraudulent testimony alone. In effect, perjury became legal for women in sex-offence cases. The feminists were ecstatic; delirious with joy. Any woman could use the full power of the law to have any man condemned simply by pointing an accusatory finger at him. Men had been the niggers of feminism for a long time but now the niggers could be banished to prison by the flick of a feminist finger. As a bonus, the skyrocketing statistics for rape convictions were used by the feminist establishment as irrefutable evidence of how oppressed and victimised *women* were in this patriarchal society's rape culture.

Nor was this the limit of feminism's victory. They had also succeeded in enlarging the classification of rape to include any act of hetero sex in which the male had lied to the female during what feminism, in its quaint old-fashioned way, still assumed to be his 'seduction' of her. Naturally, any lies told by the female were not evidence that she had raped her male lover. Feminists took it for granted that the seduction would never be performed by the woman; she was always the seduced, never the seducer. Similarly, no woman was ever required to prove that the man had consented to sex. Male consent was taken for granted and there could be no presumption of guilt against women.

By this method feminism had achieved its long-cherished ambition of making all hetero sex an act of rape, albeit only by a purely legal definition. Under threat of false accusation and the presumption of guilt, no man would risk telling a female hook-up his real name. If she knew who he was, then he would be defenceless against a false rape charge either immediately or in the years to come. Retrospective rape accusations were a major growth industry for lawyers. Men were still required to prove consent even if the alleged crime was said to have taken place thirty years ago. So any man having sex with a female hook-up would have to lie about his identity and thereby commit an act which was, in law, rape. The feminists were delighted. It was what they'd always wanted. They strongly recommended that women should take possession of any used condoms after sex so that DNA evidence could identify the man who, having lied prior to sex, was a rapist under the law.

Feminism's rape legislation was celebrated as their most triumphant success and many men wouldn't expose themselves to this level of legal jeopardy merely for the sake of an orgasm. Cunt wasn't worth the risk, especially since there were alternatives. Traditional pornography was rapidly being replaced by high-tech virtuporn, pornographic virtual realities which made available to the general public the kind of unrestrained erotic fantasies of fabulous wantonness which had previously been the privilege of the Emperors of ancient Rome and the Caliphs of the imperial Caliphate. Masturbatory cyber-worlds opened up doorways to realms with which mere reality could not compete. In a virtuporn visor, which was not much bigger than a pair of sunglasses, the consumer experienced a 360 degree virtual reality fantasy playground constructed in accordance with their wildest dreams.

For those with a taste for the material over the intangibly imaginary, synthetics offered a release for the frustrations of lust. For some people, both women and men, a synth-lover could offer emotional comfort along with sexual relief. Although everyone knew perfectly well that the synthetic was merely a mechanised masturbatory aid, many men and women in relationships with synth-lovers actually felt a great affection for their synthetic and thought of it as a person. A few even convinced themselves that the feeling of affection was reciprocal. This was utter bullshit, of course, because synthetics had no consciousness but the belief of reciprocal affection became a part of the erotic fantasy for those who found the idea appealing. It wasn't so hard to make this fantasy work by playing with the idea of artificial intelligence. The commercial companies manufacturing synth-lovers encouraged this by making outrageously exaggerated claims about the AI capabilities of their products.

The human capacity for anthropomorphism had manifested itself in ways that made the synthetics manufacturers confident of their market. There had already been a vogue for "virtual babies" which had originated in the educative practice of giving school students a virtual baby to take care of as a way of teaching them the skills and responsibilities of childcare. A commercial application of this technology became available to meet the demand from women who wished to experience motherhood without actually undergoing the labours of pregnancy and childbirth. They bought themselves synthetic babies and were forthright in their claims that they loved their virtual children every bit as much as any biological mother loved her natural child.

So the robotics companies had rightly felt themselves to be on secure financial ground when they invested heavily in the sex industry. Their chief concern had not been the fear of any lack of demand for their product; the market for erotica had always been insatiable. No, their worry had been the predictable political backlash that would undoubtedly be unleashed. They were not wrong.

The political opposition to sexual synthetics had been colossal. Not that anyone minded women making erotic use of synthetics, any more than they had minded women using vibrators, since this could be blamed on the inadequacy of men as lovers thereby making it *men's fault* if a woman employed a machine to give herself an orgasm. But the practice of men using synth-lovers was initially ridiculed and denigrated in exactly the same way that society had always declared any man who used a masturbatory aid to be a pathetic loser who couldn't convince women to sleep with him, thereby making it *men's fault* again. The abusive insult "wanker" had only ever been used against men, never against women. If a woman masturbated, society attributed it to men's sexual inadequacy. If a man masturbated, society also attributed it to men's sexual inadequacy. Traditionalists, like feminists, had always deplored male masturbation.

The introduction of sexual synthetics had stirred up this old prejudice once again. The male-shaming was intense and ubiquitous. The reason was self-evident. Artificial sexual partners gave men a freedom from their sexual dependency upon women and this was considered to be a greater threat to women than even pornography had been. Fifth Wave feminists, who seemed to be unaware of the substantial number of women who were using male synth-lovers, declared female synthetics to be "the grossest insult to womankind since the invention of the wedding ring". Lurid tales, purporting to be anecdotal evidence, were told about the depraved effect that these degenerate products had upon the innately violent male carnal appetite.

The manufacturers of synthetics quoted statistics to show that the use of synth-lovers caused a decline in the number of sexual assaults upon women. Similar statistical evidence was presented by the software companies designing virtuporn and other pornography. The statistics were ignored. What counted was the perceived, and actual, decrease in the power that women could exercise over men.

Pornography had always had a paradoxical character. Superficially it appeared to be extremely gynocentric, with its wall-to-wall vaginas, but in practice it was politically anti-gynocentric in the way that it liberated men from the erotic pursuit of women. The power that women had always wielded as the gatekeepers of sex was seriously undermined by pornography. This was true of synthetics also, which naturally outraged the obsessive-compulsive gynocentrism of feminism. The feminist backlash had been a spit-flecked and blood-curdling explosion of sustained fury and sneering disparagement.

But it had failed to keep men contained within the prison of sexual dependency. The old male-shaming techniques didn't work any longer. Society had finally moved on, even if its establishment elites had not. Feminism had burned all its bridges. The traditional reward for conforming to the norms of masculinity had been respect. Men had been respected for their manliness and so they had lived within the narrow confines of that gender role in order to earn that respect. This reward was no longer on offer.

The women who had committed themselves to feminism, with its debasement of men to the status of guilt-objects, had no conception of how to respect manhood. They were incapable of respecting men because who could respect a guilt-object? There was a whole generation of women who had no knowledge or experience of what it meant to respect a man. The only relationships with men they'd ever had were ones in which he accepted her right to criticise and condemn him as she saw fit, whilst further accepting that he must never treat her with the same contempt with which she treated him. Women had been raised by feminism to insist upon female entitlement and a total absence of male entitlement. Men had come to understand that women had no respect for them and they had, in large numbers, decided that they did not want a relationship in which they had to continually apologise for being a man. There was no point in trying to earn a respect that would forever be withheld. So men had stopped trying. The Red Squirrels were fairly typical in this regard. They had gone their own way.

"I only mentioned the DiD's camel-toe leggings because . . ." began Gravy.

"We know why you mentioned them," interrupted Captain.

"Is that gynocentric or merely gynaecological?" queried Ritzy.

"Let's not talk vaginas," said Captain, "let's talk tits."

"Okay, let's talk tits," said Gravy laughing.

"Let's talk arses," said Ritzy with a deadpan ambiguity that the others didn't catch.

"Okay, let's talk arses," said Gravy. "Pert, curvaceous, saucy arses in skintight leggings."

"Leggings again? The boy is fixated," declared Captain.

"Paint-thin glossy lycra leggings," said Gravy.

"The boy's a fetishist," chuckled Captain.

"It is a bawdy planet," quoted Barker in the melodramatic style of a ham actor.

"A Comedy of Errors," guessed Ritzy, picking a play at random from which the quote might come.

"No, The Winter's Tale," Barker corrected him, shaking his head in sham disapproval.

Barker was fond of quoting Shakespeare. In fact he was prone to having fits of Shakespearean quotes where he interpreted the whole world through his favourite texts. He had taught himself an appreciation of the plays. The bard had not been a part of the curriculum of his schooldays, naturally, except for a crudely feminist misinterpretation of Romeo and Juliet which had been so egregiously misandrist that it had driven Barker to study the plays in his own time to find out what they were really about. He was self-taught from books on the subject which had been written prior to the turn of the century and from watching download files of cinema or television performances of a similar vintage. He viewed this as a political act of anti-establishment defiance, as indeed was the study of any of the former canon of dead white men.

"Maybe you should pop downstairs to satisfy your leggings fetish with the DiD?" said Captain to Gravy. "All it will cost you is your soul and the rest of your life."

"My fetish is my own, my soul is my own, and the rest of my life is my own," asserted Gravy with such a degree of resolution that none could have doubted him.

"Indulge your fetish with your synthetic and you'll be impervious to the DiD," advised Ritzy.

"If music be the food of love, play on, give me excess of it that, surfeiting, the appetite may sicken and so die," remarked Barker.

"Othello," guessed Captain.

"What?" scoffed Barker. "Twelfth Night, you ignoramus."

"I don't want my appetites to sicken and die, thank you very much," said Gravy. "I enjoy my appetites."

"Anyway, who's talking about love, I thought we were talking about sex," said Ritzy.

"I concede the point," murmured Barker in theatrical contrition. He prised himself off the sofa and headed for the kitchen, saying: "Shakespeare exits stage left."

"And it's a perfectly harmless fetish," said Captain. He was feeling slightly guilty at having teased Gravy too much and wanted to make up for it. "It's not like he'd ever really throw his life away in pursuit of the pedestal female."

"Have you seen Mike the Biker with his latest gold-digger on his arm?" asked Gravy. "Talk about a pedestal female. He was parading her around in the Dog and Bone last night. The man will never learn. You'd think that the way his ex took him for a bundle, what with all those gifts he bought her, he'd have given up the glamour girls."

"That chump is still trying to play the alpha-male," shouted Barker from the kitchen where he was making himself a very tasty liver and bacon late breakfast. Barker seldom ate before midday. "He likes to think that there's something wrong with his backside."

"What?" queried Gravy.

"Mike thinks he's a badass," explained Ritzy to Gravy.

"No, Mike the Biker prefers to think of himself as a PUA," observed Captain.

"Same thing. All PUAs are closet alpha-males," said Ritzy dismissively.

PUAs were Pick Up Artists who practiced various acknowledged strategies for getting uncommitted guilt-free sex from fuck-objects. They used a lot of militaristic vocabulary in their game tactics as if sex were a campaign to be fought. They invariably claimed that it worked for them. But they were not popular with men like the Red Squirrels because PUAs were particularly vicious in their male-shaming of those men who used synth-partners. As Ritzy had said, PUAs saw themselves as alpha-males. PUAs shamed other men in order to reinforce their own belief that they were better, more successful, more manly, than those other men. This, in Ritzy's opinion, was divisive.

However, most PUAs had a short shelf-life because of the legislation which held that if a man lied to a woman before she slept with him, then this constituted rape. Many women gave testimony in court which presented a PUA's game tactics as lies. She would testify how she had felt that the man had indicated a commitment to a relationship and that this was the reason why she had slept with him, which meant that the law could treat men as rapists if they had sex with a woman without demonstrating a commitment to the relationship. Casual sex, in effect, became rape. Since non-commitment was essential to the pickup lifestyle, PUAs were extremely vulnerable to this charge and a great many prison sentences were handed out.

The female equivalents to PUAs were called Hook Up Artists, but HUAs did not face the same legal penalties as PUAs, of course, because the law maintained its archaic definition of rape as a crime only perpetrated by males. Her lies did not constitute rape. Another difference between the two lifestyles was that female HUAs fucked male PUAs indiscriminately with other men, treating all cocks alike, whereas it was commonly recognised by PUAs that fucking a HUA was an inferior score, bestowing less kudos, because fucking a HUA was like pushing at an open door.

"Alpha-males are so convinced that they are superior to the rest of us," sighed Captain despairingly. "They can't break the programming which tells them that if they are scoring with more women and earning more money than other men, then they are the winners in the contest of life."

"It's always been a sign of male status to win an attractive woman," added Ritzy in as doleful a tone as his friend, "because she is seen as having intrinsic value as an object of desire. The fact that she has chosen him as her sexual partner creates the perception that he's a winner because she has awarded him the prize."

"Exactly," agreed Captain. "Women supposedly have intrinsic value just by being women but guys like us only have value for what we can achieve, for what we do, not for what we are. So we have to bust a gut to win the prize. She has all the power because she's the object of desire."

"Trophies like that gold-digger aren't won, they're rented," said Gravy. "Mike the Biker won't keep her long. I heard he's into the Russians for more than he can pay back." Gravy's vocal and facial expression was contemptuous. He wouldn't piss on an alpha-male if one was on fire, though he'd cheerfully piss on one if they weren't. "When Mike runs out of cash, little Miss Trophy will move right along."

"Base is the slave that pays!" roared Barker from the kitchen.

"Henry the 5th," Captain shouted back. They all knew where that quote came from because Barker said it so often, especially when they were all drinking together in the pub.

"Men who seek the approval of women are men who permit women to decide what a man should be," stated Ritzy with finality. "Barker is right, they are slaves. They take women's judgement of men to be what matters, not a man's judgement of himself. They allow the judgement of women to decide what status a man has, in the eyes of society and in his own eyes. But we men who go our own way understand that our self-esteem is not dependent upon the judgement of women."

"More pearls of wisdom?" commented Barker sardonically as he rattled crockery in the kitchen. Barker was inclined to think that portentous rhetoric was his speciality within the group and Ritzy was perilously close to walking on his grass and treading on his toes. But Ritzy didn't think that Barker had any prerogative on grandiloquence. He countered by shifting from sagacity to analogy:

"A man who wants to convince everyone that he's a sexual alpha-male is like someone who keeps pounding himself in the head with a hammer to show how tough he is; how much more manly he is than other men. But the reality is that he's just some poor fool who's pounding himself in the head with a hammer."

The satisfied silence which followed this whimsical piece of calculated hostility signalled a general agreement with the sentiment. The Red Squirrels rejection of the competitive alpha-male was commonplace amongst men of their age. They rejected it not simply in their sex-lives but as one aspect of a comprehensive sweeping away of all the bullshit which had perennially been imposed upon them, and expected of them, as men.

They no longer aspired to relationships with women, so they no longer had to be what women required them to be. The old fashioned notion that men must fight to gain social esteem because women valued men with high status had passed it's sell-by date. Feminism had deprived men of any social esteem no matter how hard they worked for it. So men had stopped trying. At least the men who valued their personal dignity had stopped trying.

Gravy filled the satisfied silence with the simple statement: "I am the measure of my own worth."

It was true. Gravy was an almost perfect example of this. He was, to the amazement of everyone he met, a carpenter. He didn't just have the tools, he knew how to use them. In a society where carpentry was thought of as belonging to the age of the horse and cart, Gravy's ability to craft or repair tables, chairs, shelves, furniture of all sorts and much more besides in so quaint a material as wood made him a skilled artisan in a world of intentional obsolescence. As a bespoke carpenter, he had offers of work backed up for months in advance. Unlike his housemates whose mediocre wages enabled them to get by but would never make them rich, if Gravy had devoted himself to hard work he could have made a small fortune. But Gravy had decided that he didn't need a fortune, he only needed enough to provide for his limited needs in a society which had little to offer him in return for his labour. So he worked only as much as he felt was necessary and allowed himself plenty of leisure time.

The social phenomenon of MGTOW, of Men Going Their Own Way, had been the second great gender cataclysm to re-shape society. Through the last thirty years it had grown as a natural response to society's ever more conspicuous exploitation of men. It was the same old exploitation which had been men's burden for untold generations, but the injustice of it had been brought into sharper relief as a result of late 20th century gender politics. In the same way that women had said "no" to their traditional social function, men had learned to say "no" to *theirs*. They no longer had a culture worthy of the investment of their labour, and no desire to continue to be used as a social utility by a culture which held them in contempt. They withdrew their labour. They didn't stop working. They still had to live. They still had to support themselves. They just stopped supporting everyone else. They stopped carrying the world upon their aching backs.

When a man identified as MGTOW it was a declaration of self-ownership. Men Going Their Own Way meant that each individual man had the right to decide what his own values and goals in life would be, independently of the expectations of women and society. He would not surrender himself obediently to those social expectations. The intrinsic individualism of this freedom meant that MGTOW had never been an ideology. It was not prescriptive or proscriptive, it was liberating. It was an act of rebellion. It was each individual man's refusal to condone, or cooperate in, his own oppression.

Yet, despite its non-ideological character, over time a number of variations on MGTOW had nonetheless emerged which attempted to politically orchestrate what was really just a way of trying to survive in a society that was systemically hostile to men and masculinity.

The first of these to achieve prominence was the "Sisyphus" movement which took its name from the Greek myth of a man who was condemned to work for all eternity, pushing a heavy rock up a hill only to see it roll all the way back down so that he had to push it back up the hill again. Over and over. Forever. Exhausting himself in never-ending labour. The men in the Sisyphus movement saw this imagery as a representation of the gender role of men throughout the ages.

Consequently, they held firmly to the principle of doing no work that did not immediately and directly benefit themselves. Non-payment of taxes was a strict rule within their credo because so much government spending targeted women and none of it targeted men. This was nothing more that a way of taking money from men and giving it to women in the form of publicly funded support services. Sisyphus men declared that until the state started making provision for women and men equally, they would not finance the state because they refused to work for the benefit of others in what was little more than a form of gendered slavery. Bachelor taxation was a particular target of Sisyphus outrage.

Those men in the movement who were caught and jailed for tax evasion announced in court that they welcomed being sent to prison because they had the right to refuse all work whilst incarcerated yet they would still be fed every day. They cared nothing for ambition since anything men earned could be taken from them, either indirectly to fund welfare benefits which male citizens did not themselves receive, or directly as child maintenance for children to whom they as fathers were denied access, and as so-called "ex gratia" spousal support payments to ex-wives and ex-girlfriends who received the money simply for being female.

The old alimony system, which had imposed a husband's lifelong duty of taking financial responsibility for his wife even after they had divorced, was no longer officially in operation. Central government had ended the payment of alimony when an increasing number of women had found themselves having to pay alimony to their ex-husbands because the wives had the higher paying jobs. The gynocentric backlash to the idea of women financially supporting men had forced those in power to repeal that legal requirement in short order. In its place they had initiated what they termed "ex gratia spousal support payments" which were generally only imposed upon men, almost never upon women except in extraordinary circumstances, and which were not actually "ex gratia" at all since they were legally enforced. But central government thought that "ex gratia" sounded better because then they could pretend that the extraction of financial support was performed freely from a sense of moral obligation, even though the man in question was given no choice in the matter.

The Sisyphus movement had enjoyed a huge groundswell of endorsement from those men who were escaping into the shadow economy. Predictably the misandrist establishment sought to shame the movement by calling them "sissies" but this turned out to be a mistake because the authorities were accused of homophobia and this particular shaming tactic ceased at once. They had to fall back on the ancient "failure of masculinity" strategy by propagandizing the idea that it was "unmanly" for a man to leave a woman to fend for herself. But this tactic was so lame and enfeebled by extreme old age that it had no effect.

So instead, the authorities had focused on the criminality of tax evasion. They had even dared to play the patriotism card, emphasising how men who failed to pay the necessary expenses of the state were undermining the nation by damaging the national economy. But this strategy was laughable in a country which was no longer a nation, merely a plurality of diverse communities. There was no national community so how could there be any patriotism? Besides, the political class had always despised patriotism. They were the internationalists and the advocates of mass immigration and the champions of global citizenship. It was the height of absurdity for them to appeal to a sense of nationalist solidarity when they'd spent their political careers dismantling it.

This last tactic did have one effect, however, in that its focus on criminality gave rise to a movement whose adherents styled themselves as the "Outlaws". They took their name from the two-tier legal system which existed for the protection of women and the prosecution of men, without an equivalent protection of men or prosecution of women. Historically the outlaw was a person who was denied the protection of the law. They were not merely people who broke the law, they could also be violated by others without their violators suffering any punishment for the offence. An outlaw could be robbed, raped, murdered, or otherwise abused without the wrongdoers suffering any legal penalty. The outlaw was deemed to be *outside* of the law and therefore had no right to its protection.

Drawing upon this historical precedent, the Outlaw movement said that contemporary men were in much the same position as the outlaws of the past, in being afforded no protection of the law, and so they considered themselves justified in not abiding by the law either. Consequently, they broke the law as they pleased on the grounds that they had been outlawed from it. The attempt to criminalize the men of the Sisyphus movement had generated, in response, an Outlaw movement which actively embraced a kind of romanticized criminality.

Again, the establishment fought back and this time they were more successful. Throughout the chaos of The Rupture and in the years following, society was in a constant turmoil of arson attacks and rape gangs and street violence. The media in the service of the PWKB had blamed much of this disorder on the Outlaws, who were wide open to false accusations. In this way they were a gift to the establishment who could smear the whole MGTOW phenomenon with a charge of criminality. The powers-that-be had always tried to slander MGTOW with the claim that it was a hate-crime, as if a man's decision not to marry or father children was in itself an assault upon women. The credo of Outlawry permitted those in power to misrepresent the multi-sectarian violence that was sweeping across society as a generalized male hate-crime against women. As a result, the Outlaws were considered too extreme by most MGTOWs and it remained an underground movement. Not that this bothered the Outlaws since they felt that the counter-cultural underground was their natural habitat.

There were various other derivations of MGTOW of which the most politically significant were those men who self-identified as the "Unchivalrous". The slogan of their liberation was directed toward censorious womankind. It was: "I Don't Need Your Permission and I Don't Seek Your Approval". The attractiveness of this slogan came not only from its demand for an end to misandry but also from its expression of men's righteous indignation in refusing any longer to be held accountable to women. That men might act without reference to women's feelings in the matter was deemed to be a dangerously radical notion. The establishment were quick to remind the Unchivalrous that men needed women to "civilize" them and that without the constraint of female approval men would revert to the bestial, this being their true nature. But, strangely enough, this was not an argument which carried much sway with the Unchivalrous.

Those in power were similarly appalled at the prospect of the Unchivalrous taking no responsibility for the safety of women. Men's lives had always been treated as being more expendable than women's lives, and this double-standard about the value of human life was something which men were supposed to endorse. Men had always been expected to protect women from physical danger. He would have to chivalrously escort her home after dark or defend her in a violent altercation. As a man he was required to put himself in harm's way to defend a woman's honour and protect the little lady from anyone who might disrespect her. The easiest way for a woman to manipulate a man had always been for her to play the damsel in distress. And in these violent times, with riot and civil conflict raging on all sides, it was more important than ever for men to be at the disposal of women for the latter's personal protection. If the Unchivalrous renounced their traditional gendered role of being every woman's knight in shining armour, then where was this protection to come from? It was unthinkable.

Moreover, feminism's constant gender stereotyping of women as victims had been massively successful precisely because men would always submit to feminine demands if they were couched in terms of the need to protect women from some threat of harm. Whether it was domestic violence or rape culture or sexual harassment or whatever, the special "vulnerability" of women was central to the emotional appeal made that action must be taken to defend women from this victimisation. Feminism had been exploiting this traditional sexism for decades. Without it, there was a definite possibility that feminism's constant demands that women must be given greater protection might fall on deaf ears.

Indeed, the establishment now realised that chivalry had always been essential to feminism. Why else would men have tolerated the intolerable for so long? Why had most men been willing to address every last tiny issue of misogyny, even entirely bogus ones which feminism had invented for lack of anything else to complain about, without these men ever demanding that major issues of misandry should also be addressed? Was it because a chivalrous gentleman always had to put consideration for a lady ahead of any consideration for himself or other men? The essence of gentlemanly conduct was deference to ladies. It was always ladies first. Chivalry put women on a pedestal, which is where feminism believed women belonged.

But women had long ago ceased to be ladies and the Unchivalrous likewise rejected a gentlemanly attitude toward women. They declared that chivalry was an indignity and an insult to men. In past centuries chivalry had been socially reinforced by convincing men that protecting women and providing for women made them into "real" men who were worthy of respect, and this had been a powerful motivation. Culturally it had been dishonourable for a man to fail to protect and provide. Men were made to serve the interests of women by making chivalrous conduct a source of respect, honour and pride for men. But what relevance did any of this have to contemporary culture?

This generation of men, having been raised in a feminist society which delighted in disrespecting and dishonouring men, had lived their lives in a culture of male guilt and shame. Feminist women habitually and contemptuously poured scorn upon men for being immature boys obsessed with games, for being selfishly inconsiderate domestic incompetents, for being irresponsible commitment-phobes, for being inherently violent domestic abusers, for being guilty of patriarchy and rape-culture, and for so much else besides. The former rewards of pride, honour, and respect were no longer available to men. Without the bribe of these bogus prizes chivalry stood exposed for what it had truly always been: a code of conduct to make every man the servant of every woman.

The Unchivalrous had rejected this male self-sacrifice and service to women, proclaiming boldly "I Don't Need Your Permission and I Don't Seek Your Approval". The slogan articulated the futility of trying to earn the approval of those who controlled men by withholding that approval. It asserted male independence from the passive-aggressive control of needing female permission for men's own life-choices. It was to the men of the 2030s what "A woman needs a man like a fish needs a bicycle" had been to the women of the 1970s. Feminism achieved its final victory when the Unchivalrous effectively embraced gender segregation. But, as had been said in wiser times, be careful what you wish for because you may get it.

Ritzy's channels screen beeped to signal an incoming message. He checked it idly. It was a second communication from the woman calling herself Poontang. Its arrival reminded him that he hadn't decided what to do about the first message yet. He tapped an icon to open the second one and read:

"Hello. Sorry to bother. Need to know if you willing to help get my dad out of jail. No danger to you. Can meet?"

As before, there was a sender-image attachment of an attractive young woman with short blonde hair. Her sexy pout still bothered him. He liked it too much. Ritzy decided to confess to his fellow Sparts.

"I've had two messages from an extremely erotic teenager who's the daughter of an old friend of mine," said Ritzy in an act of deliberate provocation. His voice was bland but the statement produced the desired effect. Gravy and Captain sat up in the chairs. "She wants me to get him out of the nick. He's inside for non-payment of child support."

"What old friend?" queried Captain.

"Brendan," replied Ritzy. "I don't think any of you ever met him. It's a few years back."

"And his daughter wants him out of jug? Unusual girl. Somebody actually cares about daddy," commented Captain sardonically.

"Her name is Poontang," said Ritzy matter-of-factly. He waited for the reaction. But he only had to wait about a micro-second.

"Poontang?!" chuckled Gravy, "You don't mean it?"

"I didn't christen her," said Ritzy. "She was called Sarah when she was a kid. Apparently much has changed since then."

"Sounds like a big improvement to me," smiled Gravy.

"Here he goes again," laughed Captain. "Let's not be in too much of a rush to get our boy into trouble."

Gravy asked what this Poontang looked like. He was intrigued. Ritzy held out his touch-screen to show the picture attachment. Gravy's eyebrows rose and did a little dance. He said:

"And she's a teenager?"

"By my reckoning she'd be nineteen now," Ritzy replied.

"Well, I'm convinced," said Gravy. "She's obviously been harbouring a secret lust for your body all these years and she just can't wait any longer."

"Just don't give her your real name," smirked Captain.

"The last time Brendan's daughter saw me she was only fourteen year old," said Ritzy with exaggerated patience, "and I was a friend of her father. Hardly the stuff of an adolescent girl's pubescent dreams. Now she's a woman and whatever she's after, I guarantee you that it's not sex."

"Is that a good thing or a bad thing?" asked Captain.

"The answer to that question is yes," said Ritzy wryly, looking at the photo of the blonde.

Barker came back from the kitchen with his plate of liver and bacon on a tray. He'd been listening to the conversation and as he passed Ritzy he twisted his head round to take a look at the photo. Then he plumped himself down on the sofa and began tucking in. The aroma of the meat wafted under the noses of the other three and suddenly they were all famished. They fell silent for a moment as they watched Barker stuffing his face. That was the problem with everyone cooking for themselves and eating separately, the smell of other people's meals made you feel peckish all the time.

"Another good man falls under the spell of the flirtatious twinkle in a young woman's eye," mused Captain with droll cynicism. "The goddess claims her slave."

"It's Mike the Biker all over again," sighed Gravy.

"Shouldn't this be a question of whether you want to help your friend Brendan, rather than whether you want to help this Poontang," asked Barker thoughtfully through a mouthful of liver.

"Quite right, Barker old son," said Ritzy. "There's the voice of the wise old sage of the west. I'll be led astray if I listen to these two lecherous reprobates."

None of them took seriously their ribald insinuations that Poontang's interest in Ritzy might be sexual, their banter was more of a reflex warning to him not to indulge in any such fantasies. Both the political context and the age-gap were solid reasons for Ritzy to keep his head on straight. She was nineteen and he was forty years old. Not that any of his Sparts had remembered that it was Ritzy's birthday today. Nor had he reminded anybody. The Red Squirrels didn't worry about things like that. Their birthdays came and went without anyone making a fuss.

Notwithstanding all the ribbing from his friends, Ritzy had no illusions about himself and young blondes. Little Miss Poontang might just be a timewaster, in which case she could kiss his arse, but she had piqued his curiosity and he decided to agree to a meeting. Maybe there was something he could do to help get Brendan out of jail, though he'd no idea of what that might be. Ritzy had been fond of Brendan, once upon a time, and would like to see him set free. Yes, he'd meet this Poontang. But she'd better not be trying to sucker him into anything.

Gender was always an issue, even to men who had put relationships with women behind them. Predictably, the cultural elites who were responsible for the breakdown between the sexes wanted to blame it entirely on the economic collapse, but the withdrawal of men had been underway well before the series of national bankruptcies which had ripped the global economy to pieces. All that the financial meltdown had done was to settle the dust because it had accelerated the disempowerment of the feminist establishment. They still controlled much of the centralized state machine but the authority of that machine was diminishing like water being flushed down a drain.

Feminism had always been an ideology for a privileged class and, now that there was no money for privileges, nobody had any patience with specious demands for the special pampering of women. With the crash of capitalism the public funding of feminism had ceased. Too many men were working in the shadow economy. The authorities couldn't force these men to pay for female privilege and the money wasn't coming from anywhere else. Women had to manage on their own personal resources. Even the bachelor tax had failed. Without the enforcing power of the state, the entitlement-junkies of feminism had the teat removed from their mouths. The gender studies professors were unemployed, the diversity officers were reduced to working in proper jobs, and the strident journalists had to report genuine stories about what was actually happening in the world instead of pontificating from on high about what was wrong with men. Nobody was interested in wails of protest about the sexual objectification of women and "rape culture". These days people had real problems. The rape fantasies of middle-class feminists were redundant when actual rape and violence stalked the streets.

When the bubble of feminism had burst the people who had lived their entire lives inside that cloistered environment had experienced the shock of the discovery that their privilege had been wholly dependent upon the capitalism which they had affected to despise. In common with the professional multicultis, the state-sponsored professional feminists had been financed largely by government's capacity to endlessly borrow money without paying it back. After the crash when debt-capitalism, as it was sometimes called, had been replaced by capitalism in the raw, the security which they had always taken for granted had vanished like the emperor's new clothes.

Professional feminists had previously earned their salaries by talking about women. They had spent their careers talking about themselves and getting paid for it. But when times got hard nobody was wiling to give them money for doing this because it didn't seem like a very valuable contribution to society. Nor could the professional feminists and professional multicultis retire to their comfortable abodes because the currency had been devalued, wiping out most of their personal fortunes, and the private pension companies had gone bust. No wonder it had been a shock. To them, it was the end of civilization.

But it wasn't only the professionals. The character of the economic crash had important consequences along gender lines. The worst of the job losses had been among white collar employment, the office careers, the work that was hygienic and safe but which was non-essential. Who could afford to buy pet insurance when they weren't sure where their next meal was coming from? Who needed Human Resources Administrators in a time of mass unemployment, when so many of the people still earning a living were working off-the-grid? Who needed management strategists or counselling therapists or interior designers or market researchers or merchandising analysts or any of the formerly highly paid but largely useless employees who had once unaccountably seemed so necessary? It was those white collar jobs in which women had most frequently found their livelihoods that suffered the greatest losses of staff.

In contrast, the kind of occupations that had the greatest practical value were those in which the workers were usually male. It wasn't just the high-flyers in engineering technology and science, it was much more down-to-earth that that. In a society where make-do-and-mend was the new watchword, plumbers and electricians and handymen had the type of knowledge and talent that was most in demand. The people best positioned to find work were those who had practical skills that were relevant to the changed circumstances.

Someone with the ability to cobble together an illegal access to the mains water supply, or someone with the IT skills to programme file-shares, or someone who could access the telephone system without registering, or someone who could repair an electricity generator, these were the sort of people who prospered in the cash-in-hand world of the shadow economy.

Before the societal upheavals of The Rupture those MGTOWS who had identified with the Sisyphus movement had proclaimed the slogan "Embrace Obsolescence" to taunt society's devaluation of men. But after The Rupture they had changed their slogan to "Masculine Renaissance" and this was seen by many to capture the zeitgeist.

Those women who had the maturity to face these changed circumstances with equanimity rolled up their sleeves and set about learning the skills necessitated by life as it must now be lived. There was nothing to stop them from learning how to be scientists and plumbers and engineers and all the rest. But, unsurprisingly perhaps, there were others who sought an alternative solution. Suddenly a great many women were looking to find themselves a traditional man: a capable protector and provider who would raise her children and take care of her in a marriage that lasted until death do they part.

It was a vain hope. Feminist society had long since destroyed the traditional man. They had shunned him as an "unreconstructed" male. They had replaced him with the much derided "man-boy" and the vilified "deadbeat dad". They had degraded him into a male guilt-object who was to blame for the oppression of women. They had cast him out amid a storm of misandrist gender stereotypes for women to take pleasure in despising. So he wasn't around when he was needed. Looked for, he could not be found. When women once again required men to embody the traditional male virtues, precious few such men were forthcoming. It was much too late for women to decide that they wanted him now. It was too late to apologise.

Men, especially young men, had no experience of performing the traditional masculine role that women were increasingly demanding that men re-adopt. This expectation was foolhardy. How could they learn overnight to be the very thing which they had always been told they must not be? Why should they try? Some couldn't and the rest wouldn't.

Questions were now raised perforce which had never been asked by any of the gender studies professors in all their decades of naval gazing. They were tough questions like: what psychological scars had the feminist education system inflicted upon the male children in their care? These were boys who had been raised by their female teachers at school and by their mothers at home, estranged from their excluded fathers, trying to cope with their own feminisation and thwarted masculinity in a culture which told them daily that they would grow up into rapists and wife-beaters, obsolete labour and idiotic clowns. What consequences follow from generations of young men deliberately being raised to see themselves through a feminist lens? With the state propaganda machine raising boys to view men as nothing more than a social problem, to what alternatives would these boys turn to seek some self-esteem? When the day came that these young men finally saw feminism in its true light, how would they react?

One answer to this last question was evident after the collapse. Young men would not be able to take up the burden of male responsibilities which their grandfathers had carried because, quite literally, they were not the men their grandfathers had been. These were feminised men. All they had ever been taught about masculinity was to feel guilty and ashamed of their maleness. And with the bursting of the feminist bubble, they had no intention of trying to re-adopt traditional masculinity. The young men were resolved that they would not carry the burden of supplying women's needs, of fulfilling women's entitlements. They reminded anyone who suggested such a thing that a woman needed a man like a fish needs a bicycle. Sisters could do it for themselves. The young men would not. They had learned from their fathers that there was no reward for doing so. No reward of respect, no reward of gratitude, no reward of public acknowledgment. Nothing but endless insults and abuse. That had been their father's experience. The young men had no desire to become their fathers.

Was it any wonder that bachelor taxation had failed so miserably? Single male taxation was the forlorn hope upon which central government had placed its future. This was one of the reasons that it didn't have a future. The policies of the elites had turned out to be self-defeating. Their education policies over the preceding decades had created an army of unqualified and unemployable male waste-labour; the female population had invested their lives in their careers, causing a plummeting birth-rate which mass immigration had failed to solve; and the old folk lingered on into geriatric bewilderment at public expense. How could the unemployable waste-labour be expected to finance anything? What value did ex-careers have for the ageing careerists who had seen their savings and pensions disappear in the economic collapse? Only the old folk were doing their bit for the country, in that the suicide rate among the elderly was sky-high in these troubled times. Men like the Red Squirrels had escaped into the shadow economy rather than accept the responsibility of funding the state by the sweat of their brow because it was a state which had always despised them and had never made any secret of that fact. Were the young men, the unemployable waste-labour, going to step into the breach?

Male youth had flocked to the banners of the Sisyphus movement, the Outlaws, the Unchivalrous, and all the others. They had refused their traditional gendered role to protect women and provide for women. They found other ways to value themselves. They resolved that, as men, they were persons in their own right. They declared: "Anti-feminism is the radical notion that men are people, not guilt-objects or beasts of burden." They decided on their own authority, without society's permission, that they had no responsibility for women. Women must be responsible for themselves. There must be equality. No one should have to carry anyone else. Men had their own lives. They moved on. They went their own way. They were unorganised, for they needed no organisation. They had no leadership because they desired no leadership. They were not following some demagogue on a political platform. Men were going their own way.

Chapter 4

Alf in the year 1975

What really changed everything was the war. How could it not? Such a cataclysmic interruption to the lives of millions, and the ending of the lives of hundreds of thousands, was a wiping of the slate in England. It didn't wash the slate clean because the washcloth was drenched not in water but in blood, yet it left the country with a sense that one society had ended and now a new one must be built; a new country for a people who had suffered much and deserved better. That's why the electorate had turned their backs upon old Winston and voted for Atlee's boys who'd promised change instead of restoration.

Alf Eldridge had been ten years old when the war ended. His generation hadn't wanted anything restored, they'd wanted a fresh start. A socialist alternative. A society based not upon greed but instead upon a principle of human fellowship and equality. They'd wanted the workers in charge for the first time in history and by Christ they'd shaken up the old order, good and proper. Nationalisation, trades unions with serious clout, a national health system, no more tugging of the forelock, no more deference to the silver-spoon brigade or the middle-class toffee-nosed gits.

Alf took pride in that. Once they got around to putting an end to the House of Lords, who were a bunch of geriatric Bertie Woosters about as socially relevant as a pair of plus-fours, then there would be no more bloody toffs lording it over the rest of us. The bosses were on the back foot. Since nationalisation, with all the really important industries held in common ownership, the country had embarked upon the good years. The long steady climb toward full employment. A man could lose a job in the morning and find himself another in the afternoon. Well, maybe not the same afternoon but by the next day anyway. It had become normal for most people to work five days a week rather than six. What a blessing to have your Saturdays to yourself. The forty hour week was pretty standard these days too. Everything was on the up. Bloody marvellous.

It was Alf's birthday. He was forty years old today. Not the youngster he'd once been perhaps but still broad shouldered in his municipal workers donkey jacket. He had his dignity and that was what mattered. He had his self-respect. With that he could get whatever else he needed.

Alf walked down Palmerston Street and looked up at the spanking new Nightingale House tower block which had been built in '67 when the council had demolished all the slum housing between Briar Street and Church Road. People had somewhere cleaner to live now. The tower block symbolised the way forward; a better future. For a quarter of a century they'd been knocking down the back-to-backs and constructing a modern cityscape. What the Luftwaffe hadn't bombed into rubble we'd been flattening ourselves in the decades since and Alf felt like he'd been living amongst rubble for the whole of his life. But it was worth it. You had to clear away the detritus of the past to build the future.

Okay so living in a tower block meant that you'd lost your garden but you could still put your name down for an allotment, a plot of land for gardening and vegetable growing. The local authority maintained land right here in the city that was subdivided into allotment gardens for individual residents at a very reasonable rent. After all the years of food shortages during the war and bloody austerity rationing in the post-war period, Alf considered keeping an allotment to be both in his family's interest and in the national interest. You had to take responsibility for such things. It wouldn't do to leave it up to others to provide for you, like some scrounger, you had to provide for yourself. Besides, gardening was a part of an Englishman's heritage. Alf was on his way to the allotments now. It wasn't far. You could see the allotments from his family's flat on the eighth floor of Nightingale House.

Britain had been totally bankrupted by fighting fascism. It had been hard for the country to recover economically from the bombsite devastation of the war. The American economy had benefited from war manufacturing and they hadn't been bombed to bits like us, so they'd been in a great position to profit from a post-war boom. But in '45 when we were desperate to keep our people fed, the Americans weren't too keen on helping Britain to stay financially afloat because we'd voted in a Labour government and the Yanks thought we'd all embraced communism. It wasn't until they took fright at the thought that Stalinism would spread throughout Europe if the continent didn't recover economically that the Americans offered aid with the Marshall Plan.

So the price we'd paid in the war still wasn't enough. Defeating fascism had cost us dearly. Rationing went on, same as always, like it would never end. Kids had forgotten what sweets looked like. Alf's childhood during the war had included a lot of daydreaming about Bourneville chocolate and packets of aniseed gobstoppers.

His parents had named him Alfred Thomas because those were the names of his two grandfathers and both of the old men had been hoping for this personal acknowledgement in what was, for each of them, their first grandchild. Alfred from the paternal line and Thomas from the maternal line. Subsequent male grandchildren provided by Alf's uncles and aunts would thereby be excused this familial duty courtesy of Alfred Thomas Eldridge, except that his mother's sister Lizzie named her first child Thomas Arthur so that her dad's name could come first. These family considerations had to be considered. Without family what were you? Nobody actually called him Alfred, of course, it was always Alf, apart from his wife who called him Alfie. Since she'd seen that Michael Caine film which had tickled her so much, she'd taken to singing the theme tune at him too, the saucy minx.

Alf turned into Gladstone Road and stopped at the newsagent for a packet of Players. Mrs Caldwell wasn't behind the counter. Alf waited in the empty shop. A transistor radio was playing in the background. It was a lovely lilting song that Alf recognised. It was by the Beatle, John Lennon. He was the Beatle who got himself involved in political activism. Bed-ins and love-ins and all that. It was all a bit silly but Alf had heard Lennon being interviewed on the telly and, on the whole, he seemed a nice chap, if terribly naïve. He was typical of the attitude of the young people these days. Mrs Caldwell still didn't appear and there was nothing to do but wait. Alf listened to the lyrics of the song:

"Imagine all the people living for today."

Well, that was great for a twenty year old who had no personal responsibilities but it wouldn't do for a family man like Alf. He had to think of his kids future. And if a government were to ignore the future and just live for today it would be disastrous. Alf's long involvement in trades union activities was all about planning for a better tomorrow. It took time and patience to make real progress. You could be a hippy and live selfishly when you were young and fancy-free, fucking who you pleased and moving on, turning your back on a working life and hitting the road to Marrakesh, but somebody had to hold society together. Otherwise we'd all be living in tents and eating wild berries. Children could live for today but adults couldn't.

"Imagine there's no countries . . . . Imagine all the people sharing all the world."

That was the new policy of multiculturalism in a nutshell, thought Alf. No borders, no countries, open door immigration and no understanding of who you were any more except that you were a citizen of the world. But to have multiple cultures, to have different cultures in the same society, would mean having divisions between people. It was bad enough having class divisions without having racial divisions as well. We didn't want to become South Africa, did we? What did they call it; "separate development"? That went against everything we'd been trying to build since the war. Alf wanted fewer social divisions not additional ones.

This multiculturalism was a different thing to multiracialism. He had no ill-feeling toward the blacks. Some did, but not Alf. We should all muck in together, that was Alf's attitude. But naturally if the blacks came to live in England they should become English. What was so wrong with that? This multiculturalism lark said that Jamaicans should immigrate here but remain Jamaican, and Pakistanis should immigrate here but remain Pakistani. It didn't make sense. They wanted the immigrants to stay what they were but in this country instead of their own, so that everyone would somehow make a big melting pot society of all the different cultures.

But surely that meant that in the end there would only be one big mixture of a culture. So there wouldn't be multiple cultures after all. They couldn't have it both ways. Was it supposed to be a lot of different cultures or one big melting pot culture? Either way, it seemed like a poor lookout for Alf's own people. He was English working-class and he didn't take kindly to these young know-it-alls telling him that he mustn't be English any more.

"Imagine no possessions."

Alf smiled indulgently. No possessions? That would be plain daft if he meant it literally. Were people not to have their own clothing as their possessions? Could people take the shoes off other people's feet if they wanted because they had as much right to wear those shoes as the person currently wearing them? This is what people misunderstood about socialism, thought Alf, it wasn't that *all* property was theft, it was that some property was so important and powerful that it had to be owned collectively. That's what the nationalisation of the railways and the coal industry had been about. Socialism didn't mean you had to take the shirt off your back and give it to anyone who was more in need of a shirt than you were. It didn't mean you had to surrender your home to anyone from abroad who didn't have one, or sacrifice your own kids' best interests for somebody else's children. No possessions wasn't Alf's idea of socialism. But he was inclined to take a charitable view of Lennon's advocacy of a world without possessions. It was simply a piece of musical whimsy in keeping with the more fanciful extravagances of the hippies. It was only a song.

"You may say I'm a dreamer, but I'm not the only one."

At least Lennon admitted that it was all just a dream, you could say that much in his favour, and he was quite right about not being the only one. The popularity of the song seemed to derive from its being viewed as some sort of moral lesson rather than its being a fairy tale ditty that was to be enjoyed but not taken seriously. Living for today without countries or possessions might fit very readily into a drug-addled hippy culture but so what? Most young lads weren't hippies, they went to work every morning and watched the football team who held their allegiance every Saturday. They went to the same pubs that Alf had frequented when he was their age and they drank the same beer. They had the same loyalties to country, team, friends, and even brewery that earlier generations had valued, and they were in a much better position to enjoy these things than in the past. Yet something was prompting the young folk to chuck it all up and throw it all away.

That was the strange thing. This generation of young people had so much more reason to take the long view and plan for the future, instead of simply living for today. The war generation had the strongest reason to live for today because they knew they could be dead before they were twenty-five, they knew they might never have the chance to get married and raise a family. The war generation had no guarantee that they even had a future, so why plan for one? Alf's own youth was in the time when people lived under the shadow of the atomic bomb in the 1950s and early '60s. The world had come to the brink of destruction in '63 when Kennedy and Khrushchev had confronted each other over Cuba. But, if anything, that had proven that the two big powers at least had the sense to step back when they were brought to the brink. The shadow of the bomb had receded since then.

The young people now had plenty to live for, and plenty to look forward to, what with science inventing labour-saving machines to make work easier, new medicines to ease pain and let people live longer, and the slums being replaced by the bright new tower blocks that would guarantee homes for everybody. The bad old days of the war were past and rationing was over, the optimism and confidence of recent years and the power that the working class had today surely meant that everything was going to get better and better.

The working class had never been so powerful, not since the bloody peasants revolt. Ted Heath had just run the Tory election campaign on the slogan "Who governs Britain, the government or the unions?". Well, he'd got his answer. The Tories had lost the election and Wilson was back in office. That had shown the old Tory fart; he'd asked for it and he'd been put in his place. What was going to stop the workers now? Okay, there was some inconvenience with electricity power cuts and the three-day-week and suchlike, but that wasn't much of a price to pay for the working class taking control of the country. Anyway, we'd been through far worse during the war. What was an electricity power cut compared to the Blitz? Blimey, we weren't so soft that we'd betray socialism merely for the sake of solving some temporary inconvenience. So why would the young folk want to abandon the project of building a better future, and instead just live for today? It made no sense to Alf.

On the radio the disc jockey waffled like an idiot for a moment and then spun another record. This one was too loud and Alf didn't recognise it. At least Lennon knew how to compose a good tune. Alf decided that he should make his presence known in the shop so he rapped on the counter with a coin. Five seconds later Mrs Caldwell rushed out from the door to the back rooms and hurried behind the counter.

"Sorry, dear, I was in the scullery," she said wiping her hands on a tea towel.

"Packet of Players No 6 king size, please, Mrs Caldwell," said Alf.

There was a display of newspapers in the shop although Alf didn't need one because, like everyone else, he always had his paper delivered every morning. Alf's ten year old son Mike would soon be big enough to get a newspaper delivery round and earn himself some pocket money. It would do the boy good to be earning. It wouldn't do him any harm to have to get up in the dark every morning to get to work either. He'd be doing so for the next fifty years so he might as well get used to it. Today's headlines in the newspapers were all about the power-workers strike. Mrs Caldwell saw Alf's eyes surveying the headlines and she commented disapprovingly:

"More wildcat strikes and flying pickets."

Alf made a non-committal "humpf" noise in reply and handed her 30p. He knew that Mrs Caldwell was conservative in her opinions and took a dim view of trades union action, so he held his peace on the subject.

Puffing on a Players he continued down Gladstone Road toward the allotments. When he was younger he'd been a Woodbines man but since the introduction of filter cigarettes he'd switched to Players for some reason. Maybe Woodbines seemed a bit old fashioned now. He went through the cast iron gates into the allotments and threaded his way between the plots to his own little patch of earth. The vegetables he grew there were grown with his own hands, and they tasted all the better for it. Alf unpadlocked his shed and pottered about among his tools. He selected a spade and stuck it upright into the soil, then he saw Gilbert swinging along toward him.

He thought of Gilbert as being much older than himself but this wasn't actually true at all. Gilbert was only ten years Alf's senior but the man on crutches had fought in the war and when Alf had been a nine year old scavenger on bombsites Gilbert had been suffering crippling injuries at the battle of Arnhem. That ten year age gap had made a huge difference to their respective lives. The two of them had met when some kids were making fun of the old gent because of his disability. Alf had helped Gilbert to chase them away, giving one a good clip round the ear, because the man on crutches had been a stationary target for the little bleeders and too slow on his one remaining foot to chase them off himself. The two men had discovered that they both had plots in the same field of allotments and a friendship had developed.

Gilbert had lost a leg and his genitals at Arnhem. Thirty one years later he was still on crutches. His had been a long war. It had lasted all his life. Alf held the man in the deepest respect. Gilbert was just as working class as Alf but he was a true gentleman. While still a teenager he had worn the red beret of the 1st Airborne Division and parachuted sixty miles behind German lines to hold a bridge over the Rhine. The red berets had been supposed to hold the bridge for two or three days. They'd held it for nine brutal days. Three quarters of their men had been killed. Measured in courage, honour, and self-sacrifice it was one of those British defeats that were more glorious than our victories. There was something admirably British in this understanding that true glory was found more in the magnificence of how a soldier fought rather than whether he won or lost. Arnhem had rightly entered the pantheon of British martial glory. As far as Alf was concerned, if Gilbert had needed a kidney transplant Alf would have donated one of his own.

He offered Gilbert a fag and the wooden chair that Alf kept in his shed. The older man eased himself down off his crutches and sat while Alf leaned on his spade. They smoked companionably together. Gilbert made the joke he always made and Alf chuckled politely as he always did:

"Digging for victory?"

"From the ache I had in my back the last time I was here, I'd say the potatoes are probably winning."

"Useful addition to the family larder, though," said Gilbert.

"True enough," agreed Alf. "It's surprising how many chips you can grow in a small plot of land."

"I expect your family are grateful," said Gilbert speculatively.

"My ten year old, Michael, told me the other day that *proper* chips come in packets from the supermarket," replied Alf smiling ruefully, "and that it was disgusting to eat potatoes which had been grown in the ground because they'd been buried in mud."

"Ah, bless," grinned Gilbert.

"My two youngest don't mind eating dad's chips so long as they can have fish fingers with them. Food has to come in cardboard boxes to impress my kids. Fish fingers and American burgers are the popular idea of posh nosh in our house."

Gilbert mused silently for a moment and then said with some bitterness:

"That bloody war. I've missed my chance to have a family. Growing up, I was always told that a man is only as strong as his family. They're what gives him the strength to keep going."

Alf looked at this man who had sacrificed so much for his country and yet still found the strength to limp through his life, and it broke Alf's heart to hear him speak as if he wasn't a proper man, with a man's proper strength, because he'd lost his genitals and couldn't father children. How many men had there been like Gilbert over the generations who'd felt themselves to be inadequate in their manhood merely because they hadn't fucked a lot of women or raised kids? How many soldiers like Gilbert had died in a foreign field at the age of nineteen and died as virgins? How many men, shy and unattractive to women, had lived as solitary bachelors feeling that they had missed out on all that was most important in life?

On the other hand, how many bachelors have thought that they'd had a lucky escape? How many henpecked husbands spent their miserable lives wishing that they'd never married their shrewish wives or got themselves trapped into marrying some nagging bitch as a result of having a furtive shag one night, getting her pregnant, and then having to do the honourable thing?

Normally Alf would have supported the idea that family was more important than anything else because in his own case it was, but on this occasion he tried to view it from the other side.

"I don't necessarily see it that way," said Alf. "Maybe people tell young men that manhood is all about fulfilling their responsibilities as a husband and father because they want to keep the carthorse pulling the cart. If young men were allowed to know the truth, we'd stay bachelors all our lives, and then where would the women be? Men work harder after they're married and they sign up for overtime once the kids start to arrive."

"I think that's what they meant," said Gilbert regretfully. "It's family that gives a man his ambition and commitment. It gives him purpose in life."

"Or it puts a whip to his back," laughed the husband and father of three. "I reckon most men would say that a man doesn't get his strength from his family, he *gives* his strength *to* his family. It might be the love he feels for his wife and kids that gives him the strength to carry them on his back. But that love comes from him. He finds the strength within himself to provide for the ones he loves. He has to be strong for them, and that's what makes him find the strength to do what needs to be done. But what does that make them? They inspire a man to be strong but only because they're the weight he carries."

"A man's got to do what a man's got to do," quoted Gilbert, smiling at the cliché. "So what do you think makes a man strong?"

Alf thought for a moment, giving the honest answer time to come into his mind, and then he replied:

"I'd say a man is only as strong as his mates. I learned that in the army when I did my national service in Malaya." His voice was a mixture of the wistful and the sombre. "But I don't have to tell you that," he added to the man on crutches who'd been through the hell of Arnhem. "I learned it again working for the council. Oh, I know there are a few Bolshies about but fundamentally a trade union is a group of workmates who stand by one another. That's our strength. It's not the weight we carry that makes us strong, it's the mates who help us carry it."

Gilbert lived on a meagre disability pension and had no personal experience of trade unionism, but he thought he understood what Alf was saying. The bond between men could be strong when they had common cause, especially in adversity. His mates in the Airborne Division had been proof of that.

"Perhaps our mates are another kind of family," said Gilbert. "The lads I served with were like brothers to me, I know that."

"The trouble is, the two families can pull a man in different directions," said Alf. "Whenever there's talk of a strike at work it's always us married men who are the most reluctant, and we always say the same thing, god help us. We say that we can't afford to go on strike because we've got a wife and kids to support. The unmarried men look at us as if we've let them down. But they're still free and only have their own weight to carry."

Gilbert finished his fag and threw the butt away.

"Fancy another?" asked Alf, offering the packet.

"No, no," said Gilbert, who was always one to worry about outstaying his welcome. "I mustn't keep you. I should be letting you get on with your work."

"More chips for the nippers," chuckled Alf.

Gilbert hauled himself up on to his crutches. With a cheery "Be seeing you" he swung himself away, heading for his own allotment. Alf watched him go, then set about digging up his spuds.

Whenever he got chatting with Gilbert it invariably put Alf in mind of his own military service. The world war was over, thank god, by the time he'd had his eighteenth birthday but they were still conscripting all the young men in 1953. As a National Serviceman he'd been shipped out to Malaya to be exploited by the imperialism for which the young people of today seemed to think he was to blame. For the life of him Alf still didn't know why the regiment was sent to Malaya. They weren't told why, but when you're a conscript you're never told 'why' about anything. You're just told. With hindsight it ought to be clear why it was thought necessary, but the politics of it still escaped Alf. They went because they were sent. That was all there was to it. They were only boys.

One of his abiding memories of Malaya was of the lads in the barracks lying on their beds reading comics from home. Dan Dare in the Eagle and Wilson of the Wizard. That's how young they were. Skinny kids of eighteen. None of them had been away from home before when the government stole them from their mothers and put them in the army. Before they knew where they were, they'd been shipped out to Palestine or Malaya or Aden or wherever. They went from a cobbled street in some English town, to a parade ground in Aldershot, and from there to some sweltering foreign country where the locals wanted to shoot them or bomb them because the "police action" or the "emergency" or the "crisis" they'd been sent to deal with was really a war. Only a small war, perhaps, but you were just as dead.

The loss of empire wasn't much of a loss from Alf's point of view. Who wanted the burden of an empire, when it came right down to it? It had given Britain the foremost place in the world for a time, but Britain was fed up with being the world's bloody policeman, sending out our young men to die to preserve the peace in some wog's god-awful country. Let the Americans be the world's policeman if they wanted the job. They'd regret it soon enough. There's no gratitude for saving other people's countries for them, they just resent having needed your help. That's why the French disliked us so much. It wasn't the centuries of warfare between England and France which made them hostile toward us, it was the fact that they'd needed us to liberate them from German occupation; that's what they found so unforgivable.

But fuck the frogs, ungrateful bastards. And stuff the end of empire, too. All that really mattered was that the working class were taking their rightful place in politics and getting out from under the heel of the ruling class. Alf could build a better future for his wife and kids. There was plenty to be optimistic about. Hadn't we lived through the war and rationing to build an economic boom with plenty of jobs by the 1960s? Alf had a job for life if he wanted it, and if he didn't want it there were other jobs to be had. Men would have sold their souls for that in the 1930s. Maybe everything wasn't perfect but only a fool would demand perfection. We'd made it to 1975 and put the hardships of the past behind us. Of course there would always be problems, like the OPEC oil crisis jacking up the price of petrol over the last couple of years, but you couldn't expect a completely trouble-free life. We'd cope. Alf had high hopes for his children's future. His two sons and his daughter would inherit a better world than the one bequeathed to Alf.

The only worry was the young people themselves. Their hearts were in the right place but they had their heads screwed on backwards. All this wild talk about peace and love as if that were the basis for a sensible society. It might do well enough for a religion but not for the hard-headed business of politics. You couldn't enter into wage negotiations with your employer and argue on the basis of peace and love. The freedom rebellion of these hippies was admirable in its way but it was bloody childish when you came right down to it. Still, that was okay really, they were young and you were supposed to be a bit giddy at that age.

Alf's attitude toward them was a mixture of perplexity and sympathy. He was perplexed at the sight of men with long hair like a girl, which wasn't Alf's idea of what a man ought to look like. And this latest lot, the glam rockers in their make-up, were a fucking disgrace. Nor could he condone the sheer irresponsibility of the hippies' free sex and drug taking, especially these young women who acted like total sluts and claimed that it was a sexual liberation. Alf didn't want his daughter growing up like that. But he also felt sympathy with the young in their desire to avoid a working life of banal drudgery and instead spend their lives exploring what they called their "cosmic conscientious" and all that stuff. Their rejection of crass materialism was an ambition he could recognise as a worthy one, even if it was painfully idealistic. There had to be a better way of life than just working all hours in a factory. The dull routine could crush a man's soul. He couldn't blame these long-haired youngsters for seeking something better on their "astral plane", even if they did sound crackers. Maybe it was all rubbish but maybe they had the right idea, who knows? Time would tell.

At least he felt that he understood their desire for radical change. It was the same desire that his own generation had felt after the war when what mattered was to cast aside the old ways of politics and to be reborn as a new society, a fair society, a society with hope for the future. What his generation had demanded in the Labour landslide victory of 1945 was not so very different to what the young people were demanding now. No more war. Greater equality. A more egalitarian society. The young people nowadays had a different vocabulary but they were speaking basically the same language as when he had been their age.

But he didn't like the constant denigration of the British Empire by the young. That wasn't right. It wasn't fair. After all, if it hadn't been for the empire, Nazism would have conquered the whole of Europe, including the British Isles. In 1940 when Britain stood alone against the Nazi war machine, it was actually the British Empire that stood alone. The Aussies and Kiwis and Indians and all sorts that made up the empire had stood together to turn back the Nazi tide. And it wasn't just the men, it was the financial resources of the empire that were poured into the life and death struggle. If the empire hadn't existed, then the Germans would have won and we'd all be saluting our Nazi overlords right now. If they'd conquered the whole of Europe, the Russians would never have been able to defeat the Nazis on their own. By the time that Japan brought the Americans into the war, the war in Europe would already have been lost and a Europe-wide Nazi regime, which could've drawn upon all the industry of western Europe and all the natural resources of Russia and eastern Europe, would have been too strong for America to defeat alone, especially if they had the Japanese to fight at the same time.

Yet the young people nowadays spoke about the British Empire as if it had never done a good deed; as if it was nothing but the African slave trade, rampant militarism, and the theft of whatever the British could dig out of the ground. Their idea of the empire was nothing but skinny white men in baggy army shorts in a gunboat sailing up-river to steal black peoples countries from them. What they called 'racialism' these days. Of course the empire had involved some terrible things, what road of civilizational progress doesn't? But what about the good that it did for the peoples of the world?

The young thought nothing of the way that the empire had spread the concepts of parliamentary democracy, due legal process, freedom of speech and opinion, and civil rights all around the earth. Those places in the world today which did not value these concepts were generally places that the empire didn't conquer. It was the empire which had spread the intellectual advances of the enlightenment around the globe.

The young thought nothing of the advances in industry and technology, the railways and medicine and education and modern employment methods and much more besides which the empire had brought to places which had been living in a pre-industrial age before the British arrived.

The young didn't even seem to understand that the absence of a British Empire wouldn't have meant the lack of *any* world empire. It would just have meant that another European country would have had the dominant empire instead because the 18th and 19th centuries were Europe's time in history, when the European countries were far ahead of the rest of the globe. The French fought hard for a century to make the dominant world empire a French one rather than a British one. From the Seven Years war to the Napoleonic wars they'd tried. If they'd succeeded, would their empire have been any better? Or the Austro-Hungarian empire or the Dutch empire? Had the earlier Spanish empire been such a roaring success in the Americas? It was the British Empire which, for the first time in history, had made slavery illegal throughout a large part of the world. That wouldn't have happened otherwise. But it seemed that nothing could be said about the British empire now except total condemnation and expressions of contempt.

Alf supported the independence of the former colonies, as almost everyone else did. Independence was a good thing in principle, and in practice Britain couldn't afford to maintain an empire any more, the war had seen to that. But whether independence would actually improve the lives of the people living in those former colonies or not, that was another matter. What would happen to the countries that had been made independent in recent years? What would Nigeria and Kenya and Somalia and the Sudan be like thirty or forty years from now? Time would tell. Still, it was up to them.

Not that he approved of these race riots that had started since the immigrants had begun arriving in England in such large numbers. Alf had nothing against foreigners, they were alright by him. But the way that the students and youngsters talked about all this immigration made it sound as if Englishmen like himself had something to be ashamed of; some hereditary guilt which had to be purged by an act of masochistic cultural suicide. Let them all come, the more the merrier, we don't care a fig for the culture of our forefathers; that was their attitude. But hadn't the country just fought a shockingly terrible war against Nazism precisely to preserve that English culture from foreign overthrow? Hadn't people been through six years of heartache and bankrupted the country in order to preserve that heritage? Gilbert had lost a leg and his genitals at Arnhem, were they going to tell him: "sorry you lost your balls for your country, Gilbert, but we've decided to flush that country down the toilet"?

And who was leading the charge for this abdication of everything we had fought to preserve? The bloody Labour party, that's who; the very people who were supposed to be on our side. Alf knew their argument well enough and he didn't deny its persuasiveness. This had been the century of nationalist world wars, two of them. We needed to put an end to flag-waving nationalist patriotism to ensure that there wasn't a third world war. An atomic one. Nationalism had a tendency to slide into some form of fascism and that had to be guarded against. The argument was credible but Alf worried that they would throw the baby out with the bathwater.

As Alf saw it, you couldn't make a country out of any old mixture of different cultures. Artificial political states had been put together before but they always remained culturally divided countries. Belgium was a divided country. The Flemish and the Walloons were separated by having no national language, one culture speaking Dutch and the other culture speaking French. This left it without national newspapers, national political parties, or national universities. Everything in Belgium was divided by culture. So what was the Belgian identity, did it have one? Yugoslavia was worse, with the Serbian and the Croatian and the Bosnian and the Macedonian cultures artificially nailed together into one manufactured country called Yugoslavia. Political structures could be imposed upon a bunch of different communities to fabricate these states but the imposition could never really reconcile the people of those cultures. They continued to feel separate from each other.

That was why Alf was solidly behind Enoch Powell. What working-class man worth his salt wasn't? It was the workers who'd have to accommodate the immigrants and it was the workers who'd have to try to maintain the strength of the trades unions in spite of this flow of cheap scab labour from abroad. Of course Powell was an arch-Tory and Alf's class enemy, but he was the only one talking sense on immigration policy.

Not that Alf agreed with everything he said. Powell was convinced that the Common Market, or the European Economic Community as they called it now, was going to rob Britain of its sovereignty and we'd all be ruled by a European parliament in future. That sounded like fantasy to Alf. After all, how could foreigners order the Westminster government to do anything? How could they make us follow laws that we didn't want to follow? Would they invade us with a French army? We were our own bloody country, weren't we? So Powell's claims about us becoming a province of a federal European state in the future were a bit far-fetched in Alf's opinion. Mind you, it had caused Powell to urge people to vote Labour in the election because it had always been the Labour Party who'd opposed entry into Europe, so maybe the old Tory would eventually end up as a part of the Labour movement. Stranger things had happened. There were plenty of working men who would welcome him into it.

He was the only politician who seemed to understand what mass immigration meant. The others in both parties were all so irresponsible. When that beast Idi Amin had thrown all the Indians out of Uganda, where had they come? Here of course. But did we get any thanks? There was hardly a programme on television these days that wasn't calling the English 'racialists' and ridiculing us. It was Amin, a black African, who was the racialist. He was the one who'd expelled the Indians from his country for being Asians not Africans. Yet no one called him a racialist. The only reason they didn't was that he was black. No, it was the English who'd given those Indians a home in England who were slandered by being called racialists all the time. It pissed Alf off, it really did. The people who supported this new policy of multiculturalism seemed to really hate the English. They never had a good word for us. But giving a British passport to anyone who wanted to live in the country was a crazy policy. The world had lots of poor backward countries full of people who could improve their standard of living overnight by emigrating to Britain, but we couldn't let the whole world in, could we? What would be left of our own country if the whole world lived here? Bloody irresponsible, Alf called it.

The potential danger went far beyond just the English working class. Powell could see it because he'd witnessed the violent consequences of ethnic divisions in India and, like everyone else, he'd seen the race riots tearing America apart on the television news a few years back. It wasn't the different races that mattered, people were people, it was the different cultural identities. In India the Hindus and Muslims had hated each other since the days of the Mughal empire when Muslim rule had been imposed on the Hindus, before the British had ever discovered Ceylon tea. When the British had left India, the two cultures no longer had an authority, impartial between the two, to enforce co-existence. Predictably, the Hindus and the Muslims had set about murdering each other in the millions. Although now everybody blamed the British for that, as they blamed us for everything as far as Alf could tell. According to the modern way of thinking, in which only the British "partition" of India was to blame for the slaughter which took place after the British left, the Hindus and Muslims who had hacked one another to death and burned each other alive were in no way responsible for the murders they'd committed. It seemed barmy to Alf.

But Powell had seen it for himself and he had understood it. The "communalism" in India meant that loyalty to an ethnic or religious group would never allow the Hindus and Muslims and Sikhs to act as one people or accept democratic majority decisions that went against the interests of their own group. That was why partition had been introduced, in the belief that the Muslims needed their own country of Pakistan. Powell had expected communalism to explode into violence and it had. No wonder he was worried that excessive immigration might bring communalism to Britain.

Alf had seen something similar during his national service in Malaya. There'd been a lot of hostility between the Malays and the Chinese, especially the Chinese squatters. Having two peoples in one country was always going to create the risk of conflict between them. The British had been caught in the middle as usual.

But, in Alf's view, America's problem wasn't that it was multiracial, it was that so many black Americans didn't identify with what they saw as a white society. Alf didn't blame them for that, they had good reasons. But if that was the fact of the matter then it had to be faced. A multiracial society might work fine if all the citizens shared a sense of nationhood, if they all had a culture in common, but a society with a lot of different cultures was surely doomed to rip itself apart. The same thing would probably happen to nations like Yugoslavia and Czechoslovakia if they ever lost their Russian overlords who were artificially maintaining those countries as nations. What did the Serbs and the Croats and the Bosnians have in common except the same geographical location inside a manufactured country called Yugoslavia?

But these new multiculturalists seemed to be blithely unaware of the dangers of their own policy. They were wilfully blind, in Alf's judgement. They wouldn't listen to anyone else and just screamed "racialist" at anyone who disagreed with them. They had this childish belief that all the peoples and cultures of the world were going to hold hands and live in peace together *simply because the multiculturalists told them to*. In reality it was a leap into the dark, with not even the architects of the new society having the least idea of where it would all end.

They seemed to treat Englishness as if it were slum housing that had to be pulled down and replaced by the tower blocks of multiculturalism. You had to clear away the detritus of the past to build a better future, and the better future they envisaged was apparently one in which the English had been cleared away like condemned buildings so that a modern cityscape of foreign dwellings could be erected in their place. Alf was the detritus. Alf would be nothing but a part of the rubble to be cleared away by the bulldozers. Fuck that for a better future.

Powell seemed to be the only politician with his head screwed on straight, which is why he had such a lot of support from the working class. Not that it had done him any good. The Tory party had ostracized him and the university students screamed hysterically at him whenever he showed his face in public. Bigotry, they called it. Scaremongering, they called it. Well, again, time would tell.

The establishment had turned on Powell, despite the huge surge of support he'd received for saying what so many people were thinking and worrying about. He'd tried to speak for the ordinary people and he'd been lynched for it. And the left-wing students had led the lynching party. It was a bloody shame because anyone who was left-wing should know that it'll be the working-class in England who will pay the highest price for all this immigration. A constant flow of cheap labour from abroad, willing to take any jobs at any price, was certain to undermine working-class power. We'd spent two hundred years slowly accumulating enough political clout to defend ourselves and not have to take whatever jobs the bosses offered us at whatever wages they were prepared to pay. And now all that progress was going to be undone by the same old trick the bosses always used: bringing in scab labour to undermine the bargaining power of the workers.

The politicians all said that immigration is needed to provide more manpower to promote the economy, but that was just another way of saying that the bosses wanted a larger supply of labour to keep wages down. What was supposed to be so left-wing about undermining the working-class, Alf should like to know? Mass immigration was a right-wing policy not a left-wing policy, that was bloody obvious. It benefited the employer class at the expense of the working-class. But these middle-class students who thought that they were all so left-wing couldn't see it. All they could see was skin colour.

The middle-class didn't have immigrant neighbours, of course. Their children didn't sit next to immigrant kids in school every day. They didn't have mixed-race children or drink in the pub with black friends or discuss shop-floor trades unionism with their black co-workers in the way that the white working-class did. That was why the middle-class were so relentless in condemning the working-class as a bunch of ignorant ill-educated racialists. It was the only way they had to deflect their minds from the truth about themselves and indulge their halo-polishing. They lived outside of multiracial areas, they worked in all-white offices, their kids went to white grammar schools and the middle-class mothers would have dropped stone dead if their little princess daughter had brought home a brown boyfriend, so they had nothing else behind which to hide their mono-racial lives except condemnation of the workers.

Constantly criticising the white working-class as a bunch of primitive racialists was a form of political masturbation. The middle-class were too affluent and privileged in their own lives to demonstrate how anti-racialist they were, but they could wank-off politically by continually condemning working-class racialism and thereby parade their own moral righteousness. Then they could go out for dinner at an Indian restaurant and feel good about themselves for being so welcoming to the immigrant population by having people with brown skins serve them their meal and call them 'sir'. On their way home to their nice houses in the suburbs they could polish their halos some more by talking about what a nice chap their Indian waiter had been and then sneering at how racialist the working-class are.

These smug gits were motivated by a selfish delight in making a public exhibition their own virtue as compassionate humanitarians, ever holier than thou. But they cared nothing about the effect that all this immigration would have upon the working-class. It seemed to Alf that there was no serious thought behind their new policy at all. It was nothing more than that John Lennon song "Imagine" which he'd heard in the newsagent earlier. The sentiments expressed in that song were their manifesto and it was apparently the only justification they felt they needed. They had no more sense than the young folk who hadn't grown up yet but who wanted to rule the world; who couldn't wait until they'd achieved a bit of maturity and insisted that they wanted to be in charge right now. But you can't have a country ruled by children, they'd just make a mess of it.

Alf despaired of them sometimes. Even so, he was sure that the current policy of letting tens of thousands of immigrants into the country every year couldn't last. Common sense must prevail. Alf felt in his heart that in a few years the mass immigration would stop, just as it always had in the past. Like the Jewish immigration in the '30s. People made a fuss at the time but after a while the immigration had stopped, the Jews had assimilated, and life went on. It would be the same this time. Immigration from Pakistan and the West Indies had been alarming in recent years but before long it would slow to a trickle and then dry up. The Labour government knew that. Obviously the Labour Party wouldn't go on supporting mass immigration indefinitely because the last thing that Labour voters needed was an endless supply of scab labour for the bosses to exploit. It would completely undermine the labour movement. It stood to reason that the Labour Party couldn't support a bosses policy for very long without betraying themselves as well as the very people whose party they were. The unions had made the position plain enough since the Powell marches, and the Labour Party would be bloody fools not to listen.

A worse danger, as Alf saw it, was if the fucking Tories got back into power. Old Wilson was hanging on to Downing Street by his fingernails at the moment. But the bosses knew that moving the workers from one country to another was good for their profits. Now that they'd had a taste of it, the greedy bastards would want more. If the Tories got back into power, they might open up the borders long term. Then it could get really serious. After all, with open borders there were no natural limits to immigration. It was a lesson from history. How many times, in how many places, had migrations of people changed the character of a country in which they'd taken up residence?

Wasn't that how the English had started in the first place? A wave of immigration from the continent by the Saxons and the Angles which had eventually changed Celtic Britain into Anglo-Saxon England. What had begun with a wave of immigration could also end with a wave of immigration. Englishness would be bookended by two waves of mass immigration; one to create it and one to kill it.

And what would come after it? Who knew what the country might turn into? God help the children. And the grandchildren. But that couldn't happen, surely? The powers-that-be couldn't be that bloody stupid. Even the Tories wouldn't put the bosses profits ahead of the actual integrity and survival of the country. Not after we'd just fought the greatest war in history to keep England English?

No, the biggest worry was the attitude of the young people, especially those middle-class twats of university students. They were so infantile. That was why they engaged in their politics of juvenile name-calling. According to them the police were all "fascist pigs" and men were all "chauvinist pigs" and the English were all "racialist pigs". Everything they did in their political activism was just a lot of yah-boo-sucks-to-you. It was the political equivalent of sticking out your tongue.

They wouldn't even allow anyone to discuss the likely consequences of the policies they advocated. Whenever someone from the working class spoke his mind on the subject the students started screaming "racialist, racialist, racialist" until no one dared open their mouth. These spoilt kids at university seemed to think that if they could force everyone else to agree with them, then everything must turn out to be wonderful in the best of all possible worlds.

But they weren't half as smart as they thought they were. They had entirely the wrong idea about imperialism for a start. That was understandable, Alf supposed, given the recent conquest of half of Europe by the Nazi war machine. But imperialism could often be as much civilian as military. When the land-grabbing Americans went west and took the continent from the tribes of Red Indians, it was a civilian gold rush and civilian farmers looking to settle the land who really led the way. The blue-jackets of the US army were sent out to protect those gold miners and settlers as they travelled west. But it wasn't the soldiers who led the march westward, it was civilians.

It was the same with the French colonisation of Algeria. That was achieved by a migration of unemployed and landless French civilians, as well as Spanish and Italian civilians, who had nothing at home and were looking for a better life somewhere else. The French army had the job of dealing with the Algerians who wanted to kick the migrants out again, but would the army have been sent there if the migrants hadn't needed to be defended? Even the British presence in India had begun with a commercial enterprise, the East India Company. India had been colonised by businessmen with their own private army. It was only after the Mutiny that the British government had taken over and set up the Raj. And ninety years later the government had given it back again.

Sometimes imperialism was a military project and sometimes it wasn't. Migrant colonisers could play a major role in imperialism. But the young people only ever saw things from one perspective; their fashionably radical point of view. It wasn't enough. You had to see both sides of the coin.

It was like Churchill. He was another old Tory bastard who was naturally Alf's class enemy, but when the great war leader was given a state funeral in '65 Alf had wept a silent tear and he was prepared to bet that his shop steward had piped an eye, too. In the '20s Churchill had used troops against the workers in the general strike, but in the '30s he'd warned the world about fascism when few in government would listen. And when the enemy had a leader who could captivate and inspire his people like old Adolf, we'd needed a rousing and compelling wordsmith like Winston to lead us. You had to see the whole picture, not just the side that suited you.

Alf turned over the soil with his spade. A cluster of spuds was drawn up out of the ground. More chips for the kids. Alf smiled. There was more satisfaction in this little harvest from his allotment than in all the political wrangling at Westminster. This was where he belonged. Leave the political conundrums to the people in charge. Thank god it wasn't his job to sort out the mess. His first responsibility was to his family. At the end of the day, that was enough for him. Keeping the kids fed and keeping the wife happy. Keeping a roof over their heads. Earning a wage and teaching his sons how to follow his example. That was more than enough to keep Alf occupied. It was a man-sized job.

Chapter 5

Michael in the year 2005

Michael Eldridge was walking quickly down a corridor in the building which symbolized his life. It had been built within the last half-century, it lacked idiosyncratic character in the way that it was a carbon copy of innumerable other buildings of a similar type, and it rang with the superficial chatter of juvenile voices. The school epitomized Michael's world; it was diverse, it was feminised, and it was immature.

His parents had named him Michael after his mother's father, in acknowledgement of the newborn's sole remaining grandfather. Grandpa Mike had gotten quite misty-eyed when they told him. Baby Michael had lost his other grandfather, Grandpa Frank who'd died in an industrial accident, before the little lad was even born in 1965. Michael had never really known his Grandpa Mike but he'd always been grateful for the old man's existence because Michael would have hated to have been named after his father Alf. What a trial that would have been, having to go through life with an old-fashioned name like Alfred.

Michael had become aware of the political world around him, the world outside of the home and the school classroom, in the late 1970s when Thatcherism had swept to power. Those were the bad old days when England was too English and unrepentantly patriarchal. Sure the 1970s had been a decade of working class activism but what did that really mean? It meant white men exercising power. White men in the boardroom and white men in the union hall. At university Michael had learned that the rule of white men like himself had to be overthrown. Society had to be made to change, no matter what. Michael had taken this political agenda deeply to heart. Not just for the sake of others but for his own sake. He believed in personal redemption through multiculturalism and feminism. There was much for which he must atone.

After university he had made a career for himself as a history teacher. It offered many opportunities for redemption. Michael used the established pedagogic techniques for the interpretation of history. He laid great emphasis on "identifying bias" in the way that the practice of traditional English history selected only white males for its famous characters and "heroes". He had the children in his classes "role-play" as the victims of the white males of English history. They role-played being African slaves, unwed mothers, female industrial workers, Irish immigrants, and much more besides. There were many victims. In Michael's classes the white males of the English were always the villains of history. As a teacher, he considered it a professional duty to treat each lesson as an act of emancipation, not only for the girls and the students of colour, but also for the white boys of English heritage who could be liberated from the sins of their ancestors. It was, perhaps, especially beneficial for these boys to see the despicable racist and sexist guilt of their forebears and reject it. How else could they grow up into well-rounded decent human beings?

Gary, a colleague of Michael's in the history department, had once suggested that he try having the children role-play being an English victim of Norman oppression. Michael could portray William the Conqueror, he said, and the children could all be Anglo-Saxon peasants suffering under the Norman Yoke. That was typical of Gary, he liked to be provocative. He wasn't a bad man, he simply had the kind of sense of humour which enjoyed challenging people with unconventional ideas. It was stimulating, really. Michael didn't hold that against him. But Michael had been horrified at the suggestion of role-playing English oppression under the Norman-French. A role-play like that would surely undermine the learners' clear-cut understanding of right and wrong. It might even give rise to racism toward the French.

However, it had given Michael the idea of setting up a role-play where the children were Palestinian refugees resisting Israeli oppression. There could be no difficulty in discerning the division of right and wrong in that scenario. Michael unequivocally supported the cause of the dispossessed Palestinians, as he would expect of any moral person, demanding that their country should be returned to them.

Over the years Michael's techniques of teaching history had become the mainstream orthodoxy in his profession and, as everyone agreed, they were more necessary than ever. Many of the working-class children in his classes had fathers who had been made unemployed, firstly by immigration from the Indian sub-continent and the Caribbean, then later by immigration from Africa and Eastern Europe. Those kids from the underclass with unemployed fathers, and a probable future of unemployment themselves, came from racist white communities where there was always a lot of talk about immigrants under-pricing the local workers for the available jobs. It was made worse by some of the jobs being outsourced abroad. So it was of the greatest possible importance for these kids to learn that all this unemployment was in no way the fault of the immigrants.

Black historical role-models were a blessing and Michael used them as extensively as their limited supply would permit, for they were even more scarce than female historical role-models. There was rarely a class that went by without some mention of Mary Seacole. Lest any of his children be puzzled by the dearth of black historical figures in the face of his repeated assurances that people of colour had always played a vital role in the history of the country, Michael was careful to emphasise how white racism had caused black historical figures to be written out of history. When he said this he tried to imply that there were thousands of important people of colour in British history just waiting to be discovered by future historians.

This was something else about which Gary had challenged him. It wasn't exactly a bone of contention between them, more the sort or banter that Gary indulged in at the expense of contemporary pedagogy. Gary taught the same curriculum as every other history teacher but he would poke fun at it when he and Michael were alone. Recently Michael had been sounding off about how the wife of King Edward the third, Queen Philippa, had been a person of colour and how she hadn't featured in the standard school history curriculum until very recently.

"It hasn't been historically proven that she was anything other than white," Gary had said, "and maybe she wasn't mentioned previously because she's not very historically significant. She wasn't written out of history by anyone, there were just more important people to tell the kids about."

"Not historically significant?" expostulated Michael. "She was a queen, for goodness sake."

"Lord Frederick North was Prime Minister during the American war of independence," Gary had replied, "but how many of your students have heard of him? Does he ever get a mention in the modern schoolroom?"

"I'm sure he does," said Michael, who was not at all sure. "Anyway, there are any number of white male prime ministers."

"But Lord North is not important for being white and male," objected Gary, "he's important for being the Prime Minister during a vital period of British and American history."

"That may seem important to you," Michael came back at him, "but he adds nothing to diversity and that's what's important today."

"And when you're telling your students all about Mary Seacole in the Crimean War," smiled Gary, "do you ever tell them which Tsar was the Emperor of Russia during that war, or who was the Sultan of the Ottoman Empire at the time? The two men at the head of this clash of empires might be of some historical relevance to an understanding of the war, don't you think?"

Michael had been stumped for the moment to remember the names of the Tsar and the Sultan during the Crimean War. He wasn't certain that he'd ever known, even when he'd been studying for his degree. So he'd had to change the subject of the argument and say that social history was more relevant to his students than imperial history.

It wasn't the first time he'd relied upon on shifting the goalposts in that way when Gary was being tiresomely old-school with his knowledge of names and dates. What Gary failed to appreciate was that presenting an inclusive view of history was what mattered, not an individual person's historical importance. If they taught the children about nobody except figures of historical importance, they'd be talking about dead white men all the time. History would be His Story, as it had been in the bad old days. The learners must have women and people of colour to identify with, regardless of whether those people were significant in the historical chain of events or not. It was essential to inclusive teaching.

Michael had been a schoolteacher for eighteen years. It was the only job he'd ever had since leaving school, apart from some summer work he'd done during his university vacations. His ex-wife Iris was a schoolteacher, too, as was his present partner Rhea. For him the education system was the centre of the world. It was the forum in which young minds acquired an understanding of the beliefs and values which gave life meaning.

He was at this moment hurrying down a corridor on his way to a staff disciplinary procedure. He was not the culprit. It was his colleague Gary who was being put on the carpet for an offence against one of his students. Gary's inclination to challenge orthodoxy and engage in free-thinking had finally caught up with him. It had only been a matter of time. There was no place for intellectual dissent in the education system. The meeting that they were about to have was only the initial assessment of Gary's misconduct but he faced a very serious charge and his case was certain to be carried forward. Gary had requested that Michael be present at the meeting as his "companion colleague" accompanying the accused, as was his right.

It struck Michael that, as a fellow male in the history department, he might be the one person in the school that Gary considered a friend. Gary wasn't popular with female members of staff because his intermittent ill-advised political opinions had earned him a bad reputation. Most of the women teaching in the school had very little tolerance toward Gary's satirical observations on serious subjects. The only other male members of staff were two guys in the science department and a PE teacher, none of whom ever seemed to say anything in staff meetings and who didn't socialise with their colleagues outside of school hours. Gary and Michael usually had their lunch together and even went out for the occasional drink in the evening.

Although Gary was a dozen years older than Michael, and despite their sporadic political differences, the two men had important things in common. They were both divorced, they'd both had a child taken from them by the custody courts, and they both had an abiding sense of the failure of their personal lives. They didn't discuss these things but, curiously, just being in one another's company for a chat over a pint had a mutual feeling of consolation. They felt less alone in the world. This made them friends of a sort. In fact, Gary had been invited to Michael's fortieth birthday celebration tonight, although Rhea had only conceded this when she realised that without Gary the dinner party would have four women and two men. She had let Gary be added to their number in order to help balance the genders. Mind you, Gary might not fancy attending a birthday celebration tonight if his misconduct assessment went badly.

The five members of staff in the headteacher's office were stiff with distaste. An odious charge had been levelled against one of the school's teachers and the manner of all concerned seemed to suggest that someone had farted in church. Besides the headteacher, who nominally sat in judgement, there was Diana Bates who was the learner's representative because the learner herself wasn't permitted to be present at staff disciplinary procedures. Diana was, in effect, the voice of the prosecution. A trade union representative was also present, supposedly to ensure fair play within the rules of contract employment. Gary and Michael were the remaining two.

Gary had been accused of Islamophobia because he had tried to facilitate a discussion of the recent 7/7 bombings with his 6th formers. The terrorist attack had occurred only a month earlier and it was being talked about everywhere in the media. Gary had thought that at the age of sixteen his students ought to be able to handle a discussion on the topic in class. But one of the Muslims among his 6th formers had complained about feeling offended and distressed. Gary had been charged with "religiously aggravated threatening behaviour" which constituted a hate-crime against his student.

The trade union representative stirred in discomfort. She detested these disputes over ethnicity and religion. She always felt that it placed the union in the invidious position of being on the wrong side. She would fulfil her role as a union rep but it was odious to have to speak on behalf of a racist. Personally she had always found Gary a bit suspect; a little too free with opinions that smelled of white male attitudes. Fortunately, Diana was here as the learner's representative. Diana knew how to handle these situations.

"I had no intention of being disrespectful to Islam," said Gary in response to the charge having been formally read out to him. "I deny the accusation of Islamophobia absolutely. I merely wanted to engage my learners in a discussion of the politics of the day; the politics of the adult world which they are about to enter."

"Perhaps you were merely unaware of how offensive you were being to this student," countered Diana. "It's so easy for someone who occupies a position of unwarranted privilege in society to fail to appreciate how insensitive he's being."

"These young people see the news on television," replied Gary, "they hear these issues being discussed in their internet chat-rooms, so I think it's important that we should recognise these current events in our 'Personal Social Health & Economic Education' classes."

"I hear what you're saying, Gary," put in the headteacher, who thought it was about time that she said something, "but we must give priority to our SEAL directives. The learners 'Social Emotional Aspects of Learning' are paramount."

"I have no problem with that," acknowledged Gary in a conciliatory tone, "and nothing that was said in class was in violation of SEAL."

"I hear what you're saying, Gary," said the headteacher again. She was one of those people who used the phrase excessively because, although it was very annoying, she mistakenly believed it to be calming. "But PSHE gives the school a duty to promote the spiritual, moral, cultural, mental and physical development of our learners and of society as a whole. Let's not forget the latter part of that responsibility. Naturally we entirely support freedom of speech but it must be exercised responsibly. Irresponsible freedom of speech could have detrimental effects not only upon our learners but upon their families and the wider society."

Gary stifled the comment that rose in his throat. The headteacher typified an establishment which had never understood the concept of freedom. They saw it as a possession, much like status or reputation. It was something a person owned which had to be protected from being damaged or lost. The way to protect it was by never using it, since using it would put it at threat. If you used your freedom, someone might get upset and take it away from you. So the only way to preserve the freedom that you had was to never exercise it. You had to keep it in a shoebox under your bed. It might get a little dusty but it was safe there and you could reassure yourself that you still had it. It was something of value which you had to preserve, and the way to do that was to never take it out of the box and actually use it.

Establishment drones like the headteacher had never been able to see what was wrong with this argument. They didn't understand that the possession of freedom consisted in the exercising of freedom. If you didn't use it, you didn't have it. They failed to appreciate that freedom was something you engaged in; it was participatory. It wasn't a legal abstraction or a political state of being. The drones didn't seem to realise that by refusing to permit people to exercise their freedom, they had robbed people of their freedom.

They advocated restraint upon free speech wherever it might cause upset or offence. But the right to freedom of speech was intended precisely for statements which upset and offended people because those were the statements which other people tried to censor and suppress. If a person never said anything controversial, they wouldn't need a right to free speech because no one would be trying to stop them speaking. It was only when a person said something which caused others to want to silence them that a moral and legal *right* to freedom of speech needed to be exercised. When people like the headteacher, or for that matter the Prime Minister, said that freedom of speech must be exercised "responsibly" what they meant was that no one should say anything that would offend anyone else. But this only demonstrated that the headteacher and the Prime Minister didn't understand what a right to freedom of speech actually was.

Unfortunately, if Gary were to exercise his freedom of speech in these circumstances, he would be playing right into the hands of the people who had all the power. So he didn't say what he was thinking. Those who would pass judgement on him might know nothing about exercising freedom but they were experts at the exercising of *power*. He was in their hands and if they closed their fist they would crush him like a bug. He had to keep his temper in check no matter what the provocation.

"Nothing detrimental was said or done," said Gary.

"I hear what you're saying," repeated the headteacher and Gary wanted to scream. This phrase actually meant 'I am going to ignore everything you're saying but I want you to believe that you're being listened to so that you don't get upset'. Few things were more upsetting. You could cut the condescension with a knife.

The union representative started quoting statutes and regulations at the headteacher and the two of them began a little dialogue of their own for a while, but it was largely beside the point. The political policy directives by which schoolteachers must abide may have been the official foundation of the charge brought against Gary but these directives were not the real basis upon which a decision would be made. The student's wounded feelings, her experience of trauma, and the damage done to her emotional well-being were the heart of the issue. Interpretations of formal policy statements would be a secondary consideration.

Given that the evidence for the alleged offence of Islamophobia was the emotional suffering felt by the complainant, there was no conceivable way that Gary could offer any counter-evidence that he had not inflicted emotional suffering because it was simply a matter of somebody else's feelings. The only evidence was her personal testimony. Consequently, any facts about whether what was said was actually defamatory of Islam, or any arguments to prove or disprove whether Gary's statements in the classroom had expressed prejudice, were irrelevant to the outcome of the case. It was about feelings.

"The incident has caused the student considerable stress and has impacted not only upon her but upon her family," said Diana. She had not spoken to the family but she had been assured by the student that they were deeply upset by what had happened. "It is particularly serious because this incident occurred during the revision period for exams and the learner has said that she no longer feels positive about her chances of achieving the examination results that she was expecting."

Gary almost protested against the non-evidential nature of this evidence but he bit his lip to stifle the protest just in time. He would only make things worse if he committed the heresy of challenging the sacred pedagogical belief in student-centred learning. To suggest that how a person felt did not establish the facts of what actually happened would make him appear monstrous in their eyes. This was feminised education and ideological beliefs reigned supreme. These were the rules by which his chances of keeping or losing his job would be decided. Everyone in the room knew that pedagogy is politics and politics is pedagogy, but since no one was going to admit this there was nothing the accused could do about it except bite his lip.

"I certainly think we should ask for an Interim Prohibition Order," asserted Diana forcefully. "Where a vulnerable person's well-being is at stake we can't take any chances. Gary can't be allowed to teach any further classes until this matter has been properly settled by a Professional Conduct Panel."

"You believe that a Prohibition Order is warranted?" asked the headteacher.

"The union would have no objection to a Prohibition Order, given the seriousness of the charge," interjected the trade union representative.

Gary looked daggers at his union rep, wondering whose side she was supposed to be on. This was foolish of him since he should have known perfectly well whose side she would be on and that it wouldn't be his. She wasn't *his* union rep, she was *the* union rep, which is a very different thing. Her next question hammered this home.

"While the Prohibition Order is in force, what steps can be taken to address Gary's unacceptable conduct?" enquired the union rep, trying to be helpful and constructive.

"I haven't committed any unacceptable conduct," spluttered Gary.

"All of us who are employed in the education system have naturally gone through the requisite training including a raised awareness of multiethnic sensitivity," said the headteacher, ignoring Gary's boorish male blustering, "but it is sometimes very useful for a person to have a refresher course on correct pedagogic practices."

This recommendation had been as inevitable as rain on a bank holiday Monday. No amount of ethnic sensitivity could ever be enough ethnic sensitivity. It was to modern pedagogy what blood was to a vampire. The thirst could only be temporarily assuaged and then it returned. There was the recurrent fear that some lingering trace of incorrectness might remain within the soul of the individual or the body of the institution. Even the most committed of establishment drones was secretly haunted by the dread of discovering some sign of their own ideological inadequacy. Regular purging of the soul was required. The only way to achieve an inclusive society was to ruthlessly exclude the non-inclusive.

"I don't need a refresher on multiethnic sensitivity," said Gary.

Even as he said it, he knew he'd said the wrong thing. It was taken for granted that all white males were constantly in need of further instruction in multiethnic sensitivity. For a white male to claim that he was not in need of such instruction would be taken as the surest proof that he was in dire need of precisely that. It was, by the belief system of the culture in which he worked, a confession.

The only chance that Gary had of keeping his job was to admit his guilt unreservedly and accept additional sensitivity training. Better still, he should have requested it. The headteacher had actually been trying to be supportive with her suggestion of a refresher course on correct pedagogic practices because Gary's career would be over without it. She had been trying to give him a chance to save himself. But Gary had blown it with a show of defiance. Attempting to defend himself would only further prove his guilt and give evidence of how irredeemably he was rooted in outmoded attitudes.

"Teachers are gatekeepers," said the union rep patiently. "But we do need to remember that as educators we don't just have the power to give our students access to an inclusive society by means of correct practice, we also have the power to deny our students access if we commit error. No one should be too proud to admit they've made an error."

"But I haven't committed an error," said Gary in exasperation, thereby proving himself guilty of the sin of pride as far as the trade union representative was concerned.

"What must take precedence here," said Diana, moving the discussion toward its conclusion, "is that we have a definite policy of zero-tolerance toward all forms of Islamophobia. This makes both an Interim Prohibition Order and a Professional Conduct Panel necessary measures to demonstrate our commitment to zero-tolerance."

No one seemed to notice that she had demanded these measures, not on any evidence of Gary's guilt which might warrant them, but rather as a necessity for demonstrating the school's commitment to policy. Diana herself was only vaguely aware of the way in which she had shifted the ground. She was so adept at exploiting the malleability of language that she could fool herself with her own linguistic sleight-of-hand. It had become an engrained habit, and the concept of "zero-tolerance" was an old friend. It enabled someone to be absolutely intolerant whilst at the same time maintaining their self-image as a tolerant person. Zero-tolerance was an attitude of complete and utter intolerance. That's what it actually meant. But it avoided saying so. Instead it spoke of "tolerance", it's just that the amount of tolerance was zero. So it created the pretence that the person was talking *from a perspective of tolerance* even in the act of exercising intolerance. It made illiberalism sound liberal. It was a skilled piece of self-deceiving duplicity and one that she had used many times.

"I'm being railroaded here . . ." began Gary.

Diana interrupted with: "We can't permit the classroom to be a forum for the articulation of right-wing attitudes that belong only in the Daily Mail or some conservative rag of that sort."

Gary, a lifelong Labour Party voter and reader of the Guardian, attempted to defend himself with the truth. He should have known better. It was career suicide.

"I object to being called right-wing," he said. "I've never been any such thing. Besides, the allegation makes no sense. After all, you're accusing me of being critical of Islam, and Islam is a very conservative right-wing ideology. So why would someone who's supposedly right-wing criticise it? The term 'right-wing' is thrown about so casually and ubiquitously at critics of Islam, yet it's never applied to Islam itself. It's a case of 'if the shoe fits, throw it at someone else'."

Diana spoke the fatal words: "That's racism."

It wasn't, but that was beside the point. Gary knew what it meant. The public utterance of that word meant that he had already been found guilty and anyone who failed to endorse this verdict would share his guilt. It was a word that could never be refuted and which was never taken back. From now on, everything else would be a formality.

"That's an outrageous slander . . ." began Gary.

"I think it is now clear that Islamophobia has been committed in our school," said Diana, talking loudly over him to exercise her moral authority, "and the necessary disciplinary procedures should be implemented immediately."

The headteacher, feeling herself to have been backed into a corner by Gary's obstinate refusal to cooperate with a formal proceeding which was designed to protect him, decided to proceed as Diana had outlined. She did so with the full agreement of Gary's union rep. This verdict was held to be the only possible one in the circumstances because "safeguarding" the student must take priority over all other considerations. The judgement followed the accusation as night followed day.

The three women were already in motion, collecting up their paperwork. The disciplinary procedure was closed. The Interim

Prohibition Order would be issued and in due course a Professional Conduct Panel would be held which would dismiss Gary from his job for professional misconduct. Everyone knew that such a finding was inevitable. He was as good as fired already. Gary stood stunned as he watched his life being flushed away. He had been a schoolteacher for almost thirty years. He needn't have bothered.

Gary knew that he should be saying something. Not just docilely letting them do this to him. But he was stymied by being a man out of his time. He had learned to think in a culture that was very different to the one in which he now found himself. Gary had been taught that the goal of intellectual debate was to identify the truth. Or, at least, to try to do so. The method was to evaluate the evidence by subjecting it to the scrutiny of rational argument. That was what schoolteachers like himself meant when they said that education wasn't intended to teach you *what* to think, it was intended to teach you *how* to think. But the world had been turned on its head. Now all that mattered was endorsing the correct beliefs. Education was about teaching people *what* to think. Learning *how* to think was an irrelevance. Anachronistic ideas of truth, evidence, and rational justification were of no account at all. None of this had any place in the proceedings of the contemporary culture. His sort of thinking meant nothing these days.

That was why Gary hadn't really understood the accusation which had been levelled against him. "Islamophobia" was a brand new word. It had been coined only recently, minted in the currency of the present society, not that of Gary's dead culture. As a pejorative term it was used to bully and coerce. The actual meaning of the word wasn't important, it was how it was used which gave it significance. Its purpose was to imply racist bigotry as a way of silencing people. No one wanted to be thought a bigot, so the word had terrific power in getting them to shut up. Anyone who made an accusation of Islamophobia wasn't using the word in a literal sense. They were not actually claiming that someone who disapproved of the death penalty for homosexuality and adultery, who disapproved of the genital mutilation of children, and who disapproved of underage marriage, must therefore have an irrational fear of a religious ideology which endorsed these actions.

"Islamophobe" was simply a proxy for "racist". Most Muslims were Arabs, Asians, or Africans so to criticize Islam was to criticize a faith primarily found in cultures of non-white people, and to criticize the culture of anyone whose skin was any colour other than white must necessarily be an act of racism. This was why it didn't matter how many times it was tediously pointed out that Islam is not a race, it was associated with certain skin colours and that was enough to give the allegation the power to instil fear in the accused.

So, of course, it made not the slightest difference that a liberal like Gary ought to criticize Islam for being extremely illiberal, nor that a left-winger like Gary ought to criticize Islam for being extremely right-wing. The charge of Islamophobia had little or nothing to do with the facts about the religious ideology of Islam. It was all about the racial attitudes of the multiculturalists. It was all about the skin colour of the Muslims. This was why people who saw themselves as left-wing liberals could believe that when they treated a right-wing illiberal ideology as something which must never be criticized, this was a left-wing liberal thing to do.

Diana, for one, had no difficulty in believing that it was liberal and left-wing to give an illiberal right-wing ideology the status of being above criticism. She did not inhabit a culture in which self-contradiction was fallacious. Diana considered logic to be "masculine". She was a Social Justice Warrior. Ideology was everything. Defeating the enemy was what mattered. For Diana, telling lies was just a debating technique. Lies were words with a razor's edge. She cared very little about whether what she said was true or false, but she cared a great deal about how much power her words carried. Discussion was battle and winning was what counted. Diana was highly proficient in the McCarthyite tactic of suppressing dissident opinion through denunciation. Senator Joe had made folk unemployable by calling them a pinko or a commie or a red, and Diana was every bit as capable of making folk unemployable by calling them a racist or a misogynist or an Islamophobe. And she felt good about it. After all, racists and misogynists and Islamophobes shouldn't be permitted in the workplace.

Gary looked across at Michael, who had not spoken throughout the meeting because a "companion colleague" was not entitled to speak. Michael placed a hand on Gary's arm and accompanied his friend out of the room. Gary was the walking dead. He turned to look at Diana. He said nothing but the defeat on his face spoke for him. She stared back at Gary and silently mouthed the words:

"Right-wing prick."

It was the political equivalent of lipstick on the teeth. A child masquerading as a grown-up and making mess of it. Diana, like every other paid up member of the People Who Know Best, mistakenly believed herself to be left-wing, so she blandly assumed that anyone and everyone who disagreed with her must therefore be right-wing. All opposition was instantly put into the box marked "right-wing" regardless of what their actual politics were, or even if Diana had no idea of what their politics actually were.

*   *   *

On the way home from school Michael stopped off at the supermarket to pick up the list of items that Rhea had told him not to forget. They'd arranged a dinner party for a few friends to celebrate Michael's fortieth birthday and there were one or two bits and pieces that needed to be bought fresh. Rhea's daughter Theodora was with him. She must never be called Theo and she must never be called Dora, and these were just the first two rules on Theodora's ever-expanding list of things that were never to be done. She was a thin pale girl with lank hair and a disposition which stopped just short of being openly contemptuous of anyone who was guilty of having had the bad taste to live beyond their teenage years. Her attitude toward Michael was usually one of long-suffering martyrdom at having to waste her patience on someone who understood nothing of importance whom she only endured for the sake of her mother.

Theodora was thirteen and she attended the same school at which both Rhea and Michael worked. Rhea was the manager of the Pupil Support Guidance Team and had particular responsibility for the school's Special Educational Needs programme. But the three of them never travelled to school in the same car because Rhea's hours were at variance with Michael's and Theodora's, so the girl went to and from school in Michael's car. It bothered Michael that by using two cars to make the same journey each day they were doubling their carbon footprint but with Rhea having a managerial role there was no way around it. Besides, someone had to give Theodora a lift as Rhea wouldn't countenance the idea of her daughter walking the streets.

The supermarket was built above its car park. As Michael and Theodora travelled up the customer conveyer with their empty shopping trolley the automatic security message played over and over as each customer reached the top of the conveyer: "Please be prepared to push your trolley off the escalator". The same recorded message was repeated thousands of times a day, every day, just in case some half-witted shopper might otherwise injure themselves by bumping into their trolley. Today's mainstream culture had become very risk-averse.

Yet, contrarily, the sheer mental torture of being forced to hear the same moronically unnecessary statement being repeated endlessly must surely have put the supermarket staff at risk of suffering a psychotic breakdown. The interminable repetition of a phrase was a recognised technique of interrogation and torture amongst law enforcement agencies with a bad track record of human rights violations. Apparently, the supermarket owners were willing to send their employees stark mad rather than have a customer suffer the injury of a stubbed toe.

If a security message designed to avoid risk seemed more likely to put people at risk, of a mental seizure or perhaps a homicidal spree in the aisles of frozen fish, then the irony went unappreciated by anybody with the authority to switch the message off. But risk-averse cultures were always destined to do more harm than good because they continually lowered the bar for what risks were considered tolerable. The more overprotected and mollycoddled people were, the more protection and mollycoddling they felt they needed.

Feminism had initially demanded that women be protected from rape and domestic violence, but over a few decades it had steadily declined into the infantilism of demanding that women receive trigger warnings to protect them from unpleasant language and disturbing ideas, so that they could retreat to their "safe spaces" and cuddle their ideological teddy bears for reassurance. First wave feminism had demanded that women be treated as adults with the right to vote and to earn their own living, but by the third wave of feminism they had completely changed their minds and were demanding that women be treated like easily bruised children who had to be protected from the harsh realities of life. The new child-women had to be shielded from words and images that might cause them to experience the trauma of negative emotional responses. In their early days feminists had sung "I am woman hear me roar" but now they were hurrying to the safety of the nursery, not to take care of the infants but so that they themselves could be the infants. Feminism had proven that there was no limit to risk-aversion and its attendant privileges.

But such a criticism of contemporary culture would not have occurred to Michael. He would have strongly disapproved of any such deprecation expressed toward a "vulnerable" group. Michael thought that safe spaces were an excellent and progressive idea, although only for women. A safe space for men would be nothing more than an excuse for the misogynistic exclusion of women. Men had no reason to feel threatened and therefore they had no need of a safe space. There was almost nothing that Michael would have thought men needed. He was not in touch with his own feelings, although he was very much in touch with Rhea's and Theodora's.

He strolled down the aisles of groceries with Theodora the two of them said nothing to each other. She had her earphones plugged into her iPod and he knew better than to try to talk to her when she was listening to her downloads. Michael noticed that the background music pervading the supermarket was Bhangra, a mixture of Punjabi folk music and western pop music. He was surprised and delighted. Bhangra was a style of music which derived neither from the immigrants' home country nor from the immigrants' destination country but was created with a combination of elements from both. It was a purely immigrant music. It was, in Michael's view, a perfect representation of what multiculturalism was all about. Michael looked forward to the day when all popular music had this type of intrinsic diversity. Maybe then we would finally be rid of the cultural imperialism of American music. Bhangra was a kind of anti cultural imperialism. Not all American music was culturally imperialist, of course, because rap and hip-hop were the music of people of colour and therefore obviously couldn't be imperialistic, even if it had spread all over the planet. But he looked forward to the day when pop bands weren't just an endless series of white males.

Michael was secretly ashamed that he didn't enjoy rap music. It seemed to him a clear sign of his underlying racism. It was proof that the residue of the bigotry with which he had been born was still present inside him. He felt it like a cancer in his flesh. He knew that he would never be completely free of his engrained racism and misogyny. How could someone like himself, the recipient of so much white male privilege, ever truly understand what it meant to experience the abuse suffered by those who were oppressed?

His trolley slowly accumulated the items required for tonight's dinner party. Marinated shrimps, avocado, pasta, garlic bread, goats cheese and bottled vinaigrette for the salad. It was so splendid that ordinary supermarkets could now be relied upon to stock foodstuffs from the cuisines of the world. In Michael's childhood foreign imports had been far less readily available and often disparaged. Back then the advertising slogan had been "Buy British". How long ago that seemed. He selected some sauerkraut and dill cucumbers from the shelf. No more lumpen English cooking, thank god. He popped a jar of chilli sauce into his trolley. Michael smiled to himself as he imagined the horrified reaction there would be if his guests this evening found themselves sitting down to steak and kidney pudding. He'd never be able to show his face again.

Amid the gratifying sound of the Bhangra there arose a mournful wailing. It was the soundtrack of childhood. A four year old boy was red in the face with crying. His mother was bending down next to him, scolding and threatening her son. She grabbed him by the collar and shook him. The people around her looked rather shocked at the violence with which she manhandled him but no one felt moved to intervene. Everyone recognised that mothers have the toughest job in the world and that mothers know best how to manage their own children. The other shoppers wouldn't have felt comfortable remonstrating with a mother. It might have been different had the parent been a father, but in the circumstances nobody was prepared to interfere.

Michael hurried on to the patisserie counter with Theodora trailing along in his wake. He purchased a large chocolate gateau which would serve as a birthday cake, despite the unforgivable number of calories it contained. He moved on toward the shelves of wine. More calories. But they would need a lot of wine tonight for their guests. Michael promised himself that to make up for this sinful indulgence he would not have any wine with his dinner all next week to cut back on the calories in that way. Anyway, he thought to himself, with six or seven people at the party he probably wouldn't get to eat that much of the gateau.

This prompted the further thought that he didn't know if Gary would be joining them this evening. Gary had been withdrawn and silent after the misconduct assessment. Perhaps it would be better if he didn't attend the dinner party as Diana was going to be there and she was surely the last person that Gary would want to see at the moment.

A middle-aged man was working the checkout in the supermarket. He welcomed Michael in the manner that he welcomed every customer who passed through his checkout, as if they were a personal friend. He asked Michael if he needed any help with his packing. Michael said that he didn't. The man asked if Michael had a store card and Michael handed it over. The man said goodbye, in the same way that he said goodbye to every customer, as Michael placed his carrier bags into his trolley and walked away. The man on the checkout recited these same trite phrases in the same affable tone of voice a thousand times per shift, mindlessly mouthing the customer-friendly sycophancy which was a requirement of his job. It pleased Michael. It seemed to him that this was a sign of the feminisation of society; a new and greater concern for people's feelings. In the past a man of that sort would probably have found it humiliating to obsequiously enquire after the well-being of all his customers in this fashion. But the man on the checkout did not appear to experience it as a humiliation. He was accustomed to it now. It had become normal.

As they travelled slowly down the customer conveyer with their trolley Theodora abruptly awoke from her iPod isolation, having seen a friend of hers who was proceeding sedately upwards on the other conveyer. They communicated briefly in hand gestures, then Theodora pulled out her phone and started texting with incredible dexterity. Michael paid no heed; he was lost in thought. He felt haunted by the crying child in the supermarket. He scarcely noticed the automatic security message which issued the warning: "Please be prepared to push your trolley off the escalator". His mind was full of the image of that crying child. A small boy in tears, especially one who was being bullied by his mother, caused a sudden resurgence of Michael's fears for his son Kyle. Michael wasn't allowed to know how his ex-wife was raising his boy. Iris had told him that Kyle was no longer anything to do with him. But Michael remembered her domestic rages and he prayed that little Kyle wasn't being subjected to them now that Michael himself wasn't there to be the target for her anger.

Iris had kicked him out four years ago when Kyle was only six, and since then she had denied him any real access to his son even though she was in breach of a court order for limited access. But the court wasn't going to enforce that order because if they were to fine or imprison a single mother it would be said that they were also punishing the child. The interests of the child must come first, therefore they would never impose any penalty upon the mother regardless of how much she flouted the law by denying Michael the little bit of access that the law had said he should be permitted to have.

As a father excluded from his child by the custody court Michael felt keenly the slander of the term "absent father" whenever he heard it in the media. It was one of those phrases that was used incessantly and he could never hear it without a stab of pain. He was literally absent from his son's life but the phrase "absent father" made it sound as if this was his choice rather than something which had been done to him, and done against his dearest wish. It blamed him for his absence from Kyle's life as if it were his fault. It added insult to injury. Michael was tormented by his estrangement from his son, not least because of the impotence he felt at not being there to protect Kyle from the violent personality of his mother. But during the custody dispute, when he'd mentioned his fears about Iris' volatile temper as a danger to the child, the judge had refused to listen to his testimony and had very nearly accused Michael of malicious perjury. There was nothing in law that he could do about it.

Theodora had never met Kyle because Iris wouldn't allow it. She claimed that it was just a ruse for Michael to see more of his son. Nor was Rhea especially welcoming of the idea because she felt that Kyle was Iris' child and Rhea took the view that Michael should commit to Theodora. He sometimes wondered if Rhea was secretly pleased at his exclusion from Kyle's life because she wanted all of his parental affection to be the prerogative of the child in his new family. Neither woman seemed to waste any thought on what might be best for Kyle. But Michael couldn't help feeling that it was a pity that Theodora and Kyle would never get to know one another, he would have liked it a lot if they had. Yet even if it had been possible to get the two women to consent to the idea, he didn't suppose that Theodora would've been too thrilled by it. He doubted that she would have cooperated. Thirteen year old girls don't have much time for ten year old boys.

Rhea was equivocal about Michael's continuing financial responsibility for Kyle. On the one hand she strongly supported the legal requirement for a father to financially support the house he no longer lived in and the children he had no access to, because she firmly believed that men should not be allowed to escape their responsibilities and impose the entire burden of raising children upon women. But on the other hand, Rhea resented the fact that a significant proportion of Michael's salary was being redirected to another woman. Michael paid 12% of his income to Iris as child support plus an additional 5% as alimony. The latter was a particular annoyance to Rhea because Iris was a working schoolteacher like Michael himself. But he had incurred alimony payments because Iris had chosen to take three years away from her career when Kyle was born to bond with her child, during which time she had been supported entirely by Michael, thereby making Iris his financial dependent for a part of their marriage and in the judge's view entitling her to spousal support.

The loss of 17% of his income made a difference. Rhea was toying with the idea of having a second child whilst she was still in her thirties and time was running out. It made her angry to think that by financing his former wife and child, the loss to Michael's earning power might make the difference to Rhea being able to afford a second child. It was just another example of how the patriarchy sought to control women's reproductive rights. Not that Rhea had given up on the idea of a second child. But Michael would certainly have to buckle down if he was to make a life for his new family whilst still financially supporting his ex-wife and son.

They had discussed this issue many times but Michael found it very difficult to converse with Rhea about such things without his making the situation worse. He was inclined to explore possibilities and Rhea resented this, demanding to know why Michael was positing alternatives to decisions that she had already made. She attributed this to his controlling behaviour. Michael didn't want to appear controlling because that was a typically masculine form of domestic abuse. At the same time, when she asked him questions there seemed to be no right answer. Anything he said in response was invariably an expression of the engrained attitudes of his patriarchal conditioning. Rhea had a way of asking questions which implied that she was very interested in them, but she appeared not to listen to his answers as if she were not interested in them at all. This was entirely in keeping with her general conversation in which she paid far more attention to what she was saying than in anything which might be said to her. But if Michael failed to respond, this infuriated her. Michael lived on eggshells.

He was aware of this and yet he shielded his mind from it so that he was not consciously aware of it. The balance between what was known and what could be acknowledged as being known was delicate. Michael's only safety net was a carefully crafted ignorance of those facts which, but for his adroit doublethink, would have been forced upon his mind. He wanted to believe only the best about her, and so he was unable to admit to himself the profound selfishness which underlie her attitude.

But the reality was that Rhea's lack of humility was comprehensive. To her, everything was always about herself because everything was about her feelings. She judged everything on the basis of how she felt about it. How she felt about something was the *definition* of that something. If she felt that someone had been rude to her, then rudeness became that person's defining characteristic. If she felt that a house was ugly, then to deny its ugliness was an act of wilful contrariness. Rhea's feelings about a thing *were* that thing; they were its essential nature. This was why she became so angered by disagreement. Whenever Michael saw a situation differently to Rhea, it seemed to her that he was trying to *invalidate her feelings* about it. Whenever he disagreed, she experienced it as Michael telling her that her feelings were wrong. If he could do that, then it meant that he didn't love her or care about her. So, regardless of what the disagreement had initially been about, it rapidly descended into her making recriminations that he didn't love her. Consequently, Michael went to extreme lengths to avoid disagreements or, at least, to avoid being seen to disagree.

Michael and Theodora got back to his car in the supermarket car park, placed the two carrier bags of shopping in the boot, and drove off. The girl was still plugged into her iPod and had disappeared into her private world. Their home was only ten minutes away but out of habit Michael switched on the radio. He didn't like to drive in silence. The local radio station was broadcasting a drive-time news and phone-in discussion talk show. Michael was familiar with it. The callers were generally offensively right-wing but the show's presenter always put them in their place, which made it alright. Although Michael was disgusted by some of the callers' opinions he nonetheless found the programme educational as a window on the perverse minds of those who opposed progressivism and it could sometimes be quite amusing to listen to the presenter teach them the error of their ways. As he clicked the radio on a male voice was saying:

" . . . earlier caller tried to justify mass immigration by saying that 'they are over here because we were over there'. This old cliché really gets my goat. They say it so smugly, as if any country with an imperial past has forfeited the right to a country of their own; that mass immigration is a form of 'payback' for the country's crimes, a form of punishment for our imperialist past. But at the same time they claim that multiculturalism is a boon and a blessing to the country; that we're all much better off as a result of mass immigration. Well, if they really think that multiculturalism benefits European countries and that 'they are over here because we were over there', then this would mean that the former imperialist powers are being *rewarded* for imperialism, wouldn't it? So I think they should make up their minds whether they think that multiculturalism a 'payback' punishment for the crimes of European imperialism or whether they think that multiculturalism is a beneficial reward for European imperialism. It can't be both at the same time."

"Maybe it can," said the radio host insipidly. "Maybe we have to suffer some disadvantages to get other advantages. Maybe radical cultural changes to the identity of Europe are the only way we can get the foreign workers we need."

"Then what about the non-European imperialism of the past?" demanded the caller. "Turkey is an old imperialist power that conquered the Balkans, so should huge numbers of Rumanian and Bulgarian migrants go to live in Turkey? Is anyone going to say that Balkan migrants should be in Turkey because the Turks were in the Balkans? And would it be a reward or a punishment for the Turks, eh?"

Michael was so irked by the appalling racist arrogance of the caller that he wasn't paying proper attention to his driving and he came perilously close to a cyclist, almost touching the rear wheel. He reproached himself. Here was a cyclist doing their bit to help the environment and nearly getting injured by a carbon-fuel-burning car driver. Michael felt momentarily guilty before his ire returned.

Really! How incredibly presumptuous of that radio show caller to think that he could dictate immigration policy to the people of Turkey! What typical white European arrogance. And what nonsense to make a false comparison between the British empire and the Ottoman empire. The cultural enrichment experienced in places like Spain and the Balkans under the sophistication of Islamic conquest was completely different to the horrors experienced by the victims of the slavemongering British imperialists. The fools who phoned in to this radio show were so ill-educated.

The debate being broadcast had moved on to the next caller. It was a woman this time. To Michael's chagrin he heard her saying:

". . . is straightforward enough. The politically correct middle-class support endless immigration because it benefits them. They even employ foreign au pairs and child-minders and handymen and gardeners. They have domestic servants. But they don't give a stuff about the working class. We're the ones whose schools are overcrowded, whose healthcare system is bursting at the seams, and whose young people can't leave their parent's home because there isn't enough housing for them to find a home of their own. Yet it's the affluent middle-class with their domestic servants and their private pension plans who consider themselves to be left-wing, and when the working class complain about immigration it's those same 'champagne socialists' who claim that the workers are right-wing. It's all the wrong way round. They've got it all upside down and inside out and back to front."

The radio host cut in to say that there were lots of middle-class right-wing readers of newspapers like the Daily Mail who opposed immigration. The presenter of this show had an obsessive detestation of that particular newspaper and could always find a way to include a derisive reference to it regardless of what the topic of discussion happened to be. But Michael had mentally tuned out and was already responding to the caller's opinion inside his own head, thinking of how grossly unjust it was for the woman to claim that people like himself were not genuinely left-wing and only supported continued immigration for selfish middle-class reasons.

It was true that Rhea had once suggested to Michael that she felt they ought to employ a child-minder, but that had been at a time when she'd been taking on additional commitments in her role as the teaching liaison officer for the school governors. Michael had said that he was willing to handle being the primary child-carer but Rhea had been unhappy with the suggestion because she thought that a female would have more in common with Theodora and could occupy a "big sister" role. They could connect emotionally as sisters together, and perhaps Theodora would stop spending so much of her free time alone in her bedroom. Michael had felt crushed by this, as Rhea seemed to be implying that a female stranger could offer more to her daughter than he could. But he had kept the pain to himself. Theodora was Rhea's child and Michael didn't feel entitled to challenge her on the correct raising of her child.

In any case, it had transpired that they couldn't afford an au pair because it would have required converting the room that Rhea used as a home-office and study room into an additional bedroom, and Rhea didn't want to lose that valuable space. What it came down to in the end was that their current house simply wasn't big enough for what the radio show caller had so inappropriately described as a "domestic servant". How shockingly Victorian these racists were in their thinking and vocabulary. Anyway, it was clear that the caller didn't know what she was talking about because if Rhea and Michael, who were both professionals and had a double income, were too poor to employ a foreign child-minder, then it was obvious that their support for a policy of open door immigration had nothing to do with middle-class affluence.

His mind tuned back into the radio to find that he'd missed the end of the previous exchange of views and there was now another male voice arguing:

". . . should have let her speak. You cut her off too soon. She's only saying what we all know to be true, that immigration is cheap labour from abroad which enables employers to offer crap jobs for crap money. Mass immigration promotes the exploitation of foreign workers."

"If we bear in mind the argument of our earlier caller," interrupted the radio host chuckling at his own cleverness, "who wanted to know whether multiculturalism was 'payback' for European imperialism or a beneficial reward for European imperialism, I suppose you would conclude that it was a punishment for the working class and a reward for the middle-class."

"You could say that," replied the caller soberly, ignoring the amusement of the host, "it certainly looks that way to me. Listen, how many times have you heard some pseudo-leftie take the bosses position by telling us all that we should be grateful for mass immigration because immigrants will do the jobs that the English won't do? You've heard it a thousand times, right? And always from some university-educated idiot who thinks that he's left-wing. But they're making the classic bosses argument that if the local working class won't do a crap job for crap money, then the employers have the right to bring in scab labour to do the job. A genuinely left-wing position would be to demand that the employers improve the pay and conditions of the jobs so that English workers *will* do them. The English working class spent two centuries slowly fighting our way to the point where we no longer had to work in bad conditions for terrible money. *That's* why the English won't do those jobs, it's not because we're lazy and work-shy, it's because our grandfathers fought the battles so that we wouldn't have to do crap jobs for crap money. But the rich just brought millions of immigrant workers into the country to do them. Ask any illegal immigrant who's breaking his back for less than the minimum wage or a legal immigrant who's working double shifts at unsociable hours in a takeaway."

"But this all sounds, I'm sorry to say it, rather old-fashioned to me," objected the radio host. "I mean, all this talk about the workers and the bosses, that's so 1970s, isn't it?"

"Sadly, it is," agreed the caller despondently. "Since the political left abandoned class politics in the 1980s, when they turned their backs on the working class and became obsessed with gender and ethnicity, the distinction of left-wing and right-wing has become redundant. It's all the politics of identity now. Gender and ethnicity are not left-wing issues because they cross all economic classes. 'Left' and 'right' are terms within class politics and, like you say, nobody talks about that any more. Politics used to be divided between the working-class left and the ruling-class right, but now the divisions are between women and men, non-whites and whites, gays and straights, immigrants and non-immigrants, and all the rest of it."

"I wasn't actually suggesting that it was a bad thing to have cast off the old class attitudes," simpered the radio host, entertained by the caller's misconstrual of his comment. "I happen to think that the type of class divisions that brought about the strikes and industrial conflicts of the 1970s are something that we are better off without. We have issues that are of concern to everybody that we need to address, like climate change and globalisation."

"But globalisation is the same issue as immigration," protested the caller. "Look, the developed world has the industrialised economies and the Third World has the cheap labour. Globalisation outsources the jobs to where the cheap labour is located. Mass immigration imports the cheap labour to where the jobs are located. Either way the bosses win. Globalisation sends the work to where the cheapest workers can be found and mass immigration brings the cheapest workers to where the work is. So how can someone like yourself support mass immigration yet criticize globalisation? The two policies both serve the interests of big business. Why support one and oppose the other when they both have the same purpose?"

"I don't think they do," said the host, somewhat defensively. "Immigration benefits some of the poorest people in the world. It helps asylum-seekers find refuge from oppressive regimes and gives the people from Third World that you're talking about the chance of a better life. Surely they're working-class too?"

"Sorry," said the caller, taking his turn to be condescending, "but that just sounds like gratuitous white guilt to me. These days white people are taught that their ancestors stole all their country's wealth from the rest of the world, as if there'd never been an industrial revolution and millions of our workers in factories working their guts out to create all that wealth. So now the guilt-merchants want to give the wealth they think we stole back to the foreign countries by inviting the rest of the world to live here. Only rich people can afford to indulge that bogus sense of guilt. For them, mass immigration has never been about improving the economy or anything like that, their support for immigration has been motivated solely by their need to feel better about themselves."

As the radio host spluttered and choked, momentarily lost for words, Michael switched off the radio angrily. Right-wing filth. That wasn't his idea of infotainment. That was more like info-porn for English Nationalist wankers. Why hadn't the presenter come down harder on those far-right clowns? What a shocking farrago of ignorance and prejudice and self-serving delusion. How could a reputable radio station permit that kind of thing on their airwaves?

The host of the show should have used the mute button to shut them up. But they'd been allowed to rant on without restraint or correction. It wasn't a question of free-speech because they were engaged in hate-speech and the principle of freedom of speech didn't apply. It was perfectly legitimate to suppress hate-speech. And it couldn't be more obvious that everything being said by those people was hate-speech so there would be no problem about silencing them completely. What was wrong with that host? Did he want to promote violence against people of colour? Radio phone-in presenters were getting as bad in this country as they were in America.

     *   *   *

The dinner party to celebrate Michael's fortieth birthday was well under way. The large dining table had been set against the wall of the open-plan sitting room so that the four women and two men could pick at the food as they pleased. Wine was flowing and the cold collation buffet was a success. Everybody ate standing up and no one stopped talking the whole time. Chill-out classical music was playing on the CD and conversation was becoming increasingly unguarded. The current topic for discussion was what the party referred to as the "Islamophobic anti-Muslim backlash" following this year's multiple bombing of the London transport system.

"The BBC are so right-wing these days that the chair of Question Time actually asked the panel if they thought that terrorists born outside of the UK ought to be deported after they'd completed their prison sentence," clucked Luna censoriously. "They scarcely make any attempt to conceal their rampant desire to deport people at the first opportunity."

"Deportation is an act of racism," asserted Rhea. "It's a denial of basic human rights to refuse to allow a person to live in the country of their choice. For the chair of Question Time to suggest that migrants be deported on their release from prison is no different to these bigots who demand that migrants be deported simply because they're in the country illegally; it's a sure sign of racism."

"It's perfectly obvious that the man's a racist," said Diana. "He described Zeinah Ahmadi as a 'foreigner' merely because she's Syrian. Who but a racist would use a word like that? She's a Question Time panellist and he's making it sound as if she doesn't belong in this country just because she wasn't born here."

"Nobody is a foreigner," said Athena resolutely. "It's an out-of-date concept. This is a multicultural country and the racists have no choice but to accept that, even if they choke on it. Communities of all nations of the world now live in Britain, so the word 'foreigner' is no longer a meaningful word."

"Exactly," confirmed Diana. "Global citizenship embraces diversity and celebrates difference. The only reason anyone would use the word 'foreigner' these days is to express racist hatred. Calling someone a foreigner is a hate-crime."

The bottles of wine were emptying and Rhea was about to fetch another from the kitchen when Frank volunteered to fetch it for her.

She gave him an appreciative smile and he scuttled off. But when Rhea turned back to her friends the appreciation was replaced by scorn.

"At least there's one thing that a man is good for," she smirked.

"Why does Frank hover over people so much," asked Athena, "doesn't he realise that it makes a woman feel uncomfortable to have a man hovering like that?"

"I've told him about that so many times," said Frank's wife Luna, "but you know what men are, he never learns no matter how often you tell him."

"Just because he doesn't have a contribution to make to the discussion, that's no reason for him to loom in the background as if he were trying to pluck up the courage to raise his hand and ask to be excused to go to the toilet," cackled Diana.

"I know exactly what you mean," agreed Luna, embarrassed but willing to explain. "Actually, he does it because he has a great desire to contribute his opinions to the discussion."

"Well, why doesn't he then," enquired Rhea, "instead of hovering all the time?"

"Because nobody ever asks him for his opinions," replied Luna to a general tittering from her friends.

"God, men are so pathetic," sighed Diana. "Do they have to be invited to offer an opinion?"

"Who would be interested in their opinion?" smirked Athena.

The laughter which broke out at this sparkling witticism was sharper than knives. There was nothing unusual in these women speaking disparagingly about a man while he was out of the room. Nor was it unusual for them to do so in front of Michael, as if Michael were also not in the room. He was expected to accept it, condone it, agree with it.

Michael said nothing. As a general rule he didn't argue with women because they would only get angry with him and he'd feel guilty about having upset a woman. It would be even worse if Michael were to win an argument with a woman because then he would feel ashamed of having belittled her. He felt that winning an argument against a woman was cruel. A man ought to protect a woman, not defeat her. For a man to argue against a woman was nothing more than being a bully. So he didn't argue with them. He didn't defend Frank. Nor did anyone else.

The safety net of doublethink in Michael's mind kept him ignorant of why he felt and behaved as he did. This feeling, that a man shouldn't hurt a woman's delicate sensibilities by treating her as an adult who could be held accountable for her actions, was one of the things which had caused men to tolerate the intolerable for so long. If men had been permitted to acknowledge their equality with women, then men could have required a woman to cope emotionally with being shown that she was in the wrong on those occasions when this was the case. But, in practice, her female privilege got in the way. The belief that women were more vulnerable than men caused everyone to treat a woman as if she were too fragile for adulthood. The privilege of being assigned a special vulnerability gave her the protection appropriate to a child. Men couldn't get passed the evolutionary trait of wanting to protect women. There was a White Knight in the Y chromosome. It turned women into fairy princesses and meant that men felt obliged to continually give feminist women an unfair advantage over them.

Michael, however, was entirely unaware of this truth about himself, even though he was as badly afflicted by White Knight Syndrome as any man of his generation. Perhaps the day would eventually dawn when men would find that the innate impulse to protect women which they'd once possessed had been stomped to death under the jackboots of feminism, evolutionary psychology notwithstanding, but if this ever happened it would occur too late for Michael and for Frank.

Rhea, as a responsible hostess, brought the conversation back to serious matters. Laughing derisively at men was all well and good but whenever her social circle gathered together the talk focused mostly, and quite properly, on their agenda for the future.

"The Women in Education Conference was extremely productive," Rhea informed them. "Consensus was reached that the illegality of discrimination means that we must have legally enforceable quotas for gender, race and ethnicity. A proactive recognition by the education sector of special status for groups with protected characteristics must be the orthodoxy throughout the public sector; it must apply in education as it does in employment for enrichment through diversity."

"The issue of greatest urgency is inclusivity and equality for transgender persons," said Diana. "It is a monstrous injustice that gender is assigned at birth by the heteropatriarchy who think that they can decide what a person's gender is. They write 'male' or 'female' on a birth certificate as if heteropatriarchy had the right to assign gender identity without consent."

Michael said nothing but he was puzzled by this. The term "assigned" made it sound as if male and female were purely arbitrary descriptions or, as Diana insisted, a description socially imposed by the heteropatriarchy. But Michael couldn't quite understand how this could be. If the gender written on the birth certificate was a description of the biological sex of the child at birth, then surely it was just a report of the baby's anatomy. He was sure that his puzzlement was the result of his own failure to fully understand the heteropatriarchy, not a criticism of Diana's critique of gender assignment, and he would have liked to have asked a question so that Diana could explain it to him. He had so much still to learn. But he didn't feel comfortable about asking so foolish a question in this company. Rhea would give him one of her looks.

"But we must remember that non-inclusive gender assignment is a part of the larger issue of masculine paradigms," said Luna. "We must re-educate society to break free from the old rigid notions of logic, fact, truth, and objectivity. None of these things have any reality. Everything is a matter of perspective, subjectivity, and opinion. The patriarchy invented the idea of objective fact to lend a spurious authority to their own masculine perspectives."

Again Michael was troubled by this. The rejection of masculine notions of factual truth was a position that he had great difficulty in comprehending. For instance, when Luna asserted that there were no facts or truth, would that assertion itself be factually true? Or was it merely an alternative perspective which might be accepted or rejected?

He wondered privately if this meant that when a stick-thin emaciated anorexic looked into the mirror and saw herself as being too fat, that she therefore really was too fat because that was her perspective. If everything was a matter of subjective perspective, then how could it be objectively the case that patriarchal norms of sexual objectification had caused her to be dangerously undernourished and skinny? Rhea and her friends often criticised supermodels for being too thin, as if this were objectively true, but how could that be if objective fact was a fabrication devised by the patriarchy to justify their own masculine perspectives? Worse still, what would happen in rape cases when the woman's perspective was that she had been raped and the man's perspective was that she hadn't? Surely it must be necessary to be able to say that the woman's perspective was the objective truth about what had factually happened so that the man could be convicted?

Michael was just telling himself that his inability to understand no doubt stemmed from his masculine mind-set and his patriarchal upbringing, when the doorbell rang and Frank's voice called out from the kitchen: "I'll get it."

A few moments later Frank returned to the party with two open bottles of wine in his hands. But Frank was not alone. The ring on the doorbell had presaged the arrival of one further guest. Heads turned to see who it was, as they weren't expecting anyone else. Eyes widened as they saw the unwelcome figure of the spectre at the feast.

Gary ghosted into the room like a bad smell. A contagious air of resentment passed through the gathering. It was a breach of etiquette for someone who was in such bad odour to intrude upon people who were enjoying themselves. He should have had the decency to keep his stink to himself. There was a vague shudder of awkwardness from the assembled revellers. Except perhaps for Diana Bates who had the glint of battle in her eye. She had bested this right-wing prick in his misconduct assessment today and she would thrash him again now if he was here to cause trouble.

Gary had been drinking heavily for the last couple of hours but it hadn't had much effect. He was in that dangerous condition when a person drinks to assuage an emotional pain but no matter how much they drink they find that they can't get drunk. He had taken a lot of alcohol on board but his face was dead sober and he wasn't slurring his words at all. There was too much smouldering indignation inside him to quench it with alcohol.

Michael saw the danger at once but couldn't think what to do about it. His friend Gary was in need of sympathy and support after the events of the day. Everyone knew that Gary had certainly lost his job, although it would doubtless take several months for the authorities to go through the motions of formalising the verdict. The machinery of these things was always slow-grinding. But how could Michael offer consolation without offending his other guests?

He walked forward swiftly to intercept Gary before the new arrival reached the group of women standing next to the dining table. He gave the man as warm a welcome as he could manage in the strained circumstances and led him by the arm over to a couple of armchairs on the other side of the room. Michael dragged one of the chairs nearer to the other so that the two men could sit close together in huddled conference. In Gary's state of mental distraction he didn't notice Michael's rather furtive demeanour.

"Hello Gary," said Michael with a forced smile. "It's good of you to come."

"I should tell you, I've had a few," confessed Gary.

"So has everyone here," Michael reassured him, "it's a party."

"I've been brooding on what happened," said Gary.

It was obvious that they wouldn't be able to avoid the subject of Gary's impending dismissal from his job so Michael didn't try, his concern was to keep Gary away from the women. He didn't know if he wanted to protect them from Gary or if he wanted to protect Gary from them, but either way segregation was clearly the best and only policy.

"I should have told them exactly what I thought of them," complained Gary in self-reproach. "I was always afraid to speak freely because it would have cost me my career, but when they took my job away from me today I should have told them exactly what they are. I didn't have anything else to lose, did I?

"Maybe there's a chance that you'll keep your job," lied Michael. "They might accept an apology and a period of re-training in religious and cultural sensitivity. It's not hopeless."

"Don't sugar-coat it," said Gary, looking levelly at Michael with the cold glassy eyes of a dead fish. "Look at me. I'm an old hippy over fifty years of age who is about to be sacked from his job for the crime of Islamophobia. I'll be unemployable as a schoolteacher. Or as anything else. I've been publicly crucified by political correctness, or I soon will be. I'm a straight white male with a mind of my own. In this society I'm not just redundant as a worker, I'm redundant as a human being."

"There's still a place in this world for an old hippy," smiled Michael encouragingly. "Don't forget, you're the generation who stood up to the Colonel Blimps of the old establishment, you manned the student barricades and created the counter-culture in the first place." With a jarringly false jocularity Michael added: "There has to be a place for you, mate, you're a hero of the revolution!"

"I've been thinking a lot about the old days since they gave me the chop today," said Gary in a voice from the grave. "Look, they've accused me and condemned me for offences against Islam, right? Well, I can remember, back in the sixties and seventies, how we schoolteachers used to worry that the children of immigrants would have to cope with the confusion of having two ethnic identities. They would have to be English at school and Pakistani at home. We expected it to be a real problem. But we couldn't have been more wrong, the reality turned out to be the exact opposite of that.

The children of Pakistani immigrants experienced no identity crisis because they grew up Pakistani, not English, and they were strongly encouraged to do so by the message of multiculturalism that we were busily broadcasting. Those second generation kids have now had children of their own who are also Pakistani, growing up in Pakistani communities. Their grandchildren will be Pakistani, too."

"But what's wrong with that? That's great!" enthused Michael.

"What's wrong with it, my friend, is what happened to the kids that we didn't consider; the kids we should have been worried about but weren't," answered Gary. "It's the children of the English who have an identity crisis because they've been encouraged just as strongly to cast off their Englishness and embrace ethnic diversity. We're telling them to become global citizens. So, far from having the problem of two ethnic identities, they have the problem of not having any ethnic identity at all. We were so worried about those second generation Pakistani kids, but we couldn't have been more wrong."

This was monstrous, thought Michael. It really was Islamophobia. Maybe Diana had been right to get him removed from the classroom. It might not be safe for Gary to be around children with ideas like this in his head. On the other hand, he was badly depressed and that might account for what he was saying. Michael didn't want to give up on the poor misguided fool. He said:

"I still say that those of you who rocked the world in the sixties and seventies did great things. You made contemporary society possible."

"I didn't have anything to do with creating this," muttered Gary, gazing bitterly across the room at the circle of feminist-multiculturalists sipping wine and denouncing the heteropatriarchy. Michael's face registered incomprehension and Gary poured his heart out:

"When I was young we embraced personal freedom and alternative lifestyles and sexual permissiveness because we wanted to cast aside all the gratuitous shame and guilt that traditional society imposed upon people. But look at what they've done to that dream. Now I live in a society which is constantly telling me that it's compulsory for me to joyously welcome half a million immigrants every year, that I must uncritically accept all the foreign cultures of the world without question or limit because it is forbidden to disapprove of any of them, and that if I fail to be sufficiently joyous and welcoming it's because I'm a selfish inhumane racist. What the fuck happened to personal freedom?

Now I live in a society which is constantly telling me that if I find a woman erotic, then I'm guilty of sexual objectification and normalizing rape. Instead of free love in a society where people can get stoned and express their sexuality, I live in a society which says that if a woman is drunk when she decides to sleep with a guy then that guy is guilty of raping her. What the fuck happened to sexual permissiveness?

Like you, like every man, I'm expected to continually apologize for having been born male. I'm expected to continually apologize for having been born white. I'm expected to continually apologize for having been born heterosexual. They never tire of recounting my shame and telling me how I'm guilty of crimes I haven't committed because everything is my fault. In the sixties we wanted to create a society that was guilt-free and shame-free. But they've created a culture based upon the endless infliction of guilt and shame.

Throwing guilt and shame at people like me is the entire basis of their culture. The dream of the 1960s has been utterly betrayed."

Michael thought that Gary sounded like those right-wing bigots he'd heard on the radio phone-in show earlier but he tried to be charitable and put it all down to Gary's inebriation and the unexpected kick in the teeth he'd suffered. Thank god Gary had been speaking in a low resentful mutter, not loud enough for anyone on the other side of the room to overhear. Keeping his own voice low to prompt Gary to do the same, Michael said:

"That's not how it is. The sixties were only a first step. The progressive movement has developed and become much more sophisticated since then. We've moved on. Postmodern critical theory and standpoint theory have revolutionized contemporary understandings of gender oppression and post-colonial western imperialism. The progressive counter-culture has been put on a firm intellectual foundation. Of course, there's going to be a certain amount of collateral damage, but we're building a better future."

"The progressive counter-culture? Do you seriously think so?" Gary winced, and again he glanced over at the four implacable enemies of the demonic heteropatriarchy. Five if you counted Frank. But the popular opinion seemed to be that Frank didn't count, in this or in anything. "Their views have been dominant in the education establishment since I first became a schoolteacher in the seventies. In the intervening years their authoritarian intolerance toward dissenters has grown ever stronger and more entrenched. Knowledge-based education has been replaced by indoctrination to the correct beliefs, the correct values, the correct attitudes and the correct behaviour."

Michael was shaking his head, more in sorrow than in anger, to repudiate these atrocious and absurd misconceptions. He drew a breath, about to explain why the things that Gary was saying were nothing but egregious and delusional fallacies. He didn't get the chance. Gary had decades of pent-up despair to get off his chest and he wasn't going to be pacified with the usual platitudes. The defeated man slumped in the armchair went on:

"They don't just rule the education system. They exercise power throughout society. The entire political state and the cultural mainstream serve the beliefs of feminism and multiculturalism. They're not the counter-culture, they're the culture. They're not the progressives, they're the reactionaries of the establishment defending their own status quo. They *are* the powers-that-be. But their vanity doesn't allow them to acknowledge this obvious fact. They won't give up their romanticized self-image of being brave freedom-fighters struggling to champion the oppressed. That's why they have to keep finding ever-more trivial excuses to paint a picture of themselves as the oppressed. They *are* the system, but they have to believe that they're not. Vanity trumps reality."

"But that's nonsense. It can be refuted by the most basic evidence that's staring you in the face," said Michael in a tone of pity. "Even with a Labour government, parliament is full of white males legislating over women and people of colour."

Gary looked at his friend in the same way that he might have looked at a whipped dog. It was hard to believe that someone like Michael could have abdicated their own intelligence to such an extent that they were content to abjectly parrot this platitudinous bullshit in blind obedience to orthodoxy. Michael's submission to ideological conformity displayed a wretched impoverishment of his ability to think for himself. It was a tragedy. Gary could weep for his friend.

"That's not the politics of equality you're preaching, that's the politics of difference," said the pariah. "Don't you see, Michael, that you're accepting the idea that race and gender make people innately different, instead of their being equal in their common humanity? You're treating black people and white people as being so innately different from one another that no white politician can possibly represent black people. You're treating women and men as being so innately different from one another that no male can possibly represent females."

"But ethnic minorities must participate in their own representation, as must women . . ." began Michael, getting annoyed now.

"In politics equality is a matter of passing legislation that serves everyone equally," asserted Gary bluntly, impatiently cutting off Michael in mid-sentence. "It doesn't matter in the least whether the politicians are black or white, male or female, it only matters in whose interests they legislate. You could have a parliament made up entirely of black women or entirely of white men, if the parliament's legislation served everyone equally it wouldn't matter what sex or colour they were. Equality is only violated if, like you, the politicians believe that they have a duty to serve some groups within society more favourably than others.

For the last five decades there has been a tidal wave of legislation that is openly declared to be legislated in the interests of women. There has been nothing legislated in the interests of men. What politician would ever advocate a policy on the grounds that it will *benefit men?* They wouldn't dare. They wouldn't even think of it. Yet benefiting women is always considered a legitimate justification for any policy. The government even has a Department for Women but there's no department for men. No one cares about us, we're left to sink or swim on our own. The white male politicians aren't on the side of white males, that's just a feminist lie. We'd be the last people they'd try to help."

"That's white male paranoia," blurted out Michael, "pro-women legislation is simply a way of addressing the misogyny in a patriarchal system . . ." but his interruption was swept aside by Gary's momentum. Gary's moral outrage had been dismissed as the rantings of an Angry White Male before and this conventional contemptuous dismissal only added fuel to his fire.

"If every single politician in Westminster was male their political agenda would still be devoted to legislating in the interests of women," said Gary, his voice growing louder. "It's the same with ethnicity. Governments will openly legislate in the interests of ethnic minorities, but who could even imagine a government passing legislation that was intended to be in the interest of the ethnically English? It's unthinkable in this society. There's not the slightest attempt to create legislation that serves everyone equally. Yet you're sitting there telling me that what matters is the gender and skin colour of the politicians."

"You've had too much to drink and you're talking rubbish," Michael rebuked him sternly. "You know perfectly well that women and minorities suffer in all sorts of ways that privileged white males do not. You only have to look at the rape statistics to see that. You know that one in four women . . ."

"Falsehoods and irrelevances," interrupted Gary. Despite the alcohol inside him Gary's capacity to articulate his thoughts was unimpaired. All the alcohol had done was to embolden him. He was ready to say things he'd never said before. More than ready, he was eager.

"Even if you believe those fraudulent figures about rape they have nothing to do with sexism," he said. "You're making the usual crude mistake of thinking that *anything women suffer is therefore sexism*. No it isn't. If a man steals your wallet it's an expression of greed. If a man rapes you it's an expression of lust. If a man hits you in a rage it's an expression of that rage. An act is sexist only if it's socially imposed or socially endorsed and gender specific. That's why feminists try so hard to convince everyone that society endorses the rape of women because then they can claim that rape is sexist. But the obvious truth is that society has always totally condemned rape, sentencing convicted rapists to long prison sentences. In the past the law has even executed men for rape. Society has never approved of rape, so rape has never been sexist. It's simply a crime of violence committed by one individual against another."

"That is the most obscene rape apologist filth I have ever heard in my life!" exploded Diana. "A person could only believe that if he hates all women. We should have gotten rid of you years ago."

Diana had crept quietly over to where Gary and Michael were sitting but the two men had been too involved in their conversation to notice. Diana had overheard the last few remarks made by Gary. Her incensed repost brought the other three women hurrying over to her side to defend her against the man who clearly was attacking her with some form of inexcusable misogyny.

"It's appalling how so many men feel the need to fight a war on women," said Athena, who hadn't heard the offending remarks.

"Must you boys make trouble," said Rhea irritably, including Michael in her condemnation. Why had she allowed him to invite his disgusting friend? She been opposed to it, but then she had weakened and indulged him. Although she had naturally assumed that the issue would no longer arise after today's exposure of Gary as a closet racist. It was bad enough that Gary had turned up to the party at all after his disgrace. He ought, at least, to have the decency to accept being shunned and recognise that he fully deserved it. For him to not only show his face but to verbally assault a woman with his vile abuse was criminal.

"Let's not have this discussion now," said Michael, trying to defuse the situation, his eyes darting between Gary and Diana who were bristling at each other.

"This kind of behaviour is unacceptable. I think Gary should just apologise and leave before things get any worse," recommended Rhea.

"Perhaps that would be best," acquiesced Michael.

"Beware of a woman with a sacred cause, Michael," advised Gary. "She will crucify you on her cross."

"What does a Neanderthal like you know about causes," sneered Luna.

"I know what you're like because you're an ideologue," Gary sneered back, looking her up and down. "You're all carbon copies of each other. To know your ideology is to know you."

"Feminism is the radical notion that women are people," quoted Luna.

"No it isn't," Gary came back at her, "Feminism is the radical notion that men are *not* people. Feminism treats men as one amalgamated entity called the Patriarchy, it doesn't treat us as people."

This threw Luna for the moment. She covered her confusion by attacking. She accused:

"Why are you looking at my fucking tits instead of looking at my fucking face?!"

"Because your sagging tits are marginally more interesting than the noise coming out of your mouth," replied Gary, not bothering to deny the false accusation, as Luna squawked in outrage.

He said it deadpan but he didn't really mean it. There was nothing the least bit interesting about her sagging tits either. But as the argument was inevitably going to descend into false accusations and vulgar abuse he was in the mood to give as good as he got and dish it out as mercilessly as they dished it out to him.

"That is the grossest misogyny," hissed Diana vehemently. "You are a monument to the patriarchal oppression of women."

"How dare rich, pampered, privileged women like you play the victim?" barked Gary. "How much do your earn, Diana? How does your salary compare to the wages of the men who empty your garbage?"

It took Diana by surprise. She wasn't accustomed to having men take the offensive. In her experience men were always defending against the barbs she threw at them. Words were her weapon. They could usefully be hijacked, regardless of their true meaning, to serve her political agenda. Words like "rape apologist" and "violence against women" and "woman hater" were all ways to put the enemy on the defensive because they were forced to try to prove that they were not guilty of the things of which they'd been accused. The more the enemy was accused of bigotry, the more they had to defend against the accusations which left them with no time to make any attack of their own. The argument instantly became all about whether they were or were not a bigot. The enemy's own attacks were thereby sidelined. But Gary seemed ready to ignore her accusations and go on the offensive instead of being put in his place. Diana was unfamiliar with the shoe being on the other foot.

"There are lots of reasons why a fake victimhood appeals to you," Gary told her, rising to his feet so that he wouldn't have to look up at her. "Part of the appeal is that it provides moral ascendancy. A victimiser is clearly in the wrong. They have committed an immoral act. But you haven't because you're the victim. Therefore you are morally superior to the victimiser."

"You said it," countered Diana, who had taken a step back when Gary had stood up. "The moral superiority of women is undeniable."

"Part of the appeal," continued Gary, "is that victimhood provides absolution. If men are the victimisers, then they are to blame. They are the problem. It's their fault. You are the injured party. You are the victim and the victim is innocent. So everything is men's fault and nothing is your fault. You have been absolved of all accountability for your own actions. That's why you're always condemning what you call 'victim-blaming'. You refuse to permit women to be treated as adults who are responsible for themselves. You're a misogynist, Diana."

Diana flinched at the word as if he had struck her. Her hand twitched as if to slap him across the face but Gary tensed and Diana realised that if she hit him he might not let her get away with it. Michael realised this too and was rapidly being overcome by panic. Diana's friends were waiting to hear her put this despicable pig in his place, for the acid of her tongue was known and admired among her social circle, but Diana had delayed too long and Gary got in first.

"But the primary appeal of victimhood," he said, "is that it provides you with a spurious justification for getting your own way. Men won't stand up and answer back to your outrageous demands because you've made them feel so guilty about your victimhood. Feminist women say to men: you are the oppressor and you have injured me, so now you have to *give me what I want* to recompense me for your misbehaviour. You are a victimiser and I am your victim so you must do what I tell you to do because *you owe it to me*. It's crude emotional blackmail. It's the fundamental source of your power."

"Feminism is about gender equality, you cretin," spat Athena, "it says so in the dictionary if you bother to look it up."

"You treat women as people but you treat men as guilt-objects," responded Gary. "Don't you realise that guilt-objects can never have equality with people?"

"Men like you with tiny dicks are threatened by strong women who demand our rights," sneered Diana.

"Feminism is a licence to bitch," observed Gary. "If you want an audience for your incessant complaints, marry one."

This last comment was found so obscenely offensive that all four women were momentarily nonplussed. Not only did it insult them as feminists, it also insulted them as women and wives. In the pregnant pause that followed Gary said:

"The politics of difference has turned egalitarianism on its head. Once we believed that all people were basically alike, and that was why everyone should be treated alike. No one should be treated as some kind of superior. But now you believe that some groups of people must be given superiority over others as some kind of perpetual act of compensation for what you consider to be past wrongs."

"Consider to be?" snorted Diana. "So now you're going to deny the basic facts of life and pretend that women haven't been oppressed by men for the last five thousand years!"

"Men have kept women alive for the last five thousand years," Gary snapped back at her. "Without us you'd have starved."

There was a chorus of screeches at this, piercingly shrill in their inarticulate fury. Fists were shaken in their desire to avenge the insult but they didn't approach any closer because, like Diana, they feared he might hit them back. Michael stepped in with the intention of escorting Gary to the door, conscious only of the imperative need to get him out of there. But Gary wasn't willing to have Michael lay hands on him and he pushed his former friend away. Frank was standing rooted to the spot on the other side of the room with a bottle of wine in his hand and his mouth hanging wide open.

"It isn't only feminism that uses the politics of difference to turn egalitarianism on its head," said Gary who had gone way too far to put on the brakes now. "Multiculturalism does it too. It assigns different ethnic identities to people and treats each ethnic group differently on the basis of the primary characteristic assigned to each identity. To a multiculturalist Muslims are definitively 'religious', Indians are definitively 'industrious', black people are definitively 'economically deprived' and, of course, white people are definitively 'racist'. This ethnic and racial stereotyping is perpetrated by multiculturalists."

"Nobody assigns characteristics to ethnic minorities except racists like you," stormed Luna, finding her voice again. "Multiculturalists don't assign identities to minorities, you moron, we recognise ethnic difference."

Gary turned on her and laughed in her face: "So when the 'good' people like you acknowledge an ethnic characteristic you're 'recognising difference' but when the 'bad' people like me acknowledge an ethnic characteristic we're 'assigning racial identity', is that what you're saying? You're a joke; you don't mean to be, but you are. You're the political equivalent of Mr Bean."

"You simply don't understand what you're talking about," sniffed Athena. "Why won't you listen to us?"

"He's not capable of understanding, Athena," said Diana. "He's just a typical man."

"Typical man!? It's feminism that imposes all the social constructs of gender," said Gary, taking the battle to Diana. "You've spent half a century propagating negative constructs of masculinity. How do you describe us? You only ever speak of us as violent, sexually predatory, immature, selfish, aggressive, materialistic, domestically incompetent, and an endless recitation of other character deficiencies. Whenever you speak of a 'typical' man it's always something bad, never something good. Your generalisations about men are always negative, just as your generalisations about women are always positive. Have you ever once in your life made a *positive* generalisation about men? Have you ever said anything about men as a sex that is to our credit? Not once. To live as a man in this feminist society is a sustained indignity."

"Have you no shame?" asked Rhea in disbelief. "How can you bully a woman like this?"

"Are you appealing for feminine privilege?" enquired Gary sarcastically. "Why on earth should anyone feel ashamed of holding up a mirror to a feminist bigot and showing her the truth about herself? No one should feel guilty about opposing your sexism."

"You're the one who needs a mirror, you lout," Rhea came back at him, "so that you can see the monstrousness of your thuggish behaviour. I won't tolerate this in my home."

Rhea looked pointedly at Michael as if expecting him to come to the rescue of women who were under attack from a man so devoid of decency that he actually had the effrontery to defend himself when he was clearly in the wrong. But Michael seemed to be frozen in horror at the events unfolding before his eyes. Frank hadn't moved an inch from the other side of the room either.

"Phone the police, Rhea," suggested Athena. "If this animal won't leave your home, then the police will remove him. It's an offence for him to threaten us in this way and we have plenty of witnesses."

But Rhea didn't want the police in her house. The neighbours would all be twitching the curtains and she would become the subject of gossip. Rhea found the idea distasteful. Anyway, she shouldn't need police officers with Michael here. What was wrong with the man? Why didn't he deal with this? She was, she realised, saddled with a loser.

"No one has threatened you," said Gary.

"You threatened us with hate-speech," accused Luna.

"To you, the truth is hate-speech. You insist upon that because if the truth is hate-speech, then the truth must not be spoken."

"Why don't you just get out?" demanded Luna. "Can't you see that you're upsetting everyone?"

Gary wasn't falling for that old ploy. It was the traditional damsel in distress. It relied purely on an emotional appeal for sympathy. Women had been manipulating men with that tactic since time immemorial because men kept giving in to it. Emotional blackmail was just like criminal blackmail in that the more often you paid the price they demanded, the more often the blackmailer came back to demand more. A criminal blackmailer will bleed you financially until you don't have any money left. An emotional blackmailer will drain you dry until you can't feel anything anymore. There was even a phrase for it these days, they called it "compassion fatigue". Gary didn't hate women, it was just that he didn't hate men either. Unlike Michael and the others of his kind, Gary didn't hate himself. He knew who the real hatemongers were.

"What's wrong with upsetting you?" he asked Luna. "Why can't you take it? Are you delicate little shrinking violets? Are you the weaker sex? Are you too dainty to be told a few home-truths about yourselves? You're such hypocrites. The Victorians have a reputation for hypocrisy but you've outdone them by a mile. What was the Victorian's hypocrisy? They were very interested in sex but pretended that they weren't. Big deal. What's your hypocrisy? You say that you're totally against racism and that's why you believe that white people are born guilty. You declare that you're totally against sexism and that's why you believe that everything is men's fault. When it comes to hypocrisy the Victorians were just beginners compared to you."

"Don't you dare call us the weaker sex," snarled Diana. "Have you forgotten how I kicked your arse today? You stand here glowering at us in your drunken violence but you're finished. You're on the streets where you belong. Go sell the Big Issue, loser. You're the weaker sex."

"You've just disproved your own politics, you hypocrite," growled Gary. "Two minutes ago you were telling me how oppressed you are, and now you're telling me that you have more power than men."

"Women are oppressed, but we have empowered ourselves," proclaimed Diana. "Our generation of women has proved that we can change the world with our political consciousness. We're overturning the age-old injustices of the past and building a new society untainted by the long history of patriarchal society's archaic prejudices."

"We're putting an end to male domination," joined in Luna, "we're putting an end to white supremacism and casting out the catalogue of oppression perpetrated by straight white males like you."

"You have a very gullible moral conscience; it believes every lie you tell it," said Gary.

"Its easy enough to understand, it's hardly rocket science," lectured Diana as if to a congenital idiot. "We're against prejudice. Scum like you are motivated by prejudice. We oppose misogyny. You hate women. We fight against racism. You hate people of colour. We intend to end homophobia. You hate gays, lesbians, transgender, and every other orientation that doesn't fit your cis-gendered straight white male norms. We defend Muslims and other oppressed minorities. You are Islamophobic and hate ethnic minorities. That's why you've been thrown out of our working environment; to protect vulnerable Muslims. We are the fair, the intelligent, and the decent. You are the stupid and the bigoted. You are right-wing scum. What is there about any of this that you're having difficulty understanding?"

"And you claim that it's other people who are guilty of hate-speech," said Gary.

"You lying patriarchal misogynist pig!" stormed Athena, who had apparently not quite understood Gary's previous point of argument.

"Thanks for the confirmation," said Gary with a weary sigh. "Whenever someone shows you how wrong you are, your response is always to start talking about the degenerate personality of your opponent. You focus on their supposed character deficiencies because that shifts the discussion away from they're actually arguing. By fixating on what you claim is wrong with them personally, any argument they've made can be ignored and dismissed. You always attack the person, you never address the argument."

"Rape apologist!" scowled Diana.

"Your mind is closed and padlocked," said Gary. "A crowbar couldn't open your mind."

"Woman-hater!" snarled Rhea.

"You aren't even concerned to fix the real problems in society," he accused them. "For you, the one problem is opposition to your ideology; that's the only problem to be solved. That's why your solution to every political question is always the same: that people must conform to your ideology. For you, the only real issue is obedience. People must think what you tell them to think. If there was no disobedience, there would be no problem."

"That's just meaningless rubbish," dismissed Diana.

"You continually scapegoat the despised straight white male for all the ills of the earth," said Gary. He was tired. He was so very tired. "But it never occurs to you to wonder how the scapegoats feel. You can't afford to have any sympathy for the scapegoats because if you did you'd have to stop using them as a thing to be blamed."

"People who deny the truth of patriarchal privilege hate women," asserted Rhea.

But this unsubstantiated assertion apparently didn't mean much to Gary because he immediately replied in a voice which had begun to ache with fatigue:

"The reason you continually lie about men having all the privilege and women suffering all the oppression is so that you can claim a spurious justification for your belief that to achieve equality women and men must be treated unequally. You never treat women and men in the same way. You always favour women in everything. You always demand unequal treatment in the name of equality."

"Treating oppressed woman and privileged men equally would be inequality," shouted Athena.

"It's men who continually lie!" shouted Luna.

"You're the most sexist person I've ever met," seethed Rhea. "Get out of my house!"

"Feminism and multiculturalism own your mind," said Gary. "You can't change your mind because it doesn't belong to you. It belongs to feminism and multiculturalism."

"Your stupidity is not an excuse for your bigotry," said Rhea.

"The innocent are so sick of being falsely accused," he said. He felt worn out. The alcohol was catching up with him at last and the day had seemed to last for a thousand years. "For how long do you think men will continue to put up with it? Do you really think your double-standards can go on indefinitely? Why should men contribute to a society that insults them and slanders them so incessantly?"

"I told you to get out of my house," said Rhea, pushing him in the chest to propel him toward the door.

Gary withdrew under the pressure of Rhea's hand and as the others saw him retreating they moved in to start pushing also. In a moment Gary was shuffling backwards as the tiny mob chased him away.

"Feminism can say: I came, I saw, I conquered," muttered Gary as he was bundled out. "All I can a say is: I came, I saw, I commented."

Michael watched him go. Michael didn't understand.

Chapter 6

Utopia is Dystopia

Poontang bought Ritzy a drink. They were in a bar called the Hidey Hole in the centre of town. It was a non-cash saloon, a little too upmarket for Ritzy's taste, and Poontang was the only one of the two of them who had viable plastic. She waved her card in front of the barmaid's sensor to debit the requisite amount. This wasn't the kind of place that Ritzy felt quite comfortable in. His preference was for unlicensed cash-on-the-counter pubs like the Dog and Bone. But the young woman called Poontang had selected the Hidey Hole for their rendezvous, and since she was paying for the drinks Ritzy didn't mind.

A poster on the wall announced that the bar served food as well. The poster was headed with the words "The Best of British", which dated it because the British hadn't really existed since Scottish independence. But maybe that didn't matter in this case as from what Ritzy could see of the menu it favoured lasagne, kebabs, goulash, spaghetti bolognaise and other such staples of 'British' cuisine. He wondered what would happen if he asked for toad-in-the-hole. It might be worth it just for the look of befuddlement it would produce on the face of the barmaid. But that was the kind of joke which wasn't actually funny when you thought about it.

Poontang was the daughter of his friend Brendan, or rather his former friend because Ritzy hadn't seen Brendan in several years. They'd lost touch during The Rupture, like so many other people. Ritzy had only met the daughter a few times before, and on the last occasion the kid hadn't been more than fourteen years old. Her mother hadn't approved of Brendan's friends so Ritzy wasn't exactly a regular guest at their house. Back then the girl's name had been Sarah but clearly much had changed in the intervening years. She certainly wasn't a child any more.

One glance had told Ritzy that she was a member of a ghetto gang. Her sartorial tastes were the height of ghang eroticism for the female ghangster in a diversification neighbourhood. Her clothes served the utility of violence but were also a pointed reminder of her nubile desirability. In that sense they served the same function as the provocative pugnacity of her new name: Poontang. She was a sexually self-objectified hardcase. An eroticized female tough guy. She was squeezed into a heavily corseted bodice under a steel blue leather jacket with matching blue and white striped leggings which sheathed her ass and thighs in skintight cotton. Her biker boots laced up high at the front and were accessorised with a cluster of superfluous straps and studs. She had a crimson bandana tied around her forehead above which sprouted a thatch of short spiky blonde hair. With her slim body in its constrictive yet functional, teasingly mischievous attire she had the waiflike eroticism of the true gamine and her short hair completed the picture.

She was 120lbs of lean muscle. A cute bundle of femininity, sure enough, but Ritzy got the distinct impression that her tough guy persona was not just a pose. There were some girls who faked a ghangster image and who liked to play at talking tough but as soon as they got a stiff punch in the face they changed their minds. In Ritzy's judgement that wasn't the case with Poontang. She had a recent bruise on one of her dainty cheekbones which she hadn't bothered to try to disguise with cosmetics. Perhaps she couldn't afford luxury items like cosmetics or maybe she just didn't care. There was something in Poontang's manner which convinced Ritzy that she was the genuine article. She might be a gamine nymphet but she was also a tough little bitch. She had found a way to survive in the modern world standing on her own two feet. Ritzy warmed to her from the first. There was a reason to respect her.

Their drinks were served. They were leaning against the main bar performing the social niceties of recounting a few of the significant events which had occurred in their lives since the last time they had seen one another. Neither admitted it but each had sought information on the other prior to their meeting, however both had come up empty. The search engines online gave a nil result on their names because neither of them were on-the-grid. Their offlife left no footprint in their onlife. Their onlife was anonymous. So now Poontang told him about the Rudý and Ritzy told her about the Red Squirrels.

It turned out that they both lived in the northern quarter of the city, although in different districts with Islamic territory between them so it wasn't strange that they'd not run into each other by accident. On top of which they also had the culture gap of age-difference to divide them and the fact that Poontang lived with a bunch of ghangsters that Ritzy would have steered well clear of, like any sensible chap of forty. Mind you, had they crossed paths by chance they might not have recognised each another anyway. Ritzy was surprised that she remembered him at all, given that fourteen year old girls don't normally pay much heed to their father's friends. He had a fairly clear recollection of her as a child but it was difficult to associate that kid with the impressive nineteen year old woman standing alongside him.

As they chatted Poontang had been quietly making her own assessment of the man she was meeting, and it was a generally favourable one. His combat style trousers were blue-grey camo, colour coordinated with the bulky but sleeveless utility jacket he wore over a thick cotton tee-shirt. He was dressed all in grey with patches of blue from his hat to his ankles. She liked the hat a lot. Poontang was kinky for hats. He wasn't bad looking for a man of her father's generation. She didn't fancy him but she could appreciate the aesthetics of his taste in clothes and he was in pretty good physical shape for his age. Maybe that came from his being a mechanic and having a physically strenuous job. His eyes were as blue as her own and they gazed back steadily at her during the conversation. That was a good sign. Some men were intimidated by her overt sex appeal and their eyes would flit about nervously but this guy seemed to be able to look into her face up close without going limp at the knees or dissolving into a puddle of goo. Her first impression was that he was okay.

"Fabulous tile," said Poontang, complimenting Ritzy on his bowler hat.

"It's a statement," he explained. "We wanted something that would assert our ethnicity as Red Squirrels and we thought that nothing symbolized English ethnicity more than a bowler. Besides, we all think they're damn stylish."

"You're not wrong," smiled Poontang with just a hint of flirtatiousness. "I'd have liked to wear one myself but it would cover my feathers."

By "feathers" she meant her Rudý bandana. Ghang affiliation signs were always called feathers, though nobody seemed to know why. The origin of the term had been lost. But it wasn't a word that the Red Squirrels would have used to refer to their hats. They didn't think of themselves as a ghetto gang, more of a reciprocal self-defence union. Of course, there were plenty of folk who would've said that this description was equally applicable to a ghetto gang.

"The red bandana suits you," said Ritzy. There was nothing playful or suggestive in the way that he said it. "Everything you're wearing suits you." Again, it was just an acknowledgement of the obvious.

"Yeah? It's also a statement of allegiance," said Poontang truthfully.

Ritzy was waiting for her to get to the point. She hadn't invited him here to socialise, there was something she wanted from him. Maybe Poontang also thought that the conversation needed to be moved along because she shifted gear into talking business.

"I hope you don't mind my contacting you out of the blue like this," she said.

"You said it was about your dad," said Ritzy, "about getting him out of jail?"

"Non-payment of child support," nodded Poontang.

"Have you got a younger brother or sister?" asked Ritzy. "I thought you were Brendan's only child."

"I am," confirmed Poontang. "The unpaid child support dates back ten years. They put him in jail because he owes money to my mum from when I was a kid."

"It's child support for you?" quizzed Ritzy.

Poontang nodded again. "You know how bad things were during The Rupture when everyone was barely able to feed themselves. My dad had no money for child support so he racked up a substantial debt."

"And they've jailed him for the debt," said Ritzy.

"But while he's inside he can't earn any money," explained Poontang. "The longer they keep him in jail, the longer it'll be before he can pay."

"Lawyer's logic," summarized Ritzy.

"The thing is, I've just made a score with my Sparts and I thought I'd pay the child support for him," said Poontang, almost apologetically.

"You're going to pay the child support for your own childhood?" asked Ritzy, registering a certain amount of disbelief. He was somewhat taken aback in spite of his familiarity with the gross unfairness of the state machine.

"My generation has been paying for her generation all our lives," said Poontang glumly. Ritzy understood the "her" to be Poontang's mother. It implied a fraught relationship between mother and daughter.

"True enough," agreed Ritzy. "And not just in money."

"I want my dad out of jail," said Poontang matter-of-factly. "What could I buy with the money that's worth more than my father's freedom?"

"Good for you," said Ritzy, impressed. He was too. Genuinely impressed. "But will your mother take the money from her own daughter?"

"She would but the Metro won't. They say that as the money was intended to be paid for my living expenses, I'm the one person who can't be allowed to pay it. Well, that's not the way they said it, you know how they talk, but that's what they meant."

"You're lucky you got that much sense out of them," said Ritzy.

"I can't give my dad the money to give to my mum so I need a broker; a middle-man. You're his friend. Would you do it? Do you have an encrypted bank account?"

"Yeah I do, but I don't use it. I trade in cash," grimaced Ritzy defensively. This conversation had suddenly turned in a worrying direction.

"Doesn't matter if the account isn't normally used, so long as it's encrypted," said Poontang with a businesslike air. "I'll transfer the payment to you, you'll transfer it to him, and then he can transfer it to her. Is that okay?"

Ritzy was fairly sure that he didn't believe this rigmarole was necessary. His knowledge of the current banking system was rudimentary but it seemed to him that anyone's account could serve as an intermediary for the transfer of funds. She wouldn't need his cooperation in particular. She could have used the account of one of her friends. Ritzy was wondering about the danger of identity-theft or something like that. He had no money in his encrypted account but it was possible to run up debts using identity-theft and he was naturally wary. Ironically, the girl's sexual magnetism was working against her in this instance. Ritzy would have been more inclined to believe her if she hadn't been so young and attractive. When sexually appealing women wanted something from him, Ritzy always feared the worst.

"Can't one of your friends do that for you?" he queried.

"My friends have accounts that are unsanctioned. They have to, for the scores we make. If we transfer the money to my dad from an unauthorised account it could raise some questions that we don't want to answer. But if I transfer the funds to you, obviously you don't need to question the source, and if your account is authorised as valid then no one need question where my dad got the money from. If anyone were to ask why you were paying him the money, which they won't, then you can tell them that he's your friend, which is true. It'll look like you're simply doing a favour for a friend."

"I'm under review by the Civic Investigation," said Ritzy. "They'd certainly want to know where this money came from and they'd demand that I pay tax on it as income."

"Not a problem," said Poontang. "The transfer won't register for taxation if it's deposited and withdrawn inside an encryption. That's the point of having an encrypted account, isn't it, to prevent state interference."

She had all the answers right enough. Her blue eyes were shining with innocence and Ritzy had to remind himself that she was a ghangster and stole money for a living. Looking into that elfin countenance with it's delicate features and its alluring femininity, even a man of Ritzy's character could find it too easy to go along with her request.

"Do you trust me with your money?" he laughed.

"Hey, you wouldn't want to steal from me," she grinned. "My Sparts would skin you."

"Are they bad boys?"

"They're very bad boys," chuckled Poontang. "That's how we make our scores."

"It wouldn't arise," said Ritzy smiling. "I wouldn't steal from someone I respect. What you're doing for your dad, it does you honour as well as honouring him."

Poontang looked abashed at the compliment. She felt the truth of it and fluttered in a moment of maidenly modesty. The girlish embarrassment on her face and the steampunk aggression of her outfit were an odd combination. She might have been pleased with the surrealist effect if she could have seen herself at that moment. But she had other things on her mind and she was aware that he was reluctant to involve himself in anything which might open him up to a financial intrusion from the Civic Investigators. Poontang understood the reason for his lack of enthusiasm. She couldn't blame him for it. She didn't press the matter and deflected the conversation away from the topic of concern. She would return to her request after he'd had some time to ruminate on it.

"Can you tell me about my dad," she asked, "I mean, what he was like when you knew him? What was he like before he was in and out of jail all the time."

"Don't you remember him from your childhood?"

"Yeah, but it's hard to think of what he was like back then because I know him the way he is now. He's lost his spark, you know? He's kind of beaten down."

Ritzy could hear the undercurrent of pain in her voice. She figured that he would know more than she did about the man her father had once been. Poontang bought Ritzy another drink and he started telling her the story of the time that he and Brendan had gone to a music festival with a van full of cheap umbrellas and made an absolute fortune when it rained all week.

"We sold the brollies for five times what we'd paid for them," he said, chuckling at the memory.

"That's a nice easy score," she noted approvingly, "and pretty legitimate."

"It was your dad's idea," Ritzy said. "Brendan had a good head for a quick deal in those days. He was a chancer but he wasn't dishonest. He was what you might call 'creative' in his attitude to making money."

Poontang was fascinated. It was a side to her father that she knew nothing about. She wanted to hear more and Ritzy had some more stories to tell, but they were interrupted.

There was the sound of an enormous explosion up the street. Burglar alarms began ringing in the local shops, set off by the concussion of the blast. The ear-drum pounding volume of the sound of the detonation was followed by a half-minute of stunned hush, and then the screaming started in the distance. The customers in the Hidey Hole stirred anxiously. A woman asked if anyone was going to step outside to see what had happened. There wasn't any rush to volunteer. Everyone in the bar had lived through the violence of The Rupture and they had lost any appetite they might once have had to rubber-neck at the broken bodies that littered the road after an explosion. Their curiosity about violent death had long since been assuaged.

One man took the plunge and walked over to stand in the open doorway but he wasn't very informative. All he could tell the patrons of the Hidey Hole was that the street was full of billowing clouds of dust. But then they heard glass breaking nearby as a window was smashed, which was followed by another crash of glass even closer. The customers started to panic. They could feel the storm of human conflict approaching, hunting them down. There was a babble of distress as everyone asked everyone else what to do for the best. Where was safety?

The bar had a long frosted plate glass window facing the street. This suddenly shattered, the whole length of it, spraying glass fragments all over the customers seated beneath. Now the barely restrained panic broke loose and swept over the room like an electric charge had been shot through the assembly. Hysteria erupted. Customers run screaming for the door, barging into one another and scrambling madly to get out. Only a few, Poontang and Ritzy amongst them, remained where they were until the stampede was over. There was no advantage to acting without thinking, and it could sometimes have serious disadvantages. Neither Poontang nor Ritzy made a move until the herd had cleared the doorway. Then she looked at him and he looked at her, and they nodded. They stepped away from the counter and walked slowly out of the bar.

It was carnage outside. When Poontang and Ritzy had arrived twenty minutes earlier the centre of town had been a busy shopping gallery of metropolitan consumerism. When they left the Hidey Hole those same streets were obscured by smoke through which the shapes of citizens were running in confusion. People were coughing and choking as they staggered through the thick dust that filled the air. Missiles were being thrown. Bottles or bits of brick would fly out of the clouds of dust and smoke, leaving little time to get out of the way if they came too close. Small groups of people were making concerted attacks upon the local stores. But much more importantly, there were units of militia on the street. Some looked like they might be African-Caribbean and others were definitely Asian. This meant there was more than one sectarian community involved and that made it serious. Poontang and Ritzy had no idea what had set off the riot but it was hardly relevant what the catalyst had been. This was a survival situation.

"It hasn't just started," shouted Ritzy over the noise all around them. "The militias are out already."

"Must be a spill-over from another part of the city," Poontang yelled back.

"Might have come from any direction," said Ritzy.

"You armed?" asked Poontang as a thunder of falling masonry hit the ground from the building which had been damaged by the explosion. There were more screams and the wail of a baby crying. A patter of unknown footsteps went passed them in the dissipating dust-cloud.

Ritzy reached down to a long thigh pocket on his combats and took out an eight inch metal rod. It was an extendable baton. He flicked it out hard and the steel sections telescoped into a slender but handy twenty-inch blackjack. Poontang put a hand to her lower back under her jacket and drew a thick stubby-bladed knife from a sheath attached to the corsetry of her bodice.

"We both live in the northern quarter," shouted Poontang. "Let's travel together."

Ritzy could tell that she wasn't asking him to protect her, which was a relief. She might have been offering to protect him. That was okay with Ritzy. Despite her size, he guessed that she would probably be a more capable fighter than he was because of her youth and because Poontang was, after all, a ghangster. She might want to keep him alive because she hadn't yet got what she wanted from him to help save her dad. Be that as it may, it made sense for them to go north together. They could watch each other's backs.

"Deal," agreed Ritzy. "We could head for Tyndale Square and then take Wellesley Avenue. That's a free road."

"Yep," confirmed Poontang and they set off at a steady trot.

There was no way to know where in the city the fighting would be at its worst because the vids wouldn't have been uploaded to the channels yet. Local people would be filming now and would upload soon. Poontang and Ritzy both had their touch-pads with them, of course, and they'd probably be able to access some online information in fifteen minutes or so but in the meantime they'd have to trust to luck. With the militias on the prowl luck might be in short supply.

As they ran they passed through a few streets that were almost deserted and others that were thronged with disoriented citizens. Some people cohered into groups, others were alone amid the crowd. Every so often a rampaging mob would charge by, causing Poontang and Ritzy to take shelter in a doorway or behind a car until they'd passed. It wasn't too smart to hide behind a car because vehicles were potential targets for mobs but if there was nothing else you had to make do with what shelter was available.

It was impossible to know what had roused the mobs, and it didn't really matter anyway. They were all taking revenge for something or other. Everyone had their grievances. They were not all young. These days rioting was multi-generational. Some justification would have been given to the ethnic militias when they had been called out because, unlike the ghetto gangs, the militias were semi-legitimate armed forces. They had the formal recognition of community leaders and sometimes they even had the unofficial support of the Metro government so there was generally some kind of justification offered for their deployment, however spurious. But many of the folk in the street were just random individuals who wouldn't know or care about the reasons for the riot, they were simply taking advantage of the opportunity for looting.

It had been this way during The Rupture. For years prior to the economic collapse the underclass had been bought-off by government welfare provision. It had been a kind of protection racket. For as long as the underclass were fed and housed and supplied with mobile phones and playstations, they had more or less kept the peace. With the occasional notable exception, they had refrained from too much rioting. But they had to be paid their protection money in the form of welfare benefits if the authorities wanted them to exercise this self-restraint. If the affluent privileged class wanted a relatively peaceful and stable society in which to enjoy the pleasures of their wealth, then they had to pay for it. Governments had financed this arrangement for quite a long time, until their credit-rating expired.

When the global economic collapse had forced central government to withdraw much of the welfare provision and the Metros hadn't been able to take up the slack, the expectations of the underclass were no longer being met. In most Metros food rationing had been introduced as an interim measure following the initial financial crash. This was a breach of the conditions of the protection racket and the underclass had considered themselves justified in rioting on a scale not previously seen in living memory. If the social elites were no longer going to make the necessary pay-offs, then their society was going to be burned to the ground. This had been the beginning of what subsequently came to be known as The Rupture.

The food riots caused by the lack of foreign imports had been the worst. Central government had been living on borrowed money for years but their credit culture had burst at the seams when the national debt had passed three trillion pounds. Other countries, all of them grossly debt-laden themselves, had no longer been willing to extend credit to the UK. There was no more money to borrow. The country's service-based economy lacked the farming and food industry necessary to feed itself so, without imports, food had become painfully short. The devolution of power to the Metros had actually made things worse because these political states were too small and economically limited to be able to acquire access to international loans. Borrowing money to pay for foreign imports was beyond their capacity. Ordinary people who had never known famine in their lives were introduced to the new reality of the West. Hungry bellies had found an expression of their discontents in clenched fists.

Incoherent ethnic diversity had descended into a maelstrom of street violence. It wasn't like the riots of the previous century. There had been plenty of those, the St Pauls Bristol riot in 1980, the Brixton and Toxteth riots in 1981, the Handsworth Birmingham and Broadwater Farm London riots in 1985, and various other conflagrations in cities up and down the country. But they had all been brief explosions of rage which had spent their force within a few days, and they had been two-sided confrontations between one particular community and the state uniforms of law enforcement. 21st century riots were entirely different. Mostly they were conflicts between two or more communities, the blacks against the browns, the Euros against the Asians, the Muslims against the kufr. Multiethnic alliances were sometimes formed where cultures had common ground, but for the most part it was everybody against everybody else. The role of the police consisted mainly in trying to physically separate the communities and keep them apart. Naturally, both sides in the conflict would treat the police as the enemy. Nobody likes the referee. The police had no friends in these street battles.

It was internecine civil conflict although the political elites, entrenched in denial and clinging absurdly to their ideological convictions, continued to pretend that all this multi-sectarian violence was not a consequence of multiculturalism but merely the result of *opposition to* multiculturalism. For as long as they could they persevered with their policy of always-blame-the-white-man, in spite of the fact that the Eastern European immigrant communities were almost entirely white. But even the elites could not persist in their state of denial indefinitely. When an Islamic fascist lynch mob in London publicly hanged three gay men in the street, the crumbling elites were forced to admit that they could no longer hide their failure by blaming everything on what was left of the English population. It finally had to be acknowledged that the problem was intrinsic to multiculturalism itself.

By then it was far too late, of course. The PWKB had taught everyone the strategy of victimology. Every community declared itself the victim of every other community. Nothing was ever their own fault, everything was always the fault of the enemy. The multitude of identity-groups were all accusing one another of being in the wrong. Their own rioting was fully justified; anybody else's was mere criminality. It was cultural chaos. The long-familiar tactic employed by The Correct of throwing shame and guilt at anyone who disagreed with them was now a ploy that was used by all and sundry. The lesson had been learned and every group of rioters chanted accusations of bigotry to silence their opponents with indictments of religious intolerance and racism and misogyny and misandry and homophobia and xenophobia and Islamophobia and anti-Semitism and Nazi fascism and Islamic fascism and anything else that seemed useful at the time.

There seemed to be no way out of the cycle of violence. When a copycat Jihadi lynch mob in the East Midlands Metro hanged a lesbian couple alongside a gay couple, both of whom had been easily identifiable because they'd been married in civil partnerships, the police's attempt to investigate the murders had been hopelessly hampered by their awareness that any arrests would have produced more rioting by the Jihadis. So despite the video footage filmed by members of the lynch mob themselves which was posted on the channels, the police failed to find the perpetrators. This duly produced one of last anti-homophobia riots.

Gays and lesbians had for several years been retreating back into the closet as a result of colonialist violence against LGBT organisations, including the firebombing of activist offices. But after the lynchings began they were forced underground for fear of their lives. Central government declared that they were going to hold a summit conference of community leaders from all ethnic colonies including the largest of the Muslim communities, and the two Metros in the Midlands declared their support for the conference. But everyone understood that if the politicians were talking and making a big show of how they were engaged in dialogue, then nothing practical was going to be done about the murders. This gave various imams the confidence to speak out and denounce the proposed conference as an Islamophobic witch-hunt. They claimed that the people hanged had been duly punished in strict accordance with Sharia law and for the politicians to attempt to punish anyone for this was an insult to true religion.

Yet that was only one cultural divide among a multitude. People had tried to clarify their ethnic and religious allegiances to identify who they were and whose side they were on in any inter-communal clashes. It was easier for some than for others. Sikh men always wore the turban, not only to profess their faith but also to distinguish themselves from their fellow Asians who were Muslim and Hindu. But many Somalis were both a part of residential African-Caribbean communities and a part of the ummah which included the Asian Muslim communities. The Somalis were conflicted, trapped between ethnicity and religion. They had tried to resolve the issue by treating the Pakistani Muslims as apostates but that hadn't worked because the majority of both Somali and Pakistani Muslims were Sunni. So the Somalis remained caught between their fellow Muslims and their fellow Africans. Russian and Ukrainian immigrants were at daggers drawn because they had inherited an ethnic conflict from their compatriots in the Crimea, yet alliances were often made between East European communities including Poles, Latvians, and Estonians which welcomed both Russians and Ukrainians, although seldom both at the same time. The situation was a mess. The sheer complexity of diversification exacerbated the internecine antagonisms.

In the few years which had passed since those dark days when the world had gone to hell some kind of social equilibrium had been reconstituted, albeit with its divisions entrenched, but society had remained precariously balanced on the brink of a second rupture. Whenever a further outbreak of rioting erupted everybody wondered if they had been tipped over the brink again. It was hard to tell when your only perspective was from ground level surrounded by smoke.

Ritzy and Poontang made it to Tyndale Square. They'd kept on the move because you were more likely to be noticed if you made yourself a target by standing still. They'd maintained a steady pace so they weren't too out of breath. Ritzy's lean body was keeping up with Poontang's youthful vigour despite his being twice her age. The multicultural dystopia was no place to be fat and out of shape. Neither was it a place to be out of touch with the news. They needed to find some reports on what was happening elsewhere in the city to get the bigger picture.

"Need to channel," shouted Poontang as they ran.

Ritzy pointed toward the recess of a disused door to the Tyndale library and they swerved into it. The building was Victorian, constructed in huge grey stonework, and the recess was deep enough to provide shelter from random projectiles. They should be able to evade detection by the militias here if they didn't loiter too long.

He kept an eye on a mob in the middle of the Square who were repeatedly chanting a phrase in a language he didn't understand while Poontang's nimble fingers brushed over the screen of her touch-pad, searching for online news updates. Someone living in an African-Caribbean district had posted a video of protesters in the street prior to the riot. It had been filmed from an upstairs window but there was no sound or voiceover, just raw footage. A channel called Sage2013 had video of battles taking place in an Asian district between African-Caribbean rioters and the local Pakistani militia. It looked bloody. Then she found a channel called Watchover on which a well-spoken man with an educated Jamaican accent was providing a slightly panicked commentary on the cause of the riot. It turned out, if what the guy on Watchover was saying could be believed, that there was a border war underway. The violence taking place where Ritzy and Poontang were located was, as they had suspected, nothing but a spill-over from a much larger riot taking place elsewhere. She held out the touch-pad so that Ritzy could see the disordered images flashing across the screen as the anonymous voiceover said:

"Rumours have been surging through the African-Caribbean districts about a Pakistani rape-gang who have been targeting young black girls from the neighbouring African-Caribbean community. I can't tell you whether these rumours are true or false, although I am told that numerous girls have testified to this. It has produced a strong response from the residents in the neighbourhoods which border Pakistani territories. The local community has organised the militia to take hostilities into the Asian area and many of our citizens have joined them to seek justice for these raped girls. I've been told that a dozen or so Muslim men have been killed but that the Islamic Militia have now been called out and they are attempting to drive the insurgents from their territory. Stay with us on Watchover for more . . ."

"S'gonna be a nasty one," remarked Poontang.

"Not our business," replied Ritzy.

One significant feature of the images they'd seen on the screen was the absence of police uniforms. Ritzy and Poontang hadn't noticed any police presence whilst they'd been running through town either. The Metro police service was apparently having trouble getting its officers mobilized. Not that it made any difference to Ritzy and Poontang. As ever, they had to take care of themselves. She continued accessing the channels and found one from the Polish district where things were comparatively quiet at the moment. She worked out the geography in her head.

"The concentration of violence is south of Nightingale Terrace and east of the Pankhurst estates," Poontang observed.

"Then we can take Wellesley Avenue, it's still open," concluded Ritzy.

"Hey listen to this," said Poontang, proffering the touch-pad again.

There was a talking head on the screen. A grey-haired woman in her sixties or seventies. She was issuing a call for calm and tolerance. It was her response to the riot but it was hardly a news update since she would doubtless have given exactly the same response to every other riot of the last decade. She was saying:

". . . to bring our communities together. If we can learn to embrace diversity and celebrate our respective cultures then we will be stronger together. When people form inclusive societies they get to know one another on a personal level and we soon learn that the differences between us are trivial compared to the common humanity we all share. Let us come together in our diversity. We all want a fair chance to make a home, to earn a living wage, to raise our children in peace and safety. The failure of capitalism, caused by the insatiable greed of the financial system, has brought misfortune upon us but we can take advantage of this opportunity to smash capitalism forever and create an inclusive eco-nurturant community of communities . . ."

"What planet is this woman from," asked Poontang, staring incredulously at the touch-pad.

"Stupid fucking idealist," said Ritzy. "They're incapable of learning. Politics should be consequentialist. Forget theory, forget ideology, you should just consider what the consequences of a particular policy will be, what the consequences of another particular policy will be, and then choose whatever has the best consequences from the available alternatives. Why can't people like her understand that?"

Poontang scratched her blonde head behind her ear. The teenager shook her head in disbelief and began to snigger softly to herself as the grey-haired woman went on:

". . . I don't regret the changes to western society that we've made during my lifetime. I don't regret smashing the patriarchy and consigning the militaristic nationalism of the bad old days to the dustbin of history. I'm proud of what we achieved. Ours is a society built upon humanitarian principles, egalitarian feminist compassion, and a belief in multiethnic global citizenship. We have our problems, I know, but our society can still be saved. Maybe it isn't everything that we hoped for, but at least we showed we cared."

"Well bully for her," said Ritzy sarcastically, "isn't her halo nice and shiny. But people have to live with the consequences of her folly."

Poontang looked up from the screen with incomprehension on her face. She had no idea of how this elderly woman could have so little understanding of the world. More than that; so little understanding of herself. The old woman seemed to be entirely lacking in self-knowledge. The ghangster was looking enquiringly at Ritzy and he got the impression that Poontang was expecting some kind of an explanation from him, but this wasn't the time or place for a history lesson.

"Multiculti," said Ritzy shrugging, as if that single word was a complete explanation. "They've betrayed our ethnic heritages, yours and mine, and they've disinherited their own posterity. They disinherited *you*. Some of them still can't admit what they've done. Even now, when the consequences of that betrayal are writ large all around us, they have to go on pretending."

Poontang pulled a face and her expression did not speak well of her disinheritor. The girl made no other reply as there didn't seem to be anything else to say. Ritzy's attention was drawn back to the mob in Tyndale Square. They had unfurled a flag. It was the black banner with the green crescent moon and star of the UK Jihad. Poontang saw it too and drew a sharp breath. The UKJ had a fearsome reputation. They were not a militia to mess with. They took no prisoners. This was nowhere for a couple of white kufr to be.

Ritzy looked from the Jihadis, with their headscarves masking the lower half of their faces, to the credulous countenance of the elderly woman on the touch-pad screen. He muttered: "They are the enemy but she is to blame."

"Can't hang around here any longer," said Poontang, jabbing an icon with her finger which closed the screen window.

Poontang slid the touch-pad into a pocket of her steel-blue leather jacket and took a glance down the street to the Wellesley Avenue exit from the Square. She had dismissed the elderly woman from her mind. Poontang was a child of the revolution and she understood that revolution far better than its feminist-multiculti architects ever had. She had to cope with the world they had created. She didn't weep for what had been lost. She was young and she had her life to live.

"Okay, go," she said.

They launched themselves into a sprint, keeping close to the stonework of the library and hoping like hell that the Jihadis didn't notice them. Poontang was dressed very sexily in her ass-hugging leggings and she could expect no mercy if they caught her. Her knife flashed in her fist as she sprinted flat out and Ritzy's extendable baton swished like a whip as he dashed along behind her, trying to keep up. Not looking behind them, they gambled everything on speed and they reached the corner without incident.

But they didn't stop, they ran on, leaving Tyndale Square and taking the free road Wellesley Avenue. A "free road" was one that was claimed by no community in particular and so it was available to all. Most roads were recognised as being owned by a specific community and some had disputed ownership, but there were a few that were recognised as being free. Wellesley Avenue was mostly shops, some of which were still trading, although they'd all been locked up when the riot had started. Ritzy and Poontang were just feeling a bit safer, and slowing down to a trot again, when Poontang suddenly dodged left into a shop doorway. She'd been in front of Ritzy and as she disappeared to the left he saw what she had seen up ahead.

A ghang of Wannabes, white boys in hair-extension dreadlocks and sporting fake Jamaican accents, had emerged from a side street and were swaggering down the avenue. There were at least twenty of them. With a riot in progress they were in search of entertainment and they were already starting to run forward, having seen easy prey down the street. Twenty against two was fun. Poontang and Ritzy were in trouble. They couldn't retreat back down the avenue to Tyndale Square without running slap bang into the fascists of the UK Jihad. But the new threat in front of them was coming on fast, whooping and hollering as they charged.

Wannabes were notorious for their malice because of their outsider status. Having flushed their heritage down the toilet they were still not accepted by their chosen community. Once upon a time they had been, but the years of conflict during The Rupture had narrowed and tightened people's ethnic allegiances and this had worked out badly for the dreadlocked white boys. They were generally shunned by the majority of the African-Caribbean community because they couldn't fake a skin pigmentation, although some of them tried with suntan in a bottle. In the same way that some hard-line feminists rejected transgender women on the grounds that they could never transcend the maleness of their birth, many in the African-Caribbean community insisted that no white boy could ever transcend the colour of his skin. This had detached the Wannabes from any and all ethnic communities. They were on their own and it tended to make them spiteful.

Ritzy ducked into the shop entrance after Poontang. The door was made of strengthened glass but she was wearing heavy biker's boots. Why the shop's manager hadn't fitted a steel shutter over the door was anybody's guess, but it was a stroke of luck that might save their lives. She kicked solidly against the door. The thick reinforced glass held. Ritzy kicked alongside her. Their boots thumped against the panel but the fucking thing was tough. No wonder they didn't bother with a shutter. The whooping and hollering was getting louder. They kicked and kicked. What kind of fucking glass was this? The thunder of feet was rattling the pavement just a few yards away. Poontang and Ritzy lashed out with their boots with the fury of desperation. The glass door shattered. The burglar alarm began shrieking.

There was a fringe of sharp fragments around the edge of the door but there was no time to worry about it. Poontang ducked inside in a second, her flexible body slipping though the gap, and Ritzy was on her heels, brushing against the edging of splinters but without cutting himself. As Poontang rushed to the back of the shop she swore. "Shit!" The front door might have lacked a steel shutter but the rear door was security fastened and utterly impassable. Nor were there any windows to the rear. The room was a sealed box.

They had imprisoned themselves in as neat a little trap as the Wannabes could have wished for, and the enemy was at the gates. They turned. It was fight or die.

Ritzy took guard to the side of the front door where he was hidden from the street because, thank god, there was a shutter on the window. Poontang stood in the centre of the shop, facing the open doorway, her knife hand extended. She would be the conspicuous target.

The first Wannabe to step through into the shop was giggling hysterically, being high on a mixture of adrenalin and ganja. He was ginger haired and, astonishingly, had copper-coloured dreadlocks. His eyes fixed on Poontang and lit up. The sexy little blonde was the only thing he saw. As he moved toward her Ritzy's baton came out of nowhere, chopping across to smash into Ginger's throat and crush his windpipe. Ginger fell forward choking.

The Wannabe behind him saw Ginger go down and he lunged at Ritzy, the butterfly knife in his right hand aiming for the face. Ritzy caught the man's forearm, swung his baton, but had his own wrist caught by his adversary's left hand. They began heaving and wrestling. The new arrival was fifteen years younger than Ritzy and he expected to be able to overpower the older man, but to his surprise he found they were evenly matched in strength.

As the two men wrestled, a third Wannabe bustled in through the door. He shuffled fast toward the girl saying something about "skank pussy". Poontang spun on her heel and thrust out a donkey kick, the heaviest blow in her repertoire of martial arts. Her leg shot out backwards and her heel caught him low in the gut, sinking deep into the internal organs. The force of the kick was amplified by his own forward momentum and it knocked all the breath out of his lungs. He slumped to his knees, his mouth open but unable to scream.

The stalemate of the wrestling match lasted only a few seconds. Ritzy wasn't a trained fighter but he knew how to win. Hit them with anything and everything you've got. He kicked hard into his opponent's shins to distract him with pain and then attempted a head butt which was only partially effective but as the man braced his legs to apply more pressure Ritzy took a chance and thrust up a knee. He caught the Wannabe in the balls and the man weakened. Ritzy tore his weapon hand free and whacked his assailant in the side of the head. Momentarily stunned, the man was defenceless as Ritzy hit him again and again in the head, clubbing him to the floor.

The shop had turned out not to be a trap but rather a defensible position. The attackers could only enter one at a time and this nullified the advantage of their numbers, although only if Poontang and Ritzy could deal with each opponent swiftly. They had to dispense with each adversary quickly enough to be able to meet the next attacker as he came through the door.

A bearded man, tall and pale with coal black dreadlocks, burst in bellowing like a bull. He wielded a saw-tooth machete that had a unusually sharp point for such weapon. Poontang was standing directly in front of him and he went for her. His long arms had several inches extra reach on Poontang and his machete was five times the length of her short stabbing knife. When he thrust with the weapon she twisted aside but could do no better than to evade the attack, not being within reach for a counter strike. She knew that she had real problems. Had he tried slashing with the blade she might have been able to avoid it and get in under his guard. But if he thrust with the point, how was she going to get within striking range?

Another Wannabe wearing knuckledusters on both his fists stood in the doorway and Ritzy stepped round the man he'd clubbed to the floor to meet this next assailant. But strangely the man did not enter. Or perhaps it was not so strange. Looking into the shop he did not see his prey helpless and weeping in terror as he'd expected. He did not see the man in the bowler hat bleeding his life out on the ground and the curvaceous young women screaming as the clothes were ripped from her body and she was raped by the first in line at a gangbangers party. Instead he saw three of his own Rasta brethren beaten senseless. The supposedly helpless prey were both on their feet and ready to fight. He paused and the man behind him in the doorway also took in the scene.

The thought shot into Ritzy's mind that a little more disincentive might change their minds about the wisdom of this enterprise, and the delay in their attack gave him the chance. He swung his baton in a wide circle to lash the tall bearded Wannabe across the back of the head. The man was confronting Poontang and so he didn't see it coming. The monstrous impact knocked the machete from his hand and broke Ritzy's baton. It was a tribute to the fellow's brute strength that he did not go down at once. His skull must have been made of concrete.

But Poontang seized the moment to rush in and stab him twice fast in the solar plexus. He punched her full in the face, the blow snapping her head back, but she took it and knifed him again. Ritzy snatched up the butterfly knife from the man he'd clubbed unconscious and used it to stab the tall Wannabe between the shoulder blades. As the man's knees buckled, Poontang's blade dug deep into his cheek and then into his eye. He fell back sprawling. The long body hit the floor heavily, bleeding from half a dozen wounds.

It was enough for his brave comrades at the door. Leaving their fallen behind them, they turned and ran. As the two fled from the doorway, the remainder of the ghang followed them without really knowing what they were running away from. But they were herd animals and if some took flight the others went with them.

There was an air of stunned shock in the small shop. It was cramped with the litter of bodies. Yet there was no doubt about the outcome of this little war. The tall bearded man was dead on his back. The clubbed man was still unconscious but the one who had suffered a kick in the guts was recovering. He was on his hands and knees sucking breath into his lungs. In a very deliberate fashion Poontang positioned herself at his side and drove a front kick into his temple. It felled him like an ox in an abattoir. Ritzy gave the clubbed man a kick in the head, too, just to make sure.

The victors assessed the damage to themselves. It was slight. The only harm done was to Poontang's nose which was streaming blood from the punch she'd taken but, amazingly, when Ritzy examined it her nose didn't seem to be broken. He told her so.

"Born lucky," said Poontang.

"I need to sit down," said Ritzy. He went behind the shop counter looking for something to sit on and found a couple of wooden folding chairs in the corner. He carried them to where Poontang was standing but she was looking at the shelves above the counter with wide eyes.

"It's a fucking grocery store, there's alcohol on the shelves," she whispered.

Ritzy hadn't even noticed. "What was that you said about being born lucky?" he quipped.

Neither wanted to return to the street just yet and the free alcohol decided them. They opened a bottle of scotch each and drank from the neck of the bottles, sitting on the wooden chairs in the middle of the shop. They didn't say much. Conversation was unnecessary. In the aftermath of a life-threatening experience it was enough merely to be alive and drinking and wondering how many bottles each of them could carry away with them when they left. The only jarring note was the deafening bloody burglar alarm which was still ringing like a mad thing.

"You handle yourself alright," said Poontang.

"So do you," replied Ritzy.

They sat comfortably, sipping steadily. Then Ritzy remembered something and made a decision. He made it without a qualm. He pulled out his touch-pad and pressed the icon to take him into the folders that he normally never used. Amongst them was a login for his empty and encrypted bank account. He looked at Poontang with a lop-sided grin on his face.

"If you've got your dad's encryptions," said Ritzy, "we can transfer your money now and you'll see the money trail reach him on my screen."

"Thanks, man," smiled Poontang, "you're a Spart."

Chapter 07

"E Pluribus Unum"

The Red Squirrels were clumping loudly down the stairs of their building on their way out. Chippy and Ritzy were carrying a recycled barrel between them. It contained Barker's home-brewed beer, a strong nut brown ale which with his usual cryptic subtlety he had named "Barker's Brew". It was a sideline of his, from which he made a little money, but his ale was mostly for personal consumption. He produced as much beer as the availability of ingredients would allow. Yeast and malt weren't that difficult to find but sugar was sometimes a problem. Occasionally he had to improvise but the results were generally very drinkable. He did a nice line in cider, too, called "Barker's Scrumpy". Apples were a fruit that it was still possible to get your hands on because they didn't have to be imported.

"This bloody barrel weighs a ton," said Chippy.

His protest wasn't meant seriously. Chippy was in a good mood today because he was taking a rare day off work and that always cheered him up. But it was his character to gratuitously find fault in trifles when he was feeling happy. He couldn't have explained why. Fortunately, the others all knew him quite well enough not to take offence.

"Rubbish," said Barker. "I've put straps on it to make it easier to carry. How can a fellow who lugs great big sacks of potatoes about, like you, make a fuss about a few pints of ale."

"Seventy-two pints," said Ritzy, shifting his grip on the strap.

"And the barrel's metal, not wood," said Chippy.

"Strictly speaking, it's not a barrel," said Barker, "it's a 'firkin' which is only a quarter of a barrel. What's a mere 9 gallons? Now if you were lugging a full-size barrel you'd really be feeling it."

"I wouldn't be feeling it," replied Ritzy, "I'd be rolling it."

In truth, the barrel wasn't as heavy as Chippy and Ritzy were making it sound. Gravy and Captain would take their turn in carrying it too, but Barker had excused himself this labour. He was adamant that as he'd brewed it and they'd all be drinking it, then the least the others could do was to carry it. This, it had to be admitted, was more than fair and so the other four men had agreed without much complaint. The brewer, however, did have a complaint.

"We're going to be late," moaned Barker.

"It's taken this long to get Gravy out of bed," said Chippy.

"I'm tired in the mornings," explained Gravy.

"It's afternoon," said Captain.

"I'm tired in the afternoons," explained Gravy.

"I'm seeing a pattern developing here," said Ritzy.

"It's just the way it is," said Gravy. "I get out of bed and it takes me so long to wake up that by the time I'm feeling properly awake I'm already starting to get tired again."

They were carrying the barrel of beer because they were going round to the "E Pluribus Unum" guys for a chinwag. The recent upsurge in civil violence had prompted them to suggest forming an alliance between the two households of men for their reciprocal protection. There wouldn't be very much in the way of details to actually discuss because the alliance would be more of a psychological boost than anything else. The "E Pluribus Unum" lived a quarter of a mile away. Neither group was likely to be able to rush to the assistance of the other if they were attacked by the militias or burned out by rioters. But each group could offer the other a place of temporary refuge if they became homeless. The last thing anyone wanted was to be vagrant when the petrol bombs were flying. If you had to bed down in a shop doorway, some bastard would probably set fire to you in your sleep. So having a bit of floor space on which to crash would come in very handy in those circumstances.

Anyway, if the main point was to establish friendlier relations and develop more of a sense of camaraderie between the two groups, then the smart thing to do was for each man to knock back several pints of Barker's home-brew and talk their heads off till dawn. The "E

Pluribus Unum" would provide the food and the venue, and the Red Squirrels would provide the beer. They had intended to also bring with them the four bottles of scotch that Ritzy had liberated from the grocery store when he was caught in the riot with Poontang, but unaccountably the scotch had all been drunk in the few days since then, so all they had was Barker's Brew.

As they descended the stairs to the next landing, the DiD stepped out from her front door. She didn't seem to have a reason for being there. Had she heard them clumping down the stairs? She tossed her brunette curls as her face registered surprise at their appearance en masse, but the five men attributed this to dissembling on her part. The coquettishness in her smile of welcome rattled a few of their hearts but they kept this shameful secret to themselves.

"Where are you off to all together?" she enquired in a neighbourly manner.

"We're just off to see some friends," replied Barker, who happened to be at the front of the party.

"It's good to have friends these days," said Abigail. "I was watching the riots a few days ago on the channels and it makes me fear for my child. There's so much violence about."

"You're right, Abbi," said Barker, "we've all got to watch out for ourselves these days."

That wasn't quite what Abbi had meant and Barker knew it perfectly well. Like his fellow Red Squirrels he had perfected the art of avoiding the implication of what any DiD said to him whilst appearing to agree with everything she was saying.

"It's such a worry, all this social upheaval," said Abbi. "A woman on her own with a child needs all the protection she can get."

This was such a pointed remark that all Barker could do was to change the subject. He said the first thing that came into his head.

"I met Terry from the ground floor the other day and he was telling me that his youngest will be starting school soon. It'll mean that Cheryl will be able to go back to work again now that both their kids are out at school all day."

"Yes," said Abbi indifferently. "Cheryl was telling me the same thing."

Abbi glanced at the barrel and it seemed to Barker, who was always on the defensive when talking to the DiD, as if she were wondering if it might contain something that could be useful to her.

"What've you got there?" she asked.

"My home-brew," replied Barker. "It's for those friends I mentioned."

"And some of us are carrying the weight," muttered Chippy meaningfully from the rear of the group.

"We'd best get on," said Barker. It was in reply to Chippy's urging but he said it to Abigail.

"Well, have a good time with your friends," said Abbi, and she went back inside her apartment.

They trudged down the next flight of stairs in silence but when they reached the ground floor there was only going to be one topic of conversation. It was Ritzy who spoke first.

"That was very deftly handled, Barker," he flattered.

"Long practice," said Barker dully.

"She's such a princess," commented Captain.

"Whore," muttered Chippy.

"No, no, let's be fair" disagreed Captain, "a princess is very far from being a whore. They're worse. Princesses sexually objectify themselves and they sleep with the men who protect and provide for them, but the power relation is completely different to that of a whore with her client. Whores offer a service for which they're paid in a buyer's market. Princesses, on the other hand, are objects of sexual worship. They have all the power in the relationship and they are very high maintenance."

"S'right," concurred Ritzy. "A whore does what *you* want. A princess convinces you to do what *she* wants."

"Their skill is in making you believe that by doing what *they* want you're really doing what *you* want," said Captain. "The most accomplished of them can convince you to like it."

"Traditional society used to say that men do like it," said Ritzy, "that we're psychologically conditioned by our evolutionary nature to like it."

"They still feed that lie to men and expect to see it swallowed," said Chippy.

"It's all part of the traditional way that men were made to serve women in the name of manhood," agreed Captain. "But there must be no more worshipping at the Altar of Cunt."

"Mind you," said Gravy, "she looked damn good in that off-the-shoulder cashmere sweater and those close-fitting yoga pants."

Bemoaning and jeering at Gravy's fetish for camel-toe, they exited the building. Gravy defended himself staunchly but the taunts and teasing continued half way down the street.

As they walked through town the signs of the recent upheaval were everywhere to be seen. Any riot was likely to spark copycat riots elsewhere and the major battle which had taken place between the Pakistanis and the African-Caribbeans had prompted some action nearer to home as well. But as there were five of them the Red Squirrels were fairly confident that they'd have no trouble. There was strength in numbers. It would have been different if they'd lived a mile in any direction but there weren't any organised militias in this district.

"Ah bugger," sighed Captain, "they've burned the old church."

He was looking across the road at a red brick Victorian building with an ornate stone doorway featuring two finely carved angels. It was St Mary's Catholic Church, originally built in 1843 although renovated several times since. The red of the brickwork was heavily blackened with smoke damage and the roof had fallen in, exposing the withered timbers burnt to cinders. Captain wasn't a Catholic but he had loved that old church simply because it had stood there for so long.

"Churches are always a target for Jihadi raids," remarked Barker. "If they can't convert them to mosques, they treat them the same way they treat pagan temples. Poor old Stonehenge, how many times has that been vandalised in the past few years?"

"But it's not so easy to burn down Stonehenge," Captain remarked wryly.

They strolled along discussing the safest route to take, although mostly out of habit because the territory they passed through wasn't badly disputed, until they reached a nondescript block in an area of diversification. The "E Pluribus Unum" shared two apartments on the top floor of a four storey firetrap. Gravy and Captain were carrying the barrel as the five men clumped heavily up the stairs. They had to use the internal fire escape staircase because, as in many residential buildings, the elevator wasn't working. They were too expensive to repair when they broke. The staircase was full of discarded furniture and the fire-doors had been removed for some reason.

"Here's a landlord with no insurance," joked Gravy.

"Must be owned by the same franchise that owns our building," said Chippy.

"Finding a landlord with insurance," opined Ritzy, "is about as probable as meeting an Asian girl with a tattoo or a white girl without one."

Their progress up the stairs grew slower with altitude. Conversation ceased as they climbed. When they arrived at the fourth floor they were grateful that there wasn't a fifth. They were breathing a little heavily from the exertion as they gathered outside one of the apartments and Chippy knocked loudly on the door.

The door opened and they were greeted by the smiling countenance of Nahas, who was one of those people who always seemed to be in a good mood. People liked him because they felt cheered up with him around. His broad symmetrical facial features were animated by his character and prompted a similar response in others.

"Good to see you, Spart," said Chippy.

His three housemates were standing behind Nahas like some sort of welcoming committee. The lofty name of "E Pluribus Unum" meant "out of many, one". It was, they claimed, intended ironically. It needed to be since the only options were irony or pomposity, and the latter is seldom congenial. But whatever trace of wit the name might contain, it was not wholly ironic because these four men were all from very different ethnic backgrounds. Their example certainly proved, as could not be denied in the face of the evidence, that people from different cultures could indeed live together in peace. The intended irony was their implied condemnation of the misconceived multiculti version of "E Pluribus Unum", the "community of communities". That concept was merely an ideological aspiration which had no basis in fact. Belief in it was an act of faith, not observation.

These four men lived together but they were not *living separately together* like multiple cultures, they were living indivisibly together as one unified group. They managed this by the simple expedient of not making a big deal out of their respective ethnicities. Nahas was a Namibian of the Owambo, Mikelis was Latvian, Derec was Welsh, and John was a mixed-race Canadian. But these distinctions of identity counted for little compared to their recognition of the overriding importance of their manhood as a unifying factor, due to the way that society treated men.

In the same way that the squatter commune on Dixon Street ignored ethnicity because they viewed themselves solely in terms of their economic class, these four men were united by their common male identity. It held them together as a group, and they argued that their example made clear why the multiculti "community of communities" was so bogus. A unifying factor was the very thing that multiculturalism had cast away when it abandoned a national identity common to all its citizens. It was the reason that countries were now so riven with discord. In contrast, the Namibian and the Latvian and the Welshman and the Canadian could live together in peace because they lived together as men in a society which had long been hostile to them as men. They had the social glue which was so lacking in the civic incohesion of the world outside their windows.

The "E Pluribus Unum" guys were an example of the latest movement to arise out of MGTOW. It was called BOBs, as an acronym for Band of Brothers, and its credo was to insist that the individual freedom enjoyed by MGTOWS meant that their crucial communal identity was as men who rejected the oppression of misandrist feminism. Each MGTOW was, by definition, an autonomous individual going his own way. All other facets of their characters were secondary to their identification as men. It was the M that preceded the GTOW which defined them. The BOBs did not surrender one iota of their individualism, they simply recognised that as men they were a Band of Brothers standing together in mutual self-defence against the establishment. The household of the "E Pluribus Unum" held precisely to this idea.

It was an attitude with which the Red Squirrels were strongly in sympathy. Although they shared a determination to preserve their English ethnicity, they also acknowledged common ground in their rejection of the guilt-ridden status that society had assigned to them as men. Not only had Englishness been under attack since before they were born, so too had masculinity. The Red Squirrels had seized the freedom to decide their own identities for themselves and they believed that it was for men to define their own concept of manhood. No feminist of the establishment elite was permitted to tell them who or what a man should be. It was a decision for men themselves and no one else. These were men who had set aside any concern for *what women want men to be*, or its cousin in disguise, *women deciding what is good for men*. They insisted that it must be left to each man to decide for himself.

The "E Pluribus Unum" spread their living space across two apartments, neither of which was big enough to house four bedrooms. Nahas and John occupied one apartment while Derec and Mikelis occupied the other, directly opposite across the narrow hallway. It had been the only way that they could get a bedroom each which, as with the Red Squirrels, was considered an absolute necessity. Bathrooms could at a pinch be shared but a man's sleeping pit must be his own. All four men were in and out of both apartments all the time and the sole drawback with this split-by-a-hallway arrangement was that they had two kitchens, which led to people's groceries being in the wrong kitchen and occasional grumbles about who had eaten whose pasta, along with further grumbles about who had left washing up in whose sink. On the other hand, it did have the advantage that their two apartments were the only ones on the fourth floor so that they had the whole fourth floor to themselves.

Today's gathering was taking place in the apartment of Nahas and John but as they didn't have enough chairs for everybody Derec and

Mikelis had brought additional seating from next door. It meant that the small flat was very cluttered; all the more so once nine men had crowded into it.

The five guests shook hands with their four hosts and there was a babble of salutations as they found places to sit. The barrel of beer was set down on the carpet at their feet in the expectation that they wouldn't want to keep getting up every time they needed a refill and it had better be close at hand. Barker did the honours of breaching his cask of ale. Glasses were filled and passed around. Nahas declined a glass because he didn't drink alcohol but he was the Master of Ceremonies for marijuana.

Nahas explained politely to Barker that he meant no disrespect to his talents as a brewer, it was simply that Nahas was a Lutheran Christian and never drank alcoholic beverages. With equal politeness Barker refrained from asking why God frowned upon alcohol but apparently had no problem with the consumption of marijuana. It wasn't mere diplomacy, Barker liked a smoke as much as anyone and didn't wish to cause offence to the man who was handing out the weed. The "E Pluribus Unum" had done the Red Squirrels proud by laying in a plentiful store of grass for this meeting of minds. There was also a pile of assorted munchies on the table by way of food for those who got the nibbles, but no one was hungry just yet. That would come later.

"Herb?" invited Nahas, offering a lumpy cigarette to Barker.

"That's most kind," said Barker, taking the joint and lighting up.

Joints were circulated and no one refused. Their pleasure in smoking was greatly enhanced by being told that the marijuana was strictly black market in this household. Nahas earned his living from growing the leaf and he was fastidious in only smoking his own. When central government had legalized grass for the sake of its tax revenues, it had been propagandized as a victory for individual freedom. Since most of the younger generation were smoking marijuana anyway, the guardians of democracy had decided that they had better take a cut for the Chancellor of the Exchequer. With so few people smoking tobacco in any quantity and with car drivers having to be parsimonious in their use of petrol, two of the government's major sources of tax revenue had been seriously curtailed and had to be replaced.

But the policy had backfired politically because it was portrayed on the channels as an attack upon the young. Non-smokers had been happy to exploit the addiction of tobacco smokers but they didn't care to exploit any other junkies, and especially not the impoverished youth. The young were seen as having been sold down the river by the previous generation's self-indulgent profligacy, so there was a certain amount of sensitivity about exploiting them still further by taxing their habits. None of the men in the room were under thirty and a couple of them were over forty but, their actual age notwithstanding, they saw themselves as belonging to the betrayed generation and they smoked their duty-free non-revenue marijuana with an air of self-righteousness.

Chippy sat looking at the foaming head of his glass of crystal clear brown beer in silent admiration for a moment and then downed the whole pint in a series of large gulps. Except for Nahas, everyone took a draught of Barker's Brew and they all declared it to be a very fine drop of ale. In fact, by the time he had finished pouring the first round of drinks, it was necessary for him to immediately set about pouring the second round of drinks. Barker enjoyed their several compliments almost as much as he enjoyed the beer itself.

In the warm good fellowship of ale and a comfortable fog of aromatic smoke, the two households agreed their alliance of mutual support should the shit hit the fan again. A glance into the street was sufficient to see that the fan was already pretty well splattered with shit, so there was no reason to resist such an alliance. It was a very simple matter to settle the few details. With that taken care of, the conversation was soon roaming over the wide prairie of their other common interests. This natural comradeship, far more than any formal agreement, was the true and binding process of forging an alliance. In the building of friendship was the construction of loyalty. Without loyalty an alliance was nothing.

They had a laugh over the Red Squirrels recent encounter with their downstairs neighbour, the DiD. If she had no other value to them she was, at least, a very effective way to bring to the two groups of men together in a mutual recognition of the way of the world.

"She was telling us that the riots a few days ago made her fear for herself and her child," explained Captain.

"She said it was good to have friends in dangerous times," added Chippy. "Friends?!"

"In other words, you guys get to be her friends and have the honour of protecting her if the violence comes in her direction," said John in his smooth-as-syrup Canadian accent.

"And what do you guys get from her in this friendship?" asked Mikelis sceptically.

"We get her cute little smile," answered Captain.

"And the pride of being a White Knight," said Barker, coughing on his joint.

"The pride of being a slave," Chippy interpreted dolefully.

"So we made our excuses and moved right along," said Captain.

"Thanks to Barker's skilful handling of the situation," Ritzy reminded them, for which he got a glance of pantomime false modesty from Barker.

It was a story that couldn't fail to find approval with its audience. All of them had experience of the women of their generation and all were single men. Mikelis had been married briefly in his twenties and Derec had lived with a girlfriend for several years, but none of them had fathered children. They had all learned the same lesson. From the cradle they had been taught that to share a domestic space with a woman was to live under her rules and her matronising tutelage *as a guest in your own home*. Consequently, their view of cohabitation with women was akin to Dante's vision of hell and they were inclined to see children as a female accessory, like a handbag or designer sunglasses. They might have felt very differently had society permitted them children of their own, independent of feminine authority, but that had never been an option.

"Women like that DiD have entirely abandoned their feminism in favour of trying to manipulate men back into our traditional role of protector and provider," said John, stretching out his legs and getting comfy. "They want the slaves back on the plantation."

"That endeavour requires a very short memory," remarked Ritzy. "Do they think that men have forgotten or forgiven feminism? That won't happen until young men are raised in a post-feminist society, and that's not going to arrive while there are still a lot of die-hard feminists in positions of political power helping us to remember. The Civic Investigation, for example."

There was a ripple of murmured endorsement from every man in the room. They had all sat before the inquisitors of the Civic Investigation. In the cramped apartment the spontaneous camaraderie which sprang up whenever groups of men got together like this was already strongly in evidence. Male competitiveness only reared its head if they strayed on to neutral subjects. Conversation flowed without friction if they kept to topics of shared experience. They were men who liked to talk and there is nothing more congenial than having your own views confirmed by others. They were settling down for a long and affable session of discoursing upon their familiar preoccupations. What could be more pleasant?

"Feminism brought out the nastiest elements of female evolutionary psychology," pontificated Derec. "It intensified their petty spite, their perennial dissatisfaction, their infantilism, their willingness to exploit men as a utility. It silenced the better angels of their nature and gave tongue to their worst devils."

"Do you think our great-grandmothers were like modern women?" asked Gravy.

"Who do you think invented the plantation?" commented John rhetorically.

"The women of the past can't have been quite like modern women, surely?" Mikelis speculated, "If they had been, then I doubt very much that we would have been born. The species would have died out by now."

"Not the whole species," John corrected him, "just the countries afflicted by feminism's entitlement-culture. I wouldn't be around, that's for sure. There'd be no Canada."

This sweeping statement was an exaggeration which reflected John's attitude toward the land of the Maple leaf. John had a grievance against the country of his birth, and it popped up in his conversation regularly. Nahas was sick of hearing about it frankly, with the two of them sharing an apartment, although he accepted that John's grievance was a legitimate one. The Canadian had been banned from returning to his own country due to his former professional association with a notorious Pick Up Artist motivational speaker. Had he been convicted of terrorist offences his passport would have remained valid but being labelled an evangelical PUA had caused Canada to disown him. It wasn't that he wanted to return home, he just resented being told that he couldn't.

"I don't think our great-grandmothers can have been anything like as bad as the women of today," said Barker, whose consuming interest in his family genealogy predisposed him toward a more benign view of his female ancestry. "Feminism is a licence to bitch and that's very corrupting. Women have betrayed men by indulging that licence to their heart's content. What could be more satisfying and more addictive than a permission to nag? Feminist malice has been the cultural norm since before we were born but it can't always have been that way, can it?"

"You may be right," agreed Captain. "After all, you can chart the progress of feminism getting steadily worse. First, men were told that we were guilty. Then we were told that we were inadequate. Then we were told that we were obsolete. Maybe women weren't so bad at the beginning."

"It didn't just bring out the worst in women, it brought out the worst in men too," said Ritzy sadly. "Our gullibility where women are concerned, our cowardice in the face of injustices committed by women, and our willingness to surrender to neoteny."

"God damn neoteny!" seethed Gravy, "It's both the most sublime thing in nature and the most terrible thing in nature. It offers bliss and delivers purgatory."

"Then god bless synthetics," said Ritzy and they all laughed.

"Ah, my sweet Angel," chuckled Gravy. "She's the greatest scientific achievement yet invented. Who needs nuclear power, vaccination, or space travel? What could be a more liberating accomplishment than a synth-lover?"

"If science ever invents an artificial womb, it will have reached its summit," said Derec. He smiled when he said it but that didn't mean he wasn't serious.

One of the most insistent campaigns by Men's Rights Activists prior to The Rupture had been the demand for all newborn babies to be

DNA tested to establish the identity of the biological father. The issue of how many women lied to men about the paternity of children had been a colossal scandal waiting to explode for decades. Child support cases in the courts had thrown up an immense profusion of fathers who had been paying financial support for children who were not their own. Everyone knew perfectly well that men were being cynically exploited in this way by many thousands of women, but exactly how many remained a mystery. No one had been sure what percentage of children were not actually the biological offspring of the men who innocently believed that they were the father, and statistical estimates had ranged widely between as little as 10% and as much as 50%.

Only the compulsory DNA testing of newborns could settle the matter but the opposition to men having parental equality in this respect was even more ferocious than feminism's usual opposition to any form of equality for men. The routine emotional blackmail was employed to heap guilt and shame upon men for viewing women in a less than unconditionally favourable light. Traditional ideas of romance and love and marital trust had been deployed like strategic military manoeuvres in the attempt to get men to obediently accept their position of having to believe whatever they were told by women, even though there was a quick and entirely painless scientific test which could provide certainty. As usual, the cultural imperative was to protect women at the expense of their menfolk.

In the end it was the increasing male reluctance to accept fatherhood at all, combined with the struggle of female single-parenthood under conditions of economic decline and welfare shortages, which had finally forced the feminist establishment to concede compulsory DNA testing of the newborn. Yet, even then, it was made clear by the authorities that this measure was not being introduced because men had demanded it but only because women who were sexually faithful to their male partners were demanding it. Whatever the reason for the concession, when DNA testing was introduced the scandal had duly erupted. This scientific proof of the sexual infidelity of women had exploded the feminist gender construct of virtuous female monogamy and, just as the government had feared, it had given rise to a plethora of acrimonious divorces. This made men even more reluctant to accept fatherhood as a life-choice.

Incubators for babies born prematurely could work wonders but science was still a long way from the creation of an artificial womb in which gestation could take place in its entirety from conception, and with abortion rights being sex-specific, the thorny problem of parental equality wasn't going to be solved any time soon. It was just one of several issues which blighted the battleground of sex and procreation.

"There's going to be another debate in the Metro Legislature to criminalize sexual synthetics," Mikelis told them, "or so I heard on the channels today."

"Another one?" expostulated Gravy. "They don't give up, do they."

"Did anyone hear about the campaign to have synthetics declared a violation of women's procreative rights on the grounds that men's use of synth-lovers denies women access to semen?" enquired John. "It's not enough for them that women already control men's fertility, now they want to control the spunk in our balls."

"What about all the women who have male synth-lovers?" asked Nahas. "Is that a violation of women's procreative rights, too?"

"The campaign will ignore women's use of synthetics, same as always," said Captain. "They just target us because they want us dependent upon cunt, like in the old days."

"All that feminists have ever offered men is a return to the old slavery, breaking our backs to earn a fuck from the gatekeepers of sex," said Chippy vehemently.

"That's why I'm a PUA," asserted John, who was the only Pick Up Artist in the room and would've welcomed an ally. "The gatekeepers of sex are our jailers so we have to fuck as many as we can and make damn sure they don't cage us. It's every man for himself. Society has never been on our side, we're on our own."

"Society had always expected men to cope alone," said Derec morosely.

The Red Squirrels all chorused together: "He's a man, he can take care of himself."

The four men of the "E Pluribus Unum" were slightly startled by this choir of voices all chanting along in unison. It was their first exposure to something which had grown into a habit among the Red

Squirrels. They would ridicule phrases which encapsulated traditional misandry, reciting them collectively with rolling eyes and comical facial expressions. These clichés were all ways in which society had controlled male behaviour to its own ends, and included things like "A man's got to do what a man's got to do" and "Boys with toys" and "Fight like a man" and "Take it like a man" and "Man up" and so on. The Red Squirrels would chorus these phrases in sarcastic mockery whenever appropriate to remind themselves that they must remain free of such coercion.

"Exactly," said Derec, recovering from being momentarily nonplussed, "and they used that expectation as an excuse to offer men no support."

"But when men became so culturally disenfranchised that we chose to abdicate all responsibility for a society which disdained us," said Ritzy grinning, "the old double-standard backfired."

"Apparently, it never occurred to those in power that if support could be withheld from men, then men might do likewise; they might withhold it from women," murmured Captain who had a lazily placid smile on his face because he was finding Nahas' marijuana very much to his taste. The Namibian was clearly a skilled gardener of the weed.

"Spart, when you get to a certain depth of disaffection and disenfranchisement," said Chippy, "you decide that society can burn. I will not cooperate. I am non-compliant. I say no."

"And then they condemn us for feeling that way," added Mikelis.

"Whereas when women feel something, that counts as factual proof that it must be true," scoffed Barker, turning the tap on his barrel to pour another pint.

"God, yes. The emotions of women have long been treated as intrinsically legitimizing of her beliefs and actions," complained Ritzy. "It's assumed that a woman's feelings are always a true account of reality. If a woman feels herself to have been harassed, then she has been harassed. If a woman feels herself to have been threatened, then she has been threatened. If a woman feels herself to have been raped, then she has been raped. If a woman feels that her culture is one of patriarchal oppression, then her culture is one of patriarchal oppression."

"That's because feminism is a faith ideology," said Barker sourly, "it's a religion. Just as Protestantism once asserted *justification by faith alone*, feminism has long practiced a belief in *justification by female feelings alone.*"

This comment was greeted by a cackle of warm appreciation from the assembly. They were all familiar with the exposure of fraudulent feminist research, which had been well-publicised on the channels. There were endless examples. When feminist researchers found that 47% of women said they did not *feel* safe on the streets, this was reported as evidence that women were not safe on the streets. When feminist researchers found that 47% of women said they *felt* undermined by colleagues at work, this was reported as evidence that women's careers were deliberately being sabotaged by sexism in the workplace. When feminist researchers found that 47% of women said that they *felt* their male partners did not do a fair share of the housework, this was reported as evidence that men were lazy bastards. The dishonesty of feminism's research methodology had become a standing joke in the years prior to The Rupture when sixty years of counterfeit data had been exposed. Not that this had stopped feminists from continuing to quote their fake statistics in all their campaigns.

"It goes all the way back to our grandfathers' time," went on Barker, taking a swallow of his beer, "when feminism rejected logic as being too masculine. You can't have justification by female feelings alone if you permit the authority of logic. So they threw away logic."

"If you throw away logic, you throw away principles," argued Nahas.

"It was worse than that," said Barker, "they also threw away the idea of an objective truth; that there is a difference between a thing being true and a thing merely being believed. For them, whatever they believe is therefore true simply because they believe it."

"That's a consequence of female nature," said John, who was far more inclined to believe in a biologically gendered nature than the rest of the men in the room. "I'll tell you how I discovered this," he said. "It was sports. Whenever an athlete wins a big race, the television interviewer always asks them the same stupid question: 'how does it feel?' Obviously, the athlete is going to be feeling great. They'll be wildly elated by their victory. They're not going to be feeling miserable or bored. So why ask such an incredibly fatuous question?"

The others were looking a bit confused at this unexpected digression into athletics but John pressed on to make his point before someone butted in:

"Then I understood. They weren't asking for information, they were asking in order to share in the emotionality of the situation. They knew perfectly well that the winning athlete was euphoric and that was precisely why they wanted the athlete to talk about this euphoria so that the television viewers could vicariously experience it too. It didn't even need to be a positive experience. It worked with the crushing disappointment of the losing athlete, too, whose despair was dramatic and had an enjoyable frisson of tragedy.

This taught me something about the masculine and the feminine. As a man, to me, a question is a way of finding out some information. But to the feminised personality, a question is a form of vicarious participation. They're not seeking to be informed by the answer to the question, they're seeking to share in the emotional experience."

"So, are you saying," asked Ritzy, who was asking for information, "that the reason feminists have no interest in what's true is because they're only concerned to validate their emotions?"

"Yes, exactly," smiled John, looking pleased. "They don't value logic or objective truth because what matters to them is to share in the emotional network of the sisterhood. And they want the emotional reassurance of everyone agreeing with them. They don't seek truth, they seek consensus."

Mikelis glanced across at the table of food, wondering if he might fancy a bite of something. There were a dozen legs of cold chicken piled up on a plate that were looking very appetizing and one of those little babies would taste pretty good with this excellent home-brew the Red Squirrels had brought with them. But he'd finish his smoke first.

"Feminists are like multicultis," said Gravy in a tone of disgust. "They divide the world up into the good people and the bad people, with themselves as the goodies and anyone who disagrees with them as the baddies, and they take it for granted that they have already won the argument simply by being the good people."

"What choice do they have, really?" agreed Captain. "By throwing away logic they have no basis for winning an argument except through superior virtue. So they have to believe that they are the virtuous people and that, from the great height of their moral superiority, whatever they judge to be correct must be right and proper. Anyone who disagrees with them must be lacking in virtue and therefore wrong."

"It makes them feel good about themselves. It's an exercise in personal vanity," concluded Barker as he buried his nose in his glass.

"Which explains why, in an argument, feminists and multicultis always make everything personal," said Ritzy. "They can never separate the argument from the person who's making the argument. For them, it's always about disparaging their opponent's character. It's why they always resort to name-calling. As you say, they don't care about logic and principle because they don't care about what's true. They only care about preening themselves as being morally and intellectually superior to their opponents, so that they can massage their inflated ego."

"They're never willing to address anything that someone else has to say which proves them wrong," grumbled Captain. "They never argue against other people's arguments, they only argue against other people."

"And hasn't that left them in a complete mess now that they've lost most of their political and cultural power," said John. "Without logic or principle, their weapon has always been emotional appeals. But nobody's listening to their hysterical diatribes any more. Maybe that explains why the Femme Armageddon resorted to social terrorism. What other course of action was available to them?"

There was a lot of derisive laughter at this mention of the Femme Armageddon, with much spluttering over beer glasses and coughing on joints. In its use of fear to exercise control over other people the concept of social terrorism had been little different from conventional terrorism, but its advocates insisted that it was entirely different because it targeted instances of misogynist societal norms. They would firebomb sex shops, or a group of them would stampede through a pro-life anti-abortion rally throwing piss-grenades at everybody, or they would trash and burn the cars parked outside businesses who'd been accused of being insufficiently pro-women, or whatever. The use of violent intimidation as a political weapon was the same as any other sort of terrorism but, according to the social terrorists, the moral status of the act was wholly dissimilar.

"That was classic!" chuckled Chippy scornfully. "The Femme Armageddon accepted no blame for all their acts of public violence, of course, on the grounds that it was a male rejection of feminism which had forced women into committing acts of terror. It was all the fault of the heteropatriarchy."

"You mean women aren't accountable for their own actions?" said Captain with deadpan drollery. "What a surprise."

"And the more violence that feminists committed," continued Chippy, "the more evidence they had of male violence because although the violence was committed by women it was actually caused by men and was therefore, properly understood, male violence. The feminist's own terror attacks proved how women were oppressed by male violence."

"There's illogic for you," snorted Mikelis.

"It was obvious that feminist terrorism was never going to last," said John dismissively. "By that stage in the social decline the police and private security services were willing to crack the heads of female terrorists as if the women had been men. Once a few of the Femme Armageddon had been beaten bloody, they ran out of volunteers. That strategy was doomed to failure because feminists weren't going to martyr themselves. Women who require safe spaces to avoid microaggressions and trigger warnings to spare themselves the emotional trauma of hearing unpleasant words spoken in their presence are not the stuff from which martyrs are made."

"So they encouraged their male feminist allies to martyr themselves for the cause," snorted Derec contemptuously. "It was so predictable that feminists would expect their men to fulfil the traditional gendered male role of putting themselves in harm's way to keep women safe."

"But even creatures as abject as male feminists weren't prepared to put up with that for very long," laughed Chippy, "and the worms turned. That put paid to feminist terrorism."

They passed around more weed and refilled their glasses. Mikelis got to his feet and went to the table of food, grabbing himself a leg of cold chicken which he ate with his fingers. Ritzy decided that perhaps he was a little peckish and he left his chair to raid the food, helping himself to some rather delicately cut salmon sandwiches that John had made. John was a bit particular about what he ate. The Canadian was into lifting weights and had an impressive physique under his expensive twill shirt and slim-fit trousers. As a PUA he was easily the best dressed man in the group and was careful with his diet.

Nahas joined them at the table, selecting a plate of store-bought quiche from the cold collation, and his decision to eat started something of a rush as everyone apparently became hungry at exactly the same moment. The conversation largely ceased while plates were filled and mouths were filled and bellies were filled. All were well-satisfied with the quality of the meal, which was excellent. Even Gravy, who for once had to eat without smothering his food with gravy, found it very tasty nonetheless.

There was the sound of raucous shouting from the street outside and the shattering of glass. Heads within the room turned toward the noise but no one interrupted their dinner. There was more hollering and another explosion of glass from outside.

"Car," muttered Mikelis through a mouthful of chicken.

Derec went to the window and looked down into the street. There wasn't much to see except a car with smashed windscreens, front and back. It was only to be expected if you parked in the street round here. But it reminded everyone of why they were meeting up today. The rioting had been escalating again lately and they all knew that it was going to get worse in the months to come.

"Another example of social enrichment through cultural diversity," mused Derec quietly.

"I was listening to a channel the other day that was seriously claiming that multiculturalism isn't a policy of colonisation," announced Chippy.

"What?!" cried Barker incredulously.

"No, really," said Chippy, "there's someone on a channel called Diverlicious who's claiming that it's wrong to describe the demographic changes caused by decades of mass immigration as colonisation."

"How very twentieth century," drawled Ritzy.

"He said that only racists use the word colonisation about multiculturalism and that it's used merely as a rhetorical device," said Chippy, trying to remember the precise quote. His paraphrase was reasonably accurate.

"But colonisation is simply the most literally descriptive term," said Nahas, frowning in puzzlement. "Obviously, colonisation occurs wherever a sufficiently large number of people from one culture migrate to the territory of another culture and settle there permanently. If they live together as an identifiable cultural community, then they're a colony."

He paused with the kind of expression on his face which conveys mystification that there are people in the world who don't know that two plus two equals four. Nahas seemed to be waiting for someone in the circle of men to solve this mystery for him, but nobody in the room was going to disagree with his statement of the obvious, so Nahas went on with his baffled protest against the bizarre idea that the demographic revolution somehow hadn't involved any colonisation.

"Surely no one could seriously deny that this is what has happened here?" he said in disbelief. "It was the first thing I noticed when I came from Namibia fifteen years ago. In a city like this one there are districts where the English are no longer to be found. Everyone in the area, the people who live there, the local shops, the local businesses, everything, all belong to the colonising cultures. It is just stupid for anyone to pretend that this isn't colonisation. It was a big disappointment to me when I arrived from Namibia and discovered that England doesn't really exist any more. I came here looking for the English and couldn't find them."

A slight air of gloom descended upon the room. Nahas, who came from a continent that knew something about colonialism, had just read the funeral oration over the corpse of a dead culture. There was a appropriately funereal hush for a moment and then Ritzy said quietly:

"In the past colonialists colonised other people's countries with their own culture. But multiculti colonialists colonise their own countries with other people's cultures."

"Multicultis never understood themselves," said Barker bitterly. "They never understood what it was that they were actually doing. They're still using a twentieth century definition of colonialism. Their thinking is so out-of-date."

"That's what I said," interrupted Ritzy, "it's very twentieth century. When I was sixteen they did a national census and it turned out, even back in 2011, that London wasn't an English city. The majority of people who lived in London at the time were not ethnically English. I've always remembered that because it was one of the events that started me questioning the indoctrination they'd given me in school. I had a blazing row with my mother about it."

"Try to find an Englishman in London these days," muttered Barker.

"Ethnic diversity forms have always been racist," said Derec, a proud Welshman. "Since I was a lad I've always refused to fill them out. They use the term "White British" as a proxy term for the English, the Welsh, and the Scottish combined as if our ethnicities were all the same thing. I won't tick their damn box because neither 'white' or 'British' is an ethnicity. They only called us that because they hated us too much to even put the names of our real ethnicities on their bloody diversity forms. They just disregarded us. They wanted to ignore us to extinction."

Derek always insisted upon the Welsh spelling of his name: Derec. However, he was one of the new generation of Welsh who felt considerable sympathy toward the English as their fellow colonized, so Derec offered no antagonism to the Red Squirrels on account of their heritage. Ironically, one consequence of pluralism's inclusion of so many foreign cultures into these islands had been for the Welsh to finally get passed their ancient resentment against the English for the latter's history of dominance over the Celts. It was the only example that anyone could bring to mind of multiculturalism actually achieving its stated purpose of overcoming ethnic hostility and bringing greater ethnic harmony. In every other case, the multiculti project had brought about only greater ethnic hostility and ethnic apartheid, but at least it could claim that the Welsh had finally forgiven the English.

"You're right," said Ritzy, "and that's my point. The Multicultis might not have understood themselves but they did know what they were doing and they did it on purpose. The less English that London became, the more that the multicultis praised the change. They were continually congratulating themselves on London being the most ethnically diverse city in the world. The more diverse it became, the more they celebrated the fact. The whole time that Englishness was a dying culture in London, the multicultis were boasting about it."

"It was the same with Birmingham and Leicester and everywhere else," said Chippy.

"Yet you say that this Diverlicious lunatic on the channels," said Nahas to Chippy, "still hasn't understood his own ideology?"

Chippy nodded and opened his mouth to reply but Gravy butted in with the angry expostulation:

"Do you mean to say that this Diverlicious guy is trying to pretend that Blackburn-Islamabad is not a colonised city? The population of the city is something like 80% Pakistani isn't it? Obviously it's a colony of Pakistan. What is the fool talking about?"

"He's got the same problem that multicultis have always had," said Barker. "He thinks it only counts as colonialism if the wicked-western-white-man does it."

"That was always my mother's opinion," said Ritzy. "Her generation believed that only racism by white people actually counted as racism, and only fascism by white people actually counted as fascism, and only imperialism by white people actually counted as imperialism. This Diverlicious clown is still peddling the same unprincipled point of view. He sees colonialism as an exclusively white crime."

"But what about the rest of history?" asked Gravy, whose childhood had evidently been less burdened by the orthodox bigotries that were personified in Ritzy's mother. "History is full of racism and colonialism and imperialism perpetrated by people of every colour against people of every colour all over the world. How did they explain all that?"

"They didn't," said Ritzy, "they just ignored it."

"What a very Eurocentric view of history these multicultis have," said Captain drily.

"But what about Islamic fascism?" asked Gravy, with a eagerness that suggested he thought he had found a flaw in this account of the political establishment before The Rupture. "They can't have thought that all fascists were white. Did they think that all Jihadis were white?"

"No, no," laughed Ritzy. "You have to remember their mind-set. Because they believed that only white people could be fascists, they just pretended that Jihadis weren't fascists. That's their idea of logic: if only white people can be fascists and Jihadis aren't white, then Islamic fascists aren't fascists."

"Our parents' generation were the biggest bloody fools in the history of the world," complained Gravy sulkily.

"They had a political ideology that required them to be bloody fools," explained Barker. "They called it a 'narrative'. Reality didn't fit into their political narrative; they had no place for it."

"Which is why the old-fashioned chump on the Diverlicious channel doesn't want to admit that multiculturalism was a policy of colonisation," added Chippy, shaking his head in dismay. "His racist double-standards don't allow him to apply the word impartially wherever colonisation occurs. He can't cope with the idea that in the present century the English are the victims of colonialism rather than the perpetrators of it."

The cheerful camaraderie of their earlier conversation had gone. When they'd been discussing the stupidity and bigoted hypocrisy of feminism they could afford to be larkish because, for all that feminism was still clinging on to power in some respects, it was unquestionably dying. It wouldn't last much longer because multiculturalism was killing it. But now that the discussion had turned to multiculturalism itself, the mood was much darker. Nothing could stand before the colossal onslaught of the pluralist juggernaut. Multiculturalism wasn't just killing feminism, it was killing everything in its path. It laid waste to civilizational heritages that were a thousand years in the making. Everyone was the loser but there was nothing that anyone could do about it.

"Whatever happened to the country of our grandfathers," reflected Barker. Like his comrades, Barker despised his father's generation and overly romanticized his grandfather's. The faults of that earlier generation had been largely forgotten, having been overshadowed by the faults of the generation which succeeded them. "From grandfather to grandson the ethnic cultures of western Europe have been largely erased. What a pity we couldn't have skipped the middle generation."

"I never knew either of my grandfathers," said Derec mournfully.

"Neither did I," said Captain consolingly. "They both lived into my teenage years but I had no real contact with them."

"I met my mother's father a few times," said Ritzy, "but all I really know about my father's father was that his name was Alf and he used to grow potatoes to make chips for the family dinner."

Chippy gave Ritzy a look and raised his eyebrows in acknowledgement of one of his unknown predecessors. Through all the demographic upheavals and cultural abandonment, chips had survived. Even if they were, more often than not, called 'fries' now.

Of the nine men, only Nahas and Mikelis had really known their grandfathers. In both cases it was back in the old country before the two men had emigrated west. Of those who had known their fathers, only Chippy and Barker had actually lived with their dads throughout their childhood.

"Our heritage never had a chance with us, did it," said Derec acidly. "Our mothers were feminists and hated our heritage because they thought it was the evil patriarchy. We barely knew our fathers. The society around us was multiculti and destroying our heritage as fast as it possibly could. Everything seems to have conspired to rob us of our inheritance."

"It wasn't just our feminist mothers," Ritzy muttered, "it was our feminist fathers, too. Mine was a schoolteacher and on the rare occasions that I think of him now I always picture him cowering cravenly under the authority of my mother. It's my abiding memory of him."

"Schoolteachers!" spat Chippy. "When I was a kid at school, in the cause of feminism they taught us to fear and despise our own male biology and in the cause of diversity they taught us to have contempt for our own ethnicity. I don't forgive them for that. I never will."

"But there's no one to take our revenge upon," said John grimacing. "You can't very well take revenge upon your own mother."

All nine men had mothers still living. But, apart from Barker, none of them were in contact with their mums. Society's umbilical cord had withered. The babies were off the breast. There was no milky fidelity any more.

"I don't want revenge," said Derec. "I just want the previous generation to admit that they were wrong. Of all their vices, it isn't their prejudice or their injustice or their profligacy that burns me up the most, it's their arrogant refusal to admit that they were wrong."

"Never happen," said Captain. "You heard what Chippy said about that channel called Diverlicious."

"There are plenty of others who'll tell them they were wrong. Multicultis are hated by everybody," asserted Gravy emphatically. "They're the enemy to the colonised, who hate them for what they've done to us, and they're the enemy to the colonisers who hate them for their feminised beliefs and values. Multicultis don't have a side to be on. They've always pretended that they are on everybody's side, but they've ended up in a situation where the only thing which all the sides can agree upon is that everybody hates the multicultis."

"The basic problem with multiculturalism," said Mikelis, "is that its fundamental premise is false. Multicultis had such total faith in the idea that if you bring diverse people together they will get to know one another and soon learn that the differences between them are trivial compared to what they share; their common humanity."

"We've all heard that a million times," interrupted Captain.

"Exactly," affirmed Mikelis. "This is their fundamental mistake. What actually happens when you bring diverse people together is that they take the things they have in common for granted and become fixated on all the things about which they disagree . . . ."

As a Latvian, Mikelis was aware that the country of his ancestors had gone through various forms of foreign rule in the past, mostly by the Germans and the Russians although the Poles and the Swedes had taken their turns as well. Yet somehow the Latvians had managed to preserve their own ethnic identity through their language and traditions. Their most recent occupiers were the Soviets and there were still a large number of ethnic Russians in Latvia. Maybe a quarter of the population. But Mikelis remained a Latvian. He felt he understood the tenacity of ethnicity when people valued it. His forefathers had never surrendered it.

". . . . In the same way that a married couple try to get along but their individual and gender differences keep causing friction between them," continued Mikelis, "when you force different cultures live together they also try to get along but their differences are constantly causing friction."

Chippy, who found this portrait of his world as hilarious as it was accurate, snorted loudly in mirthful endorsement and Ritzy slapped his thigh in agreement, but Mikelis hadn't finished yet:

"When a man and a woman set up home together there are certain things which they have in common. Perhaps they both like Chinese food and they both like to sleep late on a Sunday. Whatever. Almost immediately they take these things for granted because these are the things that never cause any friction between them.

In contrast, it's the things about which they disagree that feature most conspicuously in their relationship. If she loves romantic movies and he loves violent zombie horror films, then they're probably going to have the same argument every time they decide to see a movie. If he hates the way that she monopolizes the bathroom and she hates the way that he cuts his toenails in the bedroom, then these are the kind of things which will loom large in their relationship. This is what they'll quarrel about and this is what they'll bore their friends with when they're complaining about what they have to put up with from their inconsiderate partner."

Chippy's giggling was infecting the rest of the group and Mikelis' pet theory was rapidly turning into a stand-up routine, at least in the way that it was being received by his audience. But the laughter was very friendly and supportive so he didn't stop.

"Cultures and communities sharing a society have the same dynamic as couples sharing a home," he said. "It's the points of divergence and disagreement that claim all the attention. A Muslim and a Kufr may both be interested in starting a small business, setting up their own taxi service or something. But a shared interest in business is not how they see each other. It's the burqas and the genital mutilation of the Muslims, and it's the pornography and the pre-marital sex of the Kufr, *these* are the things that both focus on and talk about. So the fundamental premise of multiculturalism couldn't be more wrong. Far from seeing the differences between them as trivial and seeing their common humanity as important, it's the other way around. They spend all their time feeling upset about what they see as being wrong with the other cultures."

Chippy guffawed with laughter and leaned over to slap Mikelis on the shoulder. All the faces in the circle were merry with approbation, as well as with alcohol and grass. The Latvian had very neatly tied together their collective sentiments about living with women and living in pluralism. The two problems, according to Mikelis' theory, were the same problem. Too much proximity causes inevitable friction.

"It's true," Derec concurred, his normally dour face creased into a grin as he giggled along with the rest of them. "Put a devout Christian together with a secular feminist and they won't spend all their time reflecting on how they both oppose the military-industrial complex, they'll just have a flaming row about abortion and the rights of the unborn child."

"You'll never get the multicultis to admit that their basic premise is false," said Ritzy in rueful good humour, "any more than you'll ever get feminists to admit that patriarchy theory is a lie."

"They've spent too long in power to renounce their faith," said Captain.

"The lunatics took over the asylum," said John.

"No," Ritzy corrected him. "The children took over the nursery."

"It was their immaturity that made them so politically irresponsible," added Chippy, the laughter dying on his face. "The multicultis gave away the very ground we live upon; they just gave it away."

"Your own foes deliver you captive to some foreign nation without blows," quoted Barker.

The "E Pluribus Unum" guys, unfamiliar with Barker's penchant for the bard, looked baffled at this enigmatic outburst. Captain clarified the mystery:

"Shakespeare," he informed them.

"Coriolanus," Barker informed them further.

There was a hushed moment while the "E Pluribus Unum" seemed to be weighing in judgement the propriety of quoting ancient texts. They weren't accustomed to it. But then there was a flutter of affable amusement to signal that it was judged to be acceptable. If Barker wanted to affect this strange habit, then that was okay.

"We weren't the only ones delivered captive without blows, Spart," said John. "Whenever the establishment's two faith ideologies are at odds with one another, multiculturalism has always trumped feminism. Even feminists have had to walk in fear of the accusation of racism. That's why the only things they exclude from their theory of rape culture are actual rape cultures."

"You're not kidding," said Nahas laughing. "Feminist 'affirmative consent' laws make it necessary for a man to receive a woman's consent for every single act in sex. He must ask permission to touch her knee. He must ask permission to kiss her. He must ask permission to unbutton her blouse. But at the same time Muslim rape gangs are grooming underage girls for use as rape-slaves. Yet it's guys like us that feminists want to put in a cage."

"It's also why they never mounted a serious campaign against the burqa and the niqab," said Mikelis.

"They had another reason," argued Captain, making a wry face. "Muslim women wear the niqab in the belief that they need it for protection against a world full of male rapists who will pounce on them and ravish them if they show their hair or show their arms or legs or anything at all."

"Which makes the niqab an insult to every man she meets," interjected Ritzy.

"Well, every man she meets who isn't a compulsive rapist anyway," corrected Gravy pedantically.

"My point," went on Captain, disregarding the interruption, "is that feminists entirely shared the belief that they were threatened by male rapists everywhere all the time, so they sympathized with the wearing of the burqa. I think of lot of feminists would have liked to wear the niqab themselves."

"To a feminist, the burqa is a kind of mobile safe space," said John, producing a huge rowdy guffaw of laughter from everyone present.

There was a peculiar noise from the street outside. It was a kind of *whumph* sound. But, although peculiar, it was not unfamiliar. They all recognised it for what it was. The sudden burning of oxygen as a ball of fire exploded.

Carrying their glasses of beer and puffing contentedly on Nahas' excellent marijuana they rose slowly from their chairs and gathered around the window. The car which had previously been vandalized had now been set on fire. There were a lot of very young folk running up and down the road screeching enthusiastically about something. Their youthful energy was running amok. They were excited by their violence, not afraid of it. It elevated them from the level of the wretched to the level of the predatory. The scene was starting to look bad. But the nine men at the window decided not to care. Fuck it. Let the world burn.

"We're all going to be needing a safe space soon," said Ritzy.

Chapter 8

Spare a Copper

Her name was Ushna Khan but tonight she was PC522319. She put in so many hours at work that she was PC522319 Khan most of the time and only rarely was she Ushna. Her home life wasn't very rewarding, so why not put in the overtime? Work was where her friends were. Ushna was a Muslim apostate and that single fact had cut her ties with the community of her childhood. She had joined the police service in part because it had provided her with an alternative family, an alternative form of community support, when she had lost her original family and friends by leaving her religion. But by joining the police she had burned all her bridges and was now considered the very worst type of coconut; brown on the outside and white on the inside. That she was female made the offence even worse because it meant that she might be in physical confrontations with Muslim men and she would be on the side of the despised kufr. Like many other apostates, her name was on a death list. She couldn't afford to let it bother her. If she did, she'd never leave the house. PC522319 Khan couldn't stay cowering under her bed at home. She had her living to earn.

She was a Level 1 PSU officer, assigned to the unit full-time. As such she was fit enough to run 1000 metres dressed in full kit and carrying a shield weighing 17 lbs in less than 6 minutes. No one could qualify as a PSU officer until they had met the required standard of fitness. There was a lot more to the training than just the running, but it was a much-repeated joke in the service that running was likely to be the most important of a riot officers many specialist skills.

The constable was gearing up for her night's work. The changing room was all metal lockers and body odour. With ceremonial gravity PC522319 slid her helmet with its protective visor down over her head and fixed it snugly in place with its chin-strap. Her identification number was printed boldly across the front of the helmet. She wasn't wearing a yellow high-visibility jacket because those bloody things were a target for the fire-bombers to aim at, so she was looking very paramilitary in her dark blue flame-retardant assault suit. She had reinforced plastic armour on her shoulders, forearms, thighs and shins. There were steel toecaps in her boots. The radio was on her left collarbone and the handcuffs were on her belt.

She walked out of the changing room and went to collect the round shatterproof polycarbonate shield that she would carry on her left arm to complement the sleekly black riot baton that would be gripped tightly in her right fist. The baton was a solid bar of high-impact rigid nylon with a rubber grip. It was longer than a conventional police truncheon and she could do some serious damage with it, if necessary. The ritual of donning her armaments was complete. She was a 21st century warrior in formal battledress.

As a member of a Police Support Unit she had undergone specialist tactical training in the containment of public disorder and riot. This was a voluntary duty that was outside the remit of ordinary officers employed in divisional services but, although joining a PSU wasn't compulsory, there was significant pressure upon all officers to volunteer because every police service in the country was desperate to get more bodies into their tactical riot squads. Far too many officers had given up their commitment to the service, either by resigning or by just going through the motions to collect their salary. This had been especially true of the male officers. As a result, tactical riot squads were badly understaffed and were more than 50% female. The poor state of their operational readiness was a scandal that no political authority had the money to do anything about.

In the prolonged period of urban violence during The Rupture the police had been issued with water canon and rubber bullets. They had been badly outnumbered and it would have been suicide for them to have entered the combat zones without the firepower to defend themselves. Even central government had been willing to employ serious measures at the height of the widespread anarchy. The need to impose some sort of civil order had taken precedence over electoral popularity.

Those had been the glory days for the police. They'd actually been let off the leash. They'd been able to dish out a bit of stick. It had been their last hurrah. As soon as the situation had calmed down a little central government, supported by the Metro governments, had swiftly withdrawn the water canon and the rubber bullets. They'd been returned to storage, leaving the police with their trusty but sadly inadequate truncheons. Once again they were made a Police Service not a Police Force.

This decision had been premature. The recent rioting in several of the Metros was becoming endemic, just as it had been during the worst days of the economic crash. The officers on riot duty were strongly of the opinion that they should once again be equipped as armed paramilitary units, with rubber bullets and stun grenades as a basic minimum. But the opinion of the folk on the front line carried little weight. When did it ever? Decisions were made by people in offices. These days the PSU tactical squads were lucky to even get taser guns and pepper sprays to supplement their riot truncheons. Real firepower was denied to them.

They knew why. The various Metro Legislatures were so hindered by ethnic sensitivities that some of their politicians sided with the rioters and those who didn't, fearful in their political vulnerability, daren't offer unconditional support to the police. To the windbags in the Metros it was a question of consequences. The death of a police officer was a situation which called for a solemn speech and two minutes dignified silence. But the death of a citizen was a situation which called for months of expensive internal enquiries followed by an independent review. Police deaths were cheaper. Besides, when a citizen was killed by a police officer it generated further rioting which exacerbated the situation.

PC522319 Khan and her colleagues marched outside to the car park in the late twilight, all of them armoured for tonight's peace-keeping duties. The PSU squad climbed aboard three personnel carriers. The carriers were white Mercedes vans, equipped with steel mesh window guards and wheel shields, which had to be more or less rebuilt every couple of months to repair the regular damage they sustained. The paintwork on all three vehicles was blackened from fire damage. Carriers were a favourite target for the "roof bombers"; those rioters who positioned themselves on the roof or upper storey of a building to throw petrol bombs and other missiles down upon the police in the street.

The interior of the vans had a row of mounted fold-down seats along each side for the officers to sit on. Or to perch on, rather, as the foam vinyl seats were fairly small. A tactical squad was made up of an inspector, three sergeants, eighteen constables, two paramedics and the drivers of their three carriers. Of the twenty-seven officers in PC522319 Khan's squad, nineteen were female including twelve of the constables. In the final decades of the 20th century it had often been said that "The Future Is Female". This had turned out to be true. The proof of it was evident in the femaleness of the riot squad as they bolstered their courage to face the savage violence of the rioters.

The police's strategic goal in any riot was not to engage the rioters directly or attempt to suppress the riot. Had such an order been given the police would not have obeyed it. Their primary role was to protect the firefighters who were deployed to deal with the many fires which inevitably broke out. No firefighters could be expected to enter a riot area without police protection. Their secondary role was to arrest looters, although mostly the police did not pursue looters because this would split up their units and stretch their limited number of officers over too large an area of ground. They needed to keep their officers bunched together for mutual support and to present a united front.

The squad had a vigorous team spirit. They had to look out for each other if they wanted to survive the night. But at the same time it was natural that some officers formed particular attachments within the squad; a particular comrade-in-arms that they could rely upon when things got sticky. PC522319 Khan tended to partner up with another female officer, PC402783 Smith. They were compadres and they watched each other's backs.

PC402783 Smith was a stocky Englishwoman who had stood firm alongside PC522319 Khan on the defensive line at the Huntingdon riot, and that had been a real slogging match. There had been plenty of bloodshed and broken teeth that day. It had forged a powerful bond between them. Bravery in adversity does that. When two people prove to each other that each can be relied upon in a crisis, it teaches them a lesson they don't quickly forget. It has value. The other women and men on their riot squad were all staunch comrades, too, but the red-haired freckle-faced Smith had a stronger connection with the dark hirsute Khan. It had been forged in the fires of the battle of Huntington and thereafter the two of them had partnered up as far as orders permitted.

They sat side-by-side in the back of the van with the others. Smith's right knee was vibrating slightly from the nervous tension coursing through her. She was wound up tight. They all were, the whole crew. The countdown had started. The adrenalin was building inside them but could not yet be released, it had to be kept in check until it was needed. It would be needed. They'd all been here before and knew what to expect. The streets were waiting for them. The enemies on the street. The friendless zone. The troops in the blue flame-retardant assault uniforms and reinforced plastic armour had tight grim smiles on their faces. They made lame jokes to calm their nerves as the vehicle drove along the bypass toward the residential estates. The sky was rapidly darkening as night fell.

Their three vans joined up with several others from neighbouring stations to form a convoy of personnel carriers on the road as the full Operational Divisional Support Group cruised along under the yellow streetlights. They didn't use sirens. They kept their speed down. They were professionals and this was business. As the convoy got closer to the district where mobs were gathering and violence was imminent, the line of smoke-blackened white vehicles separated in multiple directions toward their specified flashpoints. There'd been rioting in this district many times before and the likely flashpoints were predictable. The three vans carrying the squad of twenty-seven officers which included PC522319 Khan and PC402783 Smith were heading for the inner-city shops along Lincoln Road where it intersected with Bedford Street. The intersections of main roads with nearby shopping precincts were always popular targets when the mayhem started.

It was an area of diversification with no dominant ethnic culture to quell the seething disaffection by imposing cultural norms. The civic incohesion of diversity didn't allow for cultural norms and this generally made those areas more unstable and explosive. Worse still, the area bordered on an Exclusion Zone from where the ethnic militia of the neighbouring district could make external sorties to protect their borders. As an Exclusion Zone had no police presence or access for any other emergency services, they were policed by their own local militia who were brutal in suppressing any riots motivated by political causes with which they did not agree. If the civil unrest reached the borderlands, it could turn into cross-cultural warfare. That eventuality was considered more serious because counter-ethnic riots were not merely crimes of violent assault against property and persons, they were also legally classified as hate-crimes. The violent assaults were an offence against the law; the hate was an offence against multiculturalism. The *act* was an offence against the state; the *motivation* for the act was an offence against the state ideology.

The officers on the tactical squads knew the ethnic geography of their city like the back of their hand. Their lives might depend upon it. They could define the ethnicity of their city street by street. But they were nonetheless required to regularly attend training sessions in which senior personnel lectured them about the importance of inter-community respect and tolerance of diversity. The senior personnel, who were paid three times the salary of a front-line officer, would regurgitate chunks of text from policy manuals written twenty years ago while the real police officers in the lecture room would impatiently grind their teeth and gaze at the ceiling.

These didactic lectures were a hangover from the pre-Rupture days. Their utter irrelevance did not deter the senior personnel from making them compulsory. The establishment elites had spent more than half a century fracturing the disunited kingdom into splinters, and comparative birth-rates would ensure that this fragmentation now continued under its own momentum, yet those elites still clung doggedly to the policies which had set this demographic revolution in motion. But at least nobody had to pretend to believe in them any more. Realists like PC522319 Khan could be openly contemptuous of their policies without losing her job. Twenty years earlier an officer would have been sacked for holding ideologically incorrect attitudes but in their present circumstances the police service knew that it couldn't afford to lose any of its tactical officers.

If the lecturers had learned nothing over the last few decades, the ordinary coppers could not afford to be so ignorant nor so complaisant. They had to cope with the situation on the ground. Since the upheaval of The Rupture civil rights had no longer been as economically viable as they once had been. The assurance of liberal freedom and equality was gone, having been pissed away by a political class who had betrayed the very ethnic cultures which had built the model of liberal freedom and equality in the first place. The systems of social welfare benefit, which had been the greatest achievement of liberalism, had crumbled as the cultures which had fostered them were dismantled. The politics of poverty had been visited upon people with avengeance, with its attendant violence. With severely limited welfare entitlements there was no security. No safety net. The underclass inhabited a bottomless pit of the economically disenfranchised. The ghetto gangs understood this far better than did the politicians, and so the front-line officers were forced to understand it too.

Large sections of the populace had, in self-preservation, retreated behind the battlements of their own ethnic cultures, among whatever they perceived as being their "own kind". When they considered it warranted, from within these ethnic fortresses skirmishing parties issued forth armed with guns, knives, and nail-bats to defend their neighbourhoods. Other communities fought back against these incursions with rampages of their own. Those left outside, in the confusion of diversification, often found refuge in localised ghangs. Under the spur of inter-communal violence, ghetto gangs were feudal in their loyalties but frequent betrayal undermined these allegiances and made the tribal social structures of gang culture inherently insecure.

The mafias tended to have a stronger ethnic integrity, usually based upon their refusal to speak English so that the language barrier of speaking only Russian, or only Urdu, or only whatever, would protect them from the kind of splits and splinter groups which beleaguered the notoriously disaffected multiethnic ghangs. The latter, having been raised in the social illiteracy of multiculturalism, had no real conception of virtues such as fidelity and trustworthiness. These virtues had to be re-learned through personal experience. In the meantime, a new morality prevailed, one which shocked and terrified those old enough to remember how it used to be before the financial upheavals in the global economy.

PC522319 Khan was twenty-three years old. She had been born in 2012 so she could remember the world before The Rupture but she was far too young to even imagine what society had been like before diversification. She knew and understood her world in a way that the senior police personnel, still clinging to the past, were incapable of appreciating. So officers like Khan just got on with the job.

She sat in the back of the van, her jaw clenched, chatting in a strained manner with PC402783 Smith. The two rows of officers in their bulky equipment swayed to the motion of the vehicle as it sped through the city. At such moments PC522319 Khan always felt like they were a squadron of paratroopers in a plane waiting to be dropped into enemy territory. It wasn't an entirely inappropriate analogy. PC473889 Crane, who was up at the driver's end, gave a holler to warn the team that they were close to their flashpoint. Thumbs were raised to confirm their readiness. It would soon be time to disembark, jumping out of the van and rallying on the inspector for dispersal. The paratroopers were about to cry "Geronimo".

The driver squinted at the road ahead of him. The streetlights were making the tarmac look strangely moist, as if it had been raining, which it hadn't. There was a glimmering sheen of something wet across the tarmac. He couldn't make out what it was, but as his headlamps played over it there was an impression of fluidity and movement.

The rioters had a talent for improvisation and they also knew a thing or two about laying their plans in advance. Ambushes were a favourite strategy. They had poured petrol all over the surface of the road. A roof bomber was hanging over the edge of the flat roof of a supermarket. He was a young man of engrained malice, wearing a hoodie and a thermal cap with a scarf over the lower half of his face. When the three police carriers drove over the shallow pool of highly inflammable liquid he threw an incendiary down into the street which ignited the combustible fluid and suddenly the whole road roared into a massive sheet of flame. The blaze sprang up out of nowhere, burning fiercely from kerb to kerb.

In the cabs of the police vans there was an outburst of vociferous shouting and swearing. They'd been taken entirely unawares. But all three drivers, knowing their job, wasted no time in panic. They put their foot down hard on the pedal and instantly accelerated to get through the fire. To have hit the brakes in shock and disorientation would have been fatal. The men at the wheel couldn't see anything in the wall of flames but by speeding up they got through the fire in a few seconds. Even so, the attack had done its work. The rubber tyres of the vehicles had caught fire and the oily chassis of each van had been set aflame. The grease on the undercarriage of the vehicles was alight. Inside the carriers the police would be cooked if they didn't get out right now.

The leading van, swerving down the wrong side of the road, bumped up the kerb, went skidding over the pavement and came screeching to a halt. The second and third vehicles emerged from the cauldron of fire, grinding their gears and hitting the brakes to stop on the other side of the street. With shouts of "Go! Go! Go!" the police crashed out of the back doors of the vans, leaping into the darkness and taking up a defensive position behind their wall of shields.

The drivers unhooked their vehicle's fire extinguishers from under the dashboard and ran frantically around their vans spraying clouds of CO_2 to put out the blazing wheels and chassis. The extinguishers were barely up to the task but something had to be done before the flames that were licking all round the lower part of the vans reached the fuel tanks. By good luck and prompt action they managed. The danger appeared to have been averted for the moment but the inspector ordered her constables to keep well away from the carriers in case they reignited. There was still burning petrol on the road. Missiles began to rain down from the nearby buildings. A piss-grenade, a cardboard carton filled with urine, hit the ground a few yards away and showered piss in all directions.

The situation was far from ideal. The PSU squad were stranded on the ground in enemy territory without any transport either to take them onward or to a place of safety. But they weren't far from their designated flashpoint, perhaps a quarter of a mile. The inspector was on her radio, communicating their circumstances to the coordinating task force superintendent. His instructions came through smartly, which was just as well because the barrage of missiles wasn't showing any signs of ceasing and their accuracy was improving.

The three drivers, poor bastards, were ordered to stay with their vehicles in the hope that the Operational Aid Unit would be able to send some support trucks to tow the vans out of the area. If they couldn't, there would be nothing left of the carriers by morning. Two constables and a sergeant were detailed to remain with them as reinforcement. None of the six looked too pleased at the prospect of waiting for the Op Aid to arrive. Caught out in the open as they were, they might get rushed by a mob and then what were they supposed to do? Risk driving off in one of the vans and maybe die in an explosion if the fuel tank blew, or take to their heels and try to run all the way back to safe ground? It wasn't much of a choice. But could they rely upon the Op Aid Unit?

The remaining twenty-one officers were to press on to the flashpoint on foot. The inspector deployed her troops into two patrol groups of eight constables and a sergeant with one paramedic. That way the two groups could combine or act independently according to need. PC522319 Khan and PC402783 Smith were quick to make sure that they were both in Sergeant Kenning's troop. He was an irascible mean-spirited bugger but he had his head screwed on and he knew how to handle himself. He was the sort who was unlikely to make a mistake that got his constables hospitalised.

They set off down the road in their two lines at a slow trot, one patrol group on each side of the street. This gave them more flexibility in their response to attack from either direction and made them a smaller target for the roof bombers and projectile throwers. In the darkness the blue of their uniforms became black and they jogged through the shadows between streetlamps like menacing spectres. The yellow lights glinted on the protective visors of their helmets and on their round shatterproof polycarbonate shields. Pedestrians withdrew at their approach, ducking into shop doorways and side alleys. Verbal abuse was shouted at them from out of the hidden places of the night. Words full of hate.

Up ahead there was some trouble. A fire engine was stationary in the middle of the road but there was no fire in sight. Why had it stopped? The inspector barked a command and the squad doubled their pace, running forward in a rattling thunder of boots. The silhouetted figures moved with speed and purpose. PC522319 Khan's visor was steaming up with her breath, limiting her vision. She kept going, the rapid staccato rhythm of her feet matching those of her colleagues.

The fire engine hadn't stopped of its own accord. A car had been driven in front of it and the two machines had smashed heavily into one another. It was a deliberate collision by whomever had been driving the car, which was now wrapped around the front of the fire truck. It would have to be cut loose before the truck could move again. The crew of firefighters had survived the crash without injury but they had become trapped on their vehicle by a sizeable crowd which surged threateningly around them. There were clenched fists being shaken in the air and strident voices were baying for blood. The younger folk in the mob repeatedly attempted to climb aboard the truck and the firefighters were keeping them at a distance by using a fire hose as a water canon. But their engine only carried five hundred gallons of water and they had no access to a hydrant, so that defensive measure wasn't going to last for long.

The crowd saw the two lines of police officers coming toward them and set up an outcry of protest. The firefighters directed their powerful jet of water into the mob to carve a path for the riot squad as they charged in. PC522319 Khan was drenched from the spray as she took up a position by the rear of the truck. Smith was next to her. Screams of outrage came from the mass of citizens swelling and heaving like waves around the island of the fire engine.

Tonight's riot had been started by several hundred young multiculti activists, who were always the most energetic of the PWKB in taking their activism to the streets. Indoctrinated establishment drones like these had always been the stormtroopers of The Correct. They were automata who had been manufactured by a politicized education system which had programmed them with the software of feminism and multiculturalism and those two ideologies did all their thinking for them. Never having been permitted to have minds of their own, they thought only what they had been taught to think.

Their detractors generally referred to them by the slang term "replicants". The word was taken from the old science-fiction movie Blade Runner in which one of the biorobotic androids was unaware that it was a machine. The film's hero asks: "How can it not know what it is?" This was an apt metaphor for these young people who served the feminist-multiculti establishment but did not see themselves as the establishment reactionaries that they undoubtedly were. They always credulously believed whatever they were told by their schoolteachers and university professors, and one of the things they had been told was that their establishment beliefs were actually the anti-establishment radicalism of the progressive counter-culture. So that was what they believed. The replicants had zero self-knowledge.

Their alleged youth rebellion was, in fact, firmly in support of a political state which had been ruled by the beliefs of multiculturalism and feminism since the 1980s, fifty years ago. Their idea of revolutionary action was to be implacably hostile to anyone who opposed the ideology of the state. Their revolution was the one which had already taken place; the demographic revolution. Anyone who criticised multiculturalism was, to them, a counter-revolutionary. They agreed with, and obediently conformed to, every word that had been embedded in their brains by the indoctrination factories of the education system. They were replicas of their schoolteachers and their university lecturers. Hence the use of the slang term "replicants". Others might ask: how can it not know what it is?

The young multiculti activists of the PWKB thronged the street, cursing PC522319 Khan and her comrades who represented to them the archetype of oppression. More than that. The bodies in the blue uniforms were the very embodiment of oppression. It meant nothing to them that the police officers were as racially and ethnically diverse as the assembly of replicants who were screaming their hate. The police wore the uniforms and that was sufficient. Quite why they hated the firefighters and wanted to destroy the fire engine was less clear.

The squad had set up a barrier of blue around the fire truck, holding the line with their shields and clubs as the mob surged forward. The firefighters were standing with the police, lashing out with their fists for lack of any other weapon. It was a stand-off for the moment. Most of the mob were not armed and restricted themselves to shouting abuse. Those who got more physical were pushed back by the police. Faces glared ferociously and venom was spewed as the two forces shoved at each other but the stalemate held.

In the midst of the confusion PC402783 Smith saw a wounded firefighter on the ground in danger of being trampled by the swarming multitude. She slapped PC522319 Khan on the shoulder to draw her attention to him. The two women broke loose from the line to dash over and rescue the fallen fireman. They lifted him by the arms and half-dragged him to the engine, sitting him up against one of the rear wheels. There was a lot of blood on his collar and they swiftly examined him for wounds. He was breathing but so stunned as to be barely conscious.

The impasse in the road might have lasted long enough for the police to summon assistance by radio. It might have, if the gods of fortune had been smiling. But everyone was out of luck tonight, both the cops and the replicants. Down the broad avenue of Lincoln Road came a militia from the nearby Muslim community. This wasn't, strictly speaking, their ethnic area. At least, not yet. But it was adjacent to their borders and they had turned out to suppress the rioting lest it spread. With ardent shouts of "Allahu Akbar" they strode with evident determination toward the crashed fire truck surrounded by a milling rabble.

Flying proudly above the heads of the Muslims were several black flags with the green crescent moon and star of the UK Jihad. The militia were not all UKJ but the presence of these Islamic fascists made it certain that all of these soldiers of Allah would be Jihadis. It wasn't news. The ferocity of the cries of "Allahu Akbar" had pretty much announced that fact, with or without flags. The Jihadi Militia would be here for one purpose only, to crush the replicants.

Their sudden and fiercely aggressive arrival on the scene shifted the whole balance of power. It brought all the replicants to hurriedly gather on the same side of the fire truck as the militia. The riot squad followed, leaving PC402783 Smith and PC522319 Khan almost alone with their injured fireman on the other side of the truck. The whole horde of multiculti activists gathered before this new and formidable threat. Two hundred replicants confronted one hundred militia with the riot squad and the firefighters standing in line slightly out of the way, having seemingly become irrelevant to the proceedings.

Khan and Smith remained crouched down behind the fire engine assisting the fallen firefighter. The man had a nasty neck wound from which he was losing a great deal of blood. They were trying to stem the flow with an emergency pad-bandage from the medical kit they'd found in the cab of the fire engine. It wasn't very effective. The man was apparently concussed, too, or maybe it was just shock. Khan had noticed the replicants all rushing to the other side of the truck with her fellow coppers following them, and she grew concerned for her squad. She decided to leave Smith to it and stood up on the rear step of the truck to look across the top of the fire engine to see what was happening. Her heart stopped. The apostate saw the flags of the Muslim militia.

Khan ducked her head back down but stayed where she was to watch. She wasn't going to show herself from behind the truck. If the militia saw her brown face in its riot helmet they'd likely kill her on principle. Asian police officers were particularly targeted by Asian militias in the same way that black police officers were particularly targeted by African-Caribbean militias. They were seen as traitors to their own communities. They were judged on their skin colour and expected to identify loyally with their race. In many ways the social expectation of racial allegiance was more strongly imposed upon people now than ever before. Except, of course, for white western Europeans for whom the expectation was that they shouldn't have any racial allegiance at all, quite the contrary. In the midlands Metros of Little Asia the great majority of the police were Asian, but in all the other Metros black and Asian police officers were condemned as traitors on sight. And the militia were flying the flag of the UK Jihad. It would scarcely be of much help for Khan to pretend to be Sikh or Hindu since that would probably mean that they'd beat her to death as a pagan instead of beating her to death as an apostate. Her dark eyes surveyed the scene.

It was looking very nasty. The two armies were nose to nose and neither was willing to give ground. The Muslim militia began demanding that the replicants disperse. They declared that they had their women and children to protect, and wouldn't tolerate a riotous assembly of kufr so close to their homes. The kufr were unclean and brought degeneracy wherever they went. The militia had a sacred duty to defend the believers from the corruption of a kufr mob running amok. They commanded the multicultis to clear the streets or suffer the consequences.

The replicants may have had an advantage in numbers but they were suffering a crucial disadvantage in ideology. The Islamic fascists were passionately united in their detestation of their kufr enemies, but the young multicultis would have preferred to make friends with the Jihadis. The replicants, thoroughly versed in the false belief that only white people could be racists or fascists, saw the Muslim militia simply as the representatives of an ethnicity and religion toward which the replicants had nothing but good will. They had been taught that all communities other than the English were "ethnic minorities", no matter how much of a majority that ethnic group might be in their own area, who were thereby entitled to the support of all progressive-minded people. Consequently, the replicants could never understand why some ethnic minority communities were antagonistic to multiculturalism.

They didn't understand it now. While the Muslim spokesmen were shouting about the need to protect their families from the immorality of the multiculti kufr, the replicants kept trying to explain patiently that they were rioting in support of ethnic diversity and that it made no sense for an ethnic minority community to oppose them in this endeavour.

Had the replicants been capable of listening to what the Jihadis were explicitly telling them, they might have realised that the real world was very different to their school lessons. Militias from the colonising cultures were generally hostile to diversity because it undermined the loyalty of their own people to their own community. It threatened their ethnic unity and therefore threatened their communal strength. Anyone could see that it was the ethnic uniformity of the militias which gave them their identity and their fighting integrity. There were sometimes divisions in the African-Caribbean militias because of the rift between the ethnic Africans and the ethnic Caribbeans, and the East European militias were often only temporary alliances. The Romanians, Poles, Russians and the rest were able to come to together in a combined militia but these tended to be marriages of convenience. They didn't last. But the Muslim militias had no such problems because they had the pan-national unity of the ummah. Diversity was not in their interest.

Consequently, nothing that the replicants were saying was going to make any difference to the present situation. The Jihadis wanted the multiculti kufr gone and they were prepared to break heads to achieve their goal. The only decision that anyone in the street needed to make was whether they intended to run or fight. There wasn't a third option.

Yet this didn't stop the police inspector from trying. She spoke up to intervene in the dispute, insisting that both assemblies must disperse. A few citizens spat in her direction. She tried again, repeating her demand, to the disgust of her sergeants and constables who wished that the stupid bitch would keep her mouth shut so that the cops and firefighters could get out of this mess with a whole skin. This was no place for them. What could twenty coppers do to control three hundred hostiles?

A skinny bearded guy in a tee-shirt and chinos ran between the fire truck and the line of officers. He was fast on his feet. As he passed behind the backs of the police he dropped something on the ground and kept running. He ran for his life. He ran away from the thing that he had dropped.

A few seconds later the bomb exploded and the street disappeared. Everything was consumed by the sound and impact of the blast. The force of it hit PC522319 Khan in the face and knocked her on her arse. She flew backwards off the step of the fire truck and smacked hard into the tarmac. The air was hot and lacked oxygen. She was suffocating from the heat. A dust cloud filled the road, obscuring everything but the choking pain felt by the survivors. Khan fought for consciousness.

PC402783 Smith had been behind the fire engine attending to the wounded man when the bomb went off and so she had been sheltered from the blast. But, although she was shielded from the force of the explosion itself, her ears were ringing with the shattering noise of it. Blind from the smoke she staggered around the truck, frantic to discover what had happened to her comrades. Coughing on dust, she stumbled into a billowing cloud populated with vague human shapes. As the smoke began to clear the indistinct figures became visible and she witnessed the human wreckage. God, it was carnage.

Her squad had been slaughtered. Her friends were scattered about, their corpses torn into bloody fragments. The firefighters who had been holding the line with the police were also dead. As were a couple of dozen of the replicant protesters. Smith was seized with nausea. The bilious taste of the sick filled her throat and mouth. A single sob broke from her lips and silent tears ran down her face. But her professionalism kept her in motion, walking among the dead, checking for signs of life in the uniformed bodies. There were none.

The mob of multiculti rioters were left stupefied from the shock of the explosion. Some were reeling about in a daze. Others were stricken with terror and were scarpering. They hadn't signed up for this level of violence and they were having no more of it. Those who remained had the opposite reaction. They had taken to the streets in protest tonight because they been angry at the world. That simmering anger now became a homicidal fury. Were they to be killed like cattle? Were they to be killed without raising a hand in their own defence? Their directionless rage had been given a specific target. The murderous militia had butchered them without cause. The replicants had found a new enemy. Even as some of their number deserted them, there were still perhaps a hundred replicants crowding together in the road, confronted by as many Muslim militia. It was going to be war.

Smith rushed back to where Khan lay by the kerb. There was no time for the dead, she must concentrate on the living. The two of them were the only members of the riot squad left alive and that wouldn't last long when the mob spotted them. They had to get out of here now. Not five seconds from now but right now. Smith hauled Khan to her feet by sheer strength and was about to lift the groggy woman up over her shoulder to carry her clear when Khan looked at her friend in bleary comprehension and said "Okay. Okay." Her eyes were glassy and her head was pounding but she understood the need to get her legs moving.

They could not take the wounded firefighter with them. His weight would get them murdered. They'd have to abandon him. The fighting had broken out between the legions of hate, Jihadis versus replicants, but there were also rioters appearing from around the fire truck. The two police officers would be seen. There was no time. Smith had a tight grip on Khan's arm and they were running toward an alleyway. It was dark in that alley. They needed cover. Voices were raised behind them. There were yells of recognition and commands to pursue. The words were unintelligible but their meaning was obvious. There were further shouts, more insistent this time. Only the disorder in the mass of rioters gave the two women the precious seconds needed to flee. They hustled forward to the concealment of the alley and ran into darkness.

PC522319 Khan lumbered along clumsily as life returned to her legs. She increased her speed and Smith let go of her arm to run more freely. Behind them they could hear loud footsteps. How many? PC402783 Smith chanced a glance over her shoulder as she sprinted. All she could see was a glimpse of shadowy figures. Four or five maybe. Some masked, some bearded. All of them men as far as she could tell. Too many. But she had her shield as well as her long high-impact riot baton. Khan had only her baton. The shield was a mixed blessing. It was harder to run with that on her arm. Even so, she wasn't going to waste the advantage it gave her.

They emerged from the alley and clattered across a main road but didn't change course. They had to get well clear of the two mobs who were now engaging in battle. Once they'd put some distance between themselves and the riot they'd only have to deal with the four or five men in pursuit, which would at least give them a fighting chance. There was a narrow side street ahead of them and they went for it. Random pedestrians watched them fly by. PC402783 Smith felt the weight of the shield dragging at her left arm. She couldn't discard it. Not yet. She grit her teeth. PC522319 Khan had recovered from the bomb blast, sucking in great lungfuls of air as she rattled along, and if anything it was the more heavily laden Smith who was now the slower of the two.

The chasing pack tore out of the alley and sped on into the side street like avenging furies. One of them gave a great cry of "Allahu Akbar!" which chilled the blood of the fleeing policewomen. God damn it, they weren't replicants, they were Jihadis. Had they been multicultis they might have chased for a while and then given up. But the Islamic fascists didn't give up. They would hunt the infidel to the end, even if it cost them their lives. Martyrdom was a gift from their god.

"Need a stand!" shouted Khan breathlessly.

"Right!" Smith shouted back.

The exact same thought had struck them both. It would be a mistake to exhaust themselves in running. They were outnumbered. If fatigue slowed them to the point where their pursuers caught up with them, they'd lack the strength to defend themselves and the imbalance in numbers would decide the matter. It would be better to face the fight while they still had some energy. Better to stand their ground in a place of their own choosing than to be hunted down. They must find a defensive position where Smith could make good use of her shield.

They ran on, feeling the presence at their necks of the chasing hounds. The two women were sweating profusely in their dark blue flame-retardant assault uniforms. The material was thick and sealed, so the body's heat built up quickly got trapped inside. An officer could lose pounds of weight through perspiration on a night's riot duty. They kept running. The men were thirty yards behind them but it felt much closer.

The side street opened out into a main road, lit up by streetlamps. The frontage of various shops showed the shadowy recesses of doors. It was worth a try. The two uniformed women swerved left, which meant they were heading south, the direction home. There was no traffic and they sprinted down the middle of the road, straddling the white line. The darkened shops were all locked and shuttered, of course, and although there were lights glowing in the residential accommodation above the shops, these would offer no sanctuary for a couple of cops in trouble. It wasn't callousness, it was realism. Anyone who gave shelter to the riot squad could expect to be burned out by the next day. The cops were on their own.

Smith saw a canopied terrace outside an abandoned restaurant. It was the exterior space where middle-class multicultis had once sat at alfresco dining tables in the European fashion, feeling ever so cosmopolitan, but now it was just an empty space outside a derelict building. The brickwork entrance to the canopied terrace was only about five feet wide. Smith and Khan could make a stand there. She pointed, hollering "Restaurant!", and Khan went with her as they veered toward the terrace.

They bolted into the entranceway and turned to face their assailants who were coming on hard. There were four men, not five. Had one of them been dropped in the chase? Maybe there'd only been four to begin with. Anyway, there were four now, all glaring eyes and bared teeth and bristling beards and flapping shalwar kameez. Knives flashed in their fists as they closed the gap to their quarry. The two women filled the narrow terrace entrance with their bodies and braced themselves. They were both shaking with fear but could not surrender to it. No one would be coming to save them. Smith raised the shield to cover her upper body, standing slightly in front of Khan who didn't have a shield. They raised their long riot batons, breathing fast.

A gunshot broke the night. One of the attackers was waving a handgun. He had shot carelessly while running and sent the bullet high into the wall of the restaurant. A second shot hit the terrace brickwork to their left, much closer. A third bullet glanced off Smith's shield, cracking it and tearing a chunk out of the transparent polycarbonate. The riot shield was designed to protect against thrown projectiles, it offered very little ballistic protection, but it had done enough to save her life because of the angle of the impact. Smith and Khan retreated into the terrace area, ducking down low behind the terrace wall. The gun left them defenceless. They crouched in the darkness, trembling and biting their lips, and waited.

The man at the front of the group spread his arms out wide to slow the charge and the four men came to a halt a few yards from the cornered women. The leader snarled savagely in Urdu at the shooter. It was an order to stop firing. Khan whispered a translation to Smith, but she did not mention the likely reason why the command had been given. Maybe she didn't have to. The four Jihadis probably intended to rape these Kufr sluts before they killed them. Rape sent a message to the infidels that their women were not safe. To the Jihadis, rape was an insult to the Kufr men rather than the Kufr women. It said that the infidel men had failed as men because their women could be ravished. It was a deliberate insult to infidel men who were so cowardly that they let their women wear the uniforms and do their fighting for them. As for the Kufr sluts, they would suffer ravishment for their impious presumption at taking a man's role. If they wanted to fight, they could suffer the consequences.

Knives drawn, the four soldiers of Allah crept stealthily forward to the entrance. The leader was reciting something under his breath. Perhaps it was a prayer. He edged carefully around the opening in the brick wall. There was nowhere for the women to run. They could not escape.

PC402783 Smith lunged forward, her stocky body launched into the attack, shoulder-charging with her riot shield. She burst upwards out of the darkness like a jack-in-the-box. The shield, with her full weight behind it, caught the leader solidly in the jaw and smashed in his upper teeth, knocking him backwards into his brothers. In sudden confusion the other three men pushed him aside to get at their enemy. Smith, standing in the entranceway, brought her shield in close to her body defensively and lashed out with her long baton at the man on her right. He dodged abruptly, almost slipping over. She hoisted her club again, her freckled face contorted with aggression and fear. A man in a taqiyah on Smith's left came at her with a blade.

PC522319 Khan reared up from her crouch to emerge into the gap beside her friend, shrieking with the violence of a rage that arises from stark terror. Her fury sent her crashing bodily into the man in the taqiyah. She grabbed the forearm of the hand which held his knife. He tried to pull it loose but she clung on like grim death. With his free hand he took hold of her helmet and wrenched it off in one savage jerk. As it fell Khan brought her long nylon club swinging down at his head. She missed but hammered him in the side of the neck. His fist pounded into her eye, the knuckles thumping right into the socket, but she daren't let go of his knife hand. Her fingernails dug into the flesh of his forearm with the force of her frenzied grip. She struck again with her weapon, whacking him on the ear. He shuddered but his fist punched her hard, just below the eye this time, cracking the cheekbone. The screeching woman's high-impact baton swung down a third time and thudded into the top of his cranium. It was the decisive blow and he collapsed to his knees.

Smith's riot baton was making wide lateral sweeps to hold off the other three men. The walls of the terrace entrance prevented them from rushing in all at once. The Jihadi who'd almost slipped over had recovered his balance and the leader had spat out his front teeth in a huge gob of blood, ready to return to the fight. The leader came in low at Smith, his blade targeting her groin. The other man steadied himself for a high lunge, his knife aimed for her throat. But Smith thrust out her shield to fend off the leader and whirled her baton in an arc to keep the other man at bay.

The leader, his mouth a bloody ruin of shattered teeth, ricocheted off Smith's shield and threw himself at Khan. He gripped her shoulder with one hand while the point of his blade sank deep into her body armour. The stab-proof vest wasn't so stab proof after all, the tip of the point got through, and she felt the sharp bite of the steel in her upper chest. He was too close for her to hit him with her baton and she reacted instinctively. She jabbed her fingers at his eyes as if to rake her nails into them and luckily gouged his eyeball. He wrenched his knife out of her stab-vest and struck again but she was reeling back and his blade cut only air. Khan held her club two-handed like a baseball bat and as the leader lunged in after her she gambled her life on a do-or-die upward swipe. It was a desperate manoeuvre but, more by chance than skill, her timing was perfect. The end of the baton swept upward to connect with the leader's chin as he hurtled forward. The hideous impact of the blow hammered so hard into his jaw that it wrenched his head back on his neck and snapped his spine. The solid weight of his body slammed into her but he was already dead.

The Jihadi confronting Smith charged in like a bull, attempting to knock her over with the sheer force of his charge. She took the collision on her shield, scuffling backwards but staying on her feet. His knife embedded itself in her thigh, cutting through to the bone and slashing a gory path through the meat as he ripped the blade back out. But the long baton come over the top of her shield to catch him solidly in the temple. Smith put everything she had into the blow. It put a dent in his skull that switched off his brain.

All this time, the man with the handgun had been hanging back from the fray. Apparently, he had little taste for hand-to-hand combat. But now, as Smith reacted to the agony of the gaping wound in her thigh and her shield lowered, he stepped forward purposefully to place the muzzle of his gun up close to the red-haired woman's head and he pulled the trigger. In the confined space of the restaurant terrace the noise of the shot was colossal. At point blank range the destructive power of the weapon was devastating. The bullet went through the riot helmet like it was made of paper. There was a grotesque explosion of blood and PC402783 Smith was stone dead before her almost decapitated body hit the ground.

He was bringing the handgun around to bear upon the remaining police officer when the solid nylon bar in PC522319 Khan's fist smashed down into the gunman's wrist, shattering the bone. The shock ripped through his nervous system and he sagged at the knees. His cry of pain blended with Khan's wild screaming as she hit him on the back of the neck, stunning him. But his traumatized body had seized up and he didn't fall. Shrieking incoherently, she battered him, striking again and again until the gunman finally dropped senseless in a heap. Her sleek black club continued to rise and fall, beating his head to a pulp.

Khan staggered mindlessly out into the street as if in search of another adversary. But they were all down. She was making guttural animalistic noises, walking drunkenly around, half delirious. The man in the taqiyah wasn't dead. He groaned. The Asian woman in the riot squad uniform strode over to him and, wielding her baton two-handed, she smashed it down on to his head. The body went limp and lay still, but she gave him another whack just to make sure. As she stood upright again the street seemed to be swirling around her. The yellow streetlights were in motion, moving across the black sky. She tried to focus her mind. Then she swayed unsteadily over to Smith.

Khan sank slowly to her knees. Her mouth hung open, slack and drooling, as she knelt by the side of her friend. Then she wept. The intensity of her misery took possession of her mind and body as she surrendered herself to weeping. Her hunched shoulders shook in great heaves as the agony of her grief consumed her. Sobbing, she threw back her head and wailed in torment to the stars overhead. In that terrible moment she could have burned to the ground every last mosque in the world, she could have bombed Mecca to obliteration and cast their entire religion into the hell of their own imagination. God damn god. Smith was gone. Smith would never come back. Smith could never be replaced. Something unique and precious had died. Her friend.

Bitter sorrow transformed into smouldering hatred as Khan's homicidal apostasy raged within her. Wiping the hot tears from her eyes she leapt to her feet, picked up the gun which had ended Smith's life and pointed it at the Jihadi who had murdered her. His head was covered in blood from the battering she had given him. She wasn't trained in firearms but at this range she didn't need to be. Khan squeezed the trigger and kept squeezing. Bullets thudded into the prostrate fascist at her feet. With every lethal detonation of the weapon in her hand a shard of metal ripped through the flesh of the hellspawn, carving its way through intestines or lungs or heart or liver, to embed itself in the concrete of the ground beneath his body. She emptied the magazine into him, cleaving great lumps out of him. He was dead before the first shot but Khan just kept blazing away.

It wasn't the smart move to make. She should have kept whatever bullets remained in the gun to help her battle her way back to safe ground. She was still deep in enemy territory. But grief isn't smart.

Heartache doesn't calculate intelligently. They pour forth in a tidal wave of incoherent emotion.

PC522319 Khan stood there with the empty gun in her hand as the minutes ticked by. There were five corpses around her, strewn like litter. She hoped that four of them were suffering the torments of the damnation in which they had so fervently believed. And as for the fifth . . . ? Khan pictured Smith as she had been earlier that evening when they'd sat next to each other in the police van on their way to a night's work. Compadres, side by side. They'd not do so again. Never again.

Some instinct of self-preservation brought Khan back to her senses. She cast the gun away and found her helmet. She slid it down on to her head, then picked up Smith's shield. Her eye had swollen shut from the punch it had taken. Her broken cheekbone ached abominably and there was blood under her shirt from the stab wound. She wandered out into the road. The street was deserted. The local residents would not emerge to investigate the sound of the gunshots. They'd have more sense.

Khan tired communicating on the radio attached to her uniform but the damn thing only produced a confusion of squawk and static. It made little difference. She doubted there would be any help coming even if she got through on the radio. Her squad had been wiped out by that bomb blast and who knows what was going on elsewhere in the city tonight?

How far away was safe ground? There'd be nowhere safe until she reached the other side of the Rat Run. Beyond the shanty town she'd be in the clear. That was about five miles, probably. She would have to stay under cover as much as she could. Her riot gear made her an obvious target. But it wouldn't help to strip off her uniform because she'd be fresh meat if she was seen flitting through the city in her underwear. At least her helmet, shield, and body armour gave her some protection, and she had her riot baton. She would jog along at a steady pace and if someone wished her harm, then let them try. Smith was dead and Khan's desire for revenge wasn't yet assuaged. Let them try. She would take her revenge. On anybody, it didn't matter who.

But as she trotted away southward she passed through one deserted street after another. The rioting had erupted in several parts of the city and this had persuaded the rest of the citizenry to stay indoors. PC522319 Khan shuffled down the lanes and byways of her home town in isolation for the most part. There were no cars around. Occasional groups of people appeared in the road but they kept well clear of the one-eyed blood-splattered ghoul in the helmet and riot shield. There was a noticeable red smear on her baton and her shield was cracked. Khan looked like the lone survivor of a pitched battle, which indeed she was. She didn't look like someone it would be wise to mess with.

Khan made it as far as the Rat Run without incident. The mood of the streets changed then, with plenty of people strolling about. The shanty town was a maze of self-built hovels that was always teeming with its multitude of residents. Khan pressed on, her face set in stone. Some folk called out sarcastically as she passed by. A single riot police officer was a strange sight. They never travelled alone, only in squads. What was this stray squaddie doing wandering through the Rat Run all by herself in the middle of the night? The mocking shouts became more frequent as she progressed but she ignored them and continued at her steady pace. They hollered at her back as she went on her way, their comments lewd and antagonistic.

PC522319 Khan was getting close to the southern end of the shanty town, not far from safety, when trouble finally made its presence felt. A bunch of United Nations gangsters in their sky blue berets saw her coming and deliberately blocked her path. She had no choice but to stop. Khan looked them over with her one good eye. None of them was more than nineteen years of age. She counted six. It was odd that they were here in the Rat Run when there was so much rioting going on elsewhere in which they might have been participating. It wasn't like them to miss an opportunity for looting.

"All alone?" challenged a mixed-race youth in a Hollywood bad boy tone of voice.

"Fed's should know better than to come into our hood all on their lonesome," said his Cypriot friend.

"Specially female feds who've already taken a beating," smirked a shaven-headed woman with a small dagger tattoo on the exposed scalp of her skinhead.

Khan said nothing in reply. This wasn't a conversation. Anything they said was just a preamble to what they would do. She waited for them to decide. It wouldn't take long. The six teenagers stared menacingly at her and she knew she couldn't deal with so many. She would have to seize her moment to make a run for it. But the initial move would be theirs.

"I claim first prize," announced a hatchet-profiled Slav.

He stepped in fast, intending to make a grab at her, and Khan hit him full in the face with her baton. The youngster went down, ricocheting off her baton bloodily, his Slavic profile spread all over his face. Weapons appeared in the hands of the other five thugs as if by magic. A commonplace collection including a carving knife, a hammer, and a chain to be used as a flail. None of them showed any concern for the Slav who was sitting on the ground clutching at his bleeding nose and mouth. It wasn't a part of the ghang allegiance of the United Nations to give a damn about their fellow ghangsters. It was everyone for themselves.

PC522319 Khan shifted sideways, edging right, with the shield on her left arm toward them. Her adversaries sniggered ominously but didn't make any corresponding manoeuvre to keep her blocked. They seemed to have no knowledge of combat tactics. If they had all rushed her at once, she'd have had no chance. But Khan had managed to get half way around the group before another of them made a move, and even then it was a solo effort. The Cypriot skipped forward a yard, swinging a chain around in a circle above his head. He wasn't in any hurry, he was busy grinning and giggling and showing off for his friends. Khan waited for the strike. When it came, clumsy but dangerously brutal, she lifted her shield high to take the impact and kicked out for his balls. She missed but connected painfully with his inner thigh. He hobbled backwards swearing vociferously.

Now the penny finally dropped. Better late than never. It occurred to them that if they wanted to get passed the defences of an adversary armed with a shield and a club, they had better make use of their numerical advantage. Khan sensed them all tensing up for a concerted attack.

She had noticed a gap between some rickety structures made from what looked like corrugated plastic. These were the kind of things that were considered homes in the Rat Run. Khan had been moving closer to the gap as she had been shifting to the right. Without warning she leapt for the narrow opening and disappeared into it.

The UN saw their prey suddenly vanish and they set up a howl of protest as they plunged forward after her.

In the confined space between the hovels Khan was running like a rugby player, with her head lowered and her left shoulder foremost. The shield was in front of her and anything that got in her way was going to be bulldozered aside. A short pudgy woman was smoking a joint at the doorway of one of the flimsy habitations made of plastic sheeting. She heard Khan coming but she was slow in turning her head toward the noise. Khan's shield smacked her out of the way without the police officer even breaking stride. The pudgy woman was sent spinning in a flurry of arms and legs to crash into the plastic.

The five ghangsters yelped with excitement as they followed, sprinting like greyhounds. Khan had been on her feet all night and had spent most of it running. She was too tired to make a race of it. They were too young, too fit. To escape she must hide. But every possible place of concealment was occupied by the festering multitude of tenants who lived in the Rat Run. Khan darted passed an iron brazier, its hot coals providing heat for the three old folk standing around it. There was a pathway between an assortment of charity tents and Khan took it, scrambling over the rubbish that lay around the tents. The bestial sound of enthusiastic yips, yaps, and barks told her that the UN ghangsters were still at her heels.

Heading approximately south and taking whatever route was open in front of her, Khan thought that she must find a way out of the shanty town soon. She had no specific idea of where she was but she had been almost clear of the Rat Run when they'd started chasing her. Safety must be nearly within reach. She ran into an alley that looked more like a proper road. There were streetlights up ahead. She forced her exhausted legs onward.

PC522319 Khan came out the other end of the alley into a pedestrian precinct crowded with nightclubs just as three intimidating ghangsters were emerging from a late night bar. Khan slowed in despair, almost tripping over her own feet with fatigue. It was the finish. She was beset by enemies on all sides. It was hopeless. But maybe not. These three coming out of the bar weren't UN. They wore red bandanas, not sky blue berets.

One was a slim and attractive young woman with short spiky blonde hair. She was dressed in some kind of close-fitting grey suede bodysuit which had a lot of straps and buckles on it, and a knee-high pair of biker boots which looked heavy-duty enough for space travel. Behind her stood a man with colourful tattoos on his neck, and probably all over his body too under the black combats and the stab-proof ballistic body armour he was wearing. Behind him was a mixed-race giant who was maybe six foot five inches tall and 230lbs of muscle. No doubt all three of them were freaks and criminals but they wouldn't necessarily want to get involved in the UN's business. They might keep out of it and let the policewoman pass by unhindered.

Poontang, Painter, and Mars had been out for a few drinks at a hostelry they frequented. They were just on their way home when PC522319 Khan abruptly appeared in the pedestrian precinct, arriving in a pattering of frantic feet. The three Rudý looked up, startled. They saw a riot squad officer, alone and dishevelled, staggering out of the darkness with five ragged shanty town villains sprinting after her in hot pursuit. There was no need for explanations, the picture told its own story.

Matters could have gone either way. There were no ghetto gangs who were on good terms with the enforcers of the law but some were more hostile than others. Crucially, some ghangs were more antagonistic toward other ghangs than they were toward the uniforms of the state. It depended on a ghang's politics and their level of power. The Rudý were fairly equivocal about the police because they had very little to do with them in the ordinary course of events.

On this occasion it was Poontang's judgement which proved decisive. She didn't particularly care for the cops. In her opinion the law was for people who couldn't make moral judgements on their own authority. They needed society's permission. So they didn't act upon their own understanding of justice, they used law as a substitute for morality. Poontang despised that attitude. She had her own ideas about justice so she had no use for the law. But the police were only her enemies when they made themselves such. Otherwise they were just an irrelevance. The UN thugs, on the other hand, were a rival gang who outnumbered the Rudý by about fifty to one and who had sought to do harm to the Rudý in the past. They were unequivocally her enemies. Kicking the shit out of them was always justice. So she was naturally inclined to side with anyone against the United Nations, even cops.

Poontang took it into her head to intervene. She had no pressing reason for doing so, apart from her antagonism toward the UN. But that was reason enough. The copper didn't really feature in her decision. It wasn't a rescue, merely an intervention. Poontang drew a long serrated knife from a sheath on the inside of her boot. PC522319 Khan, still jogging along on stiff legs, saw the weapon being drawn and veered away from the blonde woman. But Poontang's attention was focused on a target behind the copper. As Khan swerved to the side Poontang ran straight at the assailants in pursuit. She would not have taken this action if she had been alone, but Poontang took it for granted that she was not alone. Mars and Painter were with her.

There were five figures ahead of her and the Rudý ghangster in the red bandana took in the sight of them in one sweeping glance, taking note of their weaponry. There was a tall young man with a carving knife; a Cypriot with a chain hanging from his hand; an Oriental with a broad forehead, a bland expression, and a butcher's cleaver; a skinhead woman with a double-edged knife; and a mixed-race youth holding a hammer. The last of these was the one who was nearest to Poontang and she went for him.

The tactics she needed to adopt were obvious: avoid the damn hammer. Any part of her body that it connected with would be badly damaged. So she used her speed. The trouble was, he was fast himself, and he was smart enough not to make wild swipes with the hammer that would allow her to counter-attack while his hammer was on the backswing. For her part Poontang kept in continuous motion, circling around, to avoid giving him a stationary target for that murderous hammer.

Mars and Painter were taken by surprise when Poontang charged the UN. They had no love for the police and would have left the copper to her fate. But when one of the Rudý was in a fight, all of the Rudý were in a fight, so there was nothing further to think about. They had to take care of their own. They didn't know why Poontang had elected to get involved but the reason no longer mattered. Mars and Painter ran forward in support of their comrade, drawing their weapons to tackle the other four UN thugs. They might later protest that Poontang should have consulted them before taking action on her own account, but that could wait. They weren't the kind of men to debate the issue when the dice had already been cast. They set to work in a businesslike fashion.

Mars rumbled ahead like a tank, swinging his great knife which was the size of a machete, and the tall guy with a carving knife found himself confronted by an adversary who was far beyond his ability to defend against. The tall guy slid to a halt and flourished his knife but the wide sweep of Mars' machete scythed through his forearm, chopping off the knife hand. The mutilated UN ghangster reeled away screeching hysterically. He was out of the fight. But Mars had already forgotten him as he squared off against the Oriental wielding a butcher's cleaver.

Poontang found herself fairly evenly matched with her opponent. The mixed-race ghangster was cagey but when he committed himself to an attack he came in hard like he meant it. He had more reach than the small blonde and this was amplified by his longer weapon. But Poontang wasn't without a trick or two up her grey suede sleeve. Instead of attacking the man, she attacked the arm which held the hammer. It meant that she had to anticipate his strike but each time he lashed out at her there was a fraction of a second when the arm was extended and exposed. That was his vulnerable moment. It was a matter of hand/eye coordination, like swatting a wasp in flight.

Poontang dodged and sidestepped perilously, evading three or four hammer blows before she tried her counter. As he struck again her knife came up and its point pierced his forearm. He felt the sting and pulled his arm back quickly. It wasn't a conscious thought, just a reflex action, but it was the worse thing he could have done. It dragged the blade through his flesh down the length of his lower arm from below the elbow to the wrist; a deep gash that came very close to the artery.

Swearing in panic, he lashed out with a foot. It almost hit her in the cunt but she just about got her free hand down to block the kick. The parry knocked his kick aside but pain exploded in her hand as his shin collided with her fingers awkwardly. A knuckle cracked. Her opponent lurched backwards, his arm spilling a trail of blood, and Poontang looked down to see one of her fingers sticking out at an unnatural angle. It was broken.

Painter was confronting the skinhead woman whose double-edged knife had a stiletto blade designed for stabbing. The tattooed man had his stun gun in one hand and an extendable baton in the other. He used the baton in defensive side sweeps to deflect the woman's swift jabs and thrusts with the knife, awaiting his chance to get in with the stun gun. The first time that his adversary overextended a knife thrust Painter would be close enough to make contact with the electric weapon and that would be the end of the skinhead.

The combat between Mars and the Oriental, machete versus butcher's cleaver, was short and lethal. Mars brought his heavy blade down at the Oriental's head. The man had the nerve to stand under it and block it with his cleaver. The sound of steel on steel rang loud and sparks flew. The Oriental was strong enough to withstand the blow but it rooted him to the spot and Mars stepped into him, punching solidly. The fist caught the man flush on the nose and he rocketed back, too stunned to maintain his footing and went crashing to the ground. Mars was still moving forward under the momentum of his attack and he leapt into the air over the supine figure to come down with both feet into the man's abdomen. Mars' massive weight descending crushed everything beneath it. Internal organs burst, but it made no difference. Mars' machete buried itself in the Oriental's head.

The Cypriot came at Painter from behind, swinging his chain preparatory to striking. Painter hadn't seen him and was unaware of his stealthy approach. Painter's eyes were on the skinhead woman's knife. It flashed out and Painter whipped up his flexible baton which deflected the knife hand upwards. He lunged forward, thrusting with the stun-gun, and sent a pulse of high-voltage into the woman's face. There was a crackling flash as the electric current scrambled her brain. She folded up like a puppet whose strings had been cut, landing on her arse and then sprawling senseless. But the Cypriot had stepped into range, the chain a blur above his head. He was ready to unleash and it would be goodbye Painter.

But then the chain went hurtling off into the air, flying uselessly over the pedestrian precinct toward the alley. The reason for this was the thudding blow that PC522319 Khan had delivered to the back of the Cypriot's head with her riot stick. Whilst he had been creeping up behind Painter, the police officer had been creeping up behind him. Khan had cracked his head so hard that the Cypriot had dropped like a stone. He was either dead or unconscious. Either was good enough. He was out of the fight. Khan stood over the body, feeling the glory of battle in the power of her strong right arm. The Cypriot was the ghangster that she'd fought briefly earlier and it was satisfying to finish him off.

The mixed-race youth, having stepped back to nurse his bleeding arm, saw the other UN scattered on the ground. Fear made him hesitate and take his eyes off his opponent. That was all the time that Poontang needed to double him up with a kick to the belly. He crouched over as the wind went out of him and Poontang took his ankles out from underneath him with a foot sweep. He scrambled up on to his knees but now she had manoeuvred behind him, standing above the kneeling ghangster with her long serrated knife poised for the *coup de grace*. Deftly, she slit his throat. There was a sharp pain in her knuckle as she gripped his chin with her damaged hand, slashing her blade sideways across his windpipe with the other.

Poontang had no problem with killing. She believed in capital punishment, but on the condition that she was the person that decided who deserved to get the chop. She wouldn't have supported a legal death penalty because the judiciary weren't competent to make a decision as to the justice of a killing. But when it came to capital punishment on the streets, well, that was another matter. It could be more than necessary, it could be righteous.

She had no truck with the usual objections. There were fools who claimed that executing a murderer made you just as bad as they were. In Poontang's opinion, anyone who thought that must be morally illiterate. The murder was an offence, whereas the execution was a penalty for that offence. The difference was as simple as the distinction between crime and punishment. If a kidnapper abducts someone and holds them imprisoned against their will, that's an offence. If the kidnapper is convicted of the offence and put in prison, then the kidnapper is also being imprisoned against their will. But it would be foolish to say that their imprisonment was morally equivalent to the crime of abduction which they had committed. One was an offence, the other was punishment. Administering a punishment didn't make you as bad as the person you were punishing.

Even worse was the old chestnut that there was no point in killing the murderer because it would not bring their victim back to life. That argument was an absurdity which really pissed off Poontang. No one had ever claimed that it would bring the victim back to life. Who has ever said that by executing murderers you can resurrect their victims? Nobody. The old chestnut was arguing against a position that nobody has ever taken up. The death penalty was about doing justice, it was about retribution for wrongdoing, it was about proportionate punishment, it wasn't about undoing the crime by resurrecting the dead. No, Poontang was convinced of the merit and morality of a death penalty, just so long as she was the judge and jury.

The pedestrian precinct had fallen silent in the aftermath of battle. All the UN were dead or unconscious except for the tall young man who had lost his hand to Mars' machete and he had run off down the alley shrieking his lungs out. Now there was the momentary hush of shocked survival before a few small noises could be heard. Mars was quietly growling; a canine sound which was emitted from the back of his throat. Painter was softly chuckling to himself, happy to be alive. Poontang was breathing heavily, partly from exertion but mostly from anger.

Then Poontang burst into a short tirade of much louder vocalising, swearing like a public schoolboy drunk on cherry brandy. Her middle finger had been dislocated from the knuckle when she'd blocked that kick. She was cursing herself in ferocious ill-temper, reproaching herself for getting injured so unnecessarily. There had been nothing to gain for her in the fight and therefore no real purpose. She told herself to be less headstrong in future.

Still, there were worse things than a dislocated finger. The mixed-race guy who lay at her feet was pouring what appeared to be his entire bloodstream out on to the paving stones. The red pool grew larger and wider by the second. Poontang took a step back so that she wouldn't get any of it on her boots. They were expensive and her favourites.

PC522319 Khan was standing with her shoulders drooping, looking warily at the three Rudý, uncertain whether they were enemies or allies. They had definitely saved her life, but probably for reasons of their own and she couldn't be sure that they wouldn't now turn upon her. They were ghangsters after all. She would have made a run for it if she hadn't been so utterly exhausted.

Poontang looked across at the police constable. The officer nodded her silent thanks. Poontang jerked her head to the side to indicate that the copper had better get out of here. Khan stared at the ghangster as if she hadn't understood the gesture. Then she nodded gratefully a second time and faded out of the scene. She didn't take to her heels but she went swiftly. Khan didn't look back. She should be in the clear from here onward. Even so, there was no point in hanging around.

Painter strolled over to Poontang and raised his eyebrows. She held out her damaged hand, smiling her chagrin. He grasped her wrist firmly in his left hand and gently held the dislocated finger with his right. Without pausing for any preparation he popped the finger back into its socket. He did it casually, with one quick jerk, as if it were nothing. Poontang made a point of acting very casual too, to save face. As combat wounds go, it was a bit of an embarrassment. All the same, she wouldn't be giving anyone the finger with that hand for a while.

Chapter 9

The Last Generation

He was an idiot. He should know better than to make such a mistake. The channels were full of the outbreak of street wars from Peterborough to Kings Lynn, he'd been watching them for the last two days. It was sporadic, with bits and pieces of violence here and there, but the house fires had started and there was no doubt that it was going to get worse. Yet when Ritzy had been offered a quick cash job repairing the suspension on a Toyota, temptation had led him astray. He'd needed the money and it was a new customer who might bring him more business later, so he'd taken a chance. As a result, having done the job, he now found himself out in the open on the street in the middle of urban warfare. It was stupid of him. But there was nothing for it except to try to find his way home without getting caught in the crossfire.

It could literally be crossfire because from time to time Ritzy could hear gunfire in the distance. Not too far in the distance. Pretty close in fact. The sound wasn't like in the movies, it was duller and more metallic. It was a mechanical noise, as might be expected from a machine. Thud, thud, thud, rather than bang, bang, bang. Ritzy thought of a gun as a piece of equipment. It wasn't glamorous, it was just a tool being operated to perform the task of ending a life.

The availability of firearms, or the unavailability, varied across cultures and sub-cultures. Possession of guns had largely been illegal in England for years, going back to a time long before The Rupture, so there was little access to guns outside of criminal organisations. Most people rarely even saw a gun but in some ethnic communities firearms were much more common. Most militiamen didn't have access to a gun although some did, especially if they had contacts abroad. Guns were found more frequently among the ghetto gangs than among the militia because the former were criminal in their outlook and had contempt for legality, whereas the latter saw themselves as public law enforcers. Yet even in the ghangs there were plenty of young bloods who didn't have, and couldn't afford, a firearm. The majority of rioting took place without the use of guns, but in the worst of the rioting guns would appear and that's when you knew it was going to be really bad.

The sound of gunfire in the distance gave Ritzy a nauseous ache in the pit of his stomach. This latest bout of civil disorder bore all the signs of a serious breakdown. Ordinary citizens like himself didn't stand a chance when the activists brought out the hardware. He didn't own a gun and never had. It wasn't a part of his culture. Right now, Ritzy wished it had been.

The Americans used to have a euphemism for a gun which Ritzy thought made a lot of sense at times like these. A gun was called "the old equaliser". If nobody had guns, then any physical combat was a battle of bodily strength and physical ability. In that situation, the strong can oppress the weak. But if the weak had a gun, then they were in a position to defend themselves against anybody. A gun was an "equaliser". It made the physically weak as strong as anyone else when it came to self-defence. When people had no access to guns, it didn't protect the weak, it made them vulnerable to the physically strong. But if everyone had guns, you had the seeming paradox that there were a lot of gun deaths yet the weak felt safer. It wasn't really a paradox. There were a lot of gun deaths because the strong could be killed as well as the weak. There was greater equality of death.

In England the illegality of guns meant that for years the only people who'd had them were those who were willing to break the law; the criminals. Gun ownership was very one-sided. The predators had guns and the prey didn't. If one side had guns and the other side didn't, then the game was over. The weak had no option but to surrender. Of course, it was always said that surrender was a more civilized course of action than defending yourself with violence. Sadly, the dividing line between being cowardly and being civilized had always been rather blurred.

Ritzy would have felt a lot safer on his journey home if he'd been armed with something more than just his bag of mechanic's tools. He noticed that there was no traffic in motion. The roads behind him had cars moving normally but in the road ahead of him the vehicles were parked and nothing was moving. It meant that no one was driving in the direction that Ritzy was walking. He was getting closer to the violence.

Moving fast, although not running because he didn't want to get out of breath, he scuttled down the dozen roads that stood between himself and his own front door. His touchpad would be of no use in negotiating a route. There were large mobs on the prowl, roving around, and recognised territories meant nothing when communities came out in strength. As the diverse streams of humanity shifted in the neighbourhoods, disrespecting boundaries, safety and jeopardy were like the whirling currents and eddies of a fast flowing river. A tingle went up Ritzy's back. The atmosphere was weird, the way it had been during The Rupture when everyone was in a constant state of defensive paranoia. Being a man alone it was evident that Ritzy didn't belong to any of the groups that were patrolling the streets. He was a solitary figure. Anyone could see that he wasn't part of a militia or a ghang.

He reached into his tool bag and took out the largest of his screwdrivers. It wasn't much of a weapon but it looked impressive. From here on, he carried it openly. It was more for show than anything else. He might be less likely to be set upon if he looked ready to put up a fight. The crucial thing was not to look weak; not to look like easy meat. He bowled along, walking briskly, and moving his shoulders to appear muscular and ready for action.

Ritzy lived in Anglia, the *East Anglia Metro*. It was primarily English and East European but with significant districts of greater diversity. Within that diversity there were Pakistani, Indian, Punjabi and Bengali communities but there had been a steady drain of Asian residents in the last year or two as they relocated to the adjacent *East Midlands Metro* where Asians were in the majority. Unfortunately, Ritzy's home town was close to the indeterminate border between Anglia and the East Midlands so it was the front line for the power play that was going on at the moment.

The Islamic imperialists in the two Midlands Metros were unhappy about the diminishing Muslim population in the *East Anglia Metro* and they were naturally in close contact with the UK Jihad in Anglia. As they saw it, the Polish, Russian, Romanian and Bulgarian communities were forcing the Asians out of the region and they had resolved to do something about it.

They were bussing in Jihadis from Little Asia to bolster up their presence in the neighbouring Metro. It was unusual to use buses to move people around because most folk preferred to defend their own districts rather than disperse their manpower into other areas. Besides, buses were too easy a target for petrol bombs. They were big and slow. You couldn't miss them. It was like aiming at a barn door. But the political agenda for Jihad was to claim *more* territory, not *surrender* territory by letting their people move out. So the UKJ and various other Jihad organisations had decided to offer their support to their Muslim brothers and sisters in Anglia to avoid losing any more territory in the region.

This strategy was judged by the various non-Muslim communities to be too aggressive a development for them to let it pass unchallenged. The Euros in Anglia had joined forces with the militants among the ethnically English to form a united front against the Jihadis. With a certain sense of irony they had called this union the Kufr Alliance. They mobilized in numbers, putting thousands on the streets, and from that point onwards the stakes had grown higher and higher.

Ritzy had no fear of the Kufr Alliance, of course. As an Englishman they presented no threat to him and maybe they would even defend him if they saw him in trouble. It was the UKJ and their supporters who might cut off his head if he ran into them. The other major danger was that he would come across some random group of thugs or ghangsters who happened to take a fancy to carving him up because they decided that they didn't like the look of him.

There was an explosion a few streets away. A huge plume of black smoke rose above the rooftops. Ritzy muttered a curse out loud to himself. The message in the gunfire hadn't lied, this wasn't just a riot in the offing, this was going to be war. For the next few hours the city would be a combat zone.

The noise was growing louder. From the streets behind those rooftops the burglar alarms and the car alarms were shrieking their elongated whines. Their clamour was the soundtrack of modern life. Background muzak that everyone ignored until it irked them enough to complain about it. But the whole city seemed to be screaming alarms at the moment and the ubiquity of their strident outcry demanded to be taken seriously. The closer to home he got, the worse it became. But noise was the least of it. The fear on the faces of pedestrians told the tale. Fear wasn't always a reliable indicator, the hysteria of panic being contagious, but on the features of those he passed in the street Ritzy could see that combination of fear and determination which was a sure sign that their thoughts were fixed on self-preservation.

A woman was running toward him, chivvying her two children ahead of her. They were obeying without question because they could see the haunted expression on her face, just as Ritzy could see it, and they were experiencing that special insecurity which children feel when they understand that their parent may not have the strength to protect them from the world. The authority figure in their life had been exposed as a fragile human being running scared. The anxious kids were scurrying along on their little legs, hurrying home, hoping that it might provide them with refuge.

So was Ritzy, on his longer legs. He was running now, not sprinting but keeping up a steady trot. It drew no attention to him because people had other things to look at. The fires in the buildings were getting more numerous, although many were small enough for the residents to extinguish them. The fire brigade had made no appearance yet, they were too busy elsewhere no doubt, but the locals had learned to be ready with their garden hosepipes and most of the smaller fires were being put out before they took hold properly. It was a different matter with the bombings.

Ritzy was almost home. There was pandemonium in his street. A great heaving commotion of bodies was milling about, caused by people evacuating their houses. No wonder. Half the block was in various stages of burning. Ritzy barged and elbowed his way down the street, receiving verbal abuse from many but no physical violence. People were in too much of a state of shock to do more than swear.

He guessed at once what had happened. Someone had firebombed the small synagogue that was tucked away discreetly between the furniture retail warehouse and the Polish grocery. It didn't take much guesswork. Jews had been under such sustained attacks from roving gangs of Islamic fascists for so long that most Jews in western Europe had fled to Israel or America. The authorities had done virtually nothing to halt these Jihadi pogroms and the Jewish diaspora had added another million or more to the Israeli population. But those who had remained in Europe were determined not to be driven out from the homes that their families had lived in for many generations. As an Englishman, Ritzy could sympathize, being in the same situation himself. But the Jews were a particular target of the western Jihad and so those Jews who refused to leave had the tightest security of anyone in the diversified society.

Despite this, it was almost impossible for anyone to entirely protect themselves against petrol bombs, especially as the Jews were no longer present in the country in sufficient numbers to maintain gated communities. They occupied very small areas within the nooks and crannies of diversification and kept a low profile. The local non-Jewish residents helped their neighbours to keep the secret, partly out of genuine concern and partly out of self-interest. After all, they were living next door to a prime target. But no matter how small the Jewish communities made themselves, their persecutors always seemed to find them sooner or later. The synagogue that was a few doors down from Ritzy's apartment block was so nondescript that any passing pedestrian would not have known it for what it was. Nonetheless the Jihadis had identified it and, as a result, it was ablaze. All the buildings around it were on fire too. The fascists had evidently had some petrol bombs to spare.

Then Ritzy saw it. His own apartment block was on fire. Sheets of flame filled the windows and something which was alight inside was giving the fire a deep red colour, with tongues of yellow spitting out from it. Ritzy took in the sight at a glance as he ran on toward his home. It wouldn't be his home much longer. He was a few minutes away from destitution and homelessness. But something else took precedence. Ritzy didn't know whether or not any of the Red Squirrels were inside and trapped in the fire. They might all be out at work or elsewhere but he couldn't be sure since none of them exactly kept regular working hours. He couldn't see any of them in the crowd.

He dropped his tool bag and dashed through the front door into the burning building. It wasn't bravery really, it was thoughtlessness. He just didn't stop to think. His mates might be inside. Maybe they weren't but maybe they were. Ritzy had to know, he had to check. He was through the front door before he'd even wondered whether he might get killed himself.

The heat hit him so hard it was a physical blow which almost stopped him in his tracks. He had to force his way through it, as if the weight of gravity had suddenly doubled. The arson attack had been made from ground level and the fire had apparently spread vertically up the outer shell of the building, extending inward as it climbed. But at least one bomb had been thrown through the front door because the wall up the side of the staircase was alight from floor to ceiling. Ritzy bounded up the stairs two at a time. The flames were everywhere. The scorching temperature was overpowering, the air searing his lungs. He couldn't see in the darkness of the smoke which choked him, its acrid filth making him cough. He bent low as he ran, keeping under the billowing black clouds that filled the ceiling.

He heard terrified screams coming from the apartment of the DiD and her kid as he rushed by. The question flashed through his mind: why didn't the stupid bitch get herself and her child outside? But the question was rhetorical. Ritzy wasn't here for them. Flinching as the whips of fire lashed at him, he stomped up the next flight of stairs, slowing down because of the lack of oxygen to his lungs, and reached the door of his apartment. He almost attacked the door with his screwdriver to jemmy it open by brute force but had the sense to realise that it would be quicker to just use the key in his pocket. It would be stupid to get all macho about it. Ritzy dropped the screwdriver and fished the key out of the pocket of his baggy shorts. His hand shook as he tried to insert the key and he fought to quell his panic. Nothing would kill him quicker than panic. He got the key into the lock and opened the door, shouting:

"Is anyone in here!? It's me, Ritzy! Anyone!? Anyone!?"

The apartment wasn't alight but it was full of thick smoke. It got into his eyes and was making them water. Tears were pouring down his cheeks but he wasn't aware of it, only of the stinging sensation as he blinked repeatedly trying to clear his vision. Ritzy bent so low to get underneath the smoke that he was almost crawling. It was hard to make out the geography of the room. He'd lived here for years and yet now he was completely disoriented, blundering around blindly in his own home. He searched as best he could. The place seemed to be empty.

But no it wasn't. There was Barker, asleep or unconscious on the sofa. Asphyxiation, probably. He'd already been overcome by the smoke. Ritzy tried to slap him awake but it was no use, the man was unresponsive. Lacking any alternative, Ritzy grabbed his friend under the arms and hauled Barker up over his shoulder in a fireman's lift. God, he was heavy. The body swung over Ritzy's right shoulder, the legs hanging down in front. With a thirteen stone man weighing him down, it was certain that Ritzy couldn't carry anything else out of this nightmare, so he spent no more time searching. He had his own life and Barker's life to save.

Labouriously he carried Barker out of the apartment and along the passage. There was no way to crouch low, burdened as he was, and he had to breath in the gaseous fog. It was suffocating. He staggered down the blazing stairs, almost fainting from the poisonous super-heated air and trying desperately to keep the shifting weight of Barker's body balanced on his shoulder like a sack of eels. He mustn't drop him or he'd never be able to pick him up again.

Ritzy couldn't find his footing, stamping and clumping down the steps, roaring aloud to bolster his nerve against the terror and the gruelling exertion. He bashed into the wall of the landing below but ploughed on, stumbling forward, and turned down the remaining flight of stairs. The bare flesh of his lower right arm felt like it was frying. Christ, it hurt! He felt for the next step with his foot. Where was the bloody stair? His eyes were streaming tears. Everything was smoke. He was blind! Bellowing incoherently he lumbered onward, blundering down the steps, nearly falling but keeping his feet under him by his own momentum. It was a hellishly strenuous effort. He hit the ground floor and shuffled frantically for the gap in the wall that was the open doorway.

Ritzy reeled out of the building, as soot-blackened as a coal miner, his flesh and clothing scorched. Lurching drunkenly and panting for breath, he made it passed the kerb and into the road before his knees wobbled beneath him and Barker slid off his shoulder. Ritzy caught him but struggled to hold him. A couple of guys came forward from out of the crowd to help. They eased Barker down on to the tarmac and laid him out on his back. Ritzy took a few unsteady paces, swaying dizzily, no longer in control of his limbs. He bent down, bracing his hands on his knees, and sucked air into his scalded lungs, weeping and puking.

The two guys were checking Barker's vital signs and discovered that he was still breathing. Others from the crowd gathered around him but none of them knew what medical attention they should give him and so they just hovered over him uselessly. A couple of minutes went by with everybody talking at once but nobody doing anything. Then Barker's eyes flickered and he slowly began to return to life before suddenly half-sitting up and retching his guts out in a massive fit of coughing.

Ritzy slumped down on his arse, knackered. He'd only been inside the building for ten or twelve minutes but he felt like he'd run a marathon. Everything ached. He'd strained something in his back and there were angry red patches on his bare forearms and calves where he'd been burnt. Sleeveless shirts and baggy shorts weren't the smart style for firefighting duties. He'd lost his bowler hat when he'd hoisted Barker over his shoulder. That would be ashes by now. Fuck it, he could get another one.

Someone took hold of the back of his neck but he was almost too weary to bother to see who it was. He looked up and around, squinty-eyed, and saw Captain leaning over him. His friend said something to him but there was too much pounding inside Ritzy's head to hear what it was. His pulse was like a jack-hammer beating wildly amid a blizzard of tinnitus. Chippy appeared beside Captain and they spoke, nodding agreement about something, then disappeared as they went to examine Barker. Ritzy hung his head and waited for the storm in his cranium to subside.

Chippy had been out of the house when the conflagration started because he'd had to drive his catering van to a safer location. With so many hostiles swarming, the van was too tempting a target to leave it in the little side street where it was normally parked. Captain had gone with him for protection. They'd left the vehicle in a vacant industrial unit. If it were found there, it would certainly be torched but at least it was less likely to be noticed in an abandoned area. It was a matter of luck whether the van survived the night. By the time that Chippy and Captain had walked back home, they found the building in flames with Ritzy and Barker in the road outside surrounded by their neighbours.

Some firefighters turned up but it was too late for them to do much. They moved the Red Squirrels and the rest of the crowd about fifty yards down the street because the fire was so all-consuming that it would soon undermine the structure of the building and the whole thing would come crashing down. Sure enough, fifteen minutes later there was a terrific creaking sound and the three storey structure collapsed like a house of cards. Some of the buildings adjacent had subsided into a heap too. The synagogue had been burned flat down to the ground.

By this time Barker was somewhat recovered. Captain and Chippy had carried him over to the "Adolescent" clothes and perfumery boutique and sat him up against the wall. The boutique for young women of fashion was completely unmarked, having survived the violence unscathed despite the rest of the street resembling an urban battlefield. Barker was aware of what was going on around him now. His face was pallid under the smoke-blackening but the rhythm of his rasping breathing had steadied. He stared up in appeal at Chippy.

"Gravy?" asked Barker in a hoarse voice.

"Yes, Gravy, where is Gravy?" said Chippy with deliberate over-emphasis. The street was full of noise and Barker's head must be spinning. It was necessary to speak very clearly despite the fear contained in the question. When Chippy and Captain had left home earlier Gravy had been sleeping in his bedroom. But had he remained there?

"Barker," said Chippy almost shouting, "was Gravy still in the apartment or did he leave?"

"Bedroom," said Barker. "Asleep."

So there it was. That settled it. End of story. Gravy had been in the apartment when the firebombing had occurred. They pieced together the basic facts from Barker as his ability to speak improved. There weren't many facts but they were sufficient. Barker had dozed off on the sofa whilst surfing his channels and Gravy had been snoring peacefully immediately before that. Barker had heard him because the bedroom door was open. Gravy had a habit of not closing doors. They'd made fun of him about it on many occasions. But they wouldn't be doing so in future because Gravy didn't have one. There couldn't be any doubt about it. A brother had fallen.

Although the bedroom door had been open Ritzy hadn't seen him in there because of all the smoke. In any case, Ritzy couldn't possibly have saved both Barker and Gravy, and at least he had been spared the agony of having to choose between them. As it was, they'd lost a friend.

They didn't talk about it any further. It was too painful. And there wasn't anything to say. Words couldn't change a fact. No matter how much the truth hurts, it remains true. They heard later from the firefighters that twenty-seven people from their street had been killed in the bombing all told, including the DiD and her kid. She hadn't made it out and now nobody would ever know why not. The same could be said for the other twenty-five. God knows how many had died across the city.

Captain saw John from the "E Pluribus Unum" trudging down the street through the disorderly swarm of humanity. He was carrying a large canvas bag and had a rucksack on his back. There was a peculiar stiffness to the way that he was walking. It didn't look quite natural. There was a touch of the zombie about him. But that was true of a lot of people in the crowd today. Captain drew the attention of the others to John's approach and Ritzy said: "He'll never find us amongst this lot."

Captain waved and shouted to let John see them amid the multitude but John didn't appear to notice so Captain went to fetch him. The other Red Squirrels saw him meet the Canadian and watched as they spoke together for a while. Then Captain embraced John in a sympathetic bear hug and the others immediately knew that something was wrong. Something bad.

It turned out to be even worse than they'd feared. John could scarcely get the words passed his lips when he told them. The harsh reality of it stuck in his throat.

The four "E Pluribus Unum" guys had been sharing a meal in a restaurant. It was an occasional treat they allowed themselves. But today they'd been in the wrong place at the wrong time. A suicide martyr was eating in the restaurant with a monstrous nail bomb in a plastic holdall. The weapon was well-chosen for an enclosed area full of people. The Jihadis had been very efficient about causing maximum damage. The anti-personnel explosive device could cut a swathe through human flesh as it blasted nails, ball bearings, and other small bits of metal in all directions for the maximum loss of life.

John had been halfway through his plate of shellfish when the martyr had suddenly stood up from a table in the middle of the room and bawled "Allahu Akbar!". The killer hadn't looked remotely like the usual Jihadi, he was a fat clean-shaven white guy. But you often couldn't tell nowadays, with all the reverts. Then the force of the bomb blast had knocked John out of his chair.

He'd shaken himself awake from the concussion a couple of seconds later to discover that he was the only one of the "E Pluribus Unum" left alive. He didn't have a scratch on him apart from a gash in his shoulder. Somehow all that flying shrapnel had missed him except for one small piece of metal lodged next to the end of his collarbone. The other three guys, along with most of the patrons of the restaurant, had been ripped to shreds. John's survival made no sense to him, but then these things never did.

Nahas the Namibian, Mikelis the Latvian, and Derec the Welshman, all lay in the rubble of overturned tables and shattered crockery. The death was indiscriminate. John had sleepwalked away from the corpses of his friends, having no way to deal with what had just happened. He'd walked robotically for half a mile before a recognisable thought had occurred in his head. The only thing he'd been able to think of to do amidst the turmoil of his grief and bewilderment was to find the Red Squirrels. The two groups had agreed a pact of mutual support and John had acted upon this thought simply because it was all that his mind had to hold on to. He had clung to it as a definite course of action. It gave him a place to go. Otherwise he'd have been walking around in circles.

So he'd plodded numbly home and packed a bunch of his stuff into a bag and a rucksack, scarcely aware of what he was doing. He'd almost finished before he thought to pull the little piece of shrapnel out of his shoulder and dress his wound. Dazed with shock, he'd overlooked it up until then. Curiously, it didn't seem to hurt. But he'd washed it and stuck a handkerchief over it with sticking plaster as a sort of bandage. Just to soak up the bleeding. He'd put on a clean shirt. Then he'd gone in search of the Red Squirrels. What else was there to do?

John's eyes were unfocused as he mumbled his tale, skipping over the full story and stating the essentials in a dull monotone with odd random details included arbitrarily. His face was vacant and drained of colour. His normally soft coffee skin was sallow and waxen. He looked completely shell-shocked. His friends had been dead for a little over ninety minutes and he was functioning on autopilot. It was surprising that he could function at all.

Captain put an arm around John's shoulders and told him that he could stay with them for as long as he needed to, which produced a chorus of agreement from the others. But it also raised the question of where exactly they were all going to stay. Their former home was a smoking ruin.

"Our apartments are undamaged," said John reluctantly, "you could all live there."

His reluctance derived from the strong feeling that he himself would prefer never to set foot in the place again. He'd rather live anywhere else than to take up residence in the rooms that he had shared with Derec, Nahas, and Mikelis, with the ghosts of their memory haunting every inch of the place.

"Or we could just leave the city entirely," said Ritzy in a tone of voice which suggested a similar desire to John's, that he wanted to get as far away from old memories as he could. "We've discussed it often enough. This civil war isn't over by a long shot, there'll be plenty more of this to come."

"It's time to get out of this sewer," agreed Chippy. "I've got the van. Let's make a fresh start somewhere else."

"We should go to the north-west, up to Cumbria," volunteered Barker who'd been advocating for ages that they all move to a more ethnically English part of the country. "The Lake District is the place for us."

"What about Devon and Cornwall?" asked Captain. "They're bigger. More space."

"There's a lot of poverty in the south-west," said Chippy. "Barker's right. Let's try the Lake District."

Captain might have reminded him that there was a lot of poverty everywhere. But it was pot-luck whether Cumbria or Cornwall might prove the better option. He shrugged his shoulders, accepting the majority decision.

And as quickly and simply as that, it was decided. They would get out of this city and they would take John with them. The stateless Canadian who wasn't allowed to return to his own country across the Atlantic had nowhere else to go and no other community to be a part of, so it was okay with him.

They didn't bother trying to recover any of their possessions from the smoking ruins. Everything of value would have been burnt to a cinder and they had no desire to clamber dangerously over the rubble searching for it. They didn't want to walk through Gravy's crematorium, picking the bones from his tomb. It was better to leave it all behind.

Chippy led them back to where he'd parked his catering van in the vacant industrial unit. It hadn't been disturbed in the short time since he'd left it. The vehicle had a new purpose now. It was their escape capsule. They were refugees seeking asylum. But where might they find it now that the First World had become the Third World?

They all climbed aboard for the charabanc ride. It was heigh-ho for the Lake District to find a place to live among whatever was left of the English there.

*   *   *

Diana Bates looked out from the window of her upstairs bedroom and shivered. The rioting that was sweeping the country had finally reached her own neighbourhood. Small gangs of youths, some of them little more than children, were running through the streets out there and cars were burning. She could see it from where she stood in her own home. It seemed impossible that it could happen here. How could such violence occur in her comfortable suburb? There were very few young people who even lived in this area. Where had these rioters come from?

The flickering of the fires outside cast highlights and shadows on her face as she stared through the window, her drawn and overtired features reflected in the glass. Her expression creased into fear and disgust. She felt old and weak. She was old and weak. Her glory days were over. The world had turned, as the wretched thing always did sooner or later, taking her glory with it.

Diana had married in middle age. He had been a schoolteacher like herself and the kind of man with enough sense to know that she was in charge. He didn't indulge in any puerile masculine posturing. They had shared the same political perspective, agreed on the correct way to live, and they had managed to stay together for twenty years. She and her husband had retired when The Rupture changed everything and the school system abandoned so many of the political policies which had been central to Diana's career; central to her identity. Her heart had gone out of the work. They had taken stock of their situation and since the combined assets of their marriage permitted them to retire, even without the pensions that they'd lost when the economy collapsed and the pension companies went bankrupt, they had decided that the time had come to find a safe haven to spend their declining years. This house in its suburban village setting had been their refuge. Diana had always believed in having a space to secure her own safety.

A lifelong advocate of multiculturalism, she had never actually lived in a multicultural area of the city and in retirement she had relocated even further out into the suburbs at the very edge of the urban sprawl. It was almost a rural area. She had never dreamt that the conflicts which had torn the cities apart could reach her here. She had paid close attention to the growing civil disorder in contemporary society and naturally she had always been vocally on the side of the oppressed underdog. She had blamed the white man and excused everyone else, same as always. But that had been on the tacit understanding that the oppressed underdog would never threaten her or her kind. Diana's support had been conditional on the belief that the protesters should recognise that people such as herself were inviolable. Although she was white, affluent, privileged and empowered, she had always been a vociferous campaigner and activist for the oppressed underdog, so how could they turn on her just because they were hungry and homeless? She had always been on their side.

It should never have come to this. It wasn't the political programme of multiculturalism that was at fault, it was this new attitude of multi-sectarianism, and that had been caused by the refusal of white racists to accept and embrace diversity. It was the white racists who had twisted multiethnicity into this internecine sectarianism. Even then, all this violence could have been avoided if there hadn't been an economic collapse and that was solely the fault of the capitalist 1%. Only the white racists blamed the riots on multiculturalism. Were they blind as well as ignorant and prejudiced? The true source of all this violence was the same as ever. You only had to look at who it was out there in the streets smashing and burning and looting. It was men. Young men. As always it was men who committed all the violence. Hadn't feminists like herself been telling everyone that for years?

Something had to be done about it but there didn't seem to be anyone left who was in a position to do anything. Diana couldn't even get any assistance from the authorities. She had repeatedly tried to telephone the police for protection. There were cars on fire in the street outside, for goodness sake! But she hadn't been able to get through on the phone because the police emergency number was constantly busy. The lines must be jammed by all the other calls they were receiving from people in a panic, which was understakable of course, but provision should have been made for this. The police were grossly at fault for failing to protect ordinary law-abiding citizens like her. As a sixty-eight year old woman, surely any civilized country would want to put her safety first?

It was unacceptable. But apparently there wasn't anything she could do about it. There was no one to whom she could complain. There was no one of whom she could demand that they set things right for her. All she had left to protect her now was her elderly husband and, honestly, what good was he likely to be? At his age, how was *he* going to protect her?

The problem was that with a national debt in the trillions there was no way for the country to continue to fund concessions that would buy off the discontents of minority communities. That had been the policy of the ruling elites for decades, and yet things had only gotten worse, not better. Diana couldn't comprehend how that policy had failed, but the fact remained that for years her social class had felt their grip on power slipping. Even if the state finances had been able to borrow some more money from somewhere, the ethnic minorities were no longer willing to be bought off with mere concessions, they wanted political power. So the ruling elites had increasingly been forced to surrender their authority in an attempt to placate the political leaders of the various cultures in the country. But that was a finite strategy. By incrementally conceding power to them, you eventually reached the point where they had more power than you did. So then what did you do? Could you ask for some of that power back? Concession was *your* policy, not *theirs*. Central government had become a redundant irrelevance now that the majority of power was in the hands of the Metros.

In retirement, Diana had watched horrified at the direction in which pluralism had taken society. She would not have believed it if she hadn't seen it with her own eyes. Non-negotiable features of the agenda she had endorsed all her life had been surrendered, and what made it so unbelievable was that it wasn't the cis-gendered straight white males of the patriarchy who had demanded this surrender, it was the very immigrant populations whom Diana had always championed.

She had witnessed the re-criminalisation of homosexuality, this time for lesbians as well as gay men, as a concession to the homophobia of the Islamic communities. She had seen the growth and proliferation of the ethnic militias; armed men flexing their male militarism in self-appointed power over civilian populations. She had listened to the news items about debates in the Metro legislatures in which the status of being transgender was denied legal recognition, and other debates implementing reforms to the abortion laws which set birth control back a hundred years in some regions of the country. She had read reports from reputable sources revealing the extent of the criminality and influence of Eastern European mafias in cities like London and Manchester whose control of widespread organised prostitution was fully the equal to that of any of the mafias in Moscow or St Petersburg. A generation of young women now had to live in fear. Not the type of fear which Diana had so long campaigned against; the fear of being judged by your body image or the fear of being catcalled in the street. No, this was the kind of fear which made a woman accept sex-slavery in order to avoid having her throat cut.

The political arena had been reduced to the crudest power grabs and bargain basement sell-offs and sell-outs. The major ethnic groups struggled for dominance both within Metros and between Metros. And what on earth would become of the future if the Jihadis, one of the most ubiquitous and powerful of the various cultural influences these days, were to come out on top? How had this happened? How had her own political programme, which was unquestionably ideologically correct, somehow led to a situation where people like herself were forced into a naked betrayal of their own professed beliefs?

But she didn't blame herself. Her intentions had always been pure and she judged herself on her intentions, not on the consequences of her actions. Her generation had tried their best to do what was right. If it had all gone to hell, it was none of their doing. Besides, even if others of her generation were to blame, Diana wasn't. She was convinced that she herself had never betrayed her principles, regardless of what others were now doing.

In a sense this last thought was true, although not in the way that she meant it. Diana hadn't changed. She was as rigid as she'd ever been. She remained authoritarian in the name of tolerance, illiberal in the name of liberalism, conformist in the name of diversity, and female supremacist in the name of gender equality. It was a position she had always found congenial. It defined her. She had not deviated from it.

But cultures other than her own were now in control of the Metros and could exercise more power than the former cultural establishment, so Diana and her peers had done the only thing left available to them. As a social class they had cut and run, hoping to find a refuge in the country backwaters where there were still a few pockets of the English culture which they had spent their lives despising and disparaging. It was a bitter pill to swallow. The only thought which gave Diana any comfort was that at least she had never had children. This was no world to bring children into.

She turned from the bedroom window to go downstairs to the lounge. With so much danger outside she felt fidgety and couldn't settle. She kept roaming around the house as if looking for a place to sit down but not feeling comfortable anywhere. Her husband was asleep in the spare room, the great useless lump. She could hear his snores through the door. He spent more time in there than in any other room of the house these days, but Diana wasn't going to have him reading his disgusting novels anywhere else in her home. Literature had always been his academic subject and he refused to relinquish his pleasure in the kind of books of which all decent people disapproved. Awful things like Hubert Selby's "Last Exit to Brooklyn", and Henry Miller's "Tropic of Cancer", and William Burroughs "Naked Lunch", and even Vladimir Nabikov's paedophile filth "Lolita". They all contained gender attitudes that were unacceptable to anyone with a proper appreciation of human feelings. Diana had taken the position that she wouldn't have them in her house. But he had kept whining like a little crybaby about how they were great literature. How could they be, when they objectified women and depicted scenes of violence against women?

In the end, and in a spirit of compromise that went against her better judgement, Diana had agreed to his reading them if he must, but he could do so in the spare room because she never went in there. That could be his room. She thought of it as his 'pornography room'. Yet how often did she hear him snoring away over his book? So much for their literary quality. He couldn't even stay awake while reading them, the silly old fool. But husbands were a trial. They never really understood, no matter how hard they tried, because they were men. He may have spent his life supporting feminist causes but the fact always remained that he was still a man. Even if he wasn't very much of a man when it came to protecting his wife, she thought, remembering the violence taking place outside.

As she entered the lounge there was a news report playing quietly in the background. It was on her usual channel. There was no mainstream media any more. Pluralism had located everyone within a cultural niche. The channels were the media nowadays. Diana had her favourites like everyone else.

The news report was commenting upon the recent startling statistic that Jewish emigration over the last ten years had been so extreme that it was estimated that by 2050 there would no longer be any Jews in England. They mentioned how the last time that the Jewish community had left the country entirely was in the 13th century when they were expelled by King Edward 1st, and it was for the same reason both times. Their current exodus was under the duress of a rampantly rising anti-Semitism that had grown ever worse over the last thirty years. The reporter drew a comparison between the future absence of Jews in England and many of the nations of the middle-east where, generally speaking, there were no Jews and very few Christians.

Diana had always been stridently pro-Palestinian and anti-Israeli, of course, but she still found it incredible that events could have gone so far as for the news to be discussing a Jewish pogrom in England in the 21st century. It was contrary to fundamental beliefs which for her had always been absolute certainties. Diversity made the country more tolerant. Diversity brought us all together in common cause. Diversity was our strength. For Islamic immigration to have become a force for non-inclusive religious segregation was beyond belief. Maybe it wasn't true. Maybe it was just media talk. Maybe it was the white Nazis who were driving out the Jews, not the Muslims. Yes, maybe it was the white Nazis. But, comforting though this thought was, she did not find it wholly convincing.

It made Diana think of the first time that she'd heard a member of her own social circle criticise mass immigration. It was about ten years ago and it had been such a shock to her that the incident had lodged in her memory. Diana had been at the home of her friend Juna whose daughter Rhiannon still lived with her although she was a thirty year old single mother and certainly ought to have been provided with a home of her own by the state. It was shameful the way that the government persecuted single mothers. Juna's granddaughter, Alyssa, was of primary school age and she had been sitting at the kitchen table doing her homework assignment on the question: "In how many ways does multiculturalism benefit society?"

Alyssa had asked her mother Rhiannon for an opinion on how she could best show that all opposition to multiculturalism was inspired by prejudice. She had already included the point that her schoolteacher, Ms Hassid, had emphasised in class that no one but a racist could object to, say, Brick Lane in London being totally Bengali Muslim because in an earlier generation the same area had been totally Jewish. After a time the Jewish community had moved out and the Bengali community had moved in. The only difference, she said, was the colour of their skins. So that showed how only a racist could object to the change.

To Diana's astonishment, Rhiannon had not been supportive of the teacher's position, nor did she approve of the assignment topic her daughter had been given. Rhiannon had said:

"It's a very different situation now, darling. But it's not different because of skin colour, it's different because of the numbers. Jews have been living in England, fitting in but still keeping their own identity, for absolutely ages. And after all that time there are still only a quarter of a million Jews in the country. There are four million Muslims in the country even though Muslims have had communities in this country for a much shorter time than the Jewish communities have been here. There are already sixteen times as many Muslims as Jews. Which is a poor look-out for the Jews, if you ask me."

Diana had been so taken aback that she'd just sat there and stared. It had brought home to her in one blinding instant that the world was changing radically, and not in a good way. This was the daughter of her friend Juna. This was a young woman who ought to be everything which Diana's generation had taught women to be. How could she be speaking the hate-speech of the far-right extremists? She knew Rhiannon to be a committed feminist, so where was this racist Islamophobia coming from?

Like most multicultis, Diana had never given any serious thought to what the future would actually become because she had taken it for granted that with people like herself in charge, things could only get better. They were the progressives. Their political agenda must inevitably lead to the future they envisaged. She had thought only of the future she wanted, not the future she was most likely to get. Rhiannon's refusal to endorse multiculturalism had been Diana's first indication that the future might not be everything that she had expected of it.

"But in how many ways does multiculturalism benefit society, mommy?" Alyssa had asked.

"Never mind the benefits for the moment, darling," Rhiannon had replied, "we should be more concerned with the social costs."

Diana had sat immobile and mute as her friend's daughter had guided little Alyssa toward a political standpoint that no one in Diana's social circle would have dared to think, let alone utter, in Diana's day. Incredibly, the single mother had argued an anti-multiculturalist line from a feminist perspective.

As a feminist Rhiannon rejected a policy of multiculturalism on the grounds that it was destroying women's rights and entitlements. It was in direct conflict with feminism. In the past feminists and multiculturalists had always assumed that the two ideologies were naturally and easily compatible. But Islam had proven that they were not. Attempts at Islamic-Feminism had been, as far as Rhiannon was concerned, merely a way of subsuming feminism under the patriarchal attitudes of Islam. In her view, Islamic-Feminism was all Islam and no feminism.

Rhiannon had come to understand that the policies of feminism and multiculturalism conflicted because the former lays down universal rules of conduct about the treatment of women, whereas the latter lays down culturally relative rules of conduct. The multiculturalist must respect other cultures and must not impose their own cultural beliefs upon others. But feminism required all men to obey its strictures regardless of what culture they came from. To Rhiannon's distress, whenever the two came into conflict it was always multiculturalism which took precedence. For years there had been recurrent exposures of the presence of Muslim rape gangs in cities across the country. These exposures ought to have been an opportunity for highly vocal feminist agitation against the iniquities of masculine rape-culture, but feminists had remained largely silent on the subject as if their critique of rape-culture did not extend to non-white non-western men. Feminists had said nothing because the fear of being accused of racism and Islamophobia had shut their mouths.

It had effectively silenced them, too, on Muslim women being imprisoned in the home within marriage. True, there had been a lot of feminist outrage against female genital mutilation but what had it achieved? Those communities who practiced it continued to do so. They valued the beliefs and values of their own ethnic culture above the beliefs and values of feminism. If anything, the prevalence of FGM was getting worse.

Not only that but mass immigration was promoting the occurrence of sexual offences. The statistics for rapes committed by western men were steadily declining due to the estrangement of the sexes in ethnically western communities, but the statistics for rapes committed by men from non-western immigrant communities were steadily increasing. Indeed, in some places they were skyrocketing. As a feminist, how could Rhiannon be expected to endorse a policy of importing rapists into the country?

A tirade of discontent had poured out of Rhiannon along these lines, including many issues that Diana had thought were inappropriate to be mentioned to so young a child as Alyssa. But Rhiannon had a passionate commitment to the cause of women that was the equal of Diana's at the same age. Rhiannon had a long list of injustices which she laid at the door of mass immigration, and especially Islamic immigration, and this had forced her into the realisation that feminism and multiculturalism were ideologies which were in opposition to each other.

More than that, she had even been forced to acknowledge the colonialist nature of the spread of Islam. She hadn't wanted to recognise this but with Sharia patrols on the streets, accosting western women who weren't wearing hijab, she felt that she had been left with very little choice. For this she blamed the patriarchal character of Islam. It was men again, as always. Islam was infected with patriarchal masculinity and that was why it was colonialist. However, that colonialism had been facilitated by mass immigration and a policy of multiculturalism.

In the end, for Rhiannon, it had come down to a necessary choice. As a feminist she must oppose multiculturalism. To choose otherwise would be to abandon her feminism. Her greatest worry was that it might already be too late to reverse the tide. One consequence of the increasing Islamisation of Western Europe had been that feminists found themselves confronted by non-western men who did not react to feminist agitation in the same way as western men. There was a much more physically violent reaction. Where feminist women had once been able to speak their minds to men without any fear of being assaulted in retaliation if the man felt insulted, now a woman who insulted a Jihadi might find herself hospitalised or murdered. The number of men of whom feminism could make demands seemed to be growing smaller and smaller. Women couldn't be expected to assert themselves if the man concerned might punch her in the face.

Feminists were unable to rely upon the men of their own culture to intercede on their behalf and defend them against this physical danger. Feminists had called upon them to do so, naturally, but when the social divisions of multi-sectarianism had ripped society apart, it had been painfully obvious that western feminised men were the weakest. Half of them refused to defend women and the other half didn't know how to. Rhiannon's worry was that as Islam became ever more powerful in the West, feminists would find themselves with more and more that they had to keep quiet about. There were far too few of the sisters who would take the chance of provoking a violent reaction. It was so very different to the way in which they had been raised and were accustomed to being treated.

Rhiannon had reluctantly joined those who argued that multiculturalism was actually an anti-feminist and right-wing policy. It had served the needs of corporate capitalism in providing a supply of cheap labour and clipping the wings of the trades unions but it had done nothing for women and, ultimately, had started to take back all the victories that feminism had won.

Diana had somehow managed to bite her tongue and say nothing whilst Rhiannon had filled her daughter's head with all this Islamophobic racist propaganda. Partly it was the courtesy of a houseguest but there was also an element of being unsure how Rhiannon might behave if Diana had sought to interfere with the raising of Rhiannon's child.

However, Diana had thought long and hard about what had been said in the days following this extraordinary incident. She had bridled at the suggestion that the multiculturalist programme had been driven by the employer-class who didn't mind what race or ethnicity their workers happened to be, just so long as they were easily exploitable. She was indignant that anyone might classify multiculturalism as a middle-class response to the male-oriented labour movement of the mid-twentieth century when working-class men in the West had become very resistant to their own economic oppression and were going on strike, demanding better pay and conditions, and becoming as politically powerful as the middle-class themselves.

Diana was dismissive of the notion that working-class men had ever been oppressed. Anyway, who cared if English working-class men had lost their power? It didn't prove that the reason multiculturalists had initiated a programme of mass immigration was in order to put a stop to the working-class activism of western men, and it certainly didn't mean that Diana's own moral stance of anti-racist inclusivity was bogus or sanctimonious. Multiculturalism was a moral project to oppose racism, to oppose right-wing nationalism, and to unify humanity in equality. Diana was as certain of that now as she had been fifty years ago. If the West had lost its economic hegemony, and maybe that was a good thing anyway, then it was the result of capitalist globalisation not the policy of multiculturalism.

The only reason that Diana would consider legitimate as a justification to stop a foreigner from entering the country was if that particular foreigner was someone she despised for their hate-politics. As a multiculturalist and a feminist she had supported the demand that certain writers and politicians and cultural figures must not be allowed into the country. 'Don't allow the hatemonger to come here' was the rallying cry. 'No hate-speech here' was the slogan. They were hateful and Diana hated them.

As her own reason for keeping someone out of the country was her hatred for them, she assumed that anyone who wanted to stop immigrants from coming into the country must therefore hate those immigrants. If an American wanted to limit mass immigration from Mexico, it must be because the American hated Mexicans. If an Englishman wanted to limit mass immigration from Asia, it must be because he hated Asians. If a Frenchman wanted to limit mass immigration from Africa, it must be because he hated Africans. Diana recognised no other reasons for anyone wanting to limit immigration. Hate was her only reason to refuse people entry and so she believed that it must be her opponents only reason too.

Diana had engaged in this kind of psychological projection throughout her life, although she was wholly unaware that she was doing it. As a feminist she hated men, but she had always projected this attitude on to her enemies and believed that it was men who hated women. She had supported all the feminist legislation which acted with extreme prejudice in favour of women, whilst believing that it was actually male legislators who wrote laws with extreme prejudice in favour of men. Projection had always been an essential feature of her feminism and lifelong habits are hard to break, especially if a person doesn't know that they have them. The habit had also come in handy when defending her multiculturalism.

In the lounge Diana moved over to the window to open a chink in the curtains and peek outside. In the darkness of the street there were troubling noises. She heard the guttural animalistic cries of bestial male voices. They had always been beasts to her and never more so than when you heard their brutish utterances in the street at night. Men were creatures of the jungle and the wilderness. All this rioting and violence suited their natures. They were probably enjoying themselves. She closed the curtains again, not wishing to see what was taking place beyond her front garden.

Diana had lost touch with Juna and so she had no idea what had become of Rhiannon or little Alyssa, but in the decade since that shockingly memorable revelation of a new feminist perspective Diana had heard many other young feminists expressing the same views as Rhiannon. Fifth wave feminism they were calling it; an anti-immigration, largely pro-western version of feminism. It had caused a major split in the feminist movement, generally dividing it by age, with the younger women embracing the fifth wave and the older women rejecting it. Diana still didn't agree with the fifth wave generation feminists but there was one thing which Rhiannon had said all those years ago that was ringing in Diana's head like a fire-bell tonight. The young single mother had worried that it might already be too late. It was.

Diana was appalled to countenance the thought, but when she looked at the society of 2035 she saw that none of her expectations for the future had been met. Feminism was still a dominant force in the state machinery of central government but, as a result of political devolution, central government was a spent force and all the real power lay in the Metros. So where was the advantage in dominating a mostly redundant state machine?

Take the fiasco of the Civic Investigation, for example. They were trying to get irresponsible single men to accept the duties of citizenship and pay more tax to finance those in need. The Civic Investigation was absolutely right in its ideological goals, there was no question about that, but for all practical purposes it was a joke. It cost more to fund the initiative than it generated in increased tax revenue. Single men worked in the shadow economy and shirked their responsibilities. They should be forced to pay but who could force them now? It was too late.

The pathetic little wankers and man-boys were refusing even to marry or father children. They preferred their disgustingly misogynistic synthetic sex-dolls. How decadent and degraded men were. All these sexist groups like the Unchivalrous and the Outlaws and the Sisyphus movement were nothing but a bunch of woman haters. They came out with their spurious nonsense about not wanting to break their backs at work servicing the needs of a woman. That was all rubbish and lies. But it did mean that any woman who wished to exercise her right to marry and settle down with her children was unlikely to find a suitable husband.

Those few men whose reluctance to father children could be overcome were little better than the vile man-boys. Men who were prepared to consider marriage had started to make their consent to parenthood contingent on their having an equal entitlement to occupy the role of a house-spouse. Most paid employment was boring and unrewarding, as it always had been, and the current generation of men seemed to believe that there was no reason why they should be the one in the relationship with the responsibility to earn money. Both sexes now preferred the softer option of being the partner who was financially supported by a working spouse. Men wanted an equal right to live on their wife's earnings. So a woman's desire to occupy a domestic role, whether temporarily or permanently, was stymied by men's preference for being the house-spouse themselves.

Many men were agitating for pre-nuptial legislation which would guarantee that fatherhood carried with it the mother's agreement that, if she were the higher earner, then she would financially support him and the baby so that he could raise his child as the stay-at-home parent. Some women, desperate for motherhood, had already signed such pre-nuptial agreements voluntarily. They had done so on the assumption that once the baby was born the law would make it easy for her to renege on the agreement and demand that her husband support her and her child regardless of any signature on a piece of paper. Their assumption had proven correct and the law had indeed continued to enforce financial responsibility upon men in the traditional way. This was why men were now insisting upon a change in the law to legally guarantee the father's entitlement. But surely that would never happen. Yet the horrifying thing was that, these days, you couldn't be certain.

So after more than a century of feminism, where did this leave women? Feminism had given women their entitlements but it had been unable to provide them with the resilience they needed to cope with the changed circumstances after the crash of capitalism. Under the conditions of the current financial austerity, all bets were off. With paid employment being more of a burden than a boon, western cultures were haemorrhaging young women who sought the life-choice of being a wife and mother, married to a man from one of the more traditional ethnic cultures. Female reverts to Islam from amongst the kufr were boosting the birth-rates of all the Muslim communities far beyond those of their rivals. Diana had always believed that the future was female. But now it looked as if the future of females might be Islamic.

The voices on the news channel that was playing quietly in the lounge moved on from discussing the Jewish pogrom in England to Jewish issues in international politics. A hard-line Israeli politician had recently drawn a lot of flak for his suggestion that his country's best nuclear defence strategy would be to target Mecca and Medina. He had been roundly condemned out-of-hand by statespersons from all over the world who had denounced his proposal as despicable and disgraceful, but the news channel was attempting to get at the reasoning behind his outrageous statement.

The context for his remark was well-known. Iran and Pakistan were both nuclear theocracies. Iran was a theocracy which had achieved nuclear power. Pakistan was a nuclear power which had become a theocracy. Both were busily building missiles and warheads while their people starved. The world trembled. Everyone's feet were on the very edge of the precipice of the apocalypse. Armageddon had never seemed more imminent.

It wasn't just a question of how long they could restrain themselves from a second holocaust by eradicating Israel, it was also a deadly new wrinkle on the age-old conflict between the Shia Muslims and the Sunni Muslims. It was by no means impossible that Sunni Pakistan and Shia Iran might wage nuclear war on each other. Certainly, the long-standing antagonism between Iran and Saudi Arabia left the Saudis feeling very much under the shadow of the Iranian warheads. The missiles would not have far to travel. But a nuclear attack on Arabia would threaten Mecca and Medina, the two holiest cities in Islam, so it was generally believed that this would preclude the Iranians launching a nuclear war against their hated rivals.

It was this belief which had given rise to the Israeli politician's suggestion for a stronger nuclear defence policy against the theocracies. He maintained that the Knesset should make it known that if Iran or Pakistan were to launch a nuclear attack against Israel, then Israel would launch its own missiles to strike Mecca and

Medina to obliterate them utterly. This would have vastly more deterrent effect than retaliating directly against Iran or Pakistan because their governments valued the cities of the prophet much more than they valued the lives of their own people. There was a certain logic to his argument.

The Saudi Arabians wanted the Israeli politician's head on a platter, of course, because they didn't see why they should be annihilated as a result of an attack instigated by Iran or Pakistan, especially as they had no control over either of these countries. But the Israeli politician was unrepentant. He said that it had to be acknowledged that wars were no longer about nations, they were about cultures and ideologies. Which country Mecca and Medina happened to be in was irrelevant.

"Why isn't America doing something to contain the situation in Israel?" said a voice on the channel.

"What would you expect America to do about it?" said a second voice. "It's nothing to do with them any more. America is a Latino-majority country, what do they care about Israel?"

"Are you criticising the Latinisation of America?" said the first voice, sniffing a distinct odour of racism.

"It doesn't matter what I do or don't criticise," replied the second voice. "I have no power. I'm just discussing ideas, I don't implement policy."

"But what you said about a Latinised America not caring . . . ?" queried the first voice.

"Look," said the second voice impatiently, "the Americans took the south-western territories of the USA from the Mexicans by using the 19th century method of imperialism: military force. The Mexicans have now taken those territories back from the Americans by using the 21st century method of imperialism: mass immigration. These are the tides of history. The Americans take the territory from the Mexicans, then the Mexicans take them back, and so on."

"You're actually equating immigration with imperialism?" asked the first voice, appalled.

"No, I'm not talking about immigration. I'm talking about the demographically revolutionary phenomenon of *mass* immigration. The transplantation of culturally distinct communities who demand political representation for their own cultural beliefs and values. The colonising power of mass immigration is a political annexing of foreign territory. There's a name for that, it's called imperialism."

Diana could take no more of it. Nuclear Armageddon and the death of feminism was too much for one day. The future was more than she could bear. She went over to the machine to switch off the channel. But before she reached it there was an almighty crash of glass as the window in her lounge shattered under the impact of a thrown brick. It was a brick from her own front garden wall. Diana turned toward the terrible sound of wanton destruction and screamed.

*   *   *

The Red Squirrels were travelling up the motorway in Chippy's catering van, heading for the Lake District. The vehicle was now their only home, for the time being at least. They were their own little community on wheels. Three of them white, one of them black, one of them mixed-race, four of them English, one of them Canadian, and all of them men.

Chippy was driving with Ritzy in the passenger seat beside him. Everyone else was crammed uncomfortably into the back of the van. It wasn't designed for carrying people, the rear of the vehicle was a workspace. The large stainless steel deep fat fryer and the storage areas for potatoes, cartons, sauces and the other accoutrements of Chippy's business took up most of the room. It left a narrow strip of floor space in which the three men sat. Barker was sitting on Chippy's work-stool, John was using his canvas bag as a cushion and Captain was perched on John's rucksack.

Ritzy had unanimously been voted the best seat, comfortably up front, because he was everybody's hero just at the moment for having saved Barker's life. They all thought very highly of the way that he'd risked his own life for the sake of friendship. They didn't say much about it but they showed their respect in a number of small ways, such as giving him the best seat in the van. Ritzy didn't see himself as having done anything heroic in the fire, he'd just done what had seemed necessary at the time, but he saw no reason why he shouldn't accept this reward for his alleged heroism. It was a fairly long trip and his arse was grateful for the comfy seat, although he had joked with them that he wasn't planning on running into any more burning buildings in the near future so they'd all better be careful with their matches.

Chippy's van was an electric vehicle whose Vehicle Alert System was on the blink. After all the years that cities had suffered appalling levels of traffic noise breaking ear-drums on the urban streets, and all the years that automobile manufacturers had employed acoustic engineers to find ways to make petrol car engines quieter, the invention of the electric car had finally solved this problem by manufacturing vehicles which made very little noise. But in keeping with the values of the vanguard of the establishment, this beneficial technological advance had immediately been declared "unacceptable" because it penalized the visually impaired. Quiet cars were judged to be a danger to the blind who couldn't hear them coming when crossing the street. So legislation had been passed to ensure that the satisfyingly muted cars must have loud fake engine noise, called a Vehicle Alert System, artificially added to them for the sake of the 1% of the population who were blind regardless of the effect that it had upon the 99% majority. The habit of favouring minorities over majorities had long been deeply engrained in the politics of inclusivity.

However, this legislation was very seldom enforced since The Rupture because government had other things on its mind. The Vehicle Alert System on Chippy's catering van hadn't worked the whole time he'd owned it, having bought the van second-hand several years ago. Consequently, he and Ritzy could chat pleasantly as they bowled along the motorway.

"Look at that, Spart," said Chippy pointing at the blackened shell of a car dumped at the roadside.

It wasn't the car he was pointing at but a large self-congratulatory bumper sticker on its rear-end which said COEXIST, with an Islamic crescent moon substituting for the letter C, a peace symbol substituting for the letter O, Judaism's star of David substituting for the letter X, and the crucifix of Christianity substituting for the letter T. Whereas previously this bumper sticker had merely been a sanctimonious aspiration for the self-satisfied and self-righteous, it had now finally become apposite. Coexistence was stuck on the rear-end of the burned out shell of something which used to be functional.

Ritzy and Chippy erupted into peals of sarcastic laughter. They chortled and giggled so much that Captain called out from the rear of the van to ask them if they needed medical attention. Ritzy tried to explain the reason for their amusement but he was spluttering and choking so much that he couldn't get the words out.

The state of the roads was worse than ever now that the Metros were too short of public money to repair them, but at least the motorways were less congested because people generally chose to do without a car unless it was an absolute necessity. It was a considerable saving on your annual expenses if you could get by without driving. Insurance premiums were colossal as a result of cars getting vandalised so often. The majority of drivers didn't have insurance, but that meant that if your car got trashed by vandals you lost your entire investment in the vehicle. There were still plenty of people behind the steering wheel but nothing like as many as there had been ten years ago.

After The Rupture there had been a brief craze for pushbikes but it hadn't lasted long because they were too easily stolen. No matter how securely chained up they were, with a simple pair of bolt-cutters they could be carried off and they routinely were. It got to the point where nobody who was riding a bike had actually purchased it, since everybody was riding a bicycle that they'd stolen from someone else. The same bike would go through several pairs of hands as one person stole it, only to have it stolen from them by someone else, who in turn had it stolen by another person and so on. In effect, bicycles became a kind of public property shared by anyone who cared to participate in this merry-go-round of theft. It was the reason that Ritzy preferred to walk.

During the worst of the riots Chippy had slept in his van at night in an attempt to keep guard over it. There was just enough room for one man to stretch out on the floor. Many was the cold night he'd spent in a sleeping bag in the back of his mobile chip shop. But it was just as well that he had taken the trouble to keep his property safe because he'd be sleeping in it every night for a while. As for the other five, they'd had to make other arrangements to provide themselves with some shelter. They only had the money which they'd been carrying in their pockets when disaster struck, except for John who hadn't been burned out, but they'd had enough to buy sleeping bags for themselves with a little cash left over. John had done the decent thing and bought an inflatable tent which would accommodate four, so they'd all have somewhere to sleep at night. Cumbria was a rural part of the country so they assumed they'd be able to camp out.

They had no idea what the availability of accommodation and paid employment might be like in the Lake District. They'd found no reliable information about it on the channels. Ritzy should be alright because he was a mechanic who could fix almost any kind of engine, petrol or electric. If Chippy could find a supplier of potatoes, then he had brought his own business enterprise with him. Captain, as a plumber and electrician, was fairly confident of finding work somewhere. But Barker had the idea of trying to turn his home-brewed beer and cider into a paying business, which the others thought was a bit speculative, not to say improbable. John earned his living by building personal computers and other IT equipment out of second-hand spare parts, so he might be okay if he could find some contacts for getting cheap spare parts. It was all pretty much a matter for conjecture, but that was only to be expected when you were refugees. The one thing that they all knew they'd not get was any charity. What was left of the welfare system would entitle them to nothing, and the locals wouldn't want to offer handouts to strangers.

All their worldly goods now consisted of the contents of the catering van and the clothes on their backs. They'd have something to eat for the next several days, if they didn't mind chips for breakfast, lunch, and dinner. John was a little more prosperous than the others because he'd had time to gather up some clothes and a few possessions from his apartment but, as these had only been such as would fit into the canvas bag and the rucksack, it wasn't going to cause any envy. John, Captain and Chippy still had their channels tablets but Ritzy and Barker had lost theirs. Ritzy still had his touchpad so he wasn't entirely offline. What mattered most, of course, was that he still had his tool bag. His tools were his livelihood. Thank god he'd been out working when the arsonists had set fire to the building.

In the back of the van Barker, Captain, and John passed the time by viewing the channels. Riding bumpily on the luggage, they balanced the tablets on their laps, their earphones plugged in. Barker had borrowed Chippy's tablet and was watching a channel which was reporting on an apparently continual series of climate disasters from around the world. Everywhere seemed to be full of floods and hurricanes and tsunamis and earthquakes; everywhere but here. In the former England there was barely any weather left. The winters were mild and the summers lacked any real heat, there was as much rain in August as in April and as much sunshine in March as in July. It was almost as if there was only one season and it lasted all the year round. But too little weather was better than too much weather. The English had once been ridiculed for their preoccupation with the weather but if they'd been around today they would have appreciated the real benefits of an equable climate.

Not that Barker had anything more than an academic interest in the alleged apocalypse taking place in the global climate. The planet could burn to a crisp or freeze over with ice or drown under tidal waves or whatever it was that climate change was supposedly bringing about; he didn't really give a toss. Barker was much more interested in what was happening to the broken remains of what used to be his country. His fingertips punched a few icons and his screen shifted to a channel where people uploaded local news. Today the footage was all of civil chaos. There were numerous videos of what was taking place in the major cities. He opened up a channel that he often used because it summarised the breaking news. It was even worse in these pictures. Barker waved a hand to attract the attention of Captain and John, then held up his screen for them to see. Their eyebrows rose. They both switched channels from the porn sites they'd been viewing and joined him in contemplating what looked like the end of civilization. There was news from all parts of the country.

The Red Squirrels had fled from the growing conflict between the *East Midlands Metro* and the *East Anglia Metro*, and they were travelling broadly northwest toward the Lake District. But they hadn't left the violent disorder and internecine warfare behind them. The channels were showing them the turmoil that was taking place in the north-western Metros also. As Chippy's van trundled up the motorway, it was passing by regions of Metropolitan government that were splitting at the seams. The channels were full of it. People had uploaded reports that parts of Manchester and Liverpool were in flames. There was no predominant ethnicity in either the *Greater Manchester Metro* or the *Greater Merseyside Metro* and the competition for tribal ascendancy was getting very nasty. The government districts where the political administration of these

Metros was conducted had been placed under curfew with armed police on every street corner. The channels depicted images of beleaguered firefighters in Manchester trying to extinguish a burning ambulance and a bus that was a huge tower of flame. In Liverpool the two cathedrals on Hope Street were packed with local refugees from besieged communities seeking asylum from the militias who battled for command of the ground, street by street and even house by house.

The two cities were spiralling ever deeper into the ruinous consequences of social unintelligibility. The total diversification of these great conurbations had passed through what the demographers, in their understated fashion, had called "civic incohesion" and these cities were now entering the choppy and uncharted waters of multi-sectarian divergence. The Red Squirrels wanted no part of that. They kept heading north.

By evening they had left the motorway and were following their GPS navigation unit on the road to Lake Windermere, the first of the serenely beautiful lakes in the district that included Coniston water, Derwentwater, Ullswater, and all the others. Their surroundings became agreeably rural, their route winding through narrow lanes with fields and woodlands on either side. The steep hills around the lakes were craggy and precipitous, making the whole area seem quite separate from the country of motorways and cities which they had driven through that day. It was a world apart.

They had intended to continue on to the delightfully named town of Cockermouth. The end of the line would be Whitehaven on the west coast. But Chippy decided that he was tired of driving and the rest of them were getting cramped and disgruntled from having been stuck in the back of the van for so long, and this caused them to change their plan. They were all content to stop by the roadside and camp for the night. There was plenty of space out here in the countryside. There was no great hurry and it would be easier to complete their journey in the morning.

They built a small campfire, mostly from food packaging and other litter from the van but supplemented by the remains of a broken wooden sign from a ramblers footpath. Splashing some chip fat on the wood they set the fire going nicely and settled down. With their sleeping bags inside their inflatable tent they'd be reasonably warm. The food packaging burned to nothing very quickly but it lasted just long enough to get the wood alight, and that smouldered and crackled very pleasantly for quite a while. It didn't give out much heat but it looked cosy. The five of them talked aimlessly into the night, curled up snugly in their bags, the conversationalists decreasing in number as they slowly fell asleep.

They woke up cold in the very early morning. There was still mist hanging in the vales and hollows between the peaks. The sky was streaks of pale blue flanked by light grey clouds. The hills were so sharply vertical that they felt like mountains. There was a body of water in the distance which glinted under the soft sunlight. There was no sound except the cry of a bird. The glimmer of the lake and the ghostly mists and the majestic hills were a vision. It was ethereally beautiful. It was like awakening in the midst of an ancient fantasy of gods and swordsmen, of shield-maidens and sorcerer kings. It was the dream of an England from a thousand years past, an Anglo-Saxon legend of a Celtic myth from a time before history when fables were realities. But it was also wet and bloody cold.

They packed up their meagre campsite quickly and got the kettle boiling to brew the tea. They were all a bit stiff from sleeping under canvas but there was a fresh feeling to the morning that was invigorating. Everyone felt optimistic for some reason, though they couldn't have explained why. They exchanged communal smiles while they drank their hot strong tea and felt it warming their insides. They all had that tingle of excitement which comes from getting back to nature. The oppressive city environment which they had left behind them seemed already to be fading into another life.

Rather than cooking, having eaten chips twice the day before, they preferred to get going straight away. Down the road they might find a café where they could buy their breakfasts. The Lake District was, or used to be, a tourist area so they were expecting a few eateries dotted about here and there.

However, as they ploughed their way in low gear up and down the gradients of the hills, the only restaurants or pubs they saw were all closed. It was apparent that they were not just closed because it was early in the morning, they were permanently shut down. The buildings had a poignant air of desertion about them, as if they had been betrayed by the residents who had abandoned them. Maybe the tourist industry wasn't doing too well in the current economic climate. The websites on the channels were all out of date, so the Red Squirrels couldn't get any information from them. What they needed was a real-life member of the local population who might provide them with the info they required. They drove on.

"There's a typical local-yokel," said Chippy, spying a young man in an olive-green waxed waterproof jacket who was walking a dog. He couldn't have looked more like the traditional image of a English country gentleman. He had the ambling gait of the true countryman and his dog had never felt the constraint of a collar and leash. Chippy slowed the van to a halt. He lowered the side window and stuck his head out to ask:

"Morning, mate. Can you tell us if there are any cafes around here where we can buy a hot breakfast?"

The dog barked excitedly as the young man in the olive-green jacket squinted at Chippy. He looked a little confused. As a lifelong city-dweller, Chippy had the clichéd notion that country folk were all a bit suspicious of outsiders so, playing the diplomat, he didn't repeat his question but politely waited for a reply. The young man quieted his dog with a shushing noise and then looked back again at the van driver. He took a step or two toward the van. His face creased into a slightly embarrassed grin.

"Nu vorbesc engleza," he said in Romanian.

THE END

Other publications by JP Tate

http://jptate.jimdo.com

The Most Hated Man (Novel)

A series of bloody deaths is causing panic in a city in England. Someone is murdering teenagers among the underclass by disseminating a lethal recreational drug which, with morbid humour, the mainstream media have termed 'snuff'. But is the snuff-killer just some crazy drug dealer who is pushing a deadly narcotic regardless of the consequences or is he killing these young people deliberately for some deeper motivation of his own?

Two police officers, Detective Inspector Bapoto Smith and Detective Sergeant Gloria Kovač, are a part of the task force unit working the case. Lacking any forensic evidence or public support, they must pursue their investigation hindered further by the puerile restraints of the political directives, policies, and procedures that make up modern policing priorities.

At the same time a second murderer, Hereward, is on a deadly mission of his own. Hereward is abducting members of the political and cultural establishment. For fifty years these reactionaries of 'correctness' have adamantly refused to listen to anyone who disagreed with them. Now Hereward is *making* them listen. The corpses of those to whom he speaks are subsequently found dead by dehydration, bruised from the chains which had bound them. Confronted with this terror the ruling elite are frantic.

Two killers, two fatal agendas, two harassed cops, one broken nation. In a society spiralling out of control, the establishment elites have been targeted and their time is running out.

These storylines slowly come together in a chilling vision of the social alienation brought about by those who exercise authoritarian power over the ordinary citizen with the strict speech-codes and thought-police taboos of political conformity. Set against a background of economic decline, the rise of Islamic Jihad, and the social engineering imposed by the ideologies of multiculturalism and feminism, "The Most Hated Man" is unlike any other cops-and-killers thriller you have ever read. It is a story for our times.

Feminism is Sexism (Non-fiction)

For those whose mind is closed on the subject of feminism because society has told them what to think and they obediently think it, there are many hundreds of books available that will reinforce their cultural orthodoxy. This book is not for them. It is a polemic which takes a radically anti-establishment position and expresses an alternative point of view. It argues for a genuinely impartial sex equality and attempts to demonstrate that, not only has feminism always been opposed to sex equality, feminism has actually stopped us from achieving an impartial sex equality.

The book's title means just what it says. Feminism is itself sexism, and not some new kind of 'reverse' sexism but the same old sexism that operated in traditional society. Misandry is not a recent development, it has been around for as long as misogyny. Feminism endorses and exploits traditional misandry in its power-politics.

What types of traditional misandry? Most notably, the sexist double-standard about the value of human life, which treats men as the expendable sex and holds women's lives to be intrinsically more valuable than men's lives, and the sexist double-standard about human pain, which treats female pain as being more serious and important than male pain.

"Feminism is Sexism" raises many issues which, whether you agree with the arguments or not, are at least worthy of the consideration of those with an open mind. It describes feminism's perversion of the freedom movement of the 1960s. It offers argument to refute patriarchy theory (in fact, five variations of that theory), on which all feminism is based. It exposes the maxim of Equal But Different for what it is, a hypocrite's charter. Along the way it asks many uncomfortable questions, such as:

- Feminism promotes negative gender-stereotypes of men, locating the litany of men's deficiencies and vices in their biological maleness. So is feminism guilty of everything it pretends to be against?

- If the UK government's own statistics on domestic violence show that over 40% of the victims are male, why is their new policy on domestic violence called "Ending Violence Against Women and Girls"?

- Boys are being raised in a society which tells them that they are going to grow up into a cross between Jackass and Jack the Ripper. What kind of psychological damage will this do to them?

Drawing upon evidence and examples from the UK, the USA, and elsewhere, the arguments in "Feminism is Sexism" may be unsettling, but they are not going to disappear simply because the political establishment chooses to ignore them.

This is a provocative book which challenges you to doubt beliefs which you may have held all your life without really questioning them. Question them now.

Ealdræd of the Pæga
Warriors of the Iron Blade, Volume 1 (Novel)

JP Tate's radical reinvention of the Epic Fantasy saga. No flying dragons, no elves, and no magic pixie dust.

This allegorical tale is set in a world of incessant conflict; a dark age where the strong oppress the weak in the struggle for life and dignity. Amid the dangers of battle, sorcery, slavery, treachery and ethnic allegiance, only the undaunted will endure and thrive. It is a world without pity where each man and each woman must stand or fall by their own abilities, armed with no other weapons than the iron blade, the stratagems of guile, or the scented whisperings of necromancy.

Ealdræd, a spearman of the Pæga clan of Aenglia, is a tough veteran adventurer exiled from his homeland and passed forty years of age. He survives when others have long since perished. Seeking a mercenary's pay in the resurgent clash of arms along the Wehnbrian Marches, he rides south. On his journey he will meet many fascinating characters, including a notorious female spy from the Duchy of Bhel, her sexually submissive lady-in-waiting, and a magnificently volatile girl from the distant Menghis Steppes whose fate is closely entwined with his own.

'Warriors of the Iron Blade' tells of a bloody epoch of boldly adult attitudes, worldly appetites, and spiritual obscenities. It is an era when a mercenary soldier skilled in the arts of war was respected for his martial virtues, and the wanton indulgence of lusty passions brought with it no mewling guilt or shame. To each age its own beliefs and values. This is an age of violence, hunger, degradation, and courage.

Eiji of the Kajhin
Warriors of the Iron Blade, Volume 2 (Novel)

The second volume of this allegorical tale begins twenty years after the end of the first volume and two years after the death of the veteran warrior, Ealdræd of the Pæga.

His son, Hereweorc, is one of the leaders of the Pæga resistance. Informed and inspired by the campfire tales told to him by his soldier-for-hire father, the young man is a serious threat to the ruling caste. But to Clænnis, the girl who is Hereweorc's apprentice in the study of beadu-cræft (the craft of skill and strength in war), he is a strict taskmaster and the object of her erotic desire.

At the same time the story of Ealdræd's wife, the formidable Menghis warrior woman Eiji, continues as she departs from Aenglia with three companions. Eiji has resolved to return to the distant steppes of her homeland. The many dangers of the road will make the journey more than perilous; many would consider it impossible to achieve. Eiji will have to fight her way across two continents in the quest to reach her native soil, facing hazards both natural and apparently supernatural.

As their two stories unfold, Hereweorc and his comrades in the resistance must find a way to free the Pæga clan from the political oppression they suffer, and Eiji must find a way to survive as she travels across the known world.

Printed in Great Britain
by Amazon